The
Oath

The Druid Chronicles

Book One

The
Oath

A.M. LINDEN

SHE WRITES PRESS

Published 2021
Printed in the United States of America
Print ISBN: 978-1-64742-114-4
E-ISBN: 978-1-64742-115-1
Library of Congress Control Number: 2020924588

For information, address:
She Writes Press
1569 Solano Ave #546
Berkeley, CA 94707

Interior design by Tabitha Lahr

She Writes Press is a division of SparkPoint Studio, LLC.
This is a work of fiction. Names, characters, places, and incidents either are the product of the author's imagination or are used fictitiously. Any resemblance to actual persons, living or dead, is entirely coincidental.

For Mark, renaissance man
and love of my life

Author's Note

The Druid Chronicles is a historical fiction series set in Anglo-Saxon Britain during a time known alternatively as the early medieval period or the Dark Ages. Books 1, 3, 4, and 5 are primarily concerned with events that take place in 788 AD. Book 2 begins a generation earlier and recounts the events that set the main story in motion. While considerable liberty has been taken in adapting the geopolitics of the period to the needs of the story, it is generally true that:

- At the time in question, the Germanic invaders (who, for the purposes of this narrative, will be referred to as Saxons) had conquered the southeastern lowlands while indigenous Celts retained control in the mountainous northwest.
- The majority of native Britons had converted to Christianity by the end of the fourth century. The Saxon conversion was essentially complete by the late 600s.
- Before the conversion to Christianity, both ethnic groups were polytheistic, and elements of those earlier beliefs and practices persisted after that transition was nominally complete.

Atheldom and Derthwald, the Saxon kingdoms in which most of the series' actions take place, are literary creations, as is Llwddawanden, a secluded valley in which it is imagined that a secretive Druid cult has continued its traditional practices despite the otherwise relentless spread of Christianity.

About Druids: Although much has been written about Druids, there is little verifiable information regarding what this apparently elite and possibly priestly class of Celts believed or what ritual practices they may have carried out. For the purpose of this series, it is conjectured that Druids were indeed priests and priestesses and that the Druids of Llwddawanden were matriarchal, subscribing to the belief that:

- There was a supreme mother goddess at the apex of an extensive pantheon of gods and goddesses.
- The spirit of this supreme deity inhabited the body of their cult's chief priestess.
- At the chief priestess's death, the Goddess's spirit passed on to her daughter, if she had one, or else to a designated member of the priestesses' inner circle.

There is not, to the author's knowledge, any evidence that a community of practicing Druids persisted as late as the eighth century in the British Isles or elsewhere, and there is no reason to think that the views and practices ascribed to the Druids of Llwddawanden have any basis in reality.

Characters

ATHELROD . . . . King of Atheldom

GILBERTH . . . . King of Derthwald

OLFRICK . . . . Captain of King Gilberth's guards

THEOBOLD . . . . Late King of Derthwald, Gilberth's uncle

ALSWANDA . . . . Late Queen of Piffering, Theobold's wife

ALESWINA . . . . Daughter of Theobold and Alswanda,
Gilberth's cousin

MILLICENT . . . . Aleswina's first nursemaid

HILDEGARTH . . . . . Abbess of the Abbey of Saint Edeth

UDELLA . . . . Prioress

DURTHENA . . . . . . Under-prioress

IDWOLDA . . . . Novice nun

HIGBALD . . . . Bishop of Lindisfarne

WULFRIC . . . . Christian priest

ADOLPHUS . . . . Christian priest

BARNARD . . . . Wealthy landowner, previously "Benyon",
a servant in the Druid shrine

FEYWN . . . . Supreme priestess of the Shrine of the Great
Mother Goddess

RHEDWYN . . . . Druid priest, Feywn's first consort (deceased)

ARIANNA . . . . Rhedwyn and Feywn's daughter

ANNWR . . . . Priestess, midwife, Feywn's sister, enslaved
as Aleswina's nursemaid

CYRI . . . . Priestess, Annwr's daughter

CAELYM. . . . . Druid priest, bard, physician, Feywn's
second consort

ARDDWN . . . . Caelym and Feywn's son

LLIEM . . . . Caelym and Feywn's son

HERRWN . . . . The shrine's chief priest, bard

OSSIAM . . . . Druid priest, oracle

OLYRRWD . . . . Druid priest, physician (deceased)

RHONNON . . . . Priestess, the shrine's chief midwife

Author's Note: This list includes characters who are mentioned
but do not appear. Some of these characters died before the story
opens; others will appear in later books. Names of several minor
characters who appear or are mentioned in a single context have
been omitted, including Gilberth's five wives, all of whom are
deceased.

Contents

PART I

𝕻rologue

The events that took place in and around the Kingdom of Derthwald during the spring and summer of 788 AD have, understandably, been overlooked by scholars concerned with early medieval history. Even at its peak, Derthwald was never more than a minor monarchy, rising and falling within the span of forty years and leaving only a single, obscure reference to its existence in surviving documents of the period—besides which, most of those involved had good reasons for keeping silent.

By the end of the previous century, the wars between the Anglo-Saxon settlers and the native Britons had reached a standoff at the diagonal chain of mountain ridges that separated the southeastern lowlands from the northwestern uplands. Located at the northernmost edge of the Germanic territories, Derthwald was all but encircled by the larger kingdom of Atheldom. It had begun its independent existence as a land grant given by Atheldom's king, Athelrod, to Theobold, the commander of his main army, as a reward for Theobold's successful siege of the last Celtic stronghold below the mountains. Athelrod, a king as open-handed with his friends as he was iron-fisted with his enemies, had awarded Theobold the ravaged fortress along with the broad, fertile valley around it, in a proclamation that was more loosely worded than it would have been for any less trustworthy vassal.

Theobold, however, was known equally for his military prowess and his unwavering loyalty to Athelrod. Having no interest in civilian rule, he gave orders for the citadel's broken gates and ruined battlements to be repaired, renamed it Gothroc for the steep granite outcrop that held up its massive stone walls, and returned to the field for another ten years, leaving the running of his household to his widowed sister, who, along with her young son, came to live there following the death of her fourth husband.

Never intended to be a hereditary domain, Derthwald would have remained a common fiefdom had it not been for Theobold's marriage, late in life, to the queen of another realm—one even smaller, but where the royal lineage was firmly established.

Theobold was approaching sixty when he finally retired from active campaigning and returned to Derthwald. Surviving into old age was something of a miracle for a warrior of Theobold's generation, and the fact that he had managed to do so with no crippling injuries and an unbroken record of victories was taken by most as a sign of God's favor. In spite of that, Theobold began to be troubled by a recurring dream in which he came to the gates of heaven only to find them locked. Then the golden gates and shining spires vanished, leaving him standing naked on a barren hilltop surrounded by a vast multitude of ghosts—his own fallen men gathered together with slain enemies, all with fresh blood dripping from their death wounds, all of them staring at him and muttering amongst themselves.

Theobold did not tell anyone about his dream. Instead, he swore a silent oath to Jesus in which he named off the exact number of sites in Derthwald he would have consecrated in exchange for a secure place in heaven. Pursuing entry into God's kingdom with the same dark intensity that he'd put into the conquest of military objectives, he went on to endow seven churches, two monasteries, and a convent, along with thirty smaller shrines.

Preoccupied with the next world, Theobold grew increasingly withdrawn from the life going on around him. He saw his sister and nephew only at dinner—and even then, ate his unnecessarily spare meal as if he were alone at the table.

Once he'd made sure that no one in Derthwald would be more than walking distance from a place to pray, Theobold began a series of trips to increasingly distant monasteries and holy sites. Eventually, he left for what was to be a pilgrimage to Rome. He chose an indirect route through the small neighboring kingdom of Piffering, meaning to stop there briefly to pay his respects to King Alfwold, a fellow veteran of Athelrod's campaigns. Upon his arrival, he was met by a distraught servant who led him to the royal bedchamber, where his once robust, seemingly indomitable comrade lay pale and wasted, with no hope of recovery and only one surviving child, a girl of sixteen, to succeed him.

Theobold stayed at his old friend's side, talking about God, telling war stories, and conducting a tactful negotiation that culminated in his marrying the young princess. It was an arrangement that brought together their two small but prosperous domains and, at the same time, bloodlessly resolved a potentially troublesome border dispute. The most remarkable thing about the match was not the fifty-year age difference between the bride and groom but the fact that Theobold had fallen deeply in love with the slender, dark-haired girl he was about to marry.

The wedding was conducted quickly and quietly. It was followed three months later by Alfwold's funeral, and six months after that by the birth of a daughter. Once Queen Alswanda was recovered from the delivery, there was no reason not to make the journey back to Derthwald, but Theobold remained in Piffering for almost four more years.

Had he been a man to closely examine his own motives—or admit to personal weakness—Theobold would have been forced to acknowledge that he'd always been intimidated by his overbearing older sister and that her moving into Gothroc had played no small part in his decision to spend so little time there. As it was, over the course of those four years in Piffering, he simply found one excuse or another to put off his return home.

He did keep in touch, sending regular messages to his steward regarding the management of his estates but leaving out any mention of his marriage or his new family. The missives were carried by a loyal—and discreet—messenger named Hobarth, who delivered them without revealing by so much as a smirk that Theobold had not entered holy orders in Rome, as was widely assumed.

It was not until Hobarth returned to Piffering in the spring of 773 with the news that the Lady Theodosia had taken a sudden chill and died that Theobold, with an unconscious sigh of relief, packed his things and returned to Derthwald, along with his wife and nearly four-year-old daughter.

Dressed in a warrior's regalia and not looking a day over sixty, Theobold led a proud procession through the ironclad gates of Gothroc on a bright morning in May. His daughter, blond like Theobold but with her mother's luminous brown eyes, sat on a tasseled pillow propped securely in front of her nurse, who rode a light gray palfrey. Close behind, a pure white mare carried Derthwald's new queen, who was dressed in a royal blue gown that bulged out over her pregnant belly.

Hobarth had traveled ahead and arrived in time to get the palace guards busy putting up banners, the trumpeters lining both sides of the palace courtyard, ready to sound their welcome, and the cooks and kitchen servants scurrying to set out the celebratory banquet. With that done, he went, as an afterthought, to tell Theobold's nephew, Gilberth.

He found Gilberth standing in front of the wardrobe in the king's chambers, his hand outstretched towards the king's ermine-lined cloak, his fingers twitching oddly.

For a brief second after hearing the message, Gilberth looked at Hobarth as blankly as if he'd been speaking some foreign language. Then a dark shadow seemed to streak across his face but was gone before Hobarth could be sure he'd seen it. In the next moment the young nobleman beamed with fulsome goodwill, declaring this to be "good news, excellent news, wonderful news, the best possible news" before ordering Hobarth to do what he'd already done in preparation for the king's entrance.

The triumph of Theobold's homecoming was short-lived—ending less than a month later when word came of a threatened Celtic uprising on Derthwald's northern border. There'd been reports of minor troubles in that region before, but in the past, they'd been nothing more serious than small landholders complaining about missing cattle and traders claiming they'd been robbed by Britons. This time, however, Olfrick, the captain of Theobold's palace guards, burst into the dining hall in the middle of the midday meal, and, before the gathered assembly, repeated the insulting challenge that the unnamed leader of the insurgents had sent to the king.

Before Theobold could speak, his nephew, Gilberth, rose from his place at the far end of the table. "There is no need for the king, at his age, to leave the safety and comfort of his dining hall," he cried out. "I will answer this villain's foul slurs, lead our army to flush the vermin out of their den, and crush them once and for all."

Livid at his nephew's effrontery in speaking as if he, Theobold, was too feeble to wage war—to say nothing of calling attention to his age in front of Alswanda—the king rose up from the table. Pointedly ignoring Gilberth, he called for his sword, shield, and armor and sent the captain of his guard to gather his forces. An hour later, the king led his army out of the gates of Gothroc and followed Olfrick though the heavily forested foothills to a clearing large enough to camp for the night before mounting his attack in the morning.

Theobold had fought the Britons before and knew them to be an erratic and unpredictable enemy—appearing suddenly over a hilltop, charging wildly downward into the center of his battle line, then scattering and vanishing into the undergrowth, only to reappear in the crags overhead and loose a deadly barrage of rocks and arrows. With his years of experience and battalion of battle-hardened troops, the king was prepared when his scouts warned him of a war band approaching on the far side of the ridge. The actual clash was over in less time than it would take to tell about it.

Leaving a dozen of his men to despoil the enemy corpses and hunt down any survivors, Theobold sent the bulk of his troop back to Gothroc with the news of his victory. He kept only his hand-picked guard with him on his side trip to the shrine of his patron saint to give thanks—just as he'd sworn he would in front of his adored wife and detested nephew.

Instead of cheers and ovations, the contingent of troops returning through the gates of Gothroc was met by the wails of serving women, the tolling of church bells, and the news that the queen had died in labor the night before and her undelivered infant had been lost along with her.

Someone would have to tell the king.

Gilberth, his face a steely mask, ordered a delegation of Theobold's closest and most trusted retainers to carry the sad tiding to him. He urged them to go at once and intercept the king at the shrine of his patron saint, where he would have the presence of the blessed Saint Aethelbard to comfort him in his sorrow.

Riding hard, the men reached the start of the pathway that led up to the cliffside shrine just as the king was arriving from the opposite direction. As reliable witnesses told it later, "On hearing the news, King Theobold was overcome with grief. Tears flowing down his cheeks, he left us and went alone to the shrine to pray."

Theobold was old and, had he not been the king, someone might have insisted on going with him. Instead, obeying orders, they waited below for his return. They were gathered there, all of them together, when they heard a single despairing cry and rushed up the path to find the shrine empty. Fearing the worst, they looked over the edge of the cliff and saw, far below them, the body of the dead king, his once strong, straight limbs twisted at impossible angles and his proud, stern face staring vacantly at the sky.

Despite their king's dying without a grown son to succeed him, Derthwald remained intact thanks to Gilberth's stepping forward to take his uncle's place. He assumed hegemony over Piffering on his cousin's behalf and for the next fifteen years the combined territories enjoyed a period of peace and tranquility rare for small kingdoms with poorly marked borders. Good fortune, however, was not something the inhabitants of Derthwald took for granted, living as they did in the shadow of the dark, forbidding mountains where, rumor had it, devil-worshipping Druid sorcerers still lurked despite the best efforts of the church to root them out and burn them at the stake.

Chapter 1

The Clearing

𝕬 torch touched the dry tinder and the fire sprang to life, flaring up in a ring around the condemned man. At first the bound figure was just a silhouette against the night sky, but as the fire spread around the stake he was illuminated in its glow, his dark hair shining as golden red as the flames. Even bruised and bloodied, he was handsome, tall, lean, and fit—his features so fine and noble that it was hard to believe the crowd surrounding him was screaming for his death instead of pleading for his life.

Looking through the flames, he could see the shifting shapes of the mob, men with spears, women with cudgels, and children waving sticks. They were cursing him, calling him a sorcerer. If he could have made himself heard, he would have told them that he was not a sorcerer, he was a physician who could have given them the gift of healing, a singer whose songs could have soothed their rage, a bard who could have told them a thousand stories about splendid heroes from days when the world was fresh and new. If they would just stop shouting and listen, he would tell them that he'd been the last of the disciples to sit at the feet of the three greatest Druid masters of their time. He would tell them that by killing him before he could pass on what he had learned they were destroying an ancient heritage of wisdom that could never be recovered, condemning themselves to suffering and ignorance.

Their taunts and jeers seemed to fade away, lost in his longing for a swallow of water to sooth his parched throat, a bite of food to ease his aching hunger, and, above all, to die unbound. It was the fire that granted his last wish—burning through the leather cords so that, for a moment, he was free.

Instead of leaving the fire to be torn apart by the frenzied mob, he raised his arms up towards the moon like a child reaching up to his mother. A sudden breeze fanned the fire and the flames soared, engulfing him and forcing his attackers to fall back as his body turned to a soft, feathery ash that was gathered up and carried off by the wind, swirling up and away into the star-filled sky.

The crowd's angry curses quieted to grumbling complaints, and those changed to the hooting of owls and the croaking of frogs as Caelym woke up to find himself whole again, lying beside a decaying, moss-covered log at the edge of a clearing.

He'd fallen asleep in a thicket of alders, worn out from his desperate race to escape a real mob of raging Saxons. Choosing death by drowning over burning at the stake, he'd dived headlong into a river that carried him out of their reach and far out of his way. It had taken most of a day to make his way back along the river's edge to the turn in the road where he'd been discovered. From there he'd limped on, continuing the quest he'd begun the day after learning that the long-lamented Priestess Annwr, sister to their chief priestess, was alive, that Ossiam, Grand Oracle and Master of Divination had seen her in a dream . . . *Imprisoned in a high tower, her golden hair blowing in the wind and tears streaming down her cheeks, crying out for someone to save her from the bestial Saxon king who comes to ravish her night after night.*

It was Feywn herself, in the privacy of her bedchamber, who told Caelym about Ossiam's vision, and as she spoke the image of her weeping sister had seemed to hover in the air between them. Dropping to his knees, he'd sworn an oath on his life to rescue Annwr and kill the Saxon king, making with that his fifth impetuous vow since entering the room, which was—even for Caelym—a new record.

Taking his ceremonial dagger, along with a satchel of hastily gathered supplies and a map drawn for him by the shrine's eldest priest, he spent the next two months following hints and rumors, guesses and omens, until finally reaching the stronghold of the

Saxon war band that had carried Annwr off fifteen years before—only to learn that she had never been a mistress to the king but merely a nursemaid to the king's daughter, that the king was long dead, and that his daughter had left the palace and gone to a convent, taking Annwr with her.

Now, against all odds, he'd found the convent. Getting up, he stepped over the log and pushed a low-hanging branch out of his way to gaze at the cluster of roofs above a high wooden stockade. From where he stood, he could have thrown a stone and bounced it off the side of the compound's outer wall.

Before he'd fallen asleep, he'd circled the edge of clearing that surrounded the convent, searching for some way to get in. Now, looking up at the dark towers that loomed over the top of the wall, he could make out the shapes of windows and suddenly saw what he had missed before—that one of the windows was open. Still half dreaming, he thought he saw a beautiful, golden-haired woman there, reaching her arms out to him. He blinked, and the vision vanished.

The nearly full moon was sinking behind the convent, casting a shadow that crept towards him as he stared up at the window, debating what to do next. Even if he were able to scale the wall and climb in through the window, he still would have to find his way through a maze of unknown corridors and passageways, searching for a woman he hadn't seen since he was eleven years old. One part of his mind made excuses; the other part replied, *"You swore a sacred oath to save Annwr or die in the attempt."*

There was no answer to that, except that he was tired and hungry and had an arrow in his back. Swearing another oath—that he would return and either find Annwr or find out where she had gone—he stepped back over the log, picked up the damp, travel-stained leather pack that held the meager remnants of the provisions he'd taken with him on his ill-fated quest, and retreated into the forest

Not far from where he'd been standing, he came to the start of a narrow, overgrown path. With a brief invocation to any protective wood spirits that might be hovering nearby, he set off to look for something to eat and a place to hide, and to try again to pull the arrow out—hopefully without fainting this time.

◆◆◆

Caelym was hurrying along, looking from one side of the trail to the other for early berries or edible shoots, when the path took a sharp turn and he collided with a small, gray-haired woman, knocking her over and scattering the contents of her basket—a loaf of bread, a wedge of cheese, and two long sausages—on the ground.

He staggered backwards, struggling to keep his balance. He had to act quickly—either strike the woman unconscious before she started to scream or snatch the loaf of bread and run for his life. Lightheaded from hunger and fatigue, he shifted from one foot to the other, debating what to do.

"Help me up!"

He knew enough English to understand the woman's words, and he recovered his wits. Careful to keep his back turned away from her so she didn't see the arrow and become suspicious, he helped her to her feet. Then he picked up the bread, cheese, and sausages for her and brushed off the dirt with the hem of his cloak.

As he repacked the wicker basket, he apologized, saying that he was most sorry he had disturbed her walk, that he meant no harm to her or any of her people, and that he was on his way to visit a woman named Annwr who was kin to kin of his, and who might now be residing within the nearby convent, only he wasn't sure and didn't wish to disturb the Christian priestesses or their guardians by knocking at their door before breakfast. Putting together a sentence of that length in English wasn't easy, but he was pleased with it, especially with how he had dropped the hint about breakfast without actually begging for a handout.

The woman took the basket back and scowled at him.

Regretting that he hadn't slipped a sausage under his cloak when he had the chance, he tried to think of another way to ask about Annwr without giving himself away.

"Come!" The woman snapped the command in Celt before turning on her heels and going back the way she'd come, leaving the scent of freshly baked bread wafting down the path behind her.

His mind argued caution, his stomach food. His stomach won.

Rushing to catch up, he would have run into her again when she stopped to open a gate in a fence at the end of the path except that she stepped out of the way, letting him charge past her and into a garden filled with winter savory and rosemary, meadowsweet and marsh thistle, tansy and sorrel.

Grumbling something about "clumsy oafs," the woman closed the gate and elbowed past him, leaving the tangle of herbs and winding her way through freshly turned vegetable beds towards the back door of a small cottage.

Caelym started after her, only to fall back when a hissing, angry gray goose attacked him, leading a dozen more.

"Hurry up! My geese don't like men!"

Neither her words nor her tone was hospitable, but neither were the geese. So, summoning the last of his failing strength, he dashed for the door she held open for him.

Chapter 2

The Message

oing into the cottage was like entering another garden, only one that was upside down and dead. Bundles of dried flowers and herbs hung from the ceiling, well above the woman's head but low enough to hit Caelym full in the face. He ducked down, made his way past shelves lined with neat rows of jugs and pots and wooden boxes, and passed through a second door that opened into the main room of the cottage.

It was a square room with a cupboard and counter against one wall, a bed and small square table against another. The bed was covered by a plaid blanket that was laid out so that its lines were perfectly straight, both up and down and side to side. The only other furniture was another, slightly larger, square table with two matching chairs. The chairs were exactly opposite each other and exactly aligned. There was a round stone hearth in the center of the room. A polished black kettle hung over the center of the hearth, and Caelym did not need to look inside it to know that the simmering water would be bubbling with well-disciplined bubbles, each one waiting its turn and rising to the surface in orderly succession—not in the confused, churning disarray with which most kettles boil.

The woman, who had gone to the counter and started unpacking her basket, looked over her shoulder and nodded at the table.

Caelym took this as an invitation to sit down, so he did—carefully, and at an angle, to keep the arrow from hitting the back of the chair. Resting his arms on the table to steady himself, he did his best to convey no more than polite attentiveness while the woman cleaned the last specks of dust off the food, took a knife out of the cupboard, checked its edge for sharpness, and cut meticulously measured slices of the bread, cheese, and sausage, grumbling all the while about uninvited guests who expected to be waited on hand and foot. She spread butter on the bread and put the bread in the center of a round wooden platter, arranged alternating slices of cheese and sausage around the bread, and added a sprig of parsley for garnish. With the plate prepared, she took a jug out of the cupboard and poured what he guessed from the color was elderberry wine into a cup. Then, finally, she brought the plate and cup to the table and put them down directly in front of him.

Exercising a restraint acquired through years of intense training, Caelym waited for her to take her hand away before he started to eat. Even so, it took him less time to clean the plate and drain the cup than it had taken her to fill them.

Sincerely grateful for the first substantial meal he'd had in weeks, he rose from his chair to praise the woman's generosity to a stranger, only to be stopped by a dismissive wave of her hand. It was a gesture he would know anywhere—the exact same gesture that Feywn made when he came into her bedchamber uninvited. He opened his mouth, closed it, and sat back down. It was a full moment before he found his voice again.

"You are Annwr?"

"And if I am?"

"I've come with a message for Annwr from her sister and need to know that it is Annwr I am giving it to."

"Fifteen years is a long time to wait to bring this message."

Spoken in an imperious voice—as if Feywn's voice were coming from the old woman's lips—her words settled the last of Caelym's doubts. Still, it was not fair that he should have to answer for Ossiam's failure to have his vision sooner, and he recovered himself enough to say so.

"I began searching from one end of the land to the other, climbing snow-covered mountains and descending into desolate valleys, swimming across raging rivers, and wading through perilous swamps, with little food and no rest, the very moment it was revealed that Ossiam, Grand Oracle and Master of Divination, had seen in his dreams that . . . that . . ."

Caelym faltered. The vision that Ossiam had seen was of a beautiful girl held captive in a king's palace, not a bad-tempered old woman living comfortably in a common cottage that was too clean but otherwise quite pleasant. He finished awkwardly, "That you were still alive."

The realization of just how far off the mark their Grand Oracle and Master of Divination had been shook Caelym to his core, leaving him speechless.

Annwr broke the silence. "Ossiam couldn't divine his way to the latrine in broad daylight and downwind of it!" She fixed Caelym in a direct glare. "So now you are finally here, suppose you say what it is you have come to say."

Challenged to get to the point, he did. "To my sister, Annwr—greetings. In your absence, much has come to pass. It is imperative that you come without delay. Caelym, son of Caelendra, who bears this message, will be your guide. All will be revealed at the equinox."

"Spring or fall?"

Her words hit hard—harder, maybe, than she intended. Refusing to acknowledge Annwr's unwelcome reminder that he'd spent over two months searching for her and still had a long road ahead of him, Caelym spoke in his most imposing and masterful voice—a voice befitting an emissary of the Great Mother Goddess—as he changed the subject.

"Of course, you must be overcome with eagerness to hear of all that has come to pass in your long, sad years of separation. If there were but time and if only I had my golden harp at hand, what stories I could tell you, what songs I could sing. For now, let it suffice to say that Cyri, brave and beautiful, conceived in the Sacred Summer Solstice Ceremony and born of your exalted loins, stands at Feywn's right side, ever yearning for your return."

He paused there, waiting for the importance of what he'd said to sink in, before adding, "Now I have found you, you need fear neither Saxon warrior nor wild beast in the forest, for I will protect you and keep you safe on our journey."

With this oath, at least, as good as fulfilled, he folded his arms on the table, put his head down, and fell asleep, the arrow in his back vibrating rhythmically with his snores.

"Caelym!"

She said his name sharply, causing him to startle.

"I remember you now! You always were a gabby little pest! I suppose that besides expecting me to feed you, you want me to pull the arrow out from between your ribs, and then go traipsing back with you so you can boast about what a brave hero you are."

While it was true that Caelym was looking forward to hearing the gasps and cheers as he recounted his adventures before the high council, it was also true that he'd suffered genuine hardship on Annwr's account, so he sulked in silence for several minutes before conceding that he would be grateful to have her help in pulling the arrow out of his back, "and pleased beyond the ability of my poor words to express for your bestowing upon me the exalted honor of escorting you out of these accursed lands to the place where your dearest kin reach out their arms wide in joyous welcome."

It was a gallant response, well phrased and flawlessly delivered, but it earned him nothing more than a cranky grumble from Annwr: "I haven't said I'm going anywhere with you."

Instead of arguing, Caelym put his head back down on his arms.

He must have dozed off again, because suddenly Annwr was next to him and helping him over to the bed. She cut the stiff, blood-soaked cloth away from the base of the arrow and eased his cloak, tunic, and shirt off around it. Then she brought him another cup of wine and a leather strap to bite on. He braced himself, gripping the checkered blanket in his fists as she took hold of the arrow, biting the strap nearly in two when she wrenched it out.

Holding a cloth to Caelym's back to stop the fresh flow of blood, Annwr led him back over to the chair by the fire. She put a basin of hot water on the floor in front of him, helped him shed the rest of his clothes, and kept a hand on his shoulder to steady him as he leaned over to wash. When he had done what he could on his own, she poured soapy water through his hair and scrubbed his back, cleaning carefully around the still-oozing wound. She had been quiet before, but somehow seemed quieter now.

Caelym guessed what she was thinking. "It would be likely to fester and bring fever, I suppose."

"And you would be some physician to be knowing about festering and fevers?"

"That I am, for six years and more."

"You never are. There'd be nobody trusting you with any healing!"

"My patients may not be trusting me with their healing, but I'm doing it whether they are trusting, or they are not."

"Well then, you are physician and I am a midwife, so I suppose we may both be thinking it could fester and bring fever, but you are young and strong and likely enough to live through it."

"Still, if it does fester, I won't be moving so well for a while, so I will get my clothes and think of where I will go next while I can still be up and about."

"And how am I to know where to find you, if I should decide to go on this trip of yours?"

"You are coming with me, then?"

"I haven't made up my mind, so you might as well be getting back into the bed, as it will be a week or more before you are going anywhere."

Caelym was not about to let the matter rest before he had an answer to his question. "A week is a long time to keep a man in your bed if you haven't decided what you're going to be doing with him."

Annwr was not about to be pushed into an answer before she was ready to give it. "I am an old woman," she snapped, "and it's been more than a week since anybody has worried about whether there was a man in my bed. Anyway, your clothes are soaking in the wash and my geese would laugh themselves egg-bound to see you walking out the door wearing nothing."

Too tired to think of a satisfactory retort, he allowed her to lead him back to the bed, but there he stood his ground, refusing to lie down, until he had repeated his pledge to save her from the Saxons. Even as the room spun around him, he spoke with a Druid's persuasive powers, choosing his words skillfully to hide his disappointment that she was no longer beautiful.

Chapter 3

The Novice

The Abbey of Saint Edeth the Enduring was a cloistered convent in the northeastern corner of the Kingdom of Derthwald. A dense forest surrounded the abbey and a narrow clearing around its outer wall was all that separated the nuns and novices inside from the wilderness, so there was a strict rule that all the doors and all the windows had to be kept closed and latched at night.

Shy, high-strung, and fearful, Sister Aleswina was an unlikely delinquent, but she eased herself out from under her blankets, tiptoed over to the window, and opened the shutters. While Caelym was looking up at her window, Aleswina was looking at the horizon, as if by staring hard enough she could make the dawn come faster. A breeze wafted in, carrying the enticing scent of spring, and she gripped the window's ledge, overcome with longing to have her trowel in her hand. If she had dared, she would have gone out in the dark to start digging her beds and planting her seeds.

While there was not much in her dress or in her features to distinguish her from any of a dozen pale, blond Saxon nuns, Aleswina was different from the other women at the convent in three ways— her passion for growing plants, her deep love for the servant who had once been her nursemaid, and in her being the cousin to the king of Derthwald. An unspoken deference to her royal status did more than save her from open reproach over the length of time it was taking her commit to her final vows; it gave her two unusual privileges within the abbey. She was allowed to work by herself in the convent's garden, and she was allowed to keep her servant, Anna, in a cottage on the edge of the convent's grounds.

While they were packing to leave the palace for the convent, Aleswina had entrusted Anna with a substantial cache of coins and jewels, and as soon as it was safe, Anna had bribed a traveling tinker to cut a secret door into the back wall of the convent garden so that Aleswina did not really work in the garden by herself. It was against the rules and, cousin to the king or not, Aleswina would have faced untold days of penance if the abbess ever found out, but every day weather allowed, Anna slipped in through their secret entrance to work along with her.

The morning promised to be exceptionally warm and balmy for so early in the year, and Aleswina was anxious to begin.

"Not our wishes but the Lord's!" was what the abbess would say if Aleswina told her how much she wanted to tend her plants instead of singing or praying. She'd tried that once and been confined in her room to pray and reflect for the rest of the day.

It was a lesson she'd taken to heart. She'd spent those long, lonely hours terrified that the abbess would send someone to the garden in her place, that Anna would be caught, and that their secret door would be discovered. Whether it was the Virgin Mary or the Mother Goddess who heard her frantic prayers, someone did; and Aleswina never said another word to the abbess about anything that really mattered to her ever again.

Now, she leaned as far out of the window as she dared, savoring the smell of fresh night air, until the bells rang for the sunrise service. As she closed the shutters—careful not to let them clatter—she realized she'd waited too long to change into her daytime habit. She snatched her wimple off its hook, pulled it on as she felt under her bed for her sandals, and was just in time to open her door and take her place in between Sister Erdorfa and Sister Idwolda as they filed past her door.

While the poorly lit passageway between the dormitory and the chapel was among the spaces exempted from convent's rule that secular exchanges were to be conducted using officially sanctioned hand signals, the nuns and novices of Saint Edeth usually went to the first office of the day in sleepy silence. That morning, however, they were wide awake, whispering,

"Did you hear?"
"Killing babies and drinking their blood!"
"Raping virgins!"
"Coming for us!"

Before Aleswina could ask who was killing babies and raping virgins, they reached the chapel. The whispering changed to shushes as they filed into their places.

After they sang the opening hymn and recited the designated psalms, the abbess stepped up to the altar, but instead of reading from the gospels, she announced that the rumors were true.

"A Druid sorcerer has been sighted near Strothford, just across the River Bense."

The nuns on either side of Aleswina gasped.

The abbess put up her hand for silence. "The king's soldiers are searching every cottage and shed. They will find the sorcerer and the rest of the devil's minions—the witches that brew his deadly potions, the demons that cavort at his feet, and the incubi that lure hapless girls into his grasping claws—and burn them at the stake."

The abbess lifted her voice in a fervent prayer for the Lord's protection before dismissing them with a final warning: "No one is to go outside of the abbey, and if you see anything suspicious—the slightest change in the behavior of any of the servants or even one of our own—you must come and tell me at once!"

The nervous chatter started up again on the way from chapel to the dining room and did not stop until the abbess took her place at the head of the table. After she said the blessing, they murmured "amen" in unison and began to eat. As Sister Aleswina moved her spoon from her plate to her mouth and back to her plate, the abbess's warning echoed in her ears.

Although she was afraid of many things, Aleswina was not frightened of Druids or witches, because Anna was both. It was no use trying to explain it to the abbess, but not all witches brewed poisons, and not all Druids were in league with the devil. There were good ones like Anna, who made healing potions to ease the pain of childbirth and who kept evil spirits away with magic sachets filled with sweet-smelling herbs and who rocked you to sleep at night with lullabies that banished nightmares and brought happy dreams of sunlit meadows blooming with beautiful flowers.

As soon as the after-breakfast benedictions and announcements were finished, Aleswina got up from the table, genuflected to the abbess, and left the room—not hurrying, hardly breathing, for fear of looking suspicious. Once she was in the hallway, she walked quicker, almost running, to the convent garden. She expected to find Anna waiting for her, but the garden was empty.

There was no time to waste. She had to tell Anna to hide her powders and potions so no one would know she was a witch and burn her at the stake. Aleswina ducked out the back way, then rushed across the clearing and into the forest, running as fast as she could along the path to Anna's cottage.

Chapter 4

The Warning

The effects of Annwr's wine had worn off, but instead of offering Caelym another cup, she fed him thin porridge, spooning it into his mouth and wiping his chin as if he were a drooling infant.

What he needed was more wine and to be left in peace to sleep and recover his strength. Instead, she made him roll over so she could spread a foul-smelling unguent on his wound, lecturing him while she worked as though she were the shrine's chief physician and he merely some ordinary patient come to injury through his own recklessness.

He was still lying face down on the bed, gritting his teeth and reminding himself that Annwr was their long-lost priestess and Feywn's beloved sister, when he heard running footsteps outside.

"The Saxons are coming!" He kept his voice low as he groped on the bedside table for his knife, only to realize that Annwr had moved it across the room to the counter where it lay polished and gleaming and out of reach.

"I told you that my geese will give warning if anyone comes—"

Annwr's hand was on his back, holding him down, helpless, as the door flew open and a Saxon—albeit a short, thin, female one—rushed into the room, gasping in English, "Anna, there are soldiers coming! They are chasing some poor Druid and searching everywhere. They are heading this way and will be—"

She came to a halt in the middle of the room and stood there, staring at Caelym.

Instead of letting him up to get his knife, Annwr kept her hand on his back and greeted the intruder like they were old friends.

"Oh, Dear Heart, I'm sorry. I was coming to see you, only this boy, who is kin to kin of mine, arrived and I had to take care of him."

"Anna, no! He cannot stay here! He must go away! The soldiers will be here any moment!"

"I'll hide him somewhere—in the loft, or maybe in the goose shed."

The two women were speaking rapidly in English, while Caelym, feeling sluggish and stupid with his rising fever, looked from one to the other trying to follow what they were saying.

"They will find him, Anna! They will search the loft and the goose shed! He must run away into the woods!"

"He is too weak to run far. They will find him in the woods and follow his tracks back here—so when they find him, they will find me too. But, Dear Heart, you have given us enough warning that we have time to take a way out of this. I'll have it mixed, and he and I will drink it, and neither of us will care what they do after that. Now, you must go straight back to the convent and be ready to say how you never suspected me of being a witch, and how glad you are that the Christian world is rid of him and me both."

"No, Anna, you must not even think of it! It is a sin!"

"Maybe so, Dear Heart, yet I will choose this sin over the virtue of being put alive into a Christian bonfire."

These last words, at least, were clear. Wrestling himself out from under Annwr's restraining hand, Caelym swung his feet over the edge of the bed and stood up. Weaving only slightly, he declared, "I will go, leading the soldiers away, leaving no tracks . . ."

He would have gone on pledging his oath to Annwr to gladly give his life for hers, but the Saxon girl let out a strangled gasp, turned away, and covered her face with her hands. Her next words almost too muffled to hear. "I will take him back with me and hide him. Only, please, Anna, tell him to put his clothes on!"

"Sit down, Caelym, and cover yourself!" Annwr said this in Celt, so sharply that Caelym hastily sat back down and pulled the blanket over his lap—offended at the girl's reaction and resentful that Annwr didn't appreciate his courageous sacrifice.

Adding further insult, the girl turned her back on him while she spoke to Annwr. "Does he know any English? Will he understand what I say to him?"

"He spoke in English when we met. Nobody would take him for a bishop, but I expect he'll understand you well enough."

Caelym started to say that he could speak English as well as any bishop could, but Annwr just told him to be quiet and get dressed, and handed him his wet clothes. With no more than a curt "and be quick about it!" she took hold of the girl's hand and led her into the back room, closing the door behind them with a resounding thud.

Curious, Caelym slipped silently across the room and put his ear to the door. He heard Annwr tell the girl what herbs and potions to mix to treat his fever and help him sleep, and—in a voice that was lower, but still audible—how much more of the poppy juice he would need to drink if the soldiers did find him after all. Then the girl, who had said almost nothing except "Yes, Anna" and "I will, Anna" until then, told Annwr to hide her potions and wear her crucifix.

Annwr (who had never once spoken to him in such an agreeable, obliging voice) answered, "I will, Dear Heart."

He'd been pulling on his pants while he was listening. When the talking stopped, he backed away and was standing by the hearth, innocently tucking in his shirt, when Annwr, with the girl following behind her, came back into the room.

Annwr looked from Caelym to the wet spot on the floor where he'd been eavesdropping, and then back at him. To his relief, the girl diverted Annwr's attention by whispering in her ear.

"His name is Caelym," Annwr said. "He is a priest among my people—a physician, too, if you can believe him."

"Then I must call him 'Father Caelym'?"

Caelym's face flushed red at the idea that he might ever be taken for the father of any Saxon, let alone one as puny and whining as this one. As usual, Annwr ignored his attempts to protest and went on talking as if he wasn't there.

"Just 'Caelym'! He is a Druid priest, and you have to watch out or he will talk you into the ground. You tell him what he is to do, and you don't let him argue back."

Annwr drew herself up to her full height and turned to Caelym. Looking him straight in the eye and switching into Celt, she declared, "Caelym, this is Sister Aleswina. She is the daughter of a king, and she is in training to be a Christian priestess. You will be going with her, and she will be hiding you at great risk. You will be grateful for it, and you will swear an oath now to give her the obedience and the service that you give to the Goddess Herself!"

"I will not!" is what Caelym would have said if Annwr hadn't been their long-lost priestess and Feywn's sister. As it was, he cast himself down flat on the floor in front of Aleswina to declare in clear and precise English: "I will sacrifice nine bulls in your honor, laying their livers and testicles at your feet, and I will obey your every wish as though you were the Goddess Herself!"

Instead of being flattered and making the proper response— giving him a bracelet from her wrist or a lock of her hair as she promised to treasure his words forever—the girl backed away, looking at Annwr and sniveling, "Please tell him that it is a sin to say such things."

"Never mind him, he's just showing off!" Annwr snapped. Fixing Caelym with her beady-eyed glare, she hissed, "Now you pick yourself up and go before you've got soldiers to be bowing to! You do what Aleswina tells you, and you keep quiet, and you stay out of trouble!"

Caelym scrambled to his feet and was searching for a fitting retort when he heard the sound of baying hounds in the distance.

"Go!" Annwr ordered.

Caelym grabbed his bag from the side of the bed and his knife from the counter and dashed after Aleswina as she ran through the back room and out the door.

Chapter 5

Abduction

The sounds of the baying hounds grew louder as Annwr sealed the gate and began to sweep away the telltale tracks. A single shrill bark rang out above the rest—then there was silence.

The broom handle grew moist in her hands as she waited, straining her ears. Out of the corner of her eye, she saw Betrys, heavy with her unborn piglets, heave herself up to look out from the door of her shed as the geese drew together into a defensive circle.

When the yowling started up again, it was jumbled and discordant, as if the dogs were arguing amongst themselves.

A loud yelp seemed to settle the pack's dispute. It was joined almost at once by a chorus of blood-curdling howls that rose up, swerved away and faded into the distance.

Suppressing a wave of pity for whatever terrified creature was now running for its life, Annwr finished sweeping and tossed out a second breakfast for the geese, watching to be sure that their eager scuffling covered over any marks she might have missed before walking deliberately around the rows and beds to lay a trail of innocent footprints. The flock followed at her heels, tutting and chuckling, while their leader stretched up his neck to nudge at her half-empty basket. Looking back later, she'd be sorry she didn't give them that final scoop of grain instead of telling Solomon he was getting too fat for his own good, shooing them off, and going inside.

After closing the inner door behind her, she looked around and saw the room as Caelym must have seen it, crude and drab, a far cry from the resplendent halls of Llwddawanden. But it was spotless. There was not a crumb on the table or a wrinkle in the bedcovers to show that he'd ever been there.

With nothing left to clean, Annwr began to pace around the hearth, clutching the silver cross Aleswina had given her to ward off evil—especially the evil of being accused of witchcraft.

Meeting him on her way to the abbey, Annwr hadn't recognized Caelym as anything except one more homeless Briton, taller than most but otherwise just another starving refugee looking for a handout. Even when he asked for her by name, she'd made no connection between the edgy, apprehensive vagabond speaking hesitant English and the willful, high-spirited boy she'd known in her other life, although the arrow in his back should have been a hint.

His proclamation that he was a messenger from Feywn had shaken her more than she let on, but she hadn't fully believed it until he plunged his face down into the washbasin and raised it up again, dripping but clean, and—for a heart-stopping moment— she'd thought Rhedwyn had surfaced instead.

Like most people in her day and age, Annwr believed in ghosts, but she was also practical. When Rhedwyn was alive, he'd never paid her any attention beyond the habitual flirtation he'd bestowed on anyone who stood still long enough—why would he take time out of his next life to pursue her now?

Still, the sight convinced her as no words could that her unexpected visitor was really Caelym, Son of Caelendra, that he'd really been sent by Feywn, and that maybe Ossiam wasn't a useless old fraud after all.

Reversing direction, she thought back over the message Caelym delivered. Stripped of its ornamentation—and there never had been a priest on the high council who could just say what he meant and get it over with—it came down to: *"I need you—so come now!"*

Whatever else had changed in Annwr's absence, her sister had not. Never a word from her for fifteen years and now imperiously calling her back, regardless of the risk and inconvenience, and making it sound as though Annwr's abduction and captivity were her own doing and not Feywn's fault in the first place.

What had they been thinking, Feywn and her swaggering consort? That Rhedwyn and his handful of play soldiers were going to win back lands lost two times over? Prove the Goddess still held sway outside the gates of Llwddawanden? Decorate the sacred grove with real severed heads as easily as counting up clay trophies from their mock battles in the pastures above the shrine? Well, Rhedwyn's decision to move up from raiding cattle and plundering trading caravans to taking on a Saxon force that outnumbered his foolhardy little war band three to one certainly settled those questions for good and all!

"Rhedwyn," even though Annwr only thought the name in her head, it came out as a snort. Too bad he didn't have the sense of a goose instead of the looks of a god! Any goose would have known better than to believe Ossiam's gibberish about some glorious destiny divined from a pile of soggy goat guts. And Feywn! Feywn should have stopped him, should have ordered him off his horse and back to her bedroom!

Instead, she'd just believed his boasting and let him go riding off—banners waving, drums beating, soon-to-be widows and orphans cheering—while she called on Ossiam to invoke spirit armies from the otherworld to rise and join the battle. Either those shadow forces had refused the oracle's entreaties or else they had no power against the Saxons who mowed down a generation of the shrine's young men like the year's last standing stalks of wheat.

Dozens of men and boys died alongside Rhedwyn, but none of them mattered to Feywn. Blind and deaf to the grief of others, she'd sent the dazed survivors out under the cover of darkness to bring Rhedwyn's body back to the shrine.

Annwr, along with her cousins, Gwennefor and Caldora, had done everything they could to appease Feywn's spiraling demands—bathing Rhedwyn's ravaged corpse with water carried down in buckets from the sacred pools, swathing him with silk and decking him with gold and precious gems, gathering armloads of flowers and herbs to be his shroud. Then she'd called for King's Heal, as if Rhedwyn was a king or there was any hope of healing him!

But there'd been no reasoning with Feywn, so they put on their fine white ceremonial robes. Leaving the safety of their hidden valley, they'd carried their little reed baskets and their little golden scissors to snip the leaves of those precious little plants growing on the banks of the sacred river just downstream from where it flowed through the blood-drenched battlefield—a place where anyone as all-seeing and all-knowing as the living embodiment of the Great Mother Goddess should have realized the Saxons would still be prowling.

They'd been caught unawares, preoccupied with their separate sorrows. Annwr had fallen behind the others, so she was the first to hear the sound of horses' hooves pounding towards them. She'd called out a warning, changed direction and started to run, hoping to give Caldora and Gwennefor a chance to escape and get help. Her next scream was cut short as a filthy, sweat-soaked cloak came down over her head and she was grappled to the ground—trapped, suffocating, feeling the earth shudder as more horses thundered past.

Carried off, bound and blindfolded, losing count of the days and the number of times she'd been raped, she'd clung to life and sanity by silently reciting the chant for the worst phase of labor, moving her mind so far away from her body that nothing they did mattered to her—so far away she never knew that she changed hands twice, once in a game of dice and once in exchange for a fresh horse, before finally being sold at the main slave market in Derthwald.

Chapter 6

Sold

Eldhelm, the slave dealer, realized almost at once that he'd made a bad bargain. Staring vacantly ahead of her, unable or unwilling to respond to the loudest and simplest of commands, Annwr drew little interest and no bids until late in the afternoon when Erbert, who'd just been appointed the under-steward of the king's chambermaids and kitchen sculleries, came looking for a nurse for the newly orphaned princess. Erbert had an intuition he should get one that was stupid and did not speak English, so he picked Annwr—answering Eldhelm's half-hearted claim that she was a trained nursemaid worth twice her asking price with, "Six sceatta, take it or leave it."

Eldhelm took it. Erbert grabbed Annwr by the wrist and dragged her out of the slave yard, shoving their way through milling, muttering crowds and clusters of guards—out of the village and up the steep road that switchbacked its way to the top of the granite outcrop that gave the name Gothroc to the central fortress and stronghold of the Kingdom of Derthwald. A portly, middle-aged man, not accustomed to strenuous activity, Erbert was sweating and out of breath by the time they'd reached the top, where a massive oak and iron gate creaked open just enough to let them in, but he forged on, hauling Annwr through the narrow passages between guardhouses, armories, stables, and storage sheds.

Stumbling along behind him, Annwr kept her eyes fixed on the knife Erbert had carelessly stuck in his belt, and if he had not been too nervous to stop off in some alley and take advantage of his temporary authority, things would have ended very differently for both of them that day. As it was, he kept hurrying on until he came to the back gate of a high-walled compound. The gate cracked open at his knock, revealing half the face of an old woman who thrust her hand out, grabbed Annwr by the sleeve, and yanked her inside.

In contrast to Erbert, who hadn't spoken a single word to Annwr, her new captor began talking as soon as the gate was latched behind them, gesturing wildly with her free hand. It would be months before Annwr would have even a rudimentary grasp of English, so the woman's guttural exhortations were totally incomprehensible to her, but there was no mistaking the urgency of their tone as she pulled Annwr through an overgrown courtyard garden and into a dark, tightly shuttered room.

It took time for Annwr's eyes to adjust to the dim light and for silhouettes and shadows around her to take recognizable shapes—a box filled with toys on the floor, a child-size table and chair next to the unlit hearth, and a small bed in the corner with a child-sized figure sitting on it. At first, Annwr thought she was seeing an amazingly lifelike doll dressed in layers of green and gold brocade, its face and hands carved of alabaster, with disks of obsidian for eyes and a smooth veil of silvery-white silk threads for hair. Then the little girl blinked, looked straight at Annwr, and reached up to her with both arms, the fingers of one hand wide open, the other clenched in a fist.

Annwr could not help herself—she shook loose from the old woman's grasp and picked the child up, expecting the crone to scream and attack her as savagely as she would have attacked any stranger who dared lay a hand on Cyri. Instead, the woman broke into a toothy smile and nodded eagerly. Annwr nodded back without any real idea of what they were agreeing about and watched in numbed bewilderment as the woman darted around the room, still babbling, and opened the doors of its several cabinets, pointing to the rows of child sized gowns as she went. When she'd opened the last cupboard, the old woman pointed to the little girl and said, "Infant Princess Aleswina." Then she pointed to Annwr. When Annwr said her own name, the woman nodded so vigorously it seemed her head might fly off her shoulders. Then, abruptly, she stopped bobbing her head, pointed to herself and said, "Millicent," then pointed to the door, ran out, and slammed it behind her.

Left standing in the dark with Aleswina clinging to her, the understanding dawned on Annwr that she was to be the child's nursemaid. She knew about nursemaids. She'd had one herself. She recalled how much liberty Nonna had had—and taken—so long as she and Feywn were quiet and happy, and so, as she rocked the little girl, humming the lullabies that Nonna used to sing, she began to plan her escape.

Within a month, she had a knife. Within a year, she had a blanket, a rope, and containers for food and water. By the end of three years, she could speak enough English to be sent out to the town market and had convinced her keepers that she could be trusted to come back again. The one thing she did not plan on was that she'd come to care so deeply for the little Saxon princess who clung to her like a limpet to a rock.

If she'd known which way to go, Annwr would have taken Aleswina and gone. If she'd had only herself to think about, she would have run off in any direction at all.

While she never actually gave up her plans to escape, she'd postponed them so often that they no longer seemed real. Meanwhile, she'd had a child to raise, babies to deliver and, in these past seven years, her own small cottage, her garden, and her animals.

It was not much, but it was what she had to show for fifteen years of hardship, and it was not as easy as some people might think to leave it all behind on a moment's notice. So now she wavered, worrying about Aleswina and also about Betrys, the pig whose regular litters gave Annwr an income of her own, and the geese, whose eggs and offspring added to her economic security as much as their militant defense of the yard added to her safety. These animals were more than livestock to Annwr; they were her friends and her family. If she left, what would happen to them?

Chapter 7

Cyri

As Annwr paced in circles, trying to decide what to do, the soft chatter of the geese outside her window seemed to change into the sounds of children at play, laughing and calling out to each other in sweet, lilting voices.

Between them, Annwr, Feywn, and their two cousins, Gwennefor and Caldora, had five girls, all born with within the space of five years. Cyri came last because Annwr was in training with the shrine's chief midwife, Rhonnon, who'd refused to give her permission to take a consort, saying, "You can learn with your mind and with your heart, but not at the same time!"

Unwilling to give up her position as Rhonnon's understudy, she'd watched with growing envy as the others chose consorts and got pregnant—assisting at each birth while wanting to have a baby so much that she pleaded, unsuccessfully, with Caldora to give over one of her twins.

Then, the spring that she was nineteen, when every living creature around the shrine had seemed to be hatching an egg or suckling a pup, she got an idea. Guessing correctly that her teacher's objection was not to having babies but to having consorts, she went to Rhonnon asking her consent to take the lead role in the Summer Solstice rites celebrating the courtship of the Earth Goddess by the Sun God and the conception of their first child together.

She returned to the women's quarter skipping and dancing to tell her cousins the news, and the three of them had barely been able to keep their composure as they sat through the speeches of the next high council, waiting for Feywn to make the official proclamation.

It had been the beginning of a wonderful, waking dream and she'd loved every part of it—the giggling sessions with Gwennefor and Caldora over which priest she should pick to stand in for the Sun, the delirious ecstasy of playing a goddess coupling with a god, the self-conscious pride in her steadily swelling belly that changed into mystic bliss as the life within her began to move and kick under her fingertips. Of course, the actual pain of giving birth had not been fun, but all memories of that vanished when Rhonnon handed the warm, squirming bundle to her and asked what she was going to name her daughter.

"Cyri."

Feywn didn't like the name and tried to get her to change it to something that sounded more elevated and fitting for a priestess destined to be her own daughter's chief assistant. But in those first wonder-filled moments when Annwr held her baby cradled in her arms, Cyri had looked up at her and said "Cu-Ree." Even though no one else heard, or believed her when she told them, Annwr was convinced that Cyri had picked her own name, and she refused to give it up for all of Feywn's badgering.

Keeping the promise she'd made to Rhonnon, Annwr returned to her training after giving birth, but she spent every spare moment with Cyri and the other four girls—Gwennefor's pretty, dark-haired daughter, Caldora's lively twins, so much like each other that even their mother couldn't tell them apart, and Feywn's daughter, Arianna, who was red-haired like Cyri and just six months older, so the two of them might have been taken from a distance for a second set of twins.

Not that Annwr would ever mistake her own daughter for any other child!

Even covered in mud and, as often as not, with her finger stuck up her nose, Cyri had always seemed to have a special radiance about her, and it had puzzled Annwr that no one else saw it as clearly as she did. But then none of the other girls got the same attention as Feywn's daughter. Not an hour went by that some

servant or priest wasn't saying how wonderful Arianna was, prais-
ing her emerald-green eyes (and Cyri's were what? Blue? Brown?),
her spiraling crown of vibrant red hair (and Cyri's wasn't just as
red and just as curly?), or her flawless skin (as if there was something wrong with a few freckles!).

The sociable chortling of the geese outside shifted briefly into
a squabble over some left-over wad of bread crusts and just as
quickly fell back to friendly chatter.

Although she was not a woman given to fanciful imaginings,
Annwr began to feel like the room was growing misty, its walls
sprouting branches and leaves to become a ring of living trees
and the bare floorboards turning into a carpet of grass sprinkled
with summer flowers. It was as if, in her impatient pacing, her
feet had carried her back to Llwddawanden and back in time to
the day she'd taken Cyri and the other little girls to play in the
meadow above the shrine. There, holding Cyri's hand on one side
and Arianna's on the other, she'd led them dancing around in
a circle, the five girls calling out "Faster! Faster!" until they all
fell laughing to the ground. Once they'd caught their breath, the
children had gotten up and run off to a new game, while she'd
sat there, a fresh breeze rustling her hair, the sun warm on her
cheeks. As she watched her daughter playing the games she'd
played as a child—singing made-up songs at make-believe stone
altars and picking flowers to weave into solstice crowns—she'd
thought that nothing could add to her happiness. And then Cyri
had broken away from the others and come running back, her face
glowing with love and her arms outstretched, holding a battered
cluster of flowers in each of her chubby little hands.

The bliss of that moment was shattered when Arianna came
tearing after Cyri, screaming, "She picked my flower! Mine! I want
it!"—and their nursemaid had actually tried to pluck that exact
blossom out of Cyri's hands, scattering the rest in a vain attempt
to mollify Arianna, who'd just screeched louder, "No, not that one!
Not that one! Not that one—"

In the pervasive web of gossip that ran from the lowest
servant's closet to the highest chambers of the elite council of
Druid elders, nothing that Arianna did went unremarked, and
that very night at supper, Ossiam, groveling toady that he was,
had gushed on and on how Arianna's "vibrant moods moved from

joyous happiness to magnificent rage and back again as the sky filled with storm clouds and parted to let the radiance of the sun shine through"—making it sound as though there were something miraculous about a spoiled child having a tantrum.

Chapter 8

Annwr Makes Up Her Mind

Coming to an abrupt halt, Annwr stood staring at the chair where Caelym had sat, spouting off about mystic visions and golden harps. She'd been so impatient with his posturing, innuendoes, and meaningful looks that she'd hardly paid attention when he said that Cyri "stands at Feywn's right side." Her right side! Where her presumptive heir would stand!

If Cyri was Feywn's heir, it could only mean that Arianna was dead.

Being a midwife, Annwr's first guess was that it must have been childbirth, and as the memories of her brash, demanding, and utterly fearless niece swept over her, Annwr thought—not for the first time—that if she had been the Goddess, she would have arranged things differently, seeing to it that starting babies was less compelling for men and that giving birth to them was less dangerous for women.

Annwr shifted her gaze from the empty chair to the open window. Most of the view was blocked by trees towering above the fence but here and there, in the gaps in the upper branches, she could just make out the purple and gray ridges of the distant mountains that hid the sacred valley of Llwddawanden—and wondered what Cyri was doing at that moment.

Of course, Feywn would have raised Cyri as her own, just as, if things had been reversed, Annwr would have raised Arianna. And, of course, with Arianna dead, Feywn would name Cyri—Feywn's closest kin except for Annwr herself—to be her heir.

But their chief midwife, Rhonnon, was actually more closely related to the past chief priestesses than Feywn . . . and while Rhonnon had no children, she had a niece born to her sister . . . and that niece had a daughter . . . theirs was a strong line going almost directly back to Feywn's revered predecessor, Caelendra.

While Feywn had never been openly challenged as chief priestess and living embodiment of the Mother Goddess, her selection had been unorthodox (and in fact unprecedented), and that departure from tradition had always been the shadow behind her otherwise unquestioned authority. Could it be, Annwr found herself wondering, that the reason her sister acted like such a tyrant was that she had some lingering doubts of her own?

Whether or not that was true, Feywn would certainly intend to head off any challenge to her power to name a successor from her own line, most likely by making Cyri her daughter by right of proclamation—a simple ritual so long as a child's real mother was dead, as, according to Caelym, they'd believed she was until Ossiam had his belated vision. But no one, not even the Goddess herself, had the power to strip a living birth mother of her natural claims without her consent.

It all fell into place.

Feywn needed Annwr to forswear her birthright claim to Cyri, freeing her to be named Feywn's daughter.

In her mind, Annwr's answer rang out: *"No! You can't have her! She's my child! Mine! I gave birth to her! I won't give her up!"*

Only, of course, she would. Who was she to say no to the will of the Goddess or to deny Cyri the greatest honor imaginable?

But did she have to go and stand at the high altar, her own heart torn out and bleeding, and declare that her child was not hers and never had been?

"NO!" She said it out loud this time and meant it, grimly glad now that she'd never actually told Caelym that she was his missing priestess. When he came back, fully recovered and twice as boastful, she would tell him that she was merely a silly old servant who'd taken advantage of his gullibility to enliven her otherwise drab and dreary existence, and that the real Annwr had died fifteen years ago. Then she'd hand him a basket of food and send him on his way.

Not happy, but relieved to have made up her mind, she looked at the room around her as if she were seeing it for the first time: the neat rows of cups and bowls on the shelves, the thick, warm quilt spread over the bed, the polished kettle simmering on the hearth.

It was peaceful and quiet.

Too quiet.

There was not a sound coming in through the window, not the clucking of geese in the yard or chirping of birds in the trees. Before she had time to worry about what that might mean, the geese sounded their shrill warning, her front door crashed open, and a dozen Saxon guards stormed in.

Half of them ransacked the room, ripping the covers off the bed, dragging boxes out from underneath and kicking them apart, tearing cupboard doors off their hinges, and pulling jars off the shelves and smashing them open—as if they expected to find a full-grown Druid hidden inside—while the other half stormed out into the garden, slashing their way through the spirited but hopelessly doomed defense offered by Solomon and the other geese.

With no chance to run or hide, Annwr dropped to her knees, closed her eyes, and clutched the silver crucifix while Betrys's terrified squeals rang in her ears, sounding like Gwennefor and Caldora's screams fifteen years before.

After the rampage was over, Annwr stayed on her knees, her head bowed as if in prayer, giving no hint that her silent invocations were not Christian appeals for mercy but pagan curses against them and all of their descendants forever after. Fortunately unable to read her thoughts, their leader, a tall, blond man with a vexed expression, muttered that they were wasting their time here and had better be going on to search the woods. Maybe he was expecting her to grovel and kiss his feet in gratitude, but she stayed where she was, certain that if she moved even a single muscle, she'd lose herself in her fury and attack him with her bare hands.

Instead, she kept her eyes cast down and began to plan what she'd need to pack for the trip back to Llwddawanden while she waited for the door to slam behind them and the tread of their boots to die off in the distance.

PART II

The Shrine of Wilfhilda

Aleswina led the way back down the path to the convent with Caelym keeping up as best he could. Reaching the alder grove at the end of the path, she whispered, "Follow me!" and darted across the clearing.

Bitterly regretting his oath to obey an enemy who was almost certainly taking him into a trap, Caelym left the safety of the trees to stagger across the open ground and flatten himself against the wall. He stood there, watching warily, as she opened a tiny doorway and crawled through it. Drawing in a deep breath, he silently invoked the seven sacred names of the Mother Goddess and followed after her.

He came out on the other side of the wall to find himself behind a small building in a garden that was so much like the one he'd just left he half expected Annwr to step out of the bushes and ask him why it had taken him so long to get there.

The girl stooped down and made a quick gesture with her right hand, touching the tips of her fingers first to her forehead, then to her midriff, then to her right shoulder, then her left. Then she lifted up a broad board from the base of the building's back wall that turned out to be another hidden door.

"It is the Shrine of Wilfhilda, Blessed Saint of Herbs and Vegetables," she whispered, as though this was an explanation for what she had just done or what Caelym was supposed to do next.

A sudden clanging of bells broke out from the tower overhead. Startled like a deer at the sound of a hunting horn, the girl thrust Annwr's basket into the chamber.

"Get in!" Almost raising her voice, she pointed a trembling finger at the hole in the wall.

He obeyed, reluctantly, squeezing through the opening and into a small, sunken chamber. There was just enough time to look around and see that its dirt walls were braced with rough posts and cross pieces and that a shelf, cut into the back wall, held an orderly assortment of cups, plates, and utensils before she closed the door, shutting out the light.

Keeping his knife drawn, he listened at the doorway, until fever and fatigue won out over suspicion and fear. Then he wrestled out of his cloak, tunic, and shirt—hitting his head on the ceiling and his elbows against the walls. After stuffing the tunic and shirt into his leather bag for a pillow, he felt around in the dark for his dagger and tucked it under his bag. Finally, pulling his cloak around him for a blanket, he lay on his side, his knees drawn up almost to his chest, and drifted off into fevered dreams.

Chapter 9

The Potion

While Caelym fell asleep under the floorboards of the Shrine of Saint Wilfhilda, Aleswina stood rigidly upright at her place in the chapel. Slipping the beads of her rosary through her fingers, she stared at the stained-glass window beyond the altar, but instead of seeing the Holy Virgin kneeling beside the body of her crucified son, she saw Anna sitting on the bed next to the Druid, her hand on his bare back, ready to die with him without hesitation or regret.

Aleswina had no memory of her life before the morning of her fourth birthday when she woke up from a nightmare to find herself cradled in Anna's arms. From then until she left her palace nursery to enter the convent, she'd slept with Anna in bed with her. Each night, just before she fell asleep, she asked Anna to promise that they would always be together, and each night Anna answered, "I will stay with you tonight, and I will be here in morning, but someday my people will come to get me, and I will go home again."

Now one of those people had come, and he was going to take Anna away with him. A black fog of dread came over Aleswina, shrouding everything around her in shadows except for the panels' glowing scene. She was still staring at Mary and Jesus when the service ended so that Sister Idwolda had to nudge her to get her moving.

◆◆◆

The rest of the day passed in odd fits and starts. One moment Aleswina was standing in the dark chapel with the sounds of the devotions around her, then she was in the garden weeding and setting out the new plants, then she was back in the chapel for the noon prayers, then she was putting her tools away behind the shrine, then she was in the common room with Sister Idwolda sitting next to her and telling rambling stories about a seemingly endless number of brothers and sisters—then, without remembering getting up or walking down the hall, Aleswina found herself alone, kneeling by her bed in her own small room.

When she began her religious instruction, Aleswina had gone straight from her first lesson to find Anna and tell her about praying to Jesus. Anna's answer had been, "This god of yours is so all-knowing, why do you have to explain to him what you want? And what good does it do? If you tell a man to do something, he will just do the opposite to be contrary."

So, with authority of the scriptures and of the Holy Church on one side and Anna's skepticism on the other, Aleswina had adopted a compromise of rote recitation of her daily prayers while she actually thought about other things. Now she was thinking that somehow she had to keep Anna from leaving her.

"God helps those who help themselves" was one of the few Christian proverbs that Anna didn't quarrel with, so Aleswina rocked back and forth on her knees, trying to think of some way she could help herself now.

Prayers to Jesus would not work because Anna did not believe in them, but Aleswina remembered that Caelym had sworn an oath promising to obey her every wish. So if she told him that she wished he'd go away and leave Anna with her, he would have to do it. For a moment her heart took wing, only to fall crashing down as she remembered Anna said that he didn't mean it, and he was just showing off.

As bitter disappointment replaced hope, a cunning, wicked idea crept into Aleswina's mind. She could go to the abbess and tell her there was a Druid under Saint Wilfhilda's shrine and the abbess would send for the king's soldiers and they would come and take him away. But almost as quickly as she thought it, she knew she couldn't, because the abbess would want to know how she knew the Druid was there.

As hard as she tried, Aleswina could not think of any way to get rid of Caelym without getting into trouble herself.

Leaving her room at night without permission was risking more trouble than she'd ever been in before, so she waited, nervously biting her lower lip, until she was certain the rest of the convent was asleep before cracking the door open. She slipped out of her room and moved swiftly along the dark hallway, down the stairs, across the central courtyard, and into the convent garden. She took a candle from the shrine, went around to the back, eased up the door to the hidden chamber, and reached in to get Anna's basket, being careful not to wake the sleeping Druid.

Sitting with her back against the side of the shrine and the basket on her lap, she looked at the small, fragile seedlings she'd planted that day, certain that they would wither and die without Anna there to help care for them.

Suddenly, she knew what to do. Anna had told her. A little poppy juice would ease the Druid's pain and help him sleep. A lot of it would end his pain and make him sleep forever. She just needed to mix the stronger recipe for the potion, and then he would drink it and she and Anna would be safe from him. It would be easy and maybe even kind, for he would be spared the suffering from his illness, or from worse suffering if the soldiers ever found him. Then she could go to Anna and tell her that he had died of his wound, and together they would . . . What would they do then?

The unlikely picture of Anna and herself digging a grave in the convent garden that was big enough for the tall Druid took shape in Aleswina's mind. Close behind came the thought of telling Anna a lie about how he'd died. She had never told Anna a lie before—what if she didn't believe her?

Aleswina continued to sit motionless, now with her eyes closed. Without her being aware of it, tears started down her cheeks. When she opened her eyes again, having given up her last hope, she expected to feel inconsolable, but instead felt at peace. Taking a deep breath, she mixed the potion, measuring the poppy juice with exacting care to the amount Anna had specified for fever and aches and not the three-times higher dose that would do that fatal harm.

Carefully setting the cup and candle to one side, she climbed down into the chamber. Most of the space was filled by the man who slept there, his knees drawn up, his leather bag under his head, and his right hand under the bag. There wasn't much spare room, but Aleswina managed to kneel next to Caelym, and she shook his shoulder to wake him up.

Chapter 10

A Druid's Cure

The instant he felt the touch, Caelym jerked up, hitting his head against the low ceiling as he thrust his right hand out. For a moment, he saw an explosion of swirling stars. Then he opened his eyes to see that Annwr's Saxon princess was backed up against the opposite wall of the chamber—staring blankly at him, apparently unable to understand what the tip of his dagger was doing a finger's breadth from the base of her throat.

His already aching head throbbed as he struggled with his limited English to explain to the unbelievably stupid girl how greatly she had endangered herself without adding to the timid anxiety that seemed to be her usual state.

"Now, Little Sister." He tried for a soothing but firm tone. "If you must be waking a hunted man—and I do not ever say that you must—then you must be doing it in a way that does not leave your throat cut."

From the look on Aleswina's face, which he would have thought could not get any paler in a living woman, he decided that he needed to be more reassuring.

"Here, I will show you." He lay back on his side, his hand holding the knife tucked under the leather bag that served as his pillow. "Now do it again; only you need to say my name and put your hand on my arm to keep it down."

When Aleswina did not either speak or put out her hand, Caelym sighed and shifted into an awkward half-kneeling position, one leg cramping under him as the other kept him more or less steady. "Like this," he said, taking Aleswina's right hand with his left and pressing it down on his own right wrist hard enough to stop its sudden jerk upwards.

Her lips moved without making any discernible sound.

"Káy·Lŭm," he said, enunciating the syllables slowly and distinctly. "My name is 'Káy·Lŭm,' and you must say it just as you are taking hold of my arm so that I know you are my friend and not a foe."

"Káy·Lŭm," she croaked in a dry whisper.

"That is good!" He nodded. "Now watch! I am you and you are me!"

He pressed the knife into Aleswina's trembling fingers and took his hand away, leaving hers suspended uncertainly in front of her. Then he trilled, "Caelym," in a high, girlish voice—simultaneously catching her wrist in his right hand and pinning her hand and the knife to the ground and holding it there for a long moment before letting go.

She did nothing but gasp and pull her hand away—leaving his beautifully engraved knife lying in the dirt.

Bound by the code of good behavior required of a guest, he sighed and said, "Again."

The second time, she actually lifted her hand on her own, kept a feeble grip on the knife's handle, and made a token show of resistance.

"That is . . ." He searched his limited list of English praise words for one that would be both encouraging and believable, and settled on 'better', and added with exaggerated hardiness, "Now we will do again with you being you and I being me." Making a show of settling himself back down, he tucked his knife-wielding hand under his makeshift pillow and closed his eyes.

"Caelym," she whispered, and grasped his wrist with a force that might, just possibly, have stopped a dying moth from flapping its wings.

Again he sighed and said, "Again."

It was only after she actually managed to keep his hand pinned in place for a moment or two that he put the knife aside and said, "Well now, as I am awake and your throat is not cut, perhaps you will tell me what is it you have come to see me about?"

"I brought you your draught." As she spoke, she picked up the half-filled cup and held it out to him. When he didn't take it, she added, "The one for fever and aches and to help you sleep."

"You have woken me up in the middle of the night to give me the draught to help me sleep?"

"And to put the healing salve on your wound, as Anna said I must."

Not a very big person to start with, Aleswina seemed to shrink as Caelym glared at her.

"So, if Annwr tells you what to do, I have nothing to say about whether I want it done or not?" Despite his rebellious tone, Caelym took the cup. He tried a mouthful, only to spit it out and bark, "Then what is it you have mixed that tastes so much like something you would be feeding to Annwr's pig?"

Aleswina's lips moved, reciting Annwr's recipe word for word. When his expression did not change, she whispered louder, "Anna is a midwife, and she knows what needs to be in potions and draughts."

"There is no doubt that Annwr is an excellent midwife," he snapped back. "And if I were a maid having my monthly cramps, then this would be just the thing for it!"

Aleswina's pallid cheeks went blotchy red. She drew back as he reached around her to toss the contents of the cup into the bushes outside of the chamber's entryway. He pulled Annwr's basket inside, looked briefly through the contents, stopping to smell or taste the powders and elixirs, and then poured a hefty portion of the poppy juice—easily three times what Aleswina had measured—into his cup, filled the cup with wine, and stirred it with his knife, muttering in his own language.

After he'd drained the cup and taken a few deep breaths, Caelym smiled at Aleswina—showing off his perfectly straight, white teeth—and said, "That, then, is a Druid's cure!"

After lying back down, his head resting on his bag and his hand holding his knife underneath it, he went on in a conciliatory tone of voice, "So now you may put the salve on my wound as you have been instructed by Annwr, high priestess of Llwddawanden, most excellent of midwives, and sister to She who is the living embodiment of the Great Mother Goddess Herself."

◆◆◆

The pot of salve was one of the things Caelym had taken out of the basket and tossed aside in his search for the poppy juice. Aleswina picked it up and pried off the lid. Biting down on her lower lip, she dabbed her fingers into the soft mound of comfrey, egg white, and goose grease. She glanced at Caelym's bare back and looked quickly away. In the nineteen years of her life, she had never been so close to a man except in the confessional where a wooden wall and heavy iron grill separated her from the elderly priest, safely covered in layers of surplices, chasubles, and vestments.

She shut her eyes and reached out to put the salve on his wound as Anna had told her she must, only to feel him flinch and hear him give a muffled groan. She tried again with her eyes open. It was not so bad—actually, it was thrilling to be doing the work of a healer just like Anna did.

By the time she left to sneak back to her room, Aleswina and Caelym were both at peace—Aleswina feeling unaccustomed bravery at having chosen martyrdom over murder, and Caelym content that he had earned the special merit gained by showing kindness to those who are born dim-witted.

Chapter 11

Prayers For The Dead

Rushing to the dormitory, Aleswina was just about to cross the courtyard when she saw a dark shape emerge from the stairwell. She stopped, stepped back into the shadows, and stood frozen, letting Sister Harthwreg, the bell ringer, pass by. Then, with only moments before she'd be discovered out of bed, she lifted her skirts and ran for the stairs. She raced up, taking two steps at a time, and reached the top gasping and out of breath. Now if only she could get down the hall and into her room before—

It was too late! At the far end of the dimly lit corridor, the unmistakable figure of the under-prioress, Sister Durthena, stood just outside Aleswina's door, her sword-straight posture making her look taller than she was.

Acting on instinct, Aleswina stepped out into plain view and walked straight down the center of the corridor. Emboldened by the startled, almost guilty, look on Durthena's face, Aleswina made the convent's hand signal for *"I had to go to the latrine."* Before the under-prioress could lift her hand to respond, Aleswina edged her way past, slipped into her room, and closed the door.

Her room was small and spare, with barely enough space for a narrow cot, a tiny side table, and a clothes cabinet in the corner by the window. She took off her night habit as she crossed the short distance from the door to the dresser and let it fall in a crumpled heap beside the bed. She was pulling her day habit on over her head when the first peal of the chapel bells rang out. By the second peal, she was tucking in her hair and straightening her veil. On the third, she opened her door just in time to join the line on its way to the chapel to say the prayers for the dead.

◆◆◆

The prayers for the dead, conducted halfway between midnight and dawn, might more precisely have been called the prayers for the royal dead. This was not because the convent's founder and namesake had any doubts that the love of Jesus was infinite and all-encompassing; it was because Edeth had promised King Theobold that in exchange for the endowment she needed to erect the abbey's bell tower, he and his family would have the nuns' exclusive prayers to speed their path through purgatory—and, realistically, including the dead of all classes in a time of frequent famines, recurring plagues, and almost constant warfare would have taken too long.

In keeping with the tradition started by the first abbess, the prayers were conducted in English instead of Latin. The current abbess, Hildegarth, presumed that this was a decision made to ensure that even the least educated of the community would be instructed in the fleeting nature of life and the need to keep their minds on the eternal life beyond this one, while, in fact, it was because Edeth had never learned Latin.

> *Lord Jesus, hear our prayers for King Theobold, who loved You, his Savior, with all his heart, grant him Your divine mercy, forgiving his sins and taking him up in Your arms that he may dwell with You in heaven forever and ever amen. Lord Jesus, hear our prayers for Queen Alswanda, beloved wife of King Theobold, who loved You, her Savior, with all her heart, grant her Your divine mercy, forgiving her sins and taking her up . . .*

As Aleswina stood in her assigned place in the chapel, between Sister Erdorfa and Sister Idwolda, the litany of names and supplications fell around her like a soft, warm spring rain, soothing her jittery nerves and helping her heart return to something more like a steady rhythm.

. . . in Your arms that she may dwell with You in heaven forever and ever amen. Lord Jesus, hear our prayers for Queen Fridwulfa, beloved wife of King Gilberth, who loved You, her Savior, with all her heart, grant her Your divine mercy, forgiving her sins and taking her up in Your arms that she may dwell with You in heaven forever and ever amen. Lord Jesus, hear our prayers for Queen Aelfgitha, beloved wife of King Gilberth, who loved you, her Savior, with all her heart, grant her Your divine mercy, forgiving her sins and taking her up in Your arms that she may dwell with You in heaven forever and ever amen. Lord Jesus, hear our prayers for Queen Redwalda, beloved wife of King Gilberth, who loved You, her Savior, with all her heart, grant her Your divine mercy, forgiving her sins . . .

The service might have been conducted in Persian, for all it meant to Aleswina, but she'd heard the litany so many times she could mumble most of it half asleep. Now, as the hot rush of panic-driven daring faded and the cold realization of just how much danger she and Anna were in took its place, she shifted her eyes to Sister Erdorfa on her left and to Sister Idwolda on her right.

. . . and taking her up in Your arms that she may dwell with You in heaven forever and ever amen. Lord Jesus, hear our prayers for Queen Witburga, beloved wife of King Gilberth, who loved You, her Savior, with all her heart, grant her Your divine mercy, forgiving her sins and taking her up in Your arms that she may dwell with You in heaven forever and ever amen.

Moving her lips in synchrony with theirs, she got through the prayer, only stumbling once, momentarily, over the newest verse—

Lord Jesus, hear our prayers for Queen Ermegdolin, beloved wife of King Gilberth, who loved You, her savior, with all her heart, grant her Your divine mercy, forgiving her sins and taking her up in Your arms that she may dwell with You in heaven forever and ever amen.

Between the flickering light of the chapel's candles and Sister Idwolda singing loud enough for both of them, Aleswina's pretense fooled even Sister Durthena, who'd spent most of the service watching Aleswina with the eyes of a wary hawk.

Of all Aleswina's religious sisters, it was Durthena who liked her least. The two were close in age and, superficially, in looks—both were short and thin, both fair-haired with pale complexions, and neither one of them smiled very much. But there the resemblance ended. Unlike Aleswina, who'd been sent to the convent against her will, Durthena wanted to be there.

The daughter of a successful merchant and the illegitimate but acknowledged daughter of a nobleman, Durthena had realized early that neither her father's wealth nor her mother's semi-aristocratic status would get her so much as a handmaiden's place in a queen's court. And she'd wanted more than that. Seeing the convent as the one place she'd have a chance to earn a position of real power and authority, Durthena had entered Saint Edeth the day she turned twelve.

From the moment she stepped inside the abbey's gate, Durthena had put her heart and soul into memorizing its rituals and upholding its rules. At fourteen, she'd been the youngest novice in the convent's history to take her final vows. By sixteen, she'd advanced from dispensing alms to the poor to overseeing the care and storage of the blessed vessels and relics. By eighteen, she'd had full charge of preparing the altar and laying out the vestments for the visiting priest to conduct mass. Now, at the age of just twenty-one, she acted as the assistant to the prioress, Sister Udella, who in turn answered only to the abbess.

Glowering from the far side of the chapel, Durthena made no effort to put down her resentment that—just because she was royal—Aleswina got the corner bedroom with the best view and she got to keep a servant on the convent grounds, despite the fact that here, at least, everyone was supposed to be equal in the eyes of God!

Any other novice who couldn't remember what day of the liturgy it was or say a simple novena from start to finish without being coached would have been sent away years ago. Instead, the abbess just coddled the stupid little bitch (this last string of words was a mental lapse on Durthena's part, and she revised it to "Dear Sister Aleswina" and continued her thought) when she should have been telling Dear Sister Aleswina that she'd burn in hell forever if she didn't learn her catechism!

Time and again, Durthena had gone to the abbess to report that Aleswina had left food on her plate, come to chapel late and with dirt under her fingernails, just hummed along with the hymns instead of singing, but the stupid little . . . Dear Sister Aleswina never got any worse penance than staying in her room. And then nobody ever checked to make sure she was actually praying for forgiveness and not adding to her sins by taking a nap. Just once, Durthena wanted to see Aleswina get really punished. (And having her burned at the stake for hiding a Druid sorcerer under the shrine of Saint Wilfhilda would have done nicely, if only Durthena had known about it.)

Somehow aware that she was under scrutiny, Aleswina resolved to do whatever she needed to do to avoid suspicion. For the next five days she became the perfect nun-to-be. What prayers she knew, she said with reverent zeal, and those she didn't know she mimed with enough fervor to convince even Durthena she understood what she was saying. And above all else, she made a careful show of attending to every word of the abbess's always erudite, usually lengthy, and often obscure noontime sermons.

Each of those days, the abbess concluded her midday discourse with a lamentation that the soldiers' ongoing search remained fruitless. Putting up her hand to silence the murmurs of disappointment (and one faint gasp of relief), she went on in an unwavering voice to say that the guards were still scouring the woods day and night. With that she launched into a closing prayer to the Lord God that He "lend His divine guidance to the king's guards, leading them to find the heathen sorcerer whereever he is hiding," finishing with an unintentionally contradictory petition for the safety of "all who dwell here within our holy walls."

After joining the others in a prolonged amen, Aleswina waited for her turn to leave the table; each time it came, she returned to the garden, barely breathing until she reached the convent garden and closed its gate behind her.

Chapter 12

A Midnight Service

Whatever Aleswina's shortcoming at other endeavors, she was a skilled gardener. She could weed with one hand, set in starts with the other, and have a row banked and watered in the time it would take most people to find their trowels and fill their buckets from the well. And that was on a day when she wasn't trying to hurry! Now her hands positively flew, and no one looking at the garden later would have any reason to suspect that she'd spent most of her time climbing in and out of Saint Wilfhilda's shrine, taking care of Caelym.

After emptying his chamber pot, refilling his water jug, and fixing a bowl of whatever she'd managed to sneak off her plate with a portion of the dwindling supplies in Annwr's basket, she mixed his draught, whispered his name, and reminded him not to cut her throat.

Caelym's mood darkened after he finished off the wine and poppy juice, and while he didn't draw his knife again, he grumbled between swallows that Anna's draught was "a poor excuse for a healing potion," and that he "might as well be a sick hare gnawing bark off a willow tree."

Muttering about midwives and their miserable tonics and foul unguents, he'd roll over on his stomach while Aleswina got the pot of salve ready to spread over his wound, but before she could begin, he'd snap at her to tell him what the wound looked like:

The first time he asked, she didn't know what to say except to stammer, "It—it looks painful."

After a long silence, he said, in more halting English than usual, "Ah, I am most grateful for your telling me this, for otherwise its being painful might have escaped my noticing." There was another long pause. Then he said, "Now, Dear Heart, beloved of she who is the most excellent of midwives, I will tell you that I, like Annwr, am a healer, and would greatly wish to have some small part in the curing of my own wound. However, since it is on my back where I cannot see it, I need you to be my eyes. So saying that, I beg, I implore, I entreat you to tell me more exactly what it is you see. How red is the wound? How swollen is it? Is the swelling hard or is it soft?"

Three times a day for next three days, he repeated those same three questions, and each time she gave the same answers: "It's very red. It's very swollen. The swelling is very hard." Whether this was good or bad, he didn't say; but he would let her spread the salve over it with only an occasional moan of pain.

On the morning of fourth day, she found him shivering and huddled in his dark cloak, groaning at her to go away and let him die in peace. When she returned in the afternoon, he was soaked in sweat, and so weak he could barely lift his head. "Water," he croaked, and gulped what she gave him, then croaked, "More," only to fall asleep before she could fill his cup again.

That night, she slipped out to the garden and crept into the underground chamber to find Caelym lying face down, his cloak thrown off to the side. He was burning with a fever that she could feel without touching him and breathing in shallow, rapid breaths. When he didn't respond to his name or her touch, she knelt next to him, holding the cup in her lap, and wondered if he was dying.

Aleswina had no personal sense of belief that went deeper than memorized prayers but, having nothing else, she started reciting those . . . mostly the Psalms, which she knew best and repeating her favorites more than once. Not knowing what else to do, she put the cup aside, picked up the jar with the last of Annwr's salve, and reached for the candle. Lifting the candle to shine so she could see the wound, she gasped and gave a strangled cry.

◆◆◆

The sharp cry, coming after the soothing stream of poetry, brought Caelym back from fevered and uncomfortable sleep to a fevered and uncomfortable wakefulness. By now he was used to Aleswina being there, so he didn't jump up or grab his knife. Instead, he took a deep breath to prepare himself for whatever it was about his back that so distressed her before asking, "How red is the wound? How swollen is it? Is the swelling hard or is it soft?"

Instead of answering, she looked at him with tears spilling out of her eyes and sobbed, "I—I think you must find Jesus now."

Speaking slowly—and as clearly as he could through gritted teeth—he replied, "I do not have the strength to look for anyone now, for I am sick and will not ever get any better if you do not tell me what it is I need to know!"

With that, he finally pried the answer from her that his wound was swollen up to the size of an apple, and that its outer edge was still very red but the center of it was an awful, horrid, dreadful greenish-yellow.

"Ah, this is good!" Feeling hope reborn, he rewarded her with his most charming smile. She, of course, looked as she usually did, blank and bewildered, so he explained, "For long days and nights, the spirits of fevers and festering have coursed through my veins, spreading out and wreaking misery where they may. Now—thinking me beaten and helpless—they have gathered together in a single force, meaning to mount their final assault, not knowing that—with you to wield my weapon—I have the means to defeat them."

With that he rolled onto his side and propped himself up on his elbow, then he dug into his stained leather bag and pulled out a rolled leather packet tied with a tight knot. After a few fumbling attempts, he managed to untie the cord and unroll the packet, revealing a collection of probes, pincers, and scalpels. He selected a small knife with a sharply pointed blade and held it up so that its point glittered in the candlelight. He ran his finger along the knife handle's intricately engraved surface, murmuring a weirdly rhythmic string of syllables, then looked straight at Aleswina, his dark eyes glowing.

"You will take this sacred healer's blade and without hesitation or fear you will stab it into the center of the enemy host, driving them out and scattering their forces into the open air so that it is they and not I who will die!"

After pantomiming what he meant a few times, he put the knife into Aleswina's hand. Still resting on his elbow, he turned away from her and said, "Now!"

Aleswina thrust the knife downwards. The wound burst open and a flood of thick, foul-smelling pus spewed out, ran down Caelym's back, and drenched the rug beneath him. Horrified, Aleswina pulled off her wimple and ripped it apart, using half to bandage the gaping wound and half to mop up as much of the gore as she could.

"That is enough," Caelym snapped.

But it was not enough! Aleswina had been raised by Anna, and Anna always kept things clean. "Move aside," she said, speaking in a voice that could have been Anna's own, and she pulled the rug out from under him and rolled it up. Not daring to take it out of the chamber, she used a wooden bowl to scrape a trench in the farthest corner covering the rug and the sodden piece of wimple with as much dirt as she could before handing him the cup of Anna's draught and leaving the chamber.

The night was crystal clear and the moon, just three days past full, lit the garden almost as if it were day. After the putrid stench of the draining wound, the air outside the chamber was pure and sweet, but Aleswina didn't dare stop to savor it. Instead, she rushed to the well to wash the residue of the gore off her hands before darting out of the garden, across the courtyard, and up the stairs—murmuring mixed pleas to Jesus and the Goddess that she would find the hall empty.

It was.

As she ran down the corridor, the echoes of her footsteps off the walls around her sounded like four feet instead of two. When she reached her room, blood pulsing in her ears, it seemed like two of the four footsteps kept going off and down the front stairs as she leaned back against the door, gasping for breath.

There was no time to wonder about it. She hurried to the cupboard, pulled out a fresh night habit and night wimple, and was dressed and under her covers in a matter of moments. Thinking

to somehow make up for her evening's disobedience by being especially good now, she adjusted the covers, smoothed her wimple,
and settled herself in the exact center of the bed, lying on her
back, her hands folded piously above the covers and clasping her
cross, the twin of the one she'd given Anna, to her breast.

Chapter 13

Durthena's Dread

The second set of footsteps were Durthena's—running so fast that she covered the length of the north hall and disappeared down the east stairway without Aleswina catching so much as a glimpse of her gray habit billowing out behind her.

When the abbess sounded the alarm about the Druid sorcerer, the abbey's under-prioress had begun to patrol the compound's buildings and grounds. Starting her nightly rounds as the rest of the nuns and novices were trudging off to bed, she scrutinized the stockade walls for cracks or crevices as she passed along the walkway to the dining hall, kitchen, and workrooms at the west end of the cloister. After looking through all the pantries and into the empty laundry tubs she went back outside, sweeping through the outbuildings and storage sheds. From there she circled around the edge of the central courtyard, checking behind every bush, returned inside to inspect the chapel, scriptorium, and infirmary, and then went on to prowl the halls of the lower and upper dormitories.

The last part of her route took her past the abbess's quarters, where she always paused to genuflect outside the closed door before climbing the east stairway stairs to the upper dormitory and walking along slowly, stopping to listen at each of the doors.

She always listened longest at door to the room at the northeast corner of the upper dormitory, picturing the miserable little . . . Dear Sister Aleswina . . . inside, not sleeping or praying but sitting up and scheming.

Aleswina was plotting something. And Durthena had thought she knew what it was! The stupid . . . *Dear* Sister Aleswina . . . had always been afraid of her own shadow, and now that there was really something to be scared about, she'd suddenly decided she wanted to be a nun after all.

For seven years, Durthena had prayed that this day would never come—that the abbess would finally see that Aleswina was unworthy of entering the Holy Order of Saint Edeth and send her back to the outside world where she belonged—but if she took her final vows, there'd be no getting rid of her ever! And because she was royal and had the biggest dowry, she might get to be the next prioress, or even the next abbess!

That was the very thought on Durthena's mind as she reached Aleswina's corner room at the end of her second round of the evening. Stopping there, she put her ear to the door and listened, hearing what she'd heard before—nothing!

Not even the sound of breathing!

The chime of a small alarm bell seemed to sound in Durthena's mind, and with it came an urgent whisper, *"Open the door!"*

Feeling a force come over her, as if she'd been entered by an angel, she lifted the latch, eased door open, and looked inside.

The room was empty. The bedcovers lay neat and straight.

Propelled by what she was certain was a divine presence, Durthena crossed the room and threw open the shutters. From where she stood she could see over the latrine and into the garden, and there she saw Aleswina—washing her hands at the well, her hair hanging loose and wild around her shoulders.

For a breathless moment Durthena stood rooted to the floor. Then, lifting up her crucifix and gasping, *Domine, libera nos a malo*, she backed out of the room, slammed the door, and ran to tell the Abbess.

Chapter 14

The Ledger

While Durthena was on her patrol of the abbey's chambers and corridors, the abbess, Hildegarth, was sitting at her writing table working on her annual report to her bishop, Higbald of Lindisfarne. The accounting sheets from the past year were stacked in twelve orderly piles in front of her, and the ledger from her first year at Saint Edeth's was lying open on her lap.

She'd gotten it out to check whether her recollection of that years' candle tally was correct and that its tripling since then could be justified by the comparing the number of illustrated pages they'd completed that year (seven psalm sheets, three saints' histories, and a psalter) with this year (one complete bible, seven saints' histories, and thirty-two prayer sheets). Feeling vindicated that the candles were fully accounted for, Hildegarth relaxed and, in an uncharacteristic loss of concentration, flipped through the pages that recorded the history of her first year as the third abbess of the Abbey of Saint Edeth the Enduring in alms and dowries, bushels of grain and bolts of cloth, blocks of salt and barrels of pickled fish.

At the same time that Durthena was putting out her hand to open the door to Aleswina's room, the abbess was turning to the page of the ledger that recorded Aleswina's promissory dowry, written in Hildegarth's steady and precise hand and dated the twenty-seventh day of June Anno Domini 773.

•◆•

Hildegarth arrived at the Abbey of Saint Edeth the Enduring at a time of crisis.

Saint Edeth had been an inspiring and charismatic figure. Born to a noble family and on the verge of marriage to a king's nephew, she'd had a vision of Jesus. He appeared to her in the middle of the night and spoke in a voice of unearthly beauty, saying, *"Find My wellsprings and you will find Me!"* as he pointed to three stars that changed before her eyes into fountains of water spouting up out of a cloud.

Defying her parents, Edeth set out alone on her mission from God, gathering disciples along the way—enraptured women who left pots burning on the hearth and husbands demanding their dinners to follow her to into the wilderness.

Undaunted by hunger, cold, or the sounds of wolves howling in the night, they'd traveled northward until finally reaching a boggy meadow, where they gathered in prayer around three sluggish springs leaking out of the cracks in half-frozen ground that Edeth proclaimed were the same holy waters she'd seen in her dream. That all but three of them survived the winter huddled in makeshift shelters was the first of Saint Edeth's many miracles. That she met Theobold, then the Earl of Derthwald, three years later, on her way to beg alms from the closest village, was another.

With the help of God and endowments from Theobold, Edeth saw her holy springs enclosed into wells, the abbey's major structures raised, and its outer walls completed in the course of five years.

Then she died.

The convent's second abbess, Freaberga, had been the first apostle to join Edeth's trek into the wilderness. As abbess, Freaberga imitated Edeth as closely as possible, answering any and all questions by quoting from her predecessor's extensive list of rules and homilies. Freaberga, however, lacked Edeth's power of persuasion, and when she died five years later, at the same age and the same day of the year that Edeth died, she left the abbey with an aging generation of nuns no longer able to do the heavier work in the convent's fields. Despite Saint Edeth's dictum that God would provide, the community could not feed itself even in good harvest years without Theobold, whose ongoing contributions allowed them to purchase what they could not gather or grow.

Sent by her bishop to revive the convent or close it down, Hildegarth arrived at the abbey's gate to be greeted by a double row of impassive faces and nervous fingers picking at the folds of threadbare habits. She hardly had time to unpack her reliquaries before the gray-faced prioress, who before this had answered Hildegarth's spoken questions with abrupt hand signals, rushed into her chambers, wailing that King Theobold had died and, in a despairing moan, adding that the king's nephew, now the king, cared only for profane earthly pleasures and would never give them the alms the old king had.

Leaving Sister Udella wringing her hands, Hildegarth took the abbey's only carthorse and went to the palace to offer her condolences and promises of prayers for the departed king's soul, along with her hope for Lord's blessings upon the new king's reign.

She'd returned to the abbey with a miracle of her own—a contract inscribed on royal parchment committing Theobold's four-year-old daughter to the convent, along with regular endowments that would double when Aleswina entered the convent at the agreed-upon age of thirteen and become permanent on the day she took her final vows.

That had been the turning point for Hildegarth and the abbey both.

As word spread that the king's own cousin was pledged to the convent, well-endowed entrants began to arrive from as far away as the capital city of Atheldom, swelling both its ranks and its coffers.

When the king's guards brought Aleswina to the abbey on the appointed day, it was obvious to Hildegarth that the thirteen-year-old princess was not there of her own free will. This did not worry the abbess unduly. She herself had struggled over relinquishing her earthly yearnings and was confident that with the right combination of firmness and patience, Aleswina could be guided along the path to true commitment—maybe not the path she would have chosen for herself, but the highest and best path, nonetheless.

◆◆◆

Nodding her head and drawing in a deep breath, Hildegarth closed the ledger. With God's help, her work had finally paid off. For almost a week now, she had watched with growing confidence as Aleswina had said her prayers with newfound conviction, sung the hymns with inspired passion, and today looked up at Hildegarth with reverent understanding throughout her elucidation of that most challenging of parables—the return of the prodigal son.

There was no question in Hildegarth's mind that Aleswina was ready to take her vows, and none too soon. Hildegarth had gotten a cold reception from the king when she went to the palace to convey the abbey's condolences for the death of his most recent wife. She'd hoped the king would not ask whether Aleswina had made her final commitment—but he had. And when she'd had to admit that after seven years of daily indoctrination, Aleswina was still a novice, she'd had an uneasy feeling that the king might be considering sending his cousin to some other convent.

Chapter 15

What Durthena Saw

ildegarth had only moments to savor her satisfaction with a job well done before her door flew open and Durthena burst in, crying, "Holy Mother, hurry! Send for the guards! Tell them she's in the garden . . . at the well . . . washing the filth of the sorcerer's sinful secretions off her hands . . . her head uncovered . . . her face lustful and licentious . . . that's why she always wants to go to the garden by herself . . . she's fornicating with her demon lover . . . coming late to chapel, the filth of rolling in the dirt still clinging to her habit . . . they must be caught and burned before they contaminate us all . . . call the guards . . . call the priest to do exorcisms of the garden . . . her room . . . everywhere she has fouled with her vile, sinful thoughts and—"

Standing up and putting out her hand, Hildegarth used her most commanding voice to break into the torrent of words.

"Sister Durthena, calm yourself! Who was in the garden?"

"Aleswina!"

"Sister Aleswina!"

"She isn't a Sister, she's an evil, sinful harlot!"

"She is the king's . . . she is a member of our holy family, a daughter of Christ, and a sister to us all. What were you doing in the garden?"

"I wasn't in the garden. I saw her from the window."

"What window?"

"The window in her room."

"What were you doing in Sister Aleswina's room?"

"An angel made me open the door, and I saw her bed was empty, and the angel told me to go the window and open the shutters and look into the garden, and that's when I saw her—"

"At the well."

"Yes, and—"

"Did you see the sorcerer?"

"No, but—"

"Did you see anyone else?"

"No, but—"

"So all you saw was Sister Aleswina washing her hands at the well in the garden!"

"Yes, but"—this time Durthena managed to rush on—"her hair was uncovered, and her habit was wrinkled, and she was out of bed in the middle of the night without permission!"

"Did you go to her and ask what she was doing in the garden in the middle of the night?"

"No, I came to warn you, and—"

"Then I think we'd best go to the garden to find what she has to say for herself!"

With that the abbess strode past Durthena and out of the room to cross the courtyard and thrust open the garden gate. Durthena hurried after her, reaching her side as she stopped and surveyed the moonlit scene. Before Durthena could catch her breath, Hildegarth said, "It appears the garden is empty—perhaps you were dreaming!"

"No! No! I wasn't dreaming I saw her! Look! There at the well! You can see the marks of her sandals!"

"Sister Aleswina works here in the garden. She draws water for the plants, so of course there are marks of her sandals there, as everywhere around us. Do you see any other prints? Cloven hooves?" Hildegarth's voice was calm, and she hesitated only slightly before she added, "A man's boots?"

Looking desperately around for some trace of proof that she'd seen what she'd seen, Durthena was forced to say, "No, but—"

"But"—Hildegarth interrupted— "what I see is a well-planted and lovingly tended garden marked with nothing but the signs of Sister Aleswina's devoted labor."

"But, but—"

"But we will go to Sister Aleswina's room and see whether she is there and whether she bears some traces of the abominations you say you saw."

Hildegard led the way back, keeping her pace steady and measured. Her face, a rigid mask, gave away nothing of her hurried calculations of what it would mean if, God forbid, there was truth behind Durthena's hysterical accusations.

Dismissing out of hand Durthena's absurd delusions of Aleswina cavorting with a demon sorcerer but grimly able to imagine an earthly lecher scaling the garden wall and seducing the innocent novice, Hildegarth had her own dread-filled vision of finding Aleswina's bedchamber empty and, beyond that, of kneeling before the king and confessing that the kinswoman he'd entrusted into her keeping had run off with some unknown lover.

The two women came to a halt outside Aleswina's door, Durthena eager to pull it open and catch her nemesis in the guilty act of changing out of the filthy, soiled habit marked with the stains of her sin, the abbess wanting one more moment to brace herself for the sight of an empty bed.

Aleswina heard the footsteps come along the hallway and stop outside her door.

Lying motionless in her bed, she pictured herself in a meadow, her head on Anna's lap—not holding a cold silver cross but a freshly gathered bundle of flowers in her hands. She breathed in slowly and easily, imagining the sweet smells of grass and flowers, the cheerful sounds of singing birds, and Anna's soothing voice promising her that she was safe and that she'd tell her one more story to help her fall asleep.

The door swung open. Light and shadows flickered across her eyelids—if they fluttered or even tensed she was lost, and Anna along with her. But she kept her mind in the meadow, listening to Anna's story about a mother fox taking her three little cubs there to play and how the cubs ran off and had one funny adventure after another until their mother found them and took them home to have supper and go to bed—and she closed her ears to the dialogue being whispered just outside her doorway.

"Do you see she is holding the blessed cross of Jesus in her hand? If she had done the evil you accuse her of, would it not burn her skin?"

"Yes, but it might not if the sorcerer cast some spell—"

"So what would you have us do? Search her room? Look under her bed and in her closet for some proof of her supposed sinfulness?"

"Yes!"

"No! We will leave Sister Aleswina in peace, sleeping the sleep of the pure and chaste! And you will go to the chapel and spend the rest of the night reading out loud the gospels of both Matthew and Mark to cleanse your mind of these lewd and lascivious thoughts."

Hildegarth's rebuke ended the argument just as Aleswina imagined she was hearing Anna's voice telling her she could go to sleep now, and she never even heard the door close or the two sets of footsteps—one brisk and relieved, the other dragging and disappointed—retreating down the hallway.

PART III

The King's Ghost

The Abbey of Saint Edeth the Enduring was either four or five leagues north of Derthwald's main town, depending on whether a traveler chose the shorter, more difficult route through forest or the longer, easier route along the river.

Named for its location at the point where the main road crossed the river, Strothford was both the gateway into the kingdom and the center of its trade. Cottages and farmsteads, occasionally coalescing into villages, spread out from there along footpaths and cartways that ran across the broad river plain like the strands of a spider's web and ended in the rugged ridges that marked the kingdom's boundaries.

Gothroc, the central fortress of Derthwald, loomed over Strothford from the top of a massive granite outcrop. Awesome by day and ominous by night, it was circled by stone walls and guarded by soldiers' garrisons. Entry was by way of a steep, exposed roadway that passed through lower and upper gates under constant watch by archers who knew they could be executed for falling asleep on duty.

The night that Aleswina so narrowly escaped being caught with Caelym in the convent garden—and at just about the same time that she was drifting off to sleep in her narrow little cot—her closest living relative, Gilberth, King of Derthwald, was awake in his royal chambers at the top of the citadel's highest tower, sitting upright in a bed the size of Aleswina's entire room.

A stray breeze had made its way through a narrow crack in the otherwise tightly sealed and barred shutters of the chamber's windows and ruffled the thick inner draperies. With only the flickering light of the hearth to see by, the motion was barely perceptible, but Gilberth stared at the swaying folds as though the spectral figure of the late King Theobold were still standing there.

Gilberth made it a point to think as little as possible about his departed uncle, but a week earlier—by coincidence on the same night that Caelym arrived at the abbey searching for Annwr—Theobold's ghost had come to him in a dream. Looking wan and frail, Theobold had walked in through the closed window wearing a monk's robe and leading a small, fair-haired boy by the hand. He hadn't said anything to Gilberth (when he was alive, he hadn't said much either), but he'd looked intently at his nephew, as he had never done in life—as though he were expecting something. Still looking straight at Gilberth, he let go of the little boy's hand to stroke the ghost-child's shimmering silky hair. Then, taking the boy's hand again, he'd turned away and walked back out through the swinging curtains.

That first night, Gilberth had dismissed the dream as an aftereffect of eating over-spiced eel at supper and settled back down to sleep. But every night since then he'd dreamed the same dream, regardless of what he'd had to eat, and even after he had the shutters of his bed chambers reinforced with iron bars.

The dream had not gotten worse and there was nothing so obviously disturbing about it—just a tall, thin, sad-faced old man holding an equally sad-looking little boy by the hand. Still, it bothered Gilberth, disturbing his sleep and leaving him jumpy and irritable during the day. And as the week passed it seemed that, even awake, Gilberth could not turn his head without catching a glimpse of the old man and the little boy, lurking in dark corners or hovering at the end of dimly lit hallways.

Whatever the dream meant, the one thing that was absolutely certain was that the boy with Theobold was not Gilberth's boyhood self. The ghost-boy was no more than four or five, and Gilberth had had been almost ten when he'd arrived at Gothroc and met his uncle for the first time—and Theobold had never once held Gilberth's hand or stroked his hair or taken him anywhere.

Gilberth's father, Gilwulf, was the first of his mother's four husbands. Like the next three, Gilwulf set out to win his fortune as a warrior and, like them, died a violent death without ever achieving more than antagonizing his neighbors. Gilberth's mother, Theodosia, didn't like Gilwulf any more than anyone else did, and after his death, she readily shifted her affections to an earl on the other side of Gilwulf's last battle.

That earl died in much the same way as Gilwulf, to be replaced in Theodosia's bed successively by his younger brother and then by an unrelated thegn. Widowed for a fourth time and approaching thirty, with no assets or suitors to speak of, Theodosia pretended a deeper affection for her only living brother than she actually felt and announced that she would refuse all future offers of marriage to live with him and oversee his household. Taking Theobold's silence for assent, she moved into Gothroc, remarking to anyone who would listen how much Gilberth resembled his childless uncle.

While it was true that Gilberth looked enough like Theobold to be his son, the two actually had little in common beyond a shared bloodline. Preoccupied first with military conquest and later with absolution, Theobold cared nothing for the things Gilberth liked to do—going to dog fights, bear baitings, and public executions—and in the brief intervals when they spent time in the same room, he rarely even glanced in his nephew's direction.

So why now, after he'd been dead for fifteen years, was Theobold looking at Gilberth from every shadow and dark corner in Gothroc?

That was one of two questions tormenting Gilberth as he sat staring at the moving curtains, his ermine robe pulled tight around him. The other was, *Why haven't any of my wives borne me a son?*

Seeing Theobold's old and decrepit ghost was an unwelcome reminder for Gilberth that time was passing. He was thirty-five years old and, despite having married five times, had no male children. He had no female children either, but that was not the problem. The problem was, as Gilberth had good reason to know, that an aging king without a grown son to defend him was never safe.

It was almost noon the next day when the answer suddenly came to him. He'd been pacing back and forth along the tower's upper walkway, muttering the two questions—"What does he want?" and "Why can't I have a son?"—over and over until they were jumbled together, sometimes coming out, "Why didn't he have a son?"

The answer to that question, at least, was obvious: Theobold's wife had died before she could give birth to the baby Theobold had been so sure was going to be a boy!

Gilberth stopped dead in his tracks and shouted, "It's the boy!"— startling the two bodyguards who'd been watching him nervously from a distance.

But, of course, that had to be it—the ghost-child was the spirit of Theobold's unborn son.

In a rare moment of looking at things from another person's point of view, Gilberth saw that Theobold had wanted an heir and the little boy had wanted to be born. That was why all of Gilberth's wives were barren! It was because Theobold, using the influence of his earthly contributions to the church coffers, stood in the way of Gilberth having an heir—just as he had once stood in the way of Gilberth being a king.

No sooner did Gilberth understand this than he saw the answer and wondered why he hadn't thought of it before. He would take Theobold's daughter back from the convent and marry her; then the little boy would be born, and he would be both Gilberth's son and Theobold's grandson, and that should make the old man happy.

Rushing back inside, practically skipping down the hallway to his throne room, Gilberth began giving orders, gleefully sending for his scribe to compose a petition to the bishop for dispensation to marry his cousin.

Chapter 16

Awakening

His abscess drained and his fever broken, Caelym had fallen into a deep sleep that lasted into the morning, when the relentless tolling of the abbey bells finally penetrated down into the depths of his slumber. Even then he refused to listen, preferring to stay as he was, swathed in a blissful sense of wellness.

It wasn't the clanging of the bells but a nagging sense of urgency, of needing to get on with the rest of what he had to do, that pulled him back towards consciousness—bringing him up to a borderland in between sleep and waking where he saw himself climbing a steep trail up the side of an otherwise sheer cliff.

In the absolute omniscience denied to a waking mind, he knew that he was dreaming and knew equally that if he got to the top and looked over the edge he would plunge headlong into an abyss of unbearable sorrow.

Rocks crumbled and slid under his feet as he clambered desperately up the trail after his other self.

Catching up just as he reached the pinnacle, he threw his arms around himself to pull himself back—only to merge together and look down.

Lying out far beneath him was a beautiful green valley. Its upper slopes were covered with stands of oak and pine mixed with open meadows. Below the forests, there were pastures thick with waving grasses, and below the pastures, where land flattened out, there were the grain fields and a cluster of thatch-roofed huts.

Sparkling brooks splashed and tumbled down the steeper slopes, turning into meandering streams that wandered across the fields before flowing into a long, sickle-shaped lake covering a third or more of the valley basin.

The valley, like the lake, was long and sickle-shaped, broader at the end that lay below him and tapering as it curved around to become a narrow gorge.

The section of the cliff where he was standing dropped straight down into the treetops, but off to his right it descended like steps in a giant's staircase and ended in a final plateau that jutted out into the bend of the lake. Dense, white mist rose up from the water's surface and swirled around the base of that lowest bluff, making it look as if the circle of white stone towers built on top of it—the shrine of Great Mother Goddess—were floating on a cloud.

Caelym's sense of dread was swept away by the surge of his longing to be home. Not stopping to think, not caring if he was dreaming or not, he jumped over the edge of the cliff, bounded downwards from one craggy foothold to the next—leaping, flying—landed lightly on his toes in a soft bed of pine needles, and then ran, sure-footed, through the forest until he came out into a meadow. It was only when he stopped to savor the sensation of Llwddawanden's earth beneath his feet and to gaze in rapture at its beloved landscape that he realized that the slopes were empty. There was not a single sheep or goat to be seen anywhere.

His sense of dread returned as he crossed pastures without flocks and fields lying fallow and grew stronger as he reached the cottages of the valley's farmers and herders. The hamlet should have been bustling with men doing their chores, women chatting and children playing games, but the cottages stood dark and silent. Afraid of what he might see if he looked inside, he didn't stop. The winding pathway that led from the village to the shrine was longer and steeper and far more overgrown than he remembered. Each step of the way seemed to take forever—then, without warning, the entrance was in front of him. Its gates gaped open, half torn from their hinges.

There was no glad outcry to welcome him—no sound at all, not even the tread of his own footsteps—as he walked through weed-infested herb gardens, past silent council chambers, and along unlit hallways to reach the arched entrance to the shrine's innermost sanctum. His knees trembled as he stepped across the threshold and into the place where even priests as high ranking as he was were forbidden to go without the permission of the priestesses who lived there. Seeing that the stool where the guardian of the women's chamber usually sat was turned over and lying on its side, he silently invoked the will of the Goddess and made his way to Feywn's chamber.

Before he could knock or try the handle, the door swung open and he walked in—expecting to find it as forlorn and desolate as everything else in his dream had been.

Instead, the room was bright and warm, glowing with the light that poured in through the open window and fragrant with the scent of sacred herbs and oils burning in pots sitting in their usual niches.

Nothing was changed or missing. The bed, with its plump, down-filled pillows and its rich silken covers, was where it belonged; the table next to it was set with golden plates and goblets, the plates piled high with the food he loved best, the goblets filled with cherry-red wine. And there by the window, bathed in sunlight, stood Feywn, dressed in a sheer, silvery gown, jewels sparkling in her hair, her eyes as blue as the sky behind her.

He must have walked over to her but had no sense that he did; he knew only that he was suddenly falling down at her feet, sobbing and consumed with grief and guilt—just as he'd done on the night of the last winter solstice. And just as she had done that night, she leaned over and touched his face, her fingers firm and cool against his burning cheek, wiped his tears, and then drew back, straightened up, and shook away the drops in a gesture that began as a flick of her fingers and ended up as a dismissive wave of her hand—as if the catastrophic betrayal of their shrine and his failure to prevent it were no more than a trifle, not important enough to merit acknowledgment.

As her lips parted and she drew in the softest of breaths, he expected her to say what she had said then—that the enemies sharpening their swords to slaughter them on their own altars would swarm through their once-secret passageway to find nothing but the empty shell of what had been their shrine, now no more than the shed skin of a sacred serpent, while they and all of those who remained faithful to the Goddess would be gone to a new and safer haven.

But this time her words came out shrill and biting: "Where are they? Where is my sister? Where are my children? Why have you not brought them back to me as you swore you would?"

Before he could explain that this was a dream and he had just forgotten to include them in it, the abbey bells sounded again, jarring him awake.

Chapter 17

Ask And It Shall Be Given

aelym was lying on his back on a dirt floor, his knees drawn up and his head resting on his leather satchel. Staring up into the darkness, he began to sort through his muddled memories and gather his scattered thoughts.

He was on a quest. He knew that even without the still-vivid vision of Feywn to remind him.

First, he had to find Annwr—and he'd done that.

Then he had to find Arddwn and Lliem. For a moment, their sweet faces floated in the darkness above him—Arddwn's a smaller version of his own, only with Feywn's blue eyes, and Lliem's more like his mother's but with eyes that, like his, were so dark a brown they seemed almost black.

The longing to hold his sons in his arms again came over him, flowing out of his heart and filling his chest so that for a moment he couldn't draw a breath. When he did, the sharp pain below his right shoulder blade reminded him of where he was and why.

Confined in this dank, dark chamber, with only the miserable clanging of those wretched bells to mark the time, there was no way to know how long he'd been there, but hopefully (and Caelym was by nature inclined to be hopeful) it had been long enough for his pursuers to give up and for Annwr to decide to let him rescue her.

Whether to return to take her rightful place as an elite priestess in the highest ranks of their sacred order or remain a Saxon's slave did not seem like a difficult decision to Caelym. The only reason he could imagine for her foot-dragging was that she had been forced to swear an oath to serve the child of her Saxon captor—an oath that, even sworn under duress to their worst enemy, was still binding, unless she was released from it by death or dispensation.

Equally binding was the absolute prohibition against a guest killing a host, so if he was to fulfill his promise to Feywn, he would have to persuade Aleswina to release Annwr from her service.

This, fortunately, was a task totally within his powers. A master bard trained by Herrwn, the greatest of all their orators, Caelym was confident that he could convince a snake, at least for a short time, that it had legs.

Slowly, cautiously, he rolled onto his side, rose up on his elbows, and then shifted into sitting as upright as the low ceiling allowed.

So far, so good. Certainly he was weak and understandably stiff, but he was no longer fevered or ailing—except for a gnawing ache in his stomach that, after a few moments' consideration, he identified as hunger.

If he was hungry, then Aleswina had not come to feed him yet and would be there soon.

And he would be ready to greet her, not as a sickly vassal here in this cramped, foul-smelling pit but out in the open air, able to sit—or even stand—upright.

He felt under his bag for his knife. Keeping a grip on it with his right hand, he crept towards where he thought the door must be. Feeling blindly along the planks and crossbars, he found it, pushed the panel upwards, and thrust it aside.

The light of day dazzled his eyes. He drew in a careful breath, savoring the fresh, clean air, as welcome as wine after the suffocating stench of the underground cell. Moving stealthily, he climbed out and peered around the corner of the shrine, then darted into a thick hedge of laurel bushes growing against the garden wall, where he could see around him without being seen. At last able to stretch his legs, he leaned back against the wall to wait for Aleswina.

◆◆◆

The midmorning prayer service had run longer than usual but, now that Aleswina was actually paying attention, the reading out of The Book of Matthew had seemed to speak directly to her, giving her a message of hope and inspiration.

"Ask and it shall be given."

Taking the Bible's words literally, she was overjoyed that it could be so easy. She just had to ask Caelym to go away and leave Anna with her—and Jesus would make him do it! Filled with hope, she hurried through the garden and around the corner of Saint Wilfhilda's shrine but came to a lurching stop at the sight of the open doorway and empty chamber.

"Over here!"

Even spoken softy, Caelym's voice coming out of the hedge startled her into dropping the handful of bread and cheese she'd brought for his breakfast. Kneeling down, she scooped what she could back into her sleeve and peered into the bushes. She first saw his feet and from there was able to make out the rest of him, sitting up and looking sternly at her—an entirely different person from the desperately ill man she'd been tending for the past week.

She started to urge him to go back into Saint Wilfhilda's shrine—but then realized that having him in the bushes meant that she could get on with the spring planting while she worked up her courage to ask him to go away.

Painfully shy and socially awkward, Aleswina was not a skilled speaker by any stretch of the imagination. Now that she had to ask for the thing she wanted most in the world, she didn't know what to say.

The little she knew about Druid customs had mostly been gleaned from the particular snorting sound Anna made—gritting her teeth and blowing sharply through her lips and her nose at the same time—whenever Aleswina tried to explain what Christians were supposed to do. This meant that practically none of the things she knew about Christian priests would help her talk to a Druid one.

At a loss to know how to begin, she picked up her trowel and started to set in her first row of bean sprouts.

It was Caelym who opened the conversation, murmuring, "Tell me about this fine garden that looks so much like Annwr's, has it been with her skill and labor that it grows so well?"

Asked for the first time in her life about the only two things that mattered to her—her plants and Anna—Aleswina began to talk, faltering at first but then with increasing ease and animation, telling him all about what Anna had showed her and taught her and how they'd planted and weeded and gathered the harvest together. Taking Caelym's nods and hums for reassurance that once he understood how much Anna meant to her everything would be all right, she went on, explaining that before she'd come to the Abbey, she and Anna had lived together in her nursery where Anna had taken care of her and told her stories and rocked her to sleep when she had bad dreams. Caught up in her happy memories, Aleswina didn't notice that Caelym's murmurs were changing tone or that his expression was growing dark.

In the chaotic aftermath of Rhedwyn's defeat, Caelym was sent back to the shrine's nursery—his defiant protests that he wasn't a baby overcome by Herrwn telling him that he was not being sent there because he was a baby but because he was grown-up enough to help take care of the little children. Once he understood how important that was, he threw himself into the task.

Almost the first thing he did was to find Annwr's orphaned daughter, Cyri, who'd wandered off from the others and gotten lost. Although seven years apart in age and only distantly related by blood, the two developed a close bond, and Caelym's affection for Cyri remained, in its own way, as strong as his love for Feywn.

Once, when they were both still children, Cyri asked Caelym to tell her what her mother looked like. Caelym didn't remember, and he blamed himself that he could not meet this forlorn request. But, he now thought—glowering at Aleswina—it was not his fault that Cyri didn't know what her mother looked like!

As Aleswina prattled on, the logical train of Caelym's planned argument was lost in his smoldering indignation over the injustice that, during all those years, this simpering Saxon girl had received the loving care that Annwr should have been giving her own child.

Finally, pausing to take a breath after having revealed far more about herself to Caelym than she had to the Christian priest who'd been taking her confessions for the past seven years, Aleswina was about to make her plea—only Caelym spoke first, in a soft, hypnotic voice, repeating back the essence of what Aleswina had just said but turning it to his own purpose and launching his challenge.

"But have you never wondered whether somewhere Annwr might have kin who were longing and weeping for her?"

Lulled into a more honest reply than she might have given otherwise, Aleswina snapped back that those kin could not love or care for Anna as much as she did, or they would have defended her better and not let her be taken away from them in the first place.

"So then you have no pity in your heart for Annwr's own little girl, left alone and crying for her mother?"

Instead of answering, Aleswina stared dumbly at Caelym, her mouth opening and closing like a fish caught and floundering on the riverbank. For all her fears of anything that might take Anna away, the possibility of Anna's having another child had simply never occurred to her.

She sank to the ground, covering her face with her hands, feeling that unknown child's pain as if it were her own.

Aleswina's muffled sobs went on long enough for Caelym to realize the debate was over and that he had won it with no real effort at all. Oddly, this added to his irritation with her. Had she at least put up a fight, he could have felt it a greater triumph than just making a foolish, simple-minded girl cry. But glorious or not, it was still a victory, and he meant to have it declared.

"So say now whether you will keep Annwr a slave to do your work for you or set her free to take her own child up in her arms again after keeping them apart these many years!"

"Anna's not a slave, she's . . ." But even if Aleswina had been able to control her quivering voice, she would not have had any word for what Anna was to her.

"Free!" Caelym filled in the word he wanted, adding, "I will go now and tell her and—"

"No! You can't! Not yet! It's too dangerous! The soldiers are still out there! You must wait until they're gone, or—or—at least until it's dark."

Realizing that she was right about the risks of leaving in the daylight, Caelym assumed the gracious demeanor of a magnanimous victor and agreed to wait until nightfall. Had she responded in kind—bowed her head in dignified defeat and acknowledged that his was the more powerful claim—he would have reached out to take her hands and thank her for saving his life, but she turned her back on him and walked off without saying a word. After the gate closed behind her, he slipped back into the underground chamber where he gathered his bag and Annwr's basket and set them just inside of the entryway. With things in readiness, he returned to the bushes and stretched out to nap in the sunlight that filtered through the leaves, getting what rest he could for the coming night's travel.

Chapter 18

The Vision

Even by her own exacting standards, the abbess had had a busy and productive morning. Up before the sunrise service, she'd finished her report to the bishop. By the second prayers of the day, she'd reviewed the contract committing Aleswina to the convent, written a letter to the abbey's visiting priest, letting him know he was needed as soon as possible to conduct the mass celebrating Aleswina's marriage to Christ, and composed the noontime sermon.

She was more than halfway through revising the Bible readings and commentaries for the coming week when a messenger arrived from the captain of the king's guard announcing that the sorcerer was driven off, and they were on their way back to Gothroc to report the mission's success to the king. She'd given him her thanks and blessing and was back at work before the man finished bowing, crossing himself, and backing out the door.

With the roads safe to travel, she sent Sister Oslynne, the one skilled rider among the younger nuns, to deliver Father Wulfric's summons by the fastest horse in the convent's stable. That done, Hildegarth returned to her plans for Aleswina's ordination, selecting the passages she liked best from Psalms of Solomon and the Book of Ecclesiastes and drafting both her own and Father Wulfric's sermons. When the bells rang for the noon prayers, she was checking the inventory of white linen.

Although Hildegarth made the decisions about the specific readings, prayers, and hymns in each of the chapel services, she followed Saint Edeth's ordering of the themes, focusing on Christ's birth at sunrise, His miracles at midmorning, His trials in the wilderness at noon, His betrayal and crucifixion in the midafternoon, and His resurrection at sunset. That day, she'd drawn heavily from Luke and Matthew, thinking that the accordance and consistency of their accounts would have a steadying effect after the worries of the past week.

Kneeling in the dark chapel, only half-listening to the Lord arguing with Satan, Aleswina fought back the tears that threatened to flow at the thought of Anna leaving with Caelym that night—never to be seen again in this life.

Or the next.

Aleswina always repeated everything she learned in her religious lessons to Anna. When she told her that you had to be Christian to enter the Kingdom of Heaven, Anna had made her snorting noise and muttered, "There'll be nobody inviting any dead Christians into the Other World either, and they can just go to their heaven and see if anyone misses them." At the time, Aleswina pleaded that she didn't want to be Christian and begged Anna to promise that she could come into the Other World too, but Annwr only said that she was too young to be worried about dying and that heaven was probably a very nice place—adding *"for Christians"* under her breath.

So once Anna left with Caelym, Aleswina would never see her again. She knew that. Now she only wished—desperately—to see Anna just once more before losing her forever.

"Just once more . . . Just once more . . ." turned into a throbbing drone in her mind as the service ended, and she walked in line out of the chapel and around the edge of the courtyard to the dining hall.

The midday meal at the Abbey of Saint Edeth the Enduring was both the largest and the longest meal of the day. This one seemed as if it was never going to end. After the abbess announced that the king's guards had driven the sorcerer off (knowing just how wrong the abbess was about that, Aleswina had to stop herself from snorting the way Anna did), the prioress said a grace thanking the Lord for everything He'd ever done. Later, Aleswina wouldn't remember what was in her bowl that day—only that it tasted like sawdust mixed with mud. She choked down her last mouthful, folded her hands, and turned her head with the others to listen as the abbess began her sermon, while *"Just once more . . . Just once more . . ."* kept humming in her ears.

Hildegarth ended her sermon with the twenty-eighth verse of the eighth chapter of Paul's letter to the Romans. A tall, solidly built woman, she stood erect at the head of the long, rough-cut dining table. Forty-six nuns and novices, twenty-three on each side of the table, looked reverently up at her. She looked straight at Aleswina, halfway down on the right-hand side, and might have been speaking only to her as she declared, "And we know that all things work together for good to them that love God, to them who are called according to His purpose."

There was rumor, widespread among the younger nuns and novices, that the abbess could see people's thoughts just by looking into their eyes. Caught in the Abbess's direct gaze, Aleswina immediately stopped thinking about Anna and filled her mind with Christian thoughts, moving her lips to silently repeat what the abbess was saying—and was relieved beyond words to see the abbess smile and nod before beginning the day's benedictions.

By the time the Abbess began the list of afternoon duties, Aleswina's heart had slowed down from a frenzied racing gallop to a brisk, steady trot. She expected to hear that she was supposed to go to work in the garden, just like every day except in the dead of winter or when it was pouring rain, only the abbess skipped over her and went on with all the other assignments.

Aleswina stayed, sitting in her place, as, one after the other, nuns and novices rose and went to their assignments. When she was the only one left, the abbess beckoned to her without speaking and walked out of the dining hall without looking back. Aleswina followed, her fears rising as she followed the abbess from the dining hall to the abbess's private chambers.

The abbess's chambers were, like the abbess herself, large and well-organized. What in Saint Edeth's time had been an oversized hut that served as chapel, dining hall, and common living quarters for the saint and her handful of followers had long since been changed as the convent grew up around it. Once a single room with a rough stone hearth in front of a drafty alcove where wood was piled, it had become the "abbess's chambers" before Hildegarth had ever arrived.

The original doors were still in place: one opened off the hall that led to the dormitories and one, on the opposite wall, opened into the central courtyard. A quarter of the space was walled off to be the abbess's bedroom and another section adjacent to the hall door had been made into a small antechamber, leaving the remainder of the room open and yet so clearly divided by function that there was no mistaking where the abbess worked and where she prayed. The work space, dominated by a heavy oak writing table and edged with shelves of manuscripts and ledgers, was on the side of the room closest to the bedroom, while the alcove in the far corner that had once been a woodshed was the room's centerpiece—the abbess's private shrine and the repository for the relics too fragile to keep in the chapel. The stone hearth had long since been replaced by a wrought-iron brazier and the walls that weren't draped with tapestries of the Last Supper, the Ascension, or Christ on the Cross were hung with paintings of the saints and apostles.

Closing the door behind them, the abbess motioned for Aleswina to go ahead of her into the room, then brushed past her and turned around so that Aleswina was trapped between the abbess's desk and the abbess herself.

"I think you know why I have called you here!"

Now certain she was caught but determined not to betray Anna even if she was tortured, Aleswina began, "I, I—" but could go no further.

"I know what you are thinking!"

A shiver of pure terror raced up and down Aleswina's spine.

"You think you are ready to take your final vows!"

Nothing could have been further from Aleswina's mind. She stammered, "M-my final vows?" Then, realizing that taking her final vows would be far better than being burned at the stake, she said, "Yes, my final vows!" and added, in what for her was a resolute voice, "I think I'm ready to take my final vows!"

Here an abbess with less strength of character might have left the question of what Durthena may or may not have seen in the garden the night before unasked. Hildegarth, however, stiffened her back and said, "But before we go on, I must ask you something and you must tell me the truth!"

The truth was, for Aleswina, whatever she had to say to keep from giving herself and Anna away, and she answered in a louder, firmer tone of voice than she'd ever used before, "I will tell the truth!"

"I have been told that you were in the garden last night without permission. If this is so, you must tell me what you were doing there."

Unable to meet Hildegarth's piercing stare, Aleswina shifted her eyes to a painting on the wall behind the abbess that showed Saint Edeth standing beside the garden well—a golden halo around her head and her hands lifted up with a fountain of water rising from each of her palms. The saint's eyes were gentle and loving and kind, like Anna's, and Aleswina found herself speaking without any effort at all.

"I had a dream that Saint Edeth came to me, called my name, and told me to come with her, and even though I woke up I could still see her and hear her so I followed her out into the garden, where she rose into the air above the well and"—thinking quickly about what anyone might have seen her doing, Aleswina gripped her cross with her—her hands!—and she went on as if she'd only paused to take a breath—"she said that I must wash my hands in the water from the well . . ." She faltered again, trying to think of some reason to wash her hands other than having to clean off the blood and pus from Caelym's wound; then, in a flash of inspiration, she continued in an almost steady voice, "to be ready to take my final vows."

"And I've heard that your hair was uncovered. Where was your wimple?"

This time, Aleswina didn't even hesitate. "Saint Edeth told me that I must take it off and wash it with holy water from the well too, and that this anointed veil was the one I must wear forever after."

Aleswina inadvertently raised her hand to touch the cloth, hoping against hope that the abbess wouldn't ask why it wasn't even damp.

It was this simple, unaffected gesture, along with the softly awed and quivering tone of Aleswina's voice in narrating what was surely an authentic moment of conversion—and maybe even a minor miracle—that relieved the last of Hildegarth's concerns. Breathing an almost audible sigh of relief, she was ready to declare the matter settled and move on to the practical things that needed to be done.

"That is wonderful. Now, then, there is only the matter of your serving woman. Once you have taken your vows, you can have no ties at all outside of this house. I will make the arrangements to send her back to the palace today to take up other duties there."

"No!" Aleswina swallowed hard. "Saint Edeth has already spoken to me about that, saying that I must set her free"—now came another flash of inspiration— "and she told me I must do this myself. So, with your permission and your blessing, I will go and tell her."

"I will send for Prioress Udella, and she will go with you—"

"No! Saint Edeth said I must go alone!"

◆◆◆

The last thing that Hildegarth wanted was to let Aleswina go out of the convent alone—especially not to see her sour-faced Celt servant. While she stopped short of calling the village midwife a witch, the abbess suspected the woman had a dark, unhealthy hold over Aleswina and that this was the real reason the novice had found one excuse after another to put off her final vows.

The abbess wavered, weighing the risks. She could, of course, insist that the ever-reliable Udella go along to make sure that Aleswina returned safely. But might she be doing more harm than good? Planting the seeds of her own doubt in the girl's soul and undermining her newfound faith? Beyond that, Hildegarth was astute enough to know that if Aleswina was to truly break free of her servant's grasp, she must do it on her own—so she set her qualms aside and gave her consent.

Chapter 19

Saying Farewell

*A*fter being dismissed by the abbess, Aleswina set out for Anna's cottage, paying no attention to the gatekeeper's startled look when she pushed the side door open and headed off along the main road that ran through the village. She hardly noticed the curious stares she got from villagers who stopped picking up after the guards' futile Druid hunt to watch her rush by. When she reached the side path that led to Anna's front door, she practically ran the rest of the way there.

The front door opened into the main room of Anna's cottage. After stepping from the midday sunlight into the darkened room, Aleswina had to stop and wait for things to take their usual shape. Only they didn't. The hearth that was always burning with warm, cheerful embers was cold and dead. The shelves that Annwr kept filled with orderly stacks of bowls and dishes were bare. There was only one table and one chair, and they were both lopsided, held upright with mismatched legs.

Anna wasn't there. But she wouldn't be inside—not on a bright, sunny day like this. She'd be outside in the garden, planting and weeding, with Solomon and the other geese following after her, snatching at the worms and bugs she dug up . . . or maybe Betrys was in labor, and Anna was helping her have her baby piglets.

Aleswina crossed the room and rushed into the garden.

Anna was there, pouring a bucket of water over a newly planted patch of meadowsweet at the edge of the fence. The rest of the garden lay in ruins. Sodden bits of gray feathers were scattered everywhere and a hint of sickish sweet stench—a scent Aleswina now knew to be the smell of clotted blood—lingered in the air.

"Anna, where are . . ." Aleswina paused mid-sentence, looking for the geese, especially for Solomon, who'd been her special favorite ever since Annwr had let her hold his hatching egg in her hands, and she'd watched as his little yellow beak pushed through a crack in the shell, his damp, fuzzy head popped up, his bright eyes blinking as he gazed into her face.

"They're dead. The guards killed them—Solomon, Betrys, all of them. They took what they wanted for their supper. I've buried what was left." Anna was looking at Aleswina as if she was having trouble recognizing her. "What are you doing here? The guards are still—"

"The guards are gone back to Gothroc. The abbess said I could come to tell you . . . to tell you . . ."

Everything Aleswina meant to tell Annwr tangled up into a lump in her throat. Choking on it, she somehow mixed the soldiers' crimes with the wrong she had done keeping Anna away from her own little girl (compounded by the unconfessed sin of thinking about poisoning Caelym), so that when she managed to speak again, it was to repent and plead for forgiveness, falling to her knees under the crushing weight of all the wrongs done by Saxons against Britons and by Christians against Druids.

It wasn't that Annwr didn't recognize who Aleswina was so much as that she was confused about *what* she was—the sweet, loving child that she had raised as her own for the past fifteen years or the spawn of Llwddawanden's worst enemy. And as for *repentance* and *forgiveness*, those were Christian notions, and Annwr only had to look around her to see how much good Christianity did for her.

Out of habit more than anything else, Annwr sat down next to Aleswina and put her arms around her. Then Aleswina started to cry, and Annwr rocked her until the sobs settled into whimpers that turned into snuffling, wet sighs.

By the time Aleswina had finished wiping her eyes and blowing her nose on Annwr's apron, the gap between them had closed, and they were talking as freely as ever. Annwr explained her plan for Caelym to travel disguised as a monk, and Aleswina told Annwr about how the abbess thought Saint Edeth had talked to her, and they both laughed until their sides ached. Together, they agreed that Aleswina would bring Caelym back to the cottage that night, and that Annwr would have everything packed and ready to go.

Aleswina was adamant in telling Anna that she was to take with her all of the coins and jewels they had brought in secret from the palace and kept hidden in the cottage loft. Annwr had refused at first, but for once Aleswina was the more stubborn and unyielding, and both of them could see that Annwr would need these funds more than Aleswina would. Having worked out their plans, they had sat with their arms around each other for as long as they dared before Aleswina got up, whispered that she'd be back after the late-night prayers, and left, fighting against a new round of tears.

Chapter 20

Idwolda

"*As our Lord chose to die on the cross out of his love for us, so each of us who make our holy vows to Him choose to live loving only him, leaving behind all lesser loves and desires.*"

Hildegarth had spent nearly an hour working and reworking that sentence until she felt satisfied that it smoothed the transition from Saint Luke's account of the dying Christ's last words to her announcement: "It is with heartfelt joy that I tell you that Sister Aleswina will be pledging herself to Him in body and spirit on Sunday."

Managing to escape from her well-wishers with the excuse that she had to finish her day's planting or lose a week's harvest, Aleswina made her way to the garden, where she set her tray of starts close enough to Caelym's bush to talk as she worked. Keeping her head down, she told him what Anna and she had decided—that she would go with him to Anna's cottage after the late-night prayers, and also about the plan for him to travel disguised as a monk.

Caelym had woken from his nap refreshed and ready to leave. He wanted to go as soon as it was dark, and he wanted to go alone, but when he said so, Aleswina's tears dripped onto the freshly turned earth and, reluctantly, he agreed to wait for her. It was generous of him in view of the pressing need he had to be on his way, but instead of thanking him she just went on working with her back to the bushes.

He endured her silence for a while, then wondered aloud whether there was anything "a person should know about being a monk?"

Aleswina answered without looking up, "Anna says you'll have to keep quiet and let her do the talking because you don't know any Christian prayers."

"*Dominus regit me; et nihil mihi deerit—*"

At the first words of the twenty-third psalm, Aleswina dropped her trowel and turned around, her mouth open in surprise.

". . . *in loco pascuae ibi me conlocavit. Super aquam refectionis educavit me, animam meam convertit. Deduxit me super semitam iustitiae propter nomen suum . . .*" Caelym went on chanting, his legs crossed in front of him, his hands, palm-side up, resting on his knees, his back straight and his eyes half closed, coming to a resonating conclusion on the last syllables, "*in perpetuum.*" Opening his eyes to see Aleswina gaping at him in what he assumed to be reproof, he said, stiffly, that he had only heard her say the incantation twice and had been, as she might recall, quite ill at the time. "So now if you will tell me how I have been in error, I will correct my mistakes and will speak these words as they should be spoken."

"But you made no mistakes! You said the whole psalm exactly as it should be said! It took me weeks and weeks to learn it!" The awe and admiration in Aleswina's voice were unmistakable.

His confidence restored, Caelym acknowledged her tribute. "Well, of course, I am both a bard and a healer, trained since youngest boyhood in careful memorization and in the precise recitation of poems, sagas, and spells." Returning to the issue at hand, he continued, "So now you will teach me what else I must know to be a monk, and I will prove myself as good as or better than a real one, betraying neither myself nor Annwr—no matter what she may have said to the contrary!"

Caught between Anna's warning and Caelym's command, Aleswina started to stammer that she'd never met a monk when the garden gate slammed open and Caelym drew back into the depths of the bushes. From the noise of the footsteps rushing towards her,

Aleswina guessed—to her dismay—that the intruder was Sister Idwolda.

Idwolda, the newest of the abbey's novices, was known for three things: her humble peasant background, her sunny good nature, and her clumsiness. It had been a challenge from the first for Hildegarth to know where to safely assign her—sent to wash dishes, the pottery bowls would break almost before she touched them; sweeping the floors, her broom handle would knock icons from their niches and saints' pictures off the walls; and it was taken as fact that she had only to walk past the door of the scriptorium for ink pots to tip over and spill on just-finished parchments. Mostly now, she worked in the laundry on the assumption that even she couldn't do too much damage there.

It was an open secret that Idwolda had been admitted to the convent just as her mother was about to sell yet another one of her numerous children to help feed the rest—and that it was Aleswina who'd supplied her dowry and pleaded with the abbess to take her in.

Overwhelmingly grateful for finding herself in the safety and the comparative luxury of the convent, Idwolda wanted more than anything to be Aleswina's friend. She always managed to sit next to Aleswina in the chapel, at the dining table, and in the common room, where, under the guise of talking about how better to serve God, she'd whisper gossip about the other nuns and novices or tell rambling stories of her life before coming to the convent, happily unaware that Aleswina had only rescued her because Anna asked her to and had never guessed that she would take it so personally.

Now Idwolda, rosy-cheeked and beaming, wisps of nut-brown hair curling out from under her wimple, came crashing around the end of the hawberry hedge. Skidding to a stop in the middle of the row that Aleswina had just finished planting, she began, "The abbess sent me to—"

Seeing Aleswina staring downwards, Idwolda looked down too, and, seeing the bent and battered seedlings crushed beneath her feet, she launched into a flood of apologies and promises to repair the damage, squashing another half-row and knocking over the water bucket as she reached for the nearest hoe.

"No, please don't! It's all right! I . . . I . . . need you to . . ." Desperate to save the rest of her plants, Aleswina said the first thing that came into her mind: "I need you to tell me about monks."

"Why?"

"Because . . ." Aleswina's newfound ability to make things up at the spur of the moment come to her rescue once again. "Because now that I am going to take my final vows, I want to learn all about our brothers in Christ and what they do to serve the Lord! And you, dear Sister Idwolda, you know so much about life outside our walls, you must tell me what monks do."

Eager to be helpful, Idwolda launched into a vivid depiction of monks—how some were good folk, not with the grandness of priests, but kind and caring, while others were no better than beggars and layabouts in brown cloaks.

Spending most of her time under Saint Edeth's rule of silence left Idwolda, a naturally talkative girl, with a build-up of words wanting to be said. Now, given the chance to break out, they got away from her, following one tangent after another, until, entirely lost and without any idea of how to find her way back to the original question, she ended up telling Aleswina not only about monks in general but about the particular monk (one of the kind and caring ones) who had stayed with her family to give comfort to her mother in those sad weeks after her father's death, and finishing with the somewhat out-of-context remark that her dear little brother, Codric, who'd come ten months after her mother was widowed, was thought by some to favor that very monk.

In a more just life, Idwolda would have been an actress on a larger stage. Still, the private performance she gave, playing the varied parts of her dying father, her grieving mother, and the solicitous monk—even emulating Brother Egred's deep bass voice singing a ballad about the Christ-child working miracles from His mother's womb—did not go unappreciated by the small but highly select audience watching it from his hiding place in the bushes. It ended abruptly, however, when she suddenly remembered what she'd been sent by the abbess to tell Aleswina.

"You need to go to the sewing room right away! They're waiting to get started on your getting-married-to-Jesus habit!"

With that, she picked up her skirts and dashed out of the garden, leaving the last stand of bean shoots crushed in her wake.

The massacre of her baby plants, so soon after seeing the devastation at Annwr's cottage, was almost more than Aleswina could bear. She got up and left through the gate Idwolda had left swinging open behind her, too downhearted to put her trowels away or remind Caelym to wait until she came to get him after the late-night prayers.

Chapter 21

Olfrick

The silence that met Aleswina when she entered the sewing chamber bristled with impatience and irritation. Sister Eardartha pointed to a footstool with one hand, holding a threaded needle in the other, while Sisters Redella and Ralfwolda looked at her sternly, their scissors snipping at the air.

As they circled around her and draped sheets of white linen over her shoulders, snatches of whispered conversations she'd overheard on the way to the noon prayer came back to her.

". . . gone on missions for the abbess . . ."

". . . Sister Durthena and Sister Fridwulfa to Lindisfarne and Sister Oslynne to find Father Wulfric . . ."

"Alone?"

"By herself!"

"The roads are dangerous even if the sorcerer is gone . . ."

". . . all sorts of men are on the roads . . ."

"No Christian man would harm a nun . . ."

". . . and besides she's got a letter of safe passage from the abbess . . ."

". . . and a fast horse!"

There was no way for Aleswina to sneak a horse out of the convent's stable, but she could and would bring one of her habits when she went to see Anna off that night—and, in a sudden surge of resolve, she made up her mind to get a letter of safe passage from the abbess as well.

Ignoring the trio of exasperated gasps, she hopped down from the box and wriggled out of the swaths of linen. Making hurried gestures for "breviary" and "need to get," Aleswina ran out of the sewing room and down the hall to the abbess's chambers.

There was no answer to her knock.

She gathered her courage, pressed the latch, and inched the door open, calling softly, "Mother Abbess?" again with no answer. Peeking through the crack, she saw a thick leather-bound bible lying open on her desk. The abbess never went to chapel without her bible.

Afraid that there might not be another chance to make her request, she slipped through the door and through the curtained entrance of the antechamber where she'd waited for her first audience with the abbess seven years earlier.

Minutes passed.

Aleswina waited, determined to have the coveted parchment to take with her when she slipped out to see Anna off that night.

The bells for the sunset service rang.

She stayed where she was.

More minutes passed.

Then, finally, there was a shuffle of movement in the hall, the latch clicked, and the door scraped open. Aleswina was about to step out when she heard a loud and demanding male voice.

"The king wants her, and he wants her now!"

Aleswina peeked through a gap in the curtains. It was Olfrick, the captain of the king's guard. He'd gotten older and fatter in the seven years since she'd last seen him, but it was him.

When they were leaving the palace to come to the convent, he'd come up behind Anna, knocked her out of his way, and called her a name so vile that Anna had refused to tell her what it meant.

Aleswina had never forgotten Olfrick's nasty, sneering face, and she hated him now every bit as much as she had then—only now he'd get his punishment! People did not demand things from the abbess in that (or in any) tone of voice and the abbess looked very, very angry. In a minute she would send Olfrick—awful, ugly Olfrick—to the worst penance ever, and Aleswina wanted to see that happen!

The abbess lowered her eyebrows, fixed Olfrick in her piercing stare, and spoke in the freezing voice that sent chills into a person's very bones. "Sister Aleswina is a betrothed bride of Christ! She will be taking her final vows—"

Olfrick obviously didn't realize the danger he was in, because he interrupted, "Not anymore! Now she's the betrothed bride of King Gilberth, and it's him she'll be marrying—so hand her over!"

The abbess drew a deep breath, and in a very low, slow voice said, "I will"—Unconsciously, Aleswina smiled a grim smile and nodded her head, confident that the abbess was going to give Olfrick one last warning before she called on Jesus to smite him into a pile of smoldering ashes—"have Princess Aleswina summoned after the evening prayers have been said, at which time I will tell her about this joyful news. In the meanwhile, you and the rest of your men may find your lodging in the village and return for her in the morning."

Aleswina's heart stopped beating. Then it started up again, pounding so loud that she thought they would hear it and find her there behind the curtain. And maybe they would have if Olfrick hadn't bellowed at the abbess, "The king said to bring her back now, not tomorrow!"

Aleswina held her breath.

The abbess spoke as calmly as if he'd asked for alms. "The bells for the evening prayers have rung. When the service is over, I will bring her to you."

"My men—"

"Your men may wait in the dining hall."

"My men will stand guard!"

"As you wish, but outside our gates. You will not disturb our sanctuary further." The abbess pointed to the door, and Olfrick turned and stalked out. The door slammed behind him.

The abbess went to her desk, picked up her bible, and clasped it to her chest—but instead of leaving for chapel, she crossed the room to stand just inside her private shrine, her back to the larger room, as still as if she'd been turned to stone.

Aleswina bit her lower lip and looked for a way to escape.

With the heat of the burning brazier adding to the unseasonable warmth of the day, the door to the courtyard had been left ajar. Acting with cautious deliberation, Aleswina took off her sandals and tiptoed across the room, keeping her eyes on the abbess's stiff back. Reaching the door, she sucked in her ribs and her stomach and slipped out. Ducking behind one bush and dashing to the next, she made her way across the courtyard. Once through the garden gate, she paused to take some gasping breaths and tie her sandals back on. Then she darted through the hedges and around to the back of the shrine.

Caelym had spent the last of the daylight hours fending off the tedium of his wait by tossing makeshift dice and moving small stones around a track he'd drawn in the dirt. Having promised to wait for Aleswina and not expecting her until well past the evening bells, he'd returned to the sunken chamber at sunset in order to continue his game by candlelight, leaving the door open for fresh air. He was deep in thought over the best strategy with which to counter his last move against himself and was startled into drawing his knife at Aleswina's sudden silent arrival.

If Aleswina noticed the dagger in Caelym's hand, she ignored it. "The guards are back, they're in the abbey and outside too," she whispered, and didn't wait for him to grab his pack, snuff out the candle, and close the chamber door behind him before hurrying to open the entryway in the wall and waving at him to follow.

He squeezed his way out. Assuming she meant to shut the opening behind him and return to her convent, he turned back to thank her for her hospitality and assure her he'd carry her final words of farewell to Annwr, but she pushed him out of the way, crawled through, and closed the entrance from the outside.

"Go back inside before—"

His warning was lost in the clatter of oncoming hooves.

"Get down!" He grabbed her arm and dove forward into the tall grass, bringing her with him, just as a mounted guard came trotting around the corner.

They were saved by the darkness and the stupidity of the Saxon guard, whose horse had to sidestep around them while its rider only spurred it on without looking down.

Slowly, cautiously, Caelym lifted his head and shifted his eyes—first to the left to watch the horse take the turn at the far corner and then back to the right to be sure the way was clear in both directions. Valiantly resolved to see Aleswina safely back inside her convent walls, whatever the risk to himself, he turned to where she'd just been cowering next to him.

She wasn't there.

Somehow, in the moments he'd looked away, she'd scurried to the edge of the woods, leaving him with no choice but to dash after her, following the fluttering of her gray veil around the bends and curves of the narrow path to Annwr's cottage.

Chapter 22

I'm Coming With You

nnwr had spent most of the past week cleaning up the wreckage the king's guards left behind. She'd dug a pit and buried the remnants of Betrys and the geese first, then staked up the plants that hadn't been pulled up by the roots. That done, she'd salvaged what she could of the broken furniture, burning what she couldn't repair in the hearth. While the kettle was heating with water to scrub the floor, she'd rehung the cupboard doors and shaken the dirt off the blankets.

The guards' ransacking had been more violent than thorough. By the time Annwr had finished picking things up and sorting them out, she had a week's worth of provisions stacked next to a cooking pot, a pouch with flints and tinder, two cups, two bowls, two spoons, two blankets, two walking poles, a knife, a sewing kit, a rope, and a monk's robe—and she had only had to venture into the village once.

There hadn't been time to find out from Caelym how long the trip was going to be, but between her own murky memories and his melodramatic account of mountains, valleys, rivers, and swamps, she guessed she'd need at least two changes of clothes, her warmest cloak, and as much food as they could carry.

She put her personal things into the smaller of two packs she'd found—scuffed but otherwise undamaged—and then, muttering to herself that Caelym could just make himself useful for something besides reciting poetry, piled the bulk of the food and gear into a larger one.

Annwr had just finished planting over the animals' grave when Aleswina arrived early that afternoon. After she left, Annwr had poured a bucket of water over the new starts and gone back inside, closing and barring windows and the front door before retrieving Aleswina's precious gift out of its hidden cache and tucking the heavy little pouch deep into the pack she planned to carry.

That done, she'd set both packs by the door to the back entry, with a walking pole by each and the hooded monk's robe folded neatly over the bigger one. She'd eaten a cold supper and washed and dried her cup and bowl, and she was putting them away when she heard the outer back door bang open.

There was barely enough time to turn around before Aleswina burst in, Caelym only a step behind her.

"You're early, Dear Heart—"

Her startled greeting was cut off as Aleswina flung herself into her arms, clinging to her and trembling like she had fifteen years before—except that then she'd made not so much as a whisper of sound, and now she gabbled between ragged, gasping breaths, "We have to go! The guards are coming! I'm coming with you!"

Caelym, equally out of breath, sputtered, "She is not!"

"I am too!"

"She is not!"

"I am! Tell him, Anna! Make him listen!"

"She isn't! Tell her she has to go back to her convent!"

Caelym was stamping his foot on the floor, his voice raised to a pitch almost as shrill as Aleswina's so that Annwr could hardly make out what either of them was saying.

"Hush, both of you! Caelym, go sit down!"

He didn't, but he at least stopped stamping and shouting. Annwr pried Aleswina's arms loose and pressed the girl's trembling hands between her own. "Now, Dear Heart, you know that I must go to my people, and you must stay with yours, take your sacred vows as a high Christian priestess, and—"

"There aren't going to be any vows! They're going to send me back and make me marry Gilberth!"

Annwr stiffened. "No."

"Yes! Olfrick told the abbess so—and she's letting him! As soon as the evening service is over, they'll know I've gone! They'll come here after me! Please, please, please, don't let them get me!"

"We won't!" She gave Aleswina a brisk hug and told Caelym to change his clothes and get his pack.

Caelym stood where he was. "Enough of this foolishness, Annwr! You are going, and I am going, and she is staying here—taking this 'Gilberth' as her consort, if she will, or giving him some courteous refusal if she wouldn't!"

Annwr's answer sounded halfway between hiss of a goose and the growl of a bear. "I am going and she is going and you may join us—or stay here to deliver her courteous refusal to the king's guards, who, I'm sure, will be glad you waited for them!"

For a long, tense moment, Annwr and Caelym glared at each other, neither of them speaking.

Finally, Caelym lowered his eyes and grumbled, "We'll decide what to do with her once we're safely away." Looking at the two packs and guessing which one Annwr meant for him to carry, he stuffed his own satchel inside the already bulging bag and heaved it up on his shoulders. Then he snatched up the coarse brown monk's robe in one hand and the longer of the two walking sticks in the other and stamped out of the door, muttering too low for Annwr to hear what he was saying.

Annwr took up her pack, which was heavy enough that Caelym didn't need to be moaning about his, took hold of Aleswina's hand, and followed Caelym out into the garden, where he stood dithering, looking at the goose pond as if he expected Solomon's ghost to appear and tell him what to do.

Instead of getting out of her way when Annwr told him to, he swung around and snapped at Aleswina, "Did these guards have hounds?"

Aleswina's voice quivered as she stammered, "I—I—don't know. . ."

Before Caelym could frighten the girl further, Annwr snapped back at him, "There are plenty of hounds in the village if the guards want them."

"There is a stream out of that pond?"

"So what if—" getting his point, she shifted midsentence to, "there is! And it runs from here to the river."

"We'll take that way out, then, and maybe have a chance of leaving the hounds behind." Having somehow decided that he was the one now in charge, he went on issuing orders. "Go, then, and open the gate so it looks as if you left that way!"

There was no more time to waste arguing. Annwr took Aleswina along with her as she hurried to unlatch the gate and shove it open. As they turned back around, Aleswina gasped and buried her face in Annwr's cloak.

"Caelym, what are you doing?" Annwr stared at him, putting her hands on her hips and shaking her head in exasperation.

"If I must be going into the water on a cool night, I'd just as soon my clothes are dry to put on when I get out."

He finished stripping to the skin and stuffed his clothes and sandals into his backpack. Pushing them down to make room for the monk's cloak, he added, "If either of you are coming with me, you'd best be doing the same."

Stifling a sigh, Annwr started to undress as well.

"Anna?" Aleswina whispered in a tiny, desperate voice.

Annwr stroked her cheek. "It's only for a little while, Dear Heart, and we'll keep your under-shift on and tuck it up a bit to keep it dry while we go wading."

Aleswina lifted her arms and let Anna pull her habit off over her head, just as she'd done as a little girl when Anna was her nurse and it was just the two of them, safe in her nursery.

Annwr packed up their clothes, then Aleswina obediently took her hand and walked with her into the pond, barely aware of Caelym, who followed after them, stepping backwards and using his pole to rub out the tracks they left in the mud.

Wading in the dark, their feet slipping on stones and sinking into soft muck, they did not make good time and were not even halfway to the river when they heard the hounds baying.

Aleswina gripped Annwr's hand, unable to tell where the sounds were coming from or which way to run. Caelym came up from behind and herded them forward to a bend where the stream had undercut the bank and carved out a deeper pool beneath it. The water came up to Aleswina's waist.

"*Get down!*" Caelym's order was barely louder than the gurgle of the current passing them, but Aleswina heard him and did as she was told, sinking down into the water until she was submerged to her chin. Annwr crouched on one side of her and Caelym on the other. Both of them bent over, keeping their heads and the packs on their backs above water, and they looked so much like a pair of oversized turtles that Aleswina felt the impulse to giggle—an urge that vanished when the next round of howls rang out, followed by yapping and shuffling in the bushes on the bank above them.

Men joined the dogs, crashing through the undergrowth, shouting back and forth. Then one voice rose over the others. It was Olfrick, cursing at the dogs and screaming orders to his men to find the bloody goddamned princess or else. Either because they'd caught an interesting scent or were fleeing Olfrick's rage, the dogs took off into the woods, howling in a single voice. The shouts of the guards followed them, fading away until even Olfrick's bellowing was too dim to make out what he was saying.

It wasn't until the last of the hounds' wails died away that Caelym stood up and started on down the stream once more. By then, Aleswina was numb to everything except for the grip of Annwr's hand. Picking one foot up and putting it in front of the other one, she sloshed along, head down.

After an eternity, they reached the river and came to a halt. Caelym and Anna began a hushed conversion in Celt while Aleswina, who'd long since forgotten the language Anna had spoken to her in their first years together, looked around, dazzled by the brilliance of the moon's reflection off the seemingly motionless expanse of water that curved in a broad arch around them.

PART IV

The River

The moon, waning but still three-quarters full, hung above the tree-tops, admiring her reflection on the shimmering river. The few faint stars that had dotted the horizon as they left Annwr's backyard to wade their way through the forest had since multiplied and spread so it now seemed that the earth had donned a night cloak made of diamonds.

Caelym put his hand out to keep Annwr and Aleswina behind him in the protective shadows of the trees and stood still, listening. The nearby sounds were reassuring—owls hooting, bats fluttering, and the occasion call of a thrush sounding—but in the distance, coming from downstream, there was a dim clanging of bells that was more likely calling on the villagers to wake and join in the hunt than summoning the Christian nuns to their nightly prayers.

A tangle of brush swept past on the far side of the river, its speed warning him of just how strong a current flowed underneath the river's deceptively smooth surface. He had dived into this same river in his desperation to escape the horde of pursuing Saxons, and he knew its strength. Neither Annwr nor Aleswina would have any chance against it.

"You packed an axe, did you?" With dogs hunting them, Caelym knew they had no choice but to stay in the water. Given the weight of the pack on his back, he felt a surge of hope that was immediately deflated by Annwr's caustic rejoinder "No, I did not! Would you be thinking of gathering wood for a bonfire to save the guards the trouble?"

"I would be thinking of making a raft so your Saxon princess could ride down the river instead of swimming, which I don't suppose she can."

"And you don't think a boat would be better?"

Looking up and down the bank for a floatable log, Caelym replied irritably, "It would be much better, only I think I'd not be wanting to go into the town just now, knocking on doors and asking whether some kind Saxon might have one to lend."

Annwr's answer was equally snide. "And I'd not be expecting you to do anything so useful, but if you'd like rowing over swimming, then I'll do what I can about it."

Dragging Aleswina along behind her, she plunged her pole into the current and started upstream.

Caelym splashed after her and came up alongside Aleswina, who, just as he'd predicted, was floundering like a drowning kitten. Grumbling the strongest invectives a priest of his rank might use in the presence of a priestess who was sister to the highest of all priestesses, he shifted his pole to his left hand and took hold of Aleswina's arm with his right to join with Annwr in keeping her upright and moving forward.

Chapter 23

Not A Word

As they fought their way against the current, Annwr relented enough to explain how she planned get the boat.

"There's an old man who works on the river, carrying freight and buying and selling boats. He has more boats than he needs, and he owes me one of them for all the times I've nursed him through hangovers. He'll be asleep now, and too drunk to notice if we took his bed out from underneath him."

With nothing better to suggest and no reason to think that Annwr would listen to him if he did, Caelym waded on, his shoulder and arm throbbing from the strain of keeping Aleswina's head above water. He was too proud to complain about the weight of his overloaded pack or to remind Annwr that he'd only recently recovered from an almost fatal arrow wound.

It was his pride against the current, and the current was on the verge of winning when they rounded a broad bend and Annwr gave a self-satisfied grunt and pointed with her staff.

Caelym's mental picture of the boathouse she'd promised was based on the only boathouse he knew—the one on the bank of the sacred lake in Llwddawanden, a fastidiously kept pier with a neat line of sleek boats tucked under the cover of a post-and-beam boat shed, each with its perfectly matched oars leaning against the wall behind it.

What he saw now was a teetering wharf, its docks battered and buckled and a clutter of boats in all states of repair crammed together under a shabby roof. On the upstream side, a heap of river debris was piled halfway up the boathouse wall. The down-stream bank was littered with the skeletons of wrecked hulls. On the bank above and behind the boathouse he saw what could have been a heap of smoldering rubbish but was actually, he guessed, the thatched roof of the hovel where the boatman was, hopefully, as sound asleep as Annwr had promised.

While Caelym was taking this in, Annwr forged on. She was about to help Aleswina climb the rickety ladder when he hissed at her to keep her hands off it and keep the girl away.

"The dogs will be set on her scent and yours too!"

"And what about yours?" she hissed back as he edged past her and gave the flimsy railing an experimental tug to see if it would take his weight along with that of his overloaded pack.

"It's the two of you they'll be after, so we'll just hope a small whiff of me won't catch their interest." He heaved himself up, wrestled off his pack, and walked gingerly along the creaking dock into the boathouse.

On a darker night or with a better repaired roof, he would have needed to risk lighting a torch to see what he was doing. As it was, the moonlight streaming down through the gaps in the moldering thatch was enough to see by. Of the dozen boats that jostled against each other, six were half sunk, two lacked oarlocks, and three of the remaining four were meant for hauling cargo and were far longer than they needed. That left one, a small, solidly built craft with two sturdy-looking oars already set in place. He untangled its tie rope and pulled it to the end of the dock where Annwr stood waist deep, holding Aleswina against her and glowering at him.

"Give your pack here!" As he'd expected, Annwr's pack was half the weight of his and the boat barely shifted as he wedged it into the prow. His own was more of a struggle, but he managed to get it over the edge of the dock and shoved back against the stern.

"Now her!"

Leaning precariously over the side, he managed to haul Aleswina up and into the boat with Annwr lifting from below. As she flopped in, the boat rocked back and forth, its pitching efforts made worse by her frenzied effort to pull away from him.

"Hold still!"

Despite saying it clearly in English, his order had no effect, in fact seemed only to add to her thrashing panic. Before she could spill both of them, along with their supplies, into the river, he wrestled her down onto the prow of the boat where she wrapped her arms around Annwr's pack, clinging to it like a drowning man to a rock in the river.

"You stay there and don't move!" He spoke more sharply than he would have if the boat weren't still tossing and pitching out of control. Once he'd gotten hold of a piling and steadied it, he added in a calmer but still firm tone of voice, "And be quiet!" Seeing nothing in the girl's dazed expression to show that she heard or understood his command, he repeated, "You must not move or make a sound! No matter what happens, you must not speak a single word—not a peep, not a whisper—until I say so."

He climbed back onto the dock, went to the workbench, found a small, sharp hatchet, and made his way around the outer deck to the piled-up tangle of brush. He hacked off as much as he could carry, then brought the armload of branches and twigs back to the boat and piled them around Aleswina and the packs. In another three trips, he'd covered the boat over well enough that in the darkness and from a distance it could easily be taken for a drift of river refuse. As he stepped back for a moment to admire his handiwork, he heard Annwr mutter, "It's lovely. Now to get me up and into the boat before I grow gills!"

"Gills would be just the thing for what comes next, so if you'd teach me how to grow my own, I'd be grateful." He snapped off a twig from the brush covering the boat and squatted down, close to where Annwr was standing, glowering at him.

"Now we must have a plan for getting past the village of savage Saxons hunting her"—he nodded towards the pile of brush covering Aleswina—"and happy to catch us in the bargain." Drawing lines in the green slime that coated the deck to illustrate what he was saying, he went on, "Here, then, is the river, and here we are, and here is the village. We will keep to the far side and in the shadow of the bank. I will swim in front, guiding the boat, and you will swim at the back, keeping it straight. We will go just with the current and no faster, since even Saxons may have sense enough to wonder at drifting brush that swims on its own accord."

Before Annwr could argue about who was to swim in front, he picked up the hatchet, inspecting it carefully while watching her out of the corner of his eye. "Now, about what this boatman owes you for all the good care you have given him in his times of need, perhaps it would include this excellent little axe as well as the boat and oars?"

Annwr's expression remained stern. "I have said he owed me a boat, which of necessity includes the oars. I will not take more than I am owed, nor rob a man while he is passed out from drinking."

Caelym suppressed a sigh. He was standing up to put the hatchet back where he found it when she said in a softer tone (not as soft as the tone she used with Aleswina, but softer than any she'd ever used with him), "Now, if your heart is set on having that axe, you may reach down on the right side of your pack and you'll find a flask of fresh mead. I . . ." Here she hesitated, cleared her throat, and went on. "I brought it along for you, as I never gave you any gift for becoming either priest or physician. If you choose, you may leave it in exchange for the axe. Were the old man here now, he would take the drink and be glad of it."

Caelym found the flask, took a long swallow from it to be sure of its quality, and made the trade. Warmed and encouraged by the drink, he lowered himself back into the water and, together with Annwr, eased the boat out into the current.

Chapter 24

The First Rapids

Τ he village of Fenwick was awake. Drifting past with their noses just above water, Caelym and Annwr could see men carrying torches rushing around with packs of hounds. The light from the flames, however, darkened the night around them, and neither men nor dogs took any notice of the brush-filled boat as they floated past on the far side of the river.

Still, they kept their heads down and stayed even with the current around another three bends before they risked landing the boat and climbing out. After shaking off like a wet dog, Caelym pulled off the tangle of twigs and branches and hoisted the packs onto the shore, leaving Aleswina to Annwr.

It was, as he'd advised them both, better to have dry clothes to get into after spending a cool night in the water. Dressed again, and with the coarse monk's robe a welcome shield against the breeze, he climbed back into the boat, set the oars into their braces, and settled himself on the seat and took some experimental strokes through the air.

"Have you taken a boat down a river before?" Annwr asked, skeptical as ever.

Of course, I have, a thousand times or more! is what he would have answered if only it were the truth. Instead, he barked back, "I have not, but how hard can it be if a drunken Saxon can do it?"

"It may have helped that he learned how when he was sober."

Unable to think of a suitably scathing rebuttal, Caelym took himself off into the bushes, both for personal reasons and to escape having to respond.

◆◆◆

Glad to have him out from underfoot, Annwr coaxed Aleswina out of the boat and into dry clothes. While she did as she was told, it worried Annwr that Aleswina kept shivering after she should have been warm, and that she didn't answer when Annwr spoke to her.

◆◆◆

Coming out of the thicket to see that Annwr still hovered over the dim-witted girl, Caelym weighed Annwr's indulgence of the stupid little Saxon princess against the harsh abuse and neglect he felt himself to be suffering. His sense of being wronged increased as he got close enough to hear Annwr telling Aleswina that she should "pay no attention to Caelym's antics, because he was always one to put on a show for the pleasure of being noticed and no doubt will be making up poetry about his own silly escapades before they're half over."

That there was some truth to this only added to Caelym's mounting resentment as he pushed the boat back into the water.

It took him a while to get the feel for rowing in the strong current and keeping the boat in a relatively straight path. Once he felt in control, he snapped "It might be better if you spent less time telling the girl that I'm a fool. As we journey together, fleeing from one danger to face another, there may be a time that I will need to tell her what she must do, and instead of doing it maybe she'll be looking at you to see if she should, and maybe by the time you tell her, it will be too late."

To Caelym's surprise, Annwr said that he was right and that she was sorry.

Another several bends of the river slipped past in oddly companionable silence, with no more than the slap and surge of the oars and the rustle of water against the sides of the boat.

◆◆◆

It was almost dawn when a change in the sound of the river caught their attention. Looking downstream, in the faint beginning of daylight, they couldn't see anything except a few rocks and some V-shaped ripples, but the sound increased to a thundering roar as the current picked up, carrying the boat faster than Caelym was rowing.

Aleswina sat up to look just as the boat came to the verge of the rapids. It teetered there for half a dozen heartbeats, held in place by Caelym's desperate backstrokes. Then it dropped its prow and plunged downwards. The two women clutched whatever there was to hold on to while Caelym heaved one oar then the other to fend off rocks or bring the boat around straight before the waves swamped it.

They were all soaked, and their packs were washing back and forth in a small lake of water in the bottom of the boat when they came out, just as suddenly, into a swift, smooth current that gave no hint of what they had just been through.

Caelym brought the boat around to look back at the cascade of water crashing behind them, his face glowing in exaltation. Even Annwr's sharp warning to look ahead or he'd be drowning them all could not dampen the triumph of that moment or keep his heart from filling with a deep and lasting love for boats and rivers.

Chapter 25

Whatever Dangers Lay Ahead

As they traveled on, passing out of inhabited lands and into steep-walled canyons, Caelym's spirits rose. Whatever sorrows lay behind him, whatever dangers lay ahead, he was, for the moment, riding on the crest of the river's current, challenging and conquering one wild rapid after another.

Kneeling in the front of the boat, Annwr gripped the rail with one hand and clutched Aleswina with the other to keep her from being pitched overboard as they careened off boulders, plunging from one roiling death trap to the next.

"Look out—"

A wave crashed over the prow of the boat, cutting off her cry. Coughing and choking, she managed to spit the water out of her mouth, but instead of finishing, "for the cliff!" she gasped out her mother's name.

Caelym could see the sheer wall of rock rising straight ahead of them perfectly well without Annwr yelling at him about it. Hauling back on his left oar and thrusting forward on the right, he brought the boat around. As it spun sideways, he brought the two oars up together and threw all his weight into his next stroke, sending the boat flying up and onto the sandy shore of an island—set there, he assumed, by the Goddess to give weary travelers a place to rest.

Annwr's first impulse, once she was able to steady her shaking limbs and climb out of the beached boat, was to curse Caelym and all of his male ancestry going back to the Sun God Himself. She settled for snapping at him that if he was done showing off just how close he could come to drowning them all without actually doing it, maybe he could make himself useful for a change.

"Get the packs! We need to hide the boat out of sight and find some shelter where we can dry off and get warm!"

Stiffening her shoulders, she surveyed the bleak, wind-swept island. A swath of grasses and brush separated the rocky shore from a scraggly stand of pine trees. It wasn't the sacred island of Cwddwaellwn, but there'd be wood for a fire and hopefully some place out of sight where they could dry their things and cook the hot meal they all needed—especially Aleswina, who was sitting motionless in her drenched clothes, her hands gripping the side rails as if she didn't realize that they'd stopped moving.

Annwr forced herself to smile as she said, "Come on, Dear Heart, you can get up now. We're landed safe and sound and need to look for somewhere to have breakfast."

Although her eyes were open, Aleswina didn't look at Annwr or loosen her grip on the side of the boat.

"Aleswina!" Annwr used her real name and said it sharply.

Aleswina blinked but made no other move.

"Caelym! Help me get her out!"

After all he'd done getting them away from the Saxons and hounds, past a dozen raging rapids, and now safely landed on a lovely tree-covered island, Caelym felt he had a right to expect at least a word or two of praise from Annwr, and he would have said so if he could have gotten a word in between her carping and complaints. As it was, he helped her pry Aleswina's hands loose from the boat rails. Together, they pulled her out of the boat and stood her on the ground, where she managed, barely, to stay upright on her own two feet. Leaving Annwr prattling to Aleswina in an irritating, high-pitched voice about how they'd gotten to this nice island all safe and sound (without so much as a mention of his part in getting them there!), he dragged the boat up the bank and hid it in the brush. Picking up the packs, he pushed his way back through the undergrowth and into the thicket.

It wasn't a large grove and it didn't take long to reach the center: a sandy basin nestled into a bank of protective grass and shrubs. Bathed in the morning sunlight and protected from the wind, it was a cozy, welcoming spot, a place so perfect it was almost surely a trap set by local sprites to snare unwary intruders.

Caelym was not unwary but knew from experience that, with the right cajoling, even the most malevolent of wood spirits could be bargained with. Stepping to the edge of the clearing, he spoke out in a strong and resonant voice, announcing that they would stop here for just as long as they needed to eat and rest, would take no more than a little dry kindling for a fire, and would leave nothing behind except for the portion of their provisions they'd gladly share with all things who made this place their home.

With that (and no more acknowledgment of his foresight and caution from Annwr than he expected, which was none at all), he set off to explore the island.

A part of Annwr's mind grumbled, *Just like a man to go off in a fit of pique when he might be of some use,* while another part chided her for not giving Caelym any thanks for saving them from Gilberth's guards. But Caelym wasn't her worry just then, Aleswina was.

She managed to get Aleswina through the tangle of undergrowth by holding her up and urging her along, but once she let go, the girl sank to her knees on the edge of the bank, her hands folded in her lap, a vacant, faraway look in her eyes, as if her spirit were on the verge of leaving her body to wander lost and alone, uncertain to which afterlife it belonged.

The first thing was to get her warm and dry. Annwr dug through the packs, pulling out flints and tinder, blankets and cloaks, pots and provisions, a flask of ale, and a rope. In almost no time at all, she had Aleswina stripped out of her wet clothes and wrapped in the least damp of the blankets, arranged stones into a serviceable hearth, had a fire burning, and had put a pot of mulled ale to heat.

Even though the deathly chill fell away and Aleswina's color (pale but pinkish) had returned, she remained mute despite all of Annwr's efforts to coax a word out of her. As much to calm herself as to comfort Aleswina, Annwr kept up her patter of baby talk, unconsciously slipping back into Celt.

"See, we've got our nice warm fire going and will make some good broth as soon as the coals are ready. Now you just watch while I tie up this rope like our clothesline at home and hang up our blankets and cloaks to keep the heat around us, and then we'll be as snug and warm as mice in their nest. Now let's just have another sip of sweet, spiced ale to give you back your strength . . ."

She was spooning the drink between Aleswina's chattering teeth when Caelym finally returned, no doubt wanting to see if his breakfast was cooked and waiting for him.

Unwilling to stand around being ignored while Annwr babbled and cooed to her stupid princess, Caelym had set out to scout for any sign of bears or Saxons. Finding no large tracks but their own, he'd made his way back to the upper end of the island where the river split into two unequal halves. The larger part crashed straight into the cliffs, curling back on itself in a churning confusion of waves with crests the height of a rearing horse, while the smaller stream threaded its way along a shallow channel between the island and a shrub-covered bank.

Taking the boat down the main branch would be the thrill of his life, but even as he thought about it, he could hear Annwr's nagging voice saying, *"The last thrill of your life!"* so he trudged back up to where the boat was hidden, pulled it out, and dragged it behind him down the bank and along the smaller stream—a piddling little trickle of water barely ankle deep—to the lower end of the island. After pulling the boat up onto the shore and into the brush, he walked down the point to where the two streams came back together to form a broad expanse of smooth, swiftly flowing water.

Muttering, "I could have done it" to himself, he picked up a flat, smooth stone, threw it, and watched as it skipped four, five, six times before coming down with a dismal plunk and sinking out of sight. Then he turned and went back to the clearing where he'd left Annwr and Aleswina.

He had, of course, assumed that Annwr would have set out their promised tribute before doing anything else. And while he had not specifically warned her that hanging her laundry up to dry was certain to offend the local sprites and require twice the remunerations they'd have to dole out, it seemed to him to go without saying!

Dodging between the blanket flaps he was appalled to realize that Annwr had yet to offer so much as a single crust of bread to their hosts, but before he could remonstrate, she ordered him off again to get more wood for the fire and a pot of water for soup.

Determined to show that he, at least, knew how to behave in someone else's home, he set out a carefully counted share of bread and apples under each of the proper trees, murmuring his apologies to whatever irritated beings were rustling in the leaves overhead. That done, he hauled two armloads of wood, and fetched Annwr her pot of water before sitting down to his own well-deserved meal (one he had to assemble himself, since Annwr was too busy fawning over her Saxon darling to put a plate out for him).

He filled his own cup and drained it three times—first for his triumph over the river, next for forgoing the glory of challenging the greatest of all the rapids, and finally, for . . . for . . .

As his thoughts began to drift, Annwr's babbling to Aleswina ceased to annoy him. Instead it was like listening to his childhood nurse, if his nurse had sounded so much like Feywn, or listening to Feywn, if Feywn had ever said such childish nonsense to him. He drew his legs up, leaned back into the soft sand, and slipped into a dream that his nurse and Feywn were blended together in one woman and she was singing him to sleep.

Chapter 26

I Will Compose A Song

It took two cups of broth and another of mulled ale, but Aleswina had finally stopped trembling. Now, wrapped in a warm blanket, she was curled up with her head on Annwr's lap, breathing slow, easy breaths.

Annwr should have been tired enough to sleep on a bed of nettles but instead she felt fidgety, bothered by something she couldn't quite put her finger on.

Caelym was dozing off on the far side of the campfire. A week's growth of beard hid his uncanny resemblance to Rhedwyn, so he now seemed to be nothing more than a stray vagabond worn out from his wandering. There was something shadowy about him, something elusive about how he changed the subject anytime she mentioned Llwddawanden.

In their rush to escape, she hadn't questioned his insistence on taking the river, but shouldn't they have left it to start the journey back up into the mountains once they were safely past the village? Even as enamored as Caelym was with riding the rapids, it didn't make sense that he would just keep rowing on in the wrong direction without thought to how far out of the way the river was taking them.

There was something he wasn't telling her.

Keeping her voice low so she didn't wake Aleswina, she called to him, only to have him grunt and mumble, turn over, and pull his cloak up around his ears.

"Caelym," she hissed louder. "Caelym! Wake up and answer me! I want to know where we're going—and don't tell me Llwddawanden, because we both know this river isn't running uphill!"

◆◆◆

Oddly, the idea of the river running uphill seemed perfectly reasonable for a moment, and Caelym was on the verge of arguing that it might if Annwr would just stop saying it couldn't. Fortunately, he woke up completely before he'd managed to organize that befuddled thought into a sentence.

He pushed himself up to sitting and returned her glare with one of his own. "We are going to find her"—he shifted his eyes to Aleswina just long enough to emphasize which "her" he was talking about—"another convent! Then we will speak of where to go next."

"Don't shout! She's sleeping!"

He hadn't shouted, just spoken in a firm, resolute voice—and more distinctly than most would be able to manage after three cups of Annwr's potent ale—so there was no need for her to chastise him when he was only answering the question she'd asked. After drawing in a breath and exhaling pointedly, Caelym repeated himself in a chirpy little voice that was, he thought, quite a clever imitation of Annwr talking to Aleswina.

"We are going to find her another nice convent where she can stay all nice and warm with all the other nice little Christian priestesses!"

Annwr, of course, failed to appreciate his humor.

"Then we don't need to go any farther, because we not leaving her in any convent, we're taking her with us back to Llwddawanden!"

"We're not going—"

One of the many irritating things about Annwr was how she kept harping on Llwddawanden. Without the long years he'd spent sitting at the feet of three great Druids, Caelym might have blurted out that they weren't going back to Llwddawanden then or ever, but with their masterful training in the art of telling the truth without telling the whole truth he didn't hesitate for more than the time it took to clear his throat to shift to saying, "to take her to Llwddawanden! We're going to take her to a convent to be with others of her kind!"

"Her kind? If by that you mean others who are sweet and gentle and loving, then I hope there will be some of her kind in Llwddawanden!"

"I mean her Saxon, Christian kind!"

"She does not care about being Christian or Saxon. She only cares that she is with me, and I will not leave her!"

"She may not care about being Christian or Saxon, but that is what she is! And someday she will care, and she will look at you and see you are her enemy, and she will forget all you have done for her, and she will betray you and all those you hold dear."

"I have raised this girl as my own daughter! She loves me and would never betray us."

Annwr was glowering at Caelym as she spoke, and she would have paid no attention to his rebuttal if it had not been for the sudden look of misery and grief—too raw to be feigned—that passed over his face in the moment before he answered her.

"I do not know what you have experienced in your years away from us, Annwr, but if you still believe that the love and care you give to another can protect against betrayal, then you have not yet learned all there is to know in this life."

Annwr, quite unfairly, evaded what Caelym considered to be an irrefutable assertion by listing off in entirely unnecessary detail the string of good deeds Aleswina had done for him—risking torture and death to save him from her fellow Saxons, hiding him, feeding him, nursing him back to health, and helping him escape his pursuers a second time.

The unspoken accusation of ingratitude hovered in the air between them and for a moment he almost wavered—but only for a moment. Then, in his mind's eye, he saw himself standing before Feywn and the high council, trying to explain how, along with Annwr, Arddwn, and Lliem, he'd also brought with him a Saxon Christian princess—and not just any Saxon Christian princess but the daughter of the king against whom, for good and valid reasons, he had sworn eternal vengeance. It was an image that strengthened his resolve and put iron into his response.

"I will compose a song commemorating her noble deeds—ending it with how she fled the lustful grasp of her evil cousin to find safety and happiness in the finest convent in Atheldom!"

Chapter 27

Who Said It Was Safe?

The name of their next destination slipped out without Caelym meaning it to, but as Annwr repeated "Atheldom!" after him, he realized that this was the answer to the problem of what to do with Aleswina and nodded vigorously.

"So you have heard of it, then, and must know that it is the one place below the mountains where Christians live alongside our folk, each conducting their own rites and leaving the other in peace."

"Who told you that?"

"One in whom we can trust absolutely and completely."

"Well, he in whom you trust absolutely is wrong! There have been Christian priests hard at work in that kingdom and those left unburned all swear that they are Christians and are ready to turn over their neighbors or their parents in exchange for themselves."

Looking at Caelym as if it were he and not Aleswina who was the simple-minded fool, Annwr brushed aside his protests, saying, "If you'd told me where we were going in the first place, I could have saved us all this trip. And now we may as well get some rest, because we'll have a long climb back the way we came."

Caelym, however, stayed sitting up, gaping at her. "You must be mistaken! He said it was safe . . ."

"Who said it was safe?"

"Benyon."

◆◆◆

"Benyon? The priest's servant?" Annwr frowned. The only memory she could dredge up on hearing the name was the vague recollection of a huffing, middle-aged man carrying an armload of the priest's robes for the women servants to wash.

"The chief of the men's servants," Caelym thrust out his chin, "trusted not only with cleaning the quarters of the priests but also with overseeing the care of the sacred vessels and the distribution of goods from the storage chambers, an excellent and loyal servant who has spent his life in our shrine and whose devotion to us is beyond question!"

"And how would a servant who spent his life in the shrine know about the world outside of Llwddawanden?"

"He has kin in the outside world, kin who live in Atheldom and who know more about it than—"

"A priestess of the shrine of the Great Mother Goddess, sister to the chief priestess who is the living embodiment of the spirit of the eternal goddess herself?"

Annwr's eyes glinted dangerously, and Caelym chose his next words with care.

"I do not say that any kinsmen of a common servant, even one so esteemed as Benyon, are as wise and all-knowing as you, only that they assured him it would be safe there for him to carry out the important mission we gave him."

"And what mission was that?"

"I will tell you that after we have found her a convent!"

"You will tell me now," Annwr snapped, "or I'll not take one more step on this mad quest of yours!"

Caelym hesitated, then decided that there was no way other than telling Annwr the truth.

"His mission was to go to Atheldom disguised as a sheepherder, taking Feywn's sons with him to foster them there so that they would learn to speak English well enough to pass among our enemies undetected. It has been two years since they left and we had expected them to return by now, as both boys are quick at learning, and it is past time for the older one to begin his training in recitation, and . . ."

Once he started talking about them, memories of Arddwn and Lliem flooded Caelym's mind. He would have gone on pouring out his longing to have them back in his arms again, only Annwr broke in.

"Now I know you are mad! Feywn has no sons. She had only the one daughter! I was at her side when Rhedwyn's body was carried in and laid at her feet, holding her back from slaying herself in her grief! She swore to me and to all the world that she would never love any other but would be true to his memory until the end of time itself. If I had been gone from Llwddawanden a hundred years, still I would know my sister and know she meant it."

"You may know your sister, Annwr, but you must also know that beyond love and beyond grief, there is need. If we are to go on, there must be children, and those children must be fathered. Nine years ago, Feywn took a second consort, and she now has two sons—Arddwn, who is eight, and Lliem, who is five."

Taken back by this unexpected news, Annwr spoke without thinking, "Only sons then? No other daughters?"

"There was a baby girl," Caelym answered, "born as beautiful as a fairy's child, but she lived only long enough to break the hearts of those who beheld her, opening her eyes but once before returning to the Otherworld."

Two dead daughters and too old to chance another pregnancy, it was no wonder Feywn wanted Cyri for her own, but Annwr did not say this out loud; instead, she changed the subject, saying as much to herself as to Caelym, "And who was it that climbed into the bed Rhedwyn left empty?"

There were three flat stones near where Annwr was sitting. She reached over and set them up in a row as she thought about the priests in the highest ranks of their order—all of them had seemed ancient to her fifteen years before, and not one of them came close to having Rhedwyn's charisma, charm, and otherworldly good looks. Tapping her finger from the first stone to second to the third and back again, she muttered, "I pity the man who dared, for the task he'd have trying to take Rhedwyn's place."

"A most difficult task indeed, but not without some small reward."

There was no mistaking the smugness in Caelym's tone, or the effort it took him to keep from smirking.

"No, Caelym, not you! You are too young! You would have been nothing more than a boy then!"

Suddenly serious, almost regal, he answered as if he were speaking out before the high council. "I was seventeen when Feywn chose me for her consort, eighteen when my first son was born, and nineteen when I buried my daughter. Maybe I started this as a boy, yet I became a man when it was required."

There was nothing to say to that except, "I'm sorry to have spoken as I did—and suppose I can see how it could be." Annwr spoke the last part of this quietly, intending the words for herself alone.

Caelym gave her a coy smile. "You would not be the first to think that, having lost the greater father, Feywn might have settled for the lesser son."

"Hush, Caelym. You were conceived at the Sacred Summer Solstice Ceremony and know full well that the mortal man who danced with your mother that night was but a vessel for the spirit of the Sun God!"

"Ah, but from what I have heard, that vessel had an uncanny resemblance to Feywn's beloved Rhedwyn, even as I do myself." Here, to Annwr's annoyance, he winked at her, and—as if reading her thoughts—added, "A resemblance that might explain why Feywn chose me as soon as I was grown enough to take my place at her side."

"Being born to Caelendra, forever mourned chief priestess and past embodiment of the Great Mother Goddess, would be reason enough for that."

Annwr's voice did not hold much conviction when she said this and Caelym did not answer. Instead, he returned to his demand that they leave Aleswina in the first convent they could find.

Caught up in their argument, neither Annwr nor Caelym noticed the flickering movement behind Aleswina's closed eyelids, or how the rate of her breathing changed depending on which of them was speaking and what was said.

Chapter 28

The Seed Of Mortal Sin

The surge of desperate courage that carried Aleswina out of the convent had ebbed away as she stumbled along the stream clinging to Anna's hand. With her feet going numb in the water and the impenetrable blackness of the forest all around her, she'd felt she was walking into the worst of her childhood nightmares.

Still, with Anna holding her up and urging her on, she'd managed to make it to the boathouse—so cold she couldn't stop shivering and so exhausted she could barely stay upright even with Anna's arms around her.

The soft splash of Caelym climbing out of the water, the creaking of planks under his feet, and the scraping of the boat against the dock as he pulled it back with him had all seemed faint and far away, not sounds that had anything to do with her. But when, with no warning, he'd pulled her away from Anna and into the boat, she'd panicked, and her panic had turned to hysteria as her struggles to break loose and get back to Anna sent the boat rocking and reeling. Caelym was bigger than she was, and stronger, but it was his angry voice ordering her to be quiet that had overcome her spasm of resistance.

"No matter what happens, you must not speak a single word, not a peep, not a whisper, until I say so."

All the way down the river, those words raced in circles inside her head, changing into three voices—one hard and commanding, one high and shrill, one soft and urgent—until Anna lifted her up out of the boat and began to croon to her in the soothing voice that had woken her up from her nightmares when she was little.

Safe inside their new shelter, finally warm again, she was on the verge of being lulled to sleep by the soft back and forth of Celtic speech between Anna and Caelym when the sounds that she remembered from earliest childhood, before Anna learned English, separated into words and phrases, and Aleswina realized that they were talking about her.

Maintaining peaceful cohabitation within the close confines of the convent had, in Hildegarth's view, required keeping gossip to a minimum. The abbess's conviction about this had led to frequent, vehement admonitions against the relatively minor sin of eavesdropping. After seven years of hearing the abbess's dire warnings that listening slyly to what others are saying was "the seed of mortal sin and must be rigorously confessed before it weakens your soul and invites the devil in," Aleswina knew that she should sit up and tell Anna she understood what they were saying.

But Caelym had ordered her not to speak—and not to move, either! So it was his fault, really, that she kept lying there as still as if she were dead even when he told Annwr, "If what you say about Atheldom is true, there is certain to be a convent there where she, at least, will be safe, while Benyon and the boys are in the gravest danger and must be rescued without further delay."

She held her breath and didn't let it out until Annwr answered, "And have you forgotten that the king's guards are pursuing her? What if word of her arrival in that convent is sent back to Derthwald?" Her breathing, along with the beat of her heart, sped up when Caelym said, meanly, "There is little need to worry about that, for by the time any message from Atheldom reaches the king's ears, his passion for her will have cooled and been forgotten in the arms of some woman more ready to welcome his affection." Both raced faster when Annwr said, "He will pursue her to her grave! And no Saxon convent is safe from him. We must at least take her to some abbey in Celtic lands where she will safe," and faster yet when Caelym said, "There is no time for that! I need to save my sons, and you need to return to your daughter—your real daughter!"

◆◆◆

Spoken openly for the first time, Caelym's accusation that she favored Aleswina over Cyri was a bitter blow, and it took Annwr several outraged moments to sort through the many answers she might make to it.

Before she was able to pick the most scathing, Caelym said in a soft, sad voice, accompanied by a dark, reproachful gaze, "You have not asked for any news of Cyri. Is that because you've no wish to hear about her?"

Knowing Caelym was doing what Druid priests always did—turning the debate from one he was losing to one he could win—Annwr snapped, "No more wish than I have to be taking another breath!" before she gave in.

"Well then, tell me! What training did she choose? Does she have a consort? Is she happy?"

"No consort yet, as there are no priests of her age and rank that are fully trained and ready for that honor. And as for her training, she is, like you, a skilled midwife, but even as she was training in the birthing chambers, she determined that she would be a physician and a bard as well."

While Annwr was sputtering that this was priest's work and how dare they allow her daughter to clutter her mind with it and was this some stupid idea of Olyrrwd's and Herrwn's, Caelym swept on.

"I had just finished my own training as a physician, with the final test of Olyrrwd's last illness, one that I correctly named but could not cure, so Cyri's training in this was given to me, while Herrwn agreed to teach her to recite our nine great sagas. From then on, he and I have been two teachers in competition for a single student. It was to become an unending rivalry between us, with me coaxing Cyri away from Herrwn's feet to learn the proper treatment of childhood fevers and him luring her back with his wondrous tales from ancient times. All the while, she would take each lesson she was given and learn it, asking no more reward than that she be given another. She is now a skilled healer in both women and men's lore and a stirring bard in her own right. As to whether she is happy or not, it is not for me to say but for you to ask her if you decide that your real daughter matters to you as much as a Saxon's spawn!"

This last was Caelym's one slip, because it brought Annwr back to the issue at hand.

"I have two real daughters, Caelym, both of them as dear to me as your two sons are to you, so first you tell me how you would choose between Arddwn and Lliem; then you may tell me how I am to choose between Aleswina and Cyri!"

If Aleswina breathed at all during Caelym's tirade, she was not aware of it, only of a growing agony in her chest that felt at first as if her lungs were on fire. Then the burning pain died away, leaving an empty, aching desolation behind. But then, into that hollow well of hurt, poured a sudden, soothing balm—Anna had two daughters, and she was one of them, no matter what Caelym said!

Caelym and Annwr continued to bicker back and forth until it was nearly noon, finally agreeing only that they were both tired and would settle the matter—by which Caelym meant Annwr would agree to leave Aleswina in the first convent they found, while Annwr meant Caelym would agree to take her along with them—after they got some sleep.

Chapter 29

Leave to Speak

Caelym woke late in the day. He got up, stretched, and took a necessary trip into the bushes. From where he stood, he could see the bright rays of the afternoon sun dancing on the river. Behind him, he could hear Annwr clanking pots and fussing over Aleswina. Instead of returning to camp, he made his way down to the lower end of the island to get the boat out of its hiding place and ready to launch.

He'd dragged the boat to the water's edge and was setting the oars into their fittings when he heard Annwr scream his name.

Saxons! It had to be! The shrillness and intensity of her outcry could only mean that they were under attack. He drew his knife and dashed back towards their camp, cursing himself for leaving the women unguarded. When he reached the edge of the clearing, he ducked behind a tree and stood still, gasping and listening.

While Annwr's shrill cries continued without let-up, he could hear nothing else—no hounds howling or men shouting. He peered cautiously out around the trunk, thinking to see how many enemies he'd be facing before he decided whether to charge into battle against them or use some stratagem to draw them off, giving Annwr and Aleswina a chance to escape.

The blanket walls of the makeshift shelter were taken down and neatly folded next to a stack of pots and bowls, all washed, dried and ready to be packed. The only Saxon in sight was Aleswina, who was sitting on a log and waving her hands in the air while Annwr stood next to her, screeching his name.

He eased his way out from behind the tree, still watching for an ambush and staying half-concealed in the underbrush, and called out softly in Celt, "I am here. What is it you would be wanting of me?"

"I want you tell Aleswina that she may speak!"

For a long moment, Caelym stood in stunned disbelief. Then he raised his voice to a pitch to that matched Annwr's. "You called me back here, sounding like some banshee being eaten alive by goblins, and I have come running thinking I must face a dozen foul Saxons with only my knife, and this just to tell me to tell this stupid coward to speak! It is nothing to me whether she speaks or not! If she cannot decide that for herself, then you may tell her—just as you tell her whether she ought to breathe or not!"

Instead of raising her voice further, Annwr lowered it ominously. "Oh, Caelym, it is something to you whether she speaks—as it was you that told her she could not!"

"I never—"

"When you first put her into the boat; you told her that she was not to speak again until you said so." Here she paused and changed to the syrupy sweet voice she reserved for her miserable little Saxon princess. "It's all right, Dear Heart, I'm telling him."

The girl, who had now stopped flapping her hands, was pointing at him.

Annwr reverted to the growl she reserved for Caelym. "And now you will tell her that she may speak, or she will go to her grave never saying any word ever again!"

Caelym stood rubbing his chin as the recollection came to him—he had said something like that, only he had not known whether the girl even heard him and never thought about it again after they were past the enemy village. For another moment, he toyed with the possibility that he might turn the blame for this away from himself and back on Aleswina for carrying on so about it . . . but, of course, there was no hope of persuading Annwr to see things from his side with Aleswina fluttering her hands and looking pitiful.

Bracing himself, he left the cover of the bushes and crossed over to them, telling Annwr that he'd take care of it and adding that she could go on with her packing and leave this to him.

Annwr backed off a few paces and stood watching him, her hands on her hips and her face set in a grim frown.

Feeling her eyes boring into his back, Caelym squatted in front of Aleswina, whose eyes widened in fear as if he, the kindest and most forbearing of men, were some ogre about to eat her alive. If, however, there was one thing in which Caelym had complete confidence, it was in his powers of charm. He reverted to English and switched into the voice he might use for comforting a small child. "Now, Little Sister, I will be giving you my leave to speak again, but before I do that, I have the need to speak myself. First, I would thank you from my heart for the honor that you have done me in carefully keeping my command. Next, I must be saying how I am sorry for keeping you silent for so long, when I only meant that you should be quiet while we passed through the village, and after that I forgot that having given you this command, I must then say when it was finished. Then we must think together about how you might remind me of this when you are forbidden to speak in words and the lovely waving of your hands does not mean more to me than the fluttering of a butterfly in the breeze."

Here Caelym paused and gave Aleswina a deeply concerned look, as though expecting some enlightenment from her. When it did not come and she only put her hands behind her back and looked over her shoulder at Annwr, he said in a firmer voice, "No! You must look at me, for I am the one who wronged you, and it is I whom you must boldly challenge to make it right!"

At this, Aleswina did look at Caelym, only with an expression that was less that of a bold challenger than of a panic-stricken mouse looking into the face of a hungry cat.

"That will not do! Seeing such a meek look as this, I should have no cause to pay attention. You must lower your eyebrows and put out your lower lip so that there can be no mistaking your displeasure with me."

To illustrate his point, Caelym demonstrated such a remarkably childish frown that, in spite of her misery, Aleswina couldn't stop a quivering smile. Caelym did not smile back.

"No, Little Sister, you must not be smiling at me! If I am to see the error of my ways, you must put your lip out and make your face as I have showed you."

Had Aleswina looked at Annwr, she would have had an

exceptionally good model of a frowning face. As it was, she did her best to rearrange her apprehensive expression into a pout. The result was feeble and wavering; still, Caelym was encouraged.

"Ah, that is good! And now I see you have something to tell me, you may use your hands to do so, even as you used them to speak with Annwr."

Aleswina bit her lip, looked down at her hands, up at Caelym, and back at her hands.

Her right hand moved as if it had a mind of its own—rising up and pointing from his mouth to hers. Then her left hand joined the right, cupping into the shape of a boat, and together they waved again up and down before coming apart, at which point the left touched her mouth and the right landed lightly on his.

"Ah, I understand!" Caelym exclaimed in apparent surprise and delight, and repeated Aleswina's gestures, reciting along with them, "I told you not to speak before we got into the boat and came down the river, and now I must say that you can!" With that, he gave her a warm and approving smile, grandly granted her permission to speak, and swept on into a superb apology that included an offer to endure whatever wrathful curses she might lay on him.

Unable to think of a single curse (and having led an exceptionally sheltered life, Aleswina actually wasn't even sure what a curse was besides something that an evil person would say to a good one), she stammered, "Thank you for letting me speak again," and darted away to cower behind Annwr.

Suppressing a smug smile, Caelym hefted his pack, swung it over his shoulder, and strode back through the trees and down to the boat. Reaching the shore minutes before the two women did, he had time to savor the satisfaction of having proven his curative powers as he stood by the boat, waiting for them to catch up with him.

The sun was warm on his face. A quickening breeze ruffled his hair. The touch of Aleswina's fingers lingered on his lips—somehow reminiscent of the caress that was Feywn's invitation to follow her to her bedchambers—and, for an odd moment, he found himself wondering just what it was about the sallow-faced girl that drew the Saxon king to pursue her with such passion.

It was at that exact moment that Annwr and Aleswina emerged from the woods. Aleswina, for once, wasn't stumbling along behind

Annwr but was walking gaily, almost skipping, at her side. Seeing her from a distance, her hair loose and glowing golden in the afternoon light, Caelym found himself thinking back to how Aleswina's soaking shift had clung to her as he'd lifted her into the boat, revealing (though he hadn't paid much attention to it at the time) that she had all the enticing attributes of a grown woman.

Something of his thoughts must have shown on his face, because Annwr spoke sharply to him in Celt. "Caelym, that oath I had you swear to serve Aleswina as if she were The Goddess—I did not know then that you were consort to Feywn, and I never meant—"

Caelym could not resist the opportunity being offered to him. He let his eyes glide appraisingly from Aleswina's face down to her ankles and up again, as he said, "Now, Annwr, you know that an oath, once sworn, cannot be taken back—" Hearing the furious intake of Annwr's next breath, he realized he'd pushed his joke far enough and hurried on before she could start screeching again—"but you need not worry, for I would give such service only on request, and I'm thinking it most unlikely that this little mouse will be asking that I, or any other man, make love to her before the fish in the ocean rise up and fly to the moon."

Annwr was still glaring at Caelym and so she did not see what he saw—that a sudden red flush brightened Aleswina's pale cheeks and that she turned her head to hide it.

Except for an almost imperceptible hardening around his mouth and eyes, Caelym's expression didn't change as he recalled his own prophetic warning—*She may not care about being Christian or Saxon, but that is what she is! And someday she will care, and she will look at you and see you are her enemy, and she will forget all you have done for her, and she will betray you and all those you hold dear*—and then numbered off, one by one, each of the vital secrets he had given away believing the girl's act that she only spoke English.

Chapter 30

Confessions

earing Caelym's mockery burst Aleswina's bubble of happiness at knowing Annwr loved her as much as her real—no, her other daughter.

As the only deity she knew anything about was Jesus—who, as best she understood it, got to be a god by being born to a virgin, being celibate himself, and dying on the cross—she did not understand what making an oath to a goddess had to do with the kind of love Caelym was talking about. Still, innocent and unworldly though she was, she couldn't miss his lewd innuendo. Well, she didn't want any service from him, now or ever!

Keeping her head down, she went to the front end of the boat and waited there, hoping Annwr would tell Caelym off for being rude.

Caelym knew treachery when he saw it. Now he had to convince Annwr. He stepped nonchalantly over to her, took her pack, strode to the boat and handed it to Aleswina, saying, "Take this, if you will, my dearest heart, and put it under the boat's front seat," in Celt as casually as if he'd merely forgotten to switch back into speaking English.

Aleswina took the pack and did as he asked. She glanced at Annwr, expecting her smile of approval, but instead saw her looking so shocked that Aleswina turned around to see what she'd done wrong with the bag.

When Annwr found her voice again, she spoke in clear and careful English. "Aleswina, you cannot know Celt! You have not spoken it since you were a small child."

All the abbess's admonitions about eavesdropping being a sign of unworthiness came back to Aleswina—redoubled by the fear that now Anna might not want her for a daughter. Desperate to make amends, she dropped to her knees. "I know that I have sinned, only there is no priest here, so how am I to confess or do penance?"

•◆•

"I told you not to take her! She's been spying on us all along!" As Caelym was about to go on—reminding Annwr that he'd warned her over and over that no Christian, no Saxon, and especially no Christian Saxon was to be trusted—he realized what Aleswina had just said and instead broke off to demand, "What does she mean there is no priest here?" Suspecting some further affront, he added, "And what is this 'sinned' and 'confess' and 'penance'?"

Annwr didn't approve of Aleswina's eavesdropping, but neither did she like Caelym's acting as though it were some heinous crime punishable by death. Unaware that this was exactly his point, she decided it was time to take him down a peg. Intentionally assuming the long-suffering but patient voice of one instructing the hopelessly ignorant, she sighed and said, "A 'sin' is something a Christian person does that is forbidden and that they feel sorry for afterwards, like touching their own male or female parts for pleasure or stealing money from the poor-box. When a Christian person has done something that is a sin, they must go to a Christian priest, who is trained and experienced in such matters, and confess that they have done that sin. Then the Christian priest judges how much of a sin it is and decides how much of a penance that the Christian person must do. Then the Christian person does that penance and promises not to do any more sins. Then the Christian priest forgives the Christian person and they are done."

Putting aside his astonishment at the idea that a person's touching their own male or female parts for pleasure was something anyone would ever feel sorry for afterwards, Caelym stayed with the main point. Considering the possibilities of sin and repentance, he asked, "And is burning Druids a sin?"

"Not if you are Christian, for it is not forbidden by their priests and so Christian people do not need to feel sorry for it afterwards."

Disappointed but not surprised, Caelym persisted, "So then the Christian person will not do any more sins after this confessing?"

Favoring Caelym with a look that was half bemused and half resigned, Annwr sighed again. "Of course, the person will do more sins. As long as people are living, they will be doing something that is forbidden and they are sorry for."

It was only when Caelym stiffened his shoulders and dropped his hand towards his dagger that Annwr realized he was serious about Aleswina being a traitor.

"Caelym," she snapped. "Nothing she has or has not done releases you from your oath, so you just forget what you are thinking . . ."

While Annwr and Caelym argued, Aleswina looked back and forth between them. She was used to kneeling in contrition, but the rocky bank was harder on her legs than the wooden floor of the confessional. When they seemed to have finished without saying whether she could get up, Aleswina looked to Annwr for some direction.

Annwr, however, did not return her look or give her any encouragement but continued staring at Caelym.

Not knowing what else to do, Aleswina looked up at Caelym, drawing in her lower lip.

Caelym glared down at her, drumming his fingers on the handle of his dagger and thinking how the simple-minded girl looked more like five than twenty. It was beyond his understanding that her only worry could be whether she was "forgiven" when she should be looking for a way to escape or preparing to fight for her life, as any reasonable person in her place would be doing.

Realizing that with her looking so innocently foolish, he couldn't make himself kill her—even if Annwr released him from his oath, which she wasn't about to do—Caelym began talking with the hope that he might come to some answer before he finished.

"Dear Heart," Caelym used Annwr's pet name but made it more serious with the gravity of his tone, "you are among Druids now, and you are doing your sinning with Druids." Pleased to see from the widening of her eyes and the raising of her eyebrows that he had the girl's proper attention, he paused briefly for emphasis before intoning, "And as I am a Druid priest and am well trained and experienced in these matters, it is I who will be judging these sins and deciding what penance there must be."

Here Caelym paused again. Having had extensive experience in committing misdeeds himself, he knew the power of letting a guilty mind have time to consider its own judgment. When he felt that Aleswina had had enough time for self-rebuke, he continued, "First, I will say that it is no sin to speak Celt, which is the first and best of all languages, nor in your keeping silent, for that was what you had been told to do—but it is most certainly a sin to lie with your head on the lap of the one who raised you, feigning sleep and listening to words you knew were never intended for your ears!"

Aleswina bowed her head and gripped her cross.

"Now, as to the amount of this sin." Caelym crossed his arms and assumed the somber expression befitting a high priest rendering his verdict. "I judge that this is a bigger sin than touching your own female parts for pleasure."

At this, Aleswina reddened to the tips of her ears.

Caelym waited for her to look back up before he went on. "Yet I think it is not so bad a sin as taking coins from the poor. It is a medium sin. Do you agree with this?"

Aleswina bit down harder on her lip and nodded.

Caelym nodded back, although his arms remained crossed as he intoned. "Now as to the penance—for this middle sin, there will be two. First, though you have confessed and are sorry, you have too much knowledge to stay here in some convent among your own people, as I would have wished. Instead, you must travel on with us until we can find some convent in Celtic lands where our Saxon enemies will never find you."

The poorly hidden happiness in both women's faces left Caelym feeling discouraged that this penance would have any benefit in preventing future sins. Taking this as one more proof that Christianity was doomed to failure, he completed the formula anyway.

"And for your second penance, while we travel together, it is you who will be speaking in Celt instead of me who must speak English."

"Mi wnaf," Aleswina whispered, barely loud enough to hear.

Shifting to Celt as well, Caelym remained stern. "You are then forgiven but are to do no more sins in my presence!"

With that, he uncrossed his arms, took hold of her hands, and pulled her to her feet.

◆◆◆

Aleswina wanted nothing more than to retreat into the boat but, as quickly as she stood up, Caelym dropped to his knees, so close to her that she stepped back, caught her legs against the edge of the boat and fell backwards—fortunately coming down on the center seat instead of landing upside-down in the bottom of the boat.

Caelym rose, pulled her back to standing, and knelt again at her feet. Then, looking solemnly up at her, he announced that he must now be confessing as well, "For I also have done sins, and it is you who must be hearing my confession and judging and giving the penance that I must do to be forgiven."

Aleswina made no audible response, but Caelym continued on as if with her approval.

"When I did not think you could understand what I was saying, I have called you unkind names. I have called you stupid, and I have called you a coward as never I should have done, and I am sorry for it. Now, will you be judging this sin, and giving me some just penance that I may do, and then I will be forgiven?"

"It doesn't matter . . . I don't mind," Aleswina stammered, barely aware that she was speaking Celt as if it were her first language. She would have edged away if Caelym had not put his arms out on either side of her and rested his hands on the side of the boat so that she was trapped there and could not move without coming into some contact with him.

Caelym remained on his knees. "Then you will not give me any penance, and I will not be forgiven but must be sorry for this ever after?" He gazed up at Aleswina with such a desolate expression that the gleam in his eyes might well have been unshed tears.

"Aleswina," Annwr snapped, "give him his penance and forgive him, or we will be here until I die of old age!"

Casting about for something to say, Aleswina recalled her years of confessions at Saint Edeth. "Father Wulfric makes me say the fifty-first psalm once for each time I have been late for services or have thought unkind thoughts."

"Then you will teach me this fifty-first psalm, and when I have said it once for each time I have called you stupid and each time I

✦ 141

have called you a fool and each time I have thought these unkind thoughts, you will forgive me?"

Annwr answered for Aleswina that she would, only later, after they were in the boat and on their way, unless Caelym wanted his sons to be old men with beards before he saw them again.

With Annwr shooing them both, Aleswina clambered into the front of the boat, and Caelym heaved his pack after her. He shoved the craft into the water, held it in place long enough for Annwr to get on board, then gave it a final thrust and leaped in. As the current took hold, he scrambled into his seat, caught hold of the flailing oars, and maneuvered the boat into the center of the channel. Keeping a firm grip on the oars to steady the boat on its course, he braced his feet, straightened his back, and looked over Annwr's head to where Aleswina was crouching in the prow of the boat. Assuming his most staunch and resolute voice, he declared, "I am ready! Recite for me this psalm fifty-one, and I will say it as decreed by your Christian priest, once for each time I have called you stupid, once for each time I have called you a coward, and once for each time I have thought these unkind thoughts."

Chapter 31

The Fifty-First Psalm

Father Wulfric, the Abby of Saint Edeth's visiting priest, was mostly a patient and uncomplaining man whose theology was deeply imbued with the kinder and more compassionate side of Christianity. He had, however, been taking confessions from the convent's nuns and novices for going on three decades, and he did not look forward to the time he spent in the chapel's cramped, stuffy confessional.

Listening to novice after nun after novice recite their litany of petty sins—coveting the biggest slice of bread at supper, inadvertently looking at a shirtless man walking past the convent's orchard, forgetting the Lord's pain on the cross for almost an hour on the Thursday before last—had, as he'd once admitted to his bishop in a confessional moment of his own, come to feel to him as if he were being slowly martyred by the pricks of a thousand embroidery needles. The bishop had chortled, given him quick absolution, and told a story of falling asleep during an abbess's confession.

Since then, Wulfric's two chief goals on his visits to Saint Edeth had been to keep from falling asleep during Hildegarth's confessions (which, like her sermons, were always erudite, usually lengthy, and often obscure), and to get through the rest as quickly as possible. Excepting the abbess, for whom he carried and consulted an annotated list of penitential prayers, he kept a count of each penitent's transgressions on his fingers, dispensed a recitation of the fifty-first psalm for each offence, forgave her, and told her to sin no more.

Then he'd close his eyes and shake his head to clear his mind of the self-excoriating fluff while he waited for the next nun or novice to send him back into a somnambulant stupor.

Having seen little of the kinder and more compassionate side of Christianity, Caelym was not expecting to have Aleswina stammer out a pitiful piffle of an invocation hardly sufficient to placate an affronted wood sprite, much less any deity as harsh and vengeful as the Christians' chief god. Determined to make up in verve and variety what the chant lacked in substance, he summoned the spirits of his bardic ancestors and began his recitations, shifting from exhortations as wild and despairing as a man's final words before he threw himself off a cliff to entreaties as soft and wistful as an errant lover wheedling his way back into his consort's bed.

Aleswina was awed.

Annwr wasn't and snapped, "That's enough! She forgives you!"

Caelym, however, had begun to relish the resonance of the psalm's long, lingering vowels so, after he finished with his estimate of the number of times he'd thought that Aleswina was a stupid coward, he went on to repent the times he'd thought she was a whiny weakling or a sniveling nuisance.

Chapter 32

Making Camp

hile Caelym was reciting, the river carried them though the saw-toothed ridges that marked the edge of Derthwald and rushed on into the rugged uplands of Atheldom as if in a race against the setting sun.

Watching the banks slip by, Annwr tried to match the passing scenery with what she'd learned from listening to every scrap of conversation in the palace kitchen or the village market that had to anything do with traveling anywhere. Although nothing she'd heard provided any hint of how to find her way back to Llwddawanden, she had accumulated an extensive knowledge of the roadways and habitations of Derthwald and the lay of lands around it. Now, seeing the dark outline of a forest looming on either side of the next ravine, she was fairly sure they were coming into the last of the wild woods before they reached the thickly populated central plains.

Atheldom, by all accounts, was ruled by a king whose notion of Christianity had nothing to do with kindness or compassion and everything to do with absolute, indisputable authority. Whether this was a good thing or a bad thing varied from one speaker to the next, but there was complete agreement that the kingdom's roads were heavily patrolled by soldiers on the lookout for bandits, rebels, and runaway slaves.

Certain that word of Aleswina's flight would have spread throughout the Saxon realms and that rewards for her capture were, even now, being proclaimed in every village and hamlet along the river, Annwr guessed that the rapidly approaching forest would be their last chance to stop and disguise themselves before they left the uplands. Besides that, she wanted to cook Aleswina another hot meal and to make sure that Caelym wasn't going to go rushing headlong into a hornet's nest when he'd not be the only one stung. It would be just like him to go on rowing and singing straight through the woods and into the laps of Gilberth's men.

"Any time you're done showing off, maybe you'll pay attention to where we're going and find us a safe place to land and make camp for the night."

Caelym had never stopped paying attention to the river and was more than a little offended by the insinuation that he could not recite poetry and row a boat at the same time. Knowing better than to argue back with a priestess in a snit, he contented himself with humming, *Miserere mei Deus secundum magnam misericordiam tuam et secundum multitudinem miserationum tuarum dele iniquitatem meam,* as he scanned the banks for a place to pull into shore.

Just as Annwr was about to repeat her command, Caelym brought the boat around, tucking it in between a sandbar and the shore where the undercut bank was just higher than the side of the boat, making a sheltered nook out of sight from any other boats that might pass by.

Despite what Annwr thought of his judgment—or lack of it— Caelym had survived on his own for nearly three months, traveling through hostile and hazardous lands, before his unfortunate encounter with that unusually alert band of Saxon guards. And even with an arrow in his back (one lucky shot out of the dozens he'd dodged), he'd escaped and made his way practically to her doorstep. He knew as well as she did that they'd need to stop, take stock, and make plans for what to do next, especially now that they had the hopelessly simple-minded Saxon princess to worry about. As he'd tried unsuccessfully to make Annwr understand, even if Aleswina didn't intentionally turn them over to their enemies, her presence was as good as waving a banner and proclaiming, *"Look! Here we are! Come and kill us!"*

Besides that, Caelym had seen the quick flashes of silver darting away when his oars struck the water. Tired of having nothing to eat except sausage, stew, and stale bread, he was ready for roasted fish, and the channel between the bank and bar ran deep enough to set a weir.

As the boat slipped into its niche, Annwr caught hold of an exposed root and tied the line to it. With the craft secured, she stood up cautiously and stepped out. Aleswina—to Caelym's surprise—handed Annwr the smaller pack without being told to do so and climbed out by herself. Caelym heaved the bigger bag onto the shore and joined Annwr and Aleswina as they looked around.

The bank itself wasn't wide. Backed by a second, steeper bank, it offered little by way of shelter, but slanting beams of sunlight pointed the way to a gap in the ridge above them where a series of flat, mossy rocks formed a stairway up and into the forest. Without so much as a word between them, Caelym and Annwr shouldered the packs. With Caelym leading the way, they made the short, easy climb and came out on at the top of a flat ridge where a towering stand of pines formed a backdrop to a semicircle of boulders that in turn enclosed a raised ring of smaller rocks.

"Here is your campsite," Caelym announced as proudly as if he'd personally planted the trees and laid the boulders to create a place that was to other campsites what a king's palace was to a peasant's hut.

Certainly they were not the first to stop there, but seeing the fire ring overgrown with moss and filled with pine needles, they were reassured that they were the first in many years. Working together, they cleared out the moss and debris—hurrying to get a fire started and banked while there was still enough light left for Caelym to go back to the river to build his weir and for Annwr and Aleswina go into the woods to gather roots and greens.

"So Caelym didn't choose such a bad place to stop after all."

It took a moment for Aleswina to place the unfamiliar note in Annwr's voice and realize that it sounded cheerful.

They'd taken a deer path that led up and over a rise and then down again into a lush glade, picking fern fronds, wild celery, and sorrel along the way. Now, coming to the edge of a wide, shallow pond grown thick with clumps of bulrushes and with birds singing all around, it seemed to Aleswina that they might be standing in the Garden of Eden.

Knowing how annoyed Annwr got at the idea of God casting Adam and Eve out of the Garden (*"For doing nothing more than eating an apple when he told them not to, which was exactly why they would and any goddess would have known it!"*), Aleswina didn't say anything about Eden. Instead, she copied what Annwr was doing. She set her basket down, slipped off her sandals, hitched up her skirt, and waded into the pond to help pull up the greenest and freshest of the stalks, which ended in the fattest and most succulent roots. She was tugging at a particularly stubborn plant when she heard Annwr snort.

Looking where Annwr was staring, Aleswina saw Caelym on the far side of the pond, cutting dry brown reeds. "Shouldn't we tell him that those are too old and tough to be any good?"

Annwr didn't answer her, just stood shaking her head and muttering something about apples and trees.

Confused because it was far too early for apples and there were none of the right trees around anyway, Aleswina started to ask again, "But shouldn't we tell Cael—"

"Never mind him!" Pulling another fresh green rush by its roots, Annwr added, "Let's get these trimmed and washed while there's still light to find our way back."

Aleswina had already lost sight of Caelym in the fading twilight, and she did as Annwr told her. After cleaning their harvest and washing her hands, she retied her sandals, hoisted her bulging basket and hurried after Annwr along the darkening trail.

As they came into camp, they were met with the smells of roasting fish and the hiss of boiling water. Caelym, who had somehow passed them unseen, stood up from the hearth and welcomed them back with a sweeping bow that ended in a wave of his hand towards a neatly spread blanket set with bowls and spoons and an open flask of Annwr's elderberry wine.

They ate Caelym's roast fish and passed a cup around in the dark as they waited for the greens and roots to cook.

Afterwards, nestled against Annwr's side, Aleswina watched golden sparks from the campfire float upward as a blanket of silver-white stars spread out across the sky. Caelym was sitting opposite her, his face glowing in the firelight. She could see he was cutting holes in his dry reed and wondered if he was going to do some Druid magic with it, even though Annwr had said over and over that if Druids could work the sorcery they were accused of, Christian priests would have turned into toads and hopped off into a bog long since—*"and a lot more sense you'd hear from them croaking in a swamp then anything they say from their indoor altars!"*

Still, Aleswina couldn't imagine what else besides magic he might be doing when he put one end of the reed to his lips and blew into it, making a sound so much like a meadow thrush that it was answered by a real bird. For a time their notes went back and forth—Caelym's flute singing out and the sweet, trilling call answering back so it seemed to Aleswina, who was getting very tired, that they were somehow back in the long-ago time Annwr had told her about, before the feud between people and animals began, and they could all still talk to each other and understand each other's language and their children still played together.

As if he was reading her thoughts, Caelym left off playing the bird's song and began a melody that skipped up and down like the sound of the children playing, and she felt herself drifting off into a story that Annwr had told her when she was a little girl afraid of falling asleep and having bad dreams.

She was just awake enough to realize that Caelym had lowered his flute and begun singing a song that was about the same thing as Annwr's story—a little girl named Gwendolwn who went into a meadow to gather flowers for her mother and met a bear cub who was looking for a honey tree.

. . . Forgetting all about her mother's flowers, Gwendolwn went along with the bear cub, looking for the honey tree. Up and down the mountains they went, and over rivers and through forests, until they came to the edge of a muddy gray marsh where they found the tree—so full of honey that they could see the honeycombs in holes in the trunk just above their heads. There were great swarms of bees circling all around the tree, buzzing and buzzing, and that should have warned them to leave the honey alone and go get their mothers, but instead the baby bear put the basket

over his head like a helmet, and Gwendolwn lifted him up, and he grabbed a honeycomb with his front paws, pulled it out, and jumped down. Together, they put the honeycomb in the basket and held it between them as they ran away. They ran fast but the bees were faster and came buzzing after them, and to escape they jumped into a muddy marsh and hid there, eating the honey and getting stickier and muddier until no one could have told by looking at them which one was the sticky, muddy little girl and which one was the sticky, muddy baby bear.

After they had eaten all the honey and the bees had buzzed away to their tree, Gwendolwn and the bear cub went back to the meadow so covered with honey and dirt that their mothers, who were searching for them, mixed them up, and it wasn't until the mother bear had taken Gwendolwn home to their cave and licked the honey off and found out she was a human child and Gwendolwn's mother had taken the bear cub back to their cottage and put him into a tub of water and washed him off with soap and water and realized he was a baby bear that the two mothers realized their mistake and rushed back to the meadow to trade children and get their own babies back. Then they all went home—the mothers scolding their children and telling them not to do that again, and Gwendolwn and the baby bear promising they wouldn't—and they both went to sleep, the little girl in her cozy bed and the little bear in his warm cave.

When she was little, Aleswina had always fallen asleep along with Gwendolwn and the baby bear, but now, determined not to let Caelym think that she was pretending to be asleep, she stayed sitting upright and pretending to be awake even though her mind was dozing off, and she actually paid no attention at all as Caelym and Annwr began talking about how to disguise themselves and where to go next. The last thing she heard before falling truly and completely asleep was Annwr saying, "So how are we to find them?" and Caelym answering, "I have a map."

Chapter 33

The Map

"And might you be willing to share this map or is it for your eyes only?"

Although this was phrased as what for Annwr was a civil inquiry, Caelym understood it was not a question but a command, and he answered accordingly. "I have been but waiting for the right moment."

If he'd been standing, he would have bowed, but as it was, he contented himself with a dignified nod and turned to open the flaps of the battered backpack that was nestled as close to his side as Aleswina was to Annwr's. The leather satchel he drew out was even more scraped and stained than the outer bag, but it had belonged to Olyrrwd, the shrine's master physician, who had bequeathed it to Caelym with his final breath. It contained Caelym's most precious possessions—his healing implements and amulets, the golden pendant that had been Feywn's gift to him when she named him her consort, and the map showing the path he must follow to find his sons.

He pulled out a roll of parchment wrapped in a layer of kid-skin, undid the ties, and spread it against his knees. Not so much as a drop of water had reached it and its inscriptions remained as distinct and clear as the day it was drawn by none other than—

But Annwr could see for herself!

He held it out before her and watched with no small satisfaction as her eyes opened wide and her mouth gaped.

◆◆◆

As Caelym guessed, Annwr recognized both the map's meaning and its maker.

Only the very highest of the priests of their order had access to ink and parchment. Of those who did, their oracle would have cast himself off the top of his tower before he would have written his prophecies down for someone to read later and compare them with what actually came to pass, and their physician's scrawl of symbols and hatch marks were barely comprehensible even to his apprentice.

The elaborately illustrated parchment that Caelym held out like a sacred offering could only be the work of their chief priest and master bard.

With the embers in their firepit crackling and flickering like a smaller version of the hearth in the shrine's great hall, Annwr could almost hear Herrwn strumming his gold-inlaid harp and singing his ancient sagas. Just for a moment, she felt a nearly unbearable longing to listen to him bringing those tales to life again. The lingering feelings of reverence she harbored for the shrine's master bard, however, were dwarfed by her recollection that Herrwn, with his mind forever caught up in the past, could get lost going from his bedroom to the dining hall—and it was dismay rather than awe that flashed across her face when she realized that a map he'd drawn was all that Caelym had to find his lost children.

"So . . ." She spoke carefully, using much the same tone of voice as she'd use to ask a child to tell her what a jumble of squiggles scratched in the mud was meant to be. "Tell me about this map and how it shows us the way to where your boys are."

After naming one after another of the main figures and symbols and explaining how each served as a warning to him of the dangers he was destined to encounter on his quest to find his beloved sons, Caelym pointed to a small sketch of a horse-drawn cart and a cluster of sheep near what Annwr had taken to a be patch of oversized mushrooms but was, it turned out, Herrwn's depiction of the peasant huts of Benyon's sheepherding kinsmen.

"See, here is the village where Benyon's kinsmen live, grazing their sheep in lush meadows and rowing their boats on a river abounding with shoals of fish and flocks of waterfowl."

"And do you know the name of this village or of Benyon's kinsmen?"

Caelym shrugged. "He said it is a village where they raise sheep and it is on the road between the mountains and the eastern sea."

"Which road?"

"Is there more than one?"

"There are . . ." Annwr bit down on her lip to stop herself from shouting at him, *There are a dozen roads and a hundred villages and thousands of sheepherders in Atheldom, so tell me how this map is going show you where to find your sons!*

Caelym's next words, "Benyon told us his kinsmen's village was in Atheldom, and we are in Atheldom! We must be almost there!" came out sounding like a plea.

Hearing the anguish in his voice, Annwr didn't tell him how hopeless she knew his search to be; nor did she reveal her growing suspicion that the man he'd sent off with his two sons and a pouch of silver and gold coins to pay their keep might not want to be found. Instead, she reached out her hand. "Give me the map, and I will see what I can make of it."

As she pretended to study the map, Annwr was actually thinking that there was only one pass that a wagon could travel over the mountain ridge separating Derthwald from Atheldom. And she was fairly certain that from there the road went around the east side of the forest, crossed over the river, and reached to a small village before it branched off in different directions. While the travelers she'd listened to had grumbled about the swill that the village innkeeper served for ale, it had been clear that they all stopped at his inn to drink it.

If she was right about that, then there was only one route Benyon and the boys could have taken into Atheldom, and Benyon, being a man with money in his pouch, would have stopped there too. While it went without saying that he would not have given either his own or the boys' real names, there was at least a chance that the innkeeper would recall them and remember which way they'd gone—especially since, never having been outside Llwddawanden before, their dress or behavior likely would have seemed odd to a Saxon villager.

As she rolled up the map and handed it back, she told Caelym what she'd been thinking, leaving out her qualms about Benyon's loyalty. Caelym didn't argue, but he had little to offer that helped. They'd taken every precaution to be sure no one would take notice of either Benyon or the boys—seeing to it that they were dressed in the most ordinary of outsiders' clothing, cautioning the boys to speak only to Benyon and say nothing of their life in Llwddawanden. As to the risk of Benyon giving away his true identity through his speech or manners, Caelym said, "He has for years gone on missions for us in the outside world without ever being discovered."

Listening to Caelym's account, a dark cloud of hopelessness settled over Annwr. What chance was there that anyone would remember a nondescript, middle-aged Celt passing through two years before?

"So there is nothing special about Benyon that anyone would notice or remember?" she pressed only to have him shake his head.

"As I have said, he is of ordinary height and appearance. His hair is brown. His eye is brown . . ."

There was something amiss in Caelym's usage, as if his struggles with English were affecting his Celt. Annwr's correction was only half-conscious. "His eyes *are* brown."

"No, his eye *is* brown. He has only one—the other was lost accidentally when he stood too close behind as the shrine's chief cook was pulling the skewer from a roasted lamb."

While Caelym went on describing how deftly Olyrrwd had removed the punctured and deflated eyeball, Annwr felt a glimmer of hope. A one-eyed man would be memorable, however ordinary he was in every other respect. After agreeing that Olyrrwd was a master of his art, she eased back to lying down and drifted off into an odd dream of walking along a forest path holding hands with Herrwn, who was wearing a monk's robe and telling her the story of Gwendolwn and the honey tree.

Chapter 34

Changing Clothes

Aleswina woke up to the sound of the birds twittering softly in the nearby bushes. Her ears and the tip of her nose were cold but the rest of her was warm, snuggled close to Annwr with a thick blanket tucked tight around them. She lay still, not praying exactly, but wishing with all her heart that she could stay exactly like this forever.

Too soon, she heard a rustle from across the hearth, and then the snapping of dry branches. A whiff of wood smoke and the crackle of burning twigs meant Caelym was up and rekindling the campfire. As his footsteps crunched off down the mossy stone path to the river, Annwr stirred and whispered, "Wake up, Dear Heart, it's morning and there's much to do."

And there was.

By the time Caelym returned with fish for breakfast, Annwr was pulling things out of the packs, talking half to herself and half to Aleswina as she sorted them into piles—"Where is that wooden bowl? I know I packed it. There it is. Now, where is that other cross . . ."

After a hurried meal, Annwr handed Caelym the robe, scapula, and cowl she'd gotten from the village seamstress in exchange for her last keg of elderberry wine. "Go make yourself into a monk!" she ordered, pointing to the bushes. Then she turned to Aleswina.

◆◆◆

Annwr didn't need Caelym to tell her that traveling with a girl fitting Aleswina's description would bring guards swarming faster than flies to a corpse. She had already thought of that, and of what to do about it.

In the early days of her captivity, she had planned to escape dressed as a boy and had secretly sewn herself a shirt, tunic, and pair of pants modeled on what she'd seen the cook's son wearing. On the off-chance that there was some truth to Caelym's tale of climbing up and down mountains on his way from Llwddawanden, she'd packed them for the journey. Now they were laid out and ready along with the scissors from her sewing kit.

"Go make yourself into a monk!" Not a bishop or some other high priest but only some low-ranking one—Caelym could tell that much from the crude, drab garments Annwr had given him. He grumbled over the affront as he followed the narrow deer path away from their campsite, down and around the pond, then up again along the edge of a trickling stream and into a fern grotto where a spring of crystal-clear water burbled out of a natural stone basin. Stepping into what was unmistakably a sacred place, his petty irritations fell away and he cleared his mind of everything except the task before him.

Whatever Annwr might think, making himself a monk was no mere matter of stripping off his own clothes and putting on another man's. Entering into the priesthood of a god who demanded that he be worshiped before all others, even temporarily, required gaining dispensation from the goddess to whom Caelym had already made this same promise—and to do so in a way that did not offend either deity. Carefully balancing his evocations to the goddess (and reminding her that it was her sons as well as his that he was doing this for) with his avowals of service to the god (being cautious to avoid any specific time commitment), he raised his arms out to each in turn, and, for good measure, scooped up water from the spring and cast it around in recognition of all the greater and lesser denizens, both known and unknown, of the ordinary and the spirit worlds. Only then did he exchange his clothes for the monk's robes, hang the wooden cross around his neck, and start back towards camp.

◆◆◆

It was no surprise to Annwr that Caelym took as long as he did to change clothes.

"He's Rhedwyn all over again and will be half the morning preening himself!"

"He will!" Aleswina agreed, not knowing who Rhedwyn was but sure Annwr was right anyway.

They were sitting together on the bank overlooking the river, putting the final touches on their own disguises after taking turns cutting each other's hair—Annwr's to fit the part of a fully ordained nun and Aleswina's to look like a boy instead of a girl. Annwr had dyed Aleswina's remaining hair dark brown with a slurry of ashes and alder bark tea and had mixed a bit of the leftover tea with dirt that she rubbed over Aleswina's face and neck before helping her change clothes. With Aleswina dressed in pants and Annwr wearing Aleswina's habit, the two were ready to pass as an elderly nun and a youthful boy.

"The river will be leaving the forest soon and coming to a bridge with a tollkeeper, and border guards too, like as not." Refining her plans as she said them out loud, Annwr muttered, "So maybe the thing to do would be to wait until nightfall and slip past like we did through Fenwick."

Aleswina nodded vigorously in agreement and was ready to jump up and start gathering brush to cover over the boat, only Annwr went on, "No! We'd do better to stop before the bridge and cross openly in broad daylight. That way we're just pilgrims traveling on foot from Derthwald, and no one will have any cause to wonder how we could appear at the tavern without being remembered crossing the bridge."

"What about our packs?" Aleswina asked, an anxious look on her face.

"The monks that I've seen don't carry anything except their staff and their begging bowls. So we'll hide them in the woods and pick them up when we come back."

"After Caelym has found his little boys."

"Yes, Dear Heart, after Caelym has found his little boys." Annwr tried to sound certain about what she knew to be a vanishingly small chance. But some chance or none, they had to try, and she shifted to muttering, "Now how much money will we need for the bridge toll and our fare at the tavern?"

When she'd packed Aleswina's cache of coins and jewels, it had seemed to Annwr like more than they'd ever need, but now she recalled the trader and merchants from Atheldom complaining about the high cost of the bridge and road tolls and innkeepers overcharging for their meals. Wishing she'd asked what they had to pay, she emptied the pouch on a cloth and set the jewelry aside. Making separate stacks of the three denominations, she counted out what they had. It came to seven gold coins, thirty-two silver ones, and forty-nine copper ones.

Seeing Aleswina looking uncomprehendingly at the coins and realizing that she'd have to learn what money was worth, Annwr pointed to the gold coins. "Those are called scillingas and they are each worth the price of five cows."

Aleswina nodded, impressed.

"These silver ones are sceattas. They are each worth a sheep."

"Just one sheep?" Aleswina asked.

"Just one. And these copper ones are penings. They are each worth a chicken."

"What if you want to buy something else?"

"That, Dear Heart, is what bargaining is for. If you want something you think is worth as much as three chickens, you offer the person who's selling it two penings and expect that they will say you have to pay four. Then you say you don't want it that much, and they will groan and say you drive a hard bargain and give it to you for three and you will both be happy."

She put the gold coins in a sock with the jewelry and put the sock into her pack, slipped the silver and copper back into the pouch and tied the pouch to her belt. "It's what we have, so it will have to be enough."

"We have the gold and jewelry too."

"But those are dangerous to flash about and are best kept well hidden, especially from . . ."

"From?" Aleswina asked when Annwr didn't finish her sentence.

"From anyone we meet." Not wanting to worry Aleswina any more than necessary, Annwr kept her suspicions of Benyon to herself. "So, Dear Heart, we'll hope the toll keeper gives us a reduced fare for being . . . pilgrims on our way to Rome." Nodding to herself, she went on. "Once we're across the bridge, we'll go to the tavern and try to find out whether anyone there recalls Benyon and the two boys. Only we will need to have some story to explain why a monk on a pilgrimage would want to find a one-eyed sheepherder."

"Maybe . . ." Aleswina started and then fell silent again.

Annwr pondered, then brightened. "Instead of a pilgrimage, I will say that our monk is on a mission for the bishop to find a one-eyed sheepherder whose name he does not know, but who may have passed this way two years ago in a horse cart with his two sons because . . . because—"

"But that it's a secret mission, and we can say no more!" Aleswina cried, looking pleased with herself for thinking of such a good excuse. She positively glowed when Annwr said, smiling, "That is the perfect answer, Dear Heart!"

"Now our next worry"—Annwr's smile turned into a frown—"is what Caelym will say."

"He can recite Psalm Twenty-three and Psalm Fifty-one—"

"Phsst!" Annwr made the snorting sound she usually reserved for Christian dogma. "And then, like as not, he'll go dancing around the room singing a hymn to the Goddess! No, we must not let Caelym say anything at all! I will tell everyone that he has taken a vow of silence, and that you are his serving boy who speaks for him—and if he opens his mouth, you must speak before he does!"

"But—"

"Don't you worry about keeping Caelym quiet—I'll take care of that. What you must remember is that you are now a boy and must act like one! Don't say more than you have to and keep your voice low. If you don't understand what's being said, just assume that it is vulgar and laugh as loudly as you can. And if you think anyone doubts you, do something a man would do—spit on the floor or scratch between your legs!"

"Spit on the floor or scratch between my legs," Aleswina repeated in a low voice, looking at Annwr to be sure she'd gotten it right.

"That's very good, Dear Heart! So then, there will likely just be men in the front room, and you will need to stay there with Caelym and ask our questions while I slip off to the kitchen to learn what I can from the gossip there." Seeing Aleswina's eyes widen in alarm, she added, "You need not worry, Dear Heart, for, as I have said, there will only be men around you and as men talk far more than they listen, once you have them started it will just take a grunt to keep them going. Can you do this for me?"

"I can, Anna!" Aleswina said and, to prove it, she grunted and spat into the grass.

"Excellent! No one will ever take you for a princess or a nun!" Annwr licked her thumb, rubbed it in the dirt and blotted out a bare spot on Aleswina's forehead. Leaning back to inspect her handiwork, she found herself almost able to believe they might survive Caelym's hopeless, foolhardy quest after all.

As if her thinking his name conjured him out of the woods, Caelym swept into the camp looking more like a Christian monk than any real one Annwr had ever seen. It was as startling a transformation as Aleswina's change from a girl to a boy and sent an involuntary shiver up Annwr's spine.

Taking Annwr's look of alarm as a compliment, Caelym announced that he would lead the way to the tavern, adding, "You, Annwr, will be a Christian priestess, and I will be your consort, and Aleswina will be our son, and we will say that we are on our way to visit a sheepherder who is kin to kin of ours . . . only we do not know his name or the name of his village."

He would've gone on with the elaborate tale he made up, explaining why they were making to visit their kinsman and how it was they happened to know nothing about him except that he was traveling with his two sons and had one eye, the other having been lost in an unfortunate accident, but Annwr rolled her eyes and interrupted him.

"You will be a monk who has taken a vow of silence and will say nothing to anyone. I will be a nun traveling with you for what little protection that might gain me. Aleswina will be your serving boy, and she will speak for you." Annwr crossed her arms and finished, "You may begin practicing your vow of silence now!" before she turned to Aleswina. "What do you think, Dear Heart? Will we pass for Christians on a mission?"

"We will!" Aleswina answered, sounding like herself only more confident. Then, remembering she was now a boy, she lowered her voice to ask, "What are our names?"

Cutting off Caelym before he could warn them that choosing names for so important a quest was a grave matter and something over which he would need time to deliberate, Annwr smiled at Aleswina. "You choose!"

Aleswina bit her lip, thinking hard, and then pointed at Caelym. "He will be 'Brother Cuthbert'—that's a common name for monks." She squinted at Annwr. "You will be 'Sister Columbina'—there are a lot of those too. And I will be 'Codric,' like Sister Idwolda's youngest brother."

Those were nothing like the names Caelym would have chosen, but seeing that Annwr wasn't going to listen to anything he said even if she did let him speak, he picked up his healer's satchel and put it back into his pack. Annwr's pack was already closed and he carried them both, without audible grumbling, down the path to the boat while Annwr and Aleswina doused the fire and refilled the pit with dirt and debris.

Chapter 35

Leaving Camp

Aleswina looked over her shoulder as she left the campsite and followed Annwr down the pathway to the river.

She had left the palace nursery where she'd spent the first thirteen years of her life caring only that Anna was with her. She had run from the convent that had been her home since then without a backward glance. Now she regretted every step back to the boat, convinced that she would never again be as happy as she had been nestled against Anna and listening to Caelym singing the story about Gwendolwn and the baby bear.

Back in the boat, she watched the trees along the banks change from oaks to birches and from birches to alders, her confidence waning as her dread of being discovered returned.

"Pull out there!"

Turning around, Aleswina saw Annwr pointing to a gap in the left bank where a creek came in to join the river. In the same moment, she was pitched to the side as Caelym jerked back on his left oar and leaned forward on his right, spinning the boat so the prow pointed straight up the side channel. She managed to catch hold of the sides in time to keep from falling over backwards when he heaved hard on both oars, sending the boat shooting up the mouth of the stream.

Caelym tucked the oars in as the boat surged forward and leaped out, calling, "The rope!"

"Toss him the rope!"

Aleswina did as Annwr said and got the line close enough to Caelym's feet that he was able to pick it up and drag them the last of the way out of sight from the river.

"Hurry along, Dear Heart!" Annwr urged, and Aleswina forced herself to climb out of the boat, trying desperately to think of some reason to stay in hiding.

"We need to put the packs in the bushes!" Annwr's next words were directed to Caelym, who grumbled that he hadn't been planning to leave them out for thieving Saxons as he picked up the larger one and shoved his way through the undergrowth.

"What if someone finds our things and steals the jewels?" Hoping what she knew was a feeble excuse would work, Aleswina took hold of Annwr's hand and stammered, "M-maybe you and I should stay here and guard packs while Caelym goes and finds out where his little boys are."

"That is a most excellent suggestion!" Caelym emerged from the bushes, nodding vigorously. "You both stay here and guard the jewels, and I will go and find where Benyon's kin live and bring him and my sons back and we will go on then to our own destinies!"

"I understand, Dear Heart," Annwr murmured, as if Caelym hadn't spoken. "Those jewels belonged to your mother, and even though they would be safe here, we will bring them along—only remember you must let no one see that you have them.

"And"—she shot a dark look in Caelym's direction—"we'll all go together so none of us get lost."

It took no more than moments for Annwr to crawl into the bushes, recover the jewelry, and make her way out again. She tucked the packet into Caelym's satchel, swatting his hand away when he reached for it.

"I am a healer," he attempted to protest, "I go nowhere without my—"

"You are a monk!" she retorted sharply. "You carry your bowl and staff! Codric is your serving boy! He carries the bag!" She gave Aleswina an encouraging smile and a loving pat on the cheek, then handed her the satchel. "Come along, Dear Heart, it's time to go."

Biting down on her lower lip, Aleswina took the bag, hung it over her shoulder, and followed Annwr and Caelym as they scrambled up the side of the ravine and onto a bluff.

"That's it! That's the road!" Caelym pointed down the hill to a wagon track just as Annwr hissed, "Get back! There's someone coming."

Instead of backing into the cover of the trees, Caelym dropped down and crawled forward on his belly to part the grass and watch the horse cart pass below. Annwr stayed behind a tree, and Aleswina stayed behind Annwr until the clopping of the horse's hooves and rattle of wagon wheels died away.

"Now!" Caelym sprang up. Holding his staff in one hand and the wooden bowl in the other, he forged his way down the slope through waist-high brush.

"Wait for us!" Annwr called after him as she grabbed Aleswina's hand and pulled her along. When they reached the road, Caelym brushed the leaves and twigs from his robe while Annwr straightened her veil and shook her skirt.

With a final, "Remember you're a monk and keep quiet!"—which Caelym answered by opening and then closing his mouth with a snap—Annwr started off.

Aleswina tucked Caelym's satchel under her arm and fell in step with the other two as they trudged first down a dip in the road and then up to the top of a rise. From there the road sloped down again, and they could see the horse cart that had passed them cross over a bridge and draw to a halt as two guards armed with pikes came out of the guard station. They were too far off the hear what the driver or the guards were saying, but close enough to see the guards pull the cover off the cart and thrust their spears into the straw before they let the wagon move on.

"We're on a quest for the bishop!" Caelym muttered between clenched teeth without slowing down.

"A mission! You're a monk! You're on a mission! And you've taken a vow of silence!" Annwr hissed as she rushed after him.

Left with no choice but to go along, Aleswina made her feet move forward. From somewhere in her frightened mind she heard the voice of the abbess reciting, *"Yea, though I walk through the valley of the shadow of death, I will fear no evil."*

Repeating, "I will fear no evil," to herself, she followed Annwr across the bridge and past the guards, and even managed to say, "God bless you," in a low voice that only quivered a little when, instead of charging a toll, the guards each tossed a penning into Caelym's wooden bowl, and the more ferocious-looking one said, "Welcome to Welsferth."

PART V

Welsferth

The village of Welsferth started out as a Saxon fort that was King Athelrod's northwestern most outpost before Theobold's successful conquest of Derthwald. Since then, its military importance had faded, and all that remained of the once heavily fortified garrison were a handful of guards who doubled as toll collectors.

Although predominantly Saxon, Welsferthers (as they called themselves) included a substantial number of native Britons who'd stayed on after their armies retreated northward. Over time, shared religion and intermarriage had blurred the distinctions between them, and although Saxons, for the most part, had the better holdings, the two groups got along surprisingly well, all things considered.

Taking advantage of their strategic location between the bridge and the crossroads where wagon traffic from the four corners of Atheldom converged, the villagers had turned to commerce so that Welsferth was now a thriving and growing community with a weekly market, two churches, and a tavern that was open from midmorning until whatever time in the evening Merna, the innkeeper's wife, got tired of cooking.

The Spotted Hound, named for the first innkeeper's boyhood pet, owed its success to being the first place travelers coming into Atheldom from Derthwald could stop before the road split in three—the main branch turning northeast toward the capital city, and other two splitting further into the maze of side roads that connected the area's outlying farms and villages.

Wilbreth, the innkeeper, ran a thriving business on three basic principles—don't water the ale so much you wouldn't drink it yourself, don't ask your customers where they got the money they're spending, and count the cost of what you serve monks and pilgrims as part of the tithe you owe to God and the church.

All in all, the Spotted Hound was as a good place as Annwr could have hoped for when she came up with her plan of tracking Benyon and the boys by word of mouth.

Chapter 36

The Spotted Hound

It was a busy day at the Spotted Hound. The first of the traders from the western coast arrived that morning, and by noon the newcomers were joined by the regular midday diners and the front room was packed and buzzing with the news from Derthwald that a Druid sorcerer had carried off a virgin princess—the king's daughter by some accounts, his betrothed bride by others.

Rushing between the kitchen, where Merna was warning him the stew was running low, and the dining room, where Frinwulf, the village smith, and Aelfgar, the potter, had come in at the same time and were each ready to take offense if the other got served first, Wilbreth was carrying two pitchers of ale in one hand and balancing Frinwulf's bowl of fried eels along with Aelfgar's platter of bread and sausage in the other when three more guests appeared at the door.

Wilbreth paused, staring at them, as he did a quick mental calculation. There was a table in the corner big enough to squeeze them in, enough of yesterday's stew left over to feed them, and he'd already compromised his first principle (regarding watering down the ale) so he'd have enough to get through the day. None of that was a problem. The nun was. Wilbreth had nothing personal against nuns—in fact, his sister was one—but having a nun in his tavern's dining room put people off and shut down the pleasantries of the tavern conversations—and while his paying customers didn't mind a monk or two (or a priest, come to that), they'd been known to clear the room entirely at the sight of a nun.

As he'd expected, his regulars looked up, saw the nun, shifted in their seats, and stopped talking.

As the room went silent, Aleswina froze with the fear that they were recognized. On her right side, she felt Caelym stiffen and sensed his hand was slipping under his cloak for his knife. Annwr's voice seemed to come from a long way off as it said, "God be with you, Sir. I am Sister Columbina, of the order of Saint Wilfhilda, and am on my way to join my sisters in Christ in a convent in the capital of Atheldom—and I am, for now, traveling with Brother Cuthbert, who is on a mission for the Bishop of Lindisfarne. As Brother Cuthbert has taken a vow of silence, his servant boy, Codric, speaks for him."

Surveying the room with an unmistakable look of disdain, Annwr went on, "My vows as a nun do not allow me to eat in the presence of men, and so I will take my meal in your kitchen."

Relieved, Wilbreth waved the way to the kitchen's curtained entrance and stepped aside to let her pass. Then, calling "Just a moment, Brother," he hurried to deliver Frinwulf's eels and Aelfgar's sausages. That done, he ushered Caelym and Aleswina to his last vacant table.

Once she got over the oddness of being in a room full of men, Aleswina found talking easier than she expected, although the topics and vocabulary here were so different from the convent that had it not been for Sister Idwolda's persistence in telling her life story, Aleswina would not have understood much of what was being said.

Remembering to keep her voice down, she took the bowl of stew the innkeeper handed her and caught his sleeve before he could rush away.

"God be with you, kind Sir. Brother Cuthbert is on a mission for the bishop to find a one-eyed sheepherder, a Briton, who may have passed this way two years ago in a horse cart with his two young sons. Pray have you any memory of such a man stopping here and saying which road he was taking or what village he was going to?"

She held her breath and sensed that Caelym wasn't breathing, either. When the innkeeper cocked his head and looked oddly at her, she added, "It's a secret mission and I can say no more, only . . . only, it is very important . . . to Brother Cuthbert . . . and to the bishop . . . and . . . and to God . . . so if you remember anything at all . . ."

She was clinging to the hope that he'd say something, anything—

"Barnard? You mean Master Barnard?"

Before she could think what to answer, a big, burly man at the next table boomed, "Nah! Couldn't be old Barnard! He's no sheepherder and never was!" Another man, who was sitting on the other side of the burly one and hidden from Aleswina's view, chimed in, "He'd milk a ram as soon as a ewe." But a third man, one sitting at the table to the left of the other two, made his voice heard over the general laughter with, "And just how many other one-eyed Britons drove into town two years ago on a horse cart with two little boys?"

Her heart beating hard against her chest, Aleswina put in, "Maybe Brother Cuthbert mistook the sheepherder part, but he's sure about the horse and cart and this man having two young sons, and"—she recalled the other thing—"he, the one-eyed man, was coming to live with his kinsman, and maybe it was they, the kinsmen, that herd sheep!"

"There'd be no one I know of claiming kin to Barnard!" This was the burly man talking again.

"Not for all his gold and silver!" That was the voice behind him.

"And least of all those two miserable little sods," added a bearded man at the table directly across from her.

A thin man with mud-splattered clothes piped up, "My wife heard it from her sister who cooks and cleans for him that they're the orphaned sons of a serving woman he had where he lived before, and that he kept them on out of Christian charity."

This was met with an outburst of raucous laughter.

The thin man held his ground. "Well, he might be . . . neither of them's old enough to be of any use to him!"

The burly man fired back, "Depends on what he'd be using them for!"

The innkeeper, who hadn't said anything until this, finally stepped in to settle the dispute.

Shifting his considerable bulk so he blocked Frinwulf and Aelfgar's view of each other, he banged his pitcher of ale down in front of Caelym with the authority of the councilman bringing a town meeting to order.

"Most likely Barnard's the man your monk is looking for," he said. "Like Albarth over there said, there's been no other one-eyed Britons coming here from Derthwald two years ago on a horse cart with two little boys."

"Where . . ." Aleswina realized that in her excitement, she'd started to speak in her own girl's voice. Catching herself, she coughed as if to clear her throat and began again in what was practically a growl, "Where do we go to find him?"

"Straight on through town to the first fork in the road, go left there, then right at the lane after the three big oaks . . ." The innkeeper's rights and lefts and landmarks went on for another several turns.

Although the talk swirling around him was in rapid and idiomatic English, Caelym had followed it well enough to understand that he had again been betrayed—this time by the man he'd trusted with his sons' lives. As the pack of boorish peasants bantered back and forth about just what sort of ill treatment Arddwn and Lliem were suffering, he sat motionless, his face hidden in the shadow of his hood, waiting for the innkeeper to finish giving his directions.

". . . just past a stand of pines, before the ridge, there'll be a fenced-off field to your left, you'll see his manor from there."

In a swift move that sent his chair clattering over behind him, Caelym stood up and went striding out of the tavern, leaving the door swinging open behind him.

Chapter 37

The Overlook

As startled as everyone else in the room, Aleswina jumped up and stammered, "Brother Cuthbert is—is—he is in a hurry to, to carry out his mission from the bishop, and—"

"—and walked off without his staff and bowl!" Annwr, who'd just emerged from the kitchen, finished for her. "Bring them along, Codric."

Aleswina grabbed the staff and bowl, along with Caelym's shoulder bag, and ran after Annwr. When they reached the far end of town, she just caught sight of Caelym turning left before disappearing behind the three oak trees.

Fifteen years earlier, Annwr had stood by and done nothing as Rhedwyn, hot-headed fool that he was, dashed off into disaster, leaving nothing but misery in his wake. That would not happen again! Tucking her own staff under her arm and lifting her habit above her knees, she put on a burst of speed that would have earned her a trophy if she'd been competing in the foot race at the summer solstice festivities.

She caught up with Caelym just as he was coming to the last turn in the road. Without slowing, she seized hold of his right arm so that their combined momentum pulled him along after her, past the turnoff. Shifting course, she dragged him off the road and a dozen paces into a thicket of scrubby brush on the side of the ridge.

When Aleswina appeared seconds later, panting and out of breath, Annwr had Caelym on his knees and was sitting uphill from him, her heels dug into the rocky ground and her two hands clenched around his wrist.

Jerking away from her, Caelym shouted, "Let me go, or I'll—"

"You'll what?" Annwr shouted back. "Go charging up to a manor defended by who knows how many guards? Get yourself killed in front of your little boys' faces? Bring the rest of the king's army down on us? You will stop and listen to me, or—"

"Or what?" Caelym wrenched his arm out of Annwr's grasp.

"Or I'll curse the part of you that fathered those boys so that it won't do you or anyone else any good ever again!"

Caelym froze where he was. "You wouldn't!"

"I would! So, are you going to listen?"

"I am going to save my sons!"

"*We* are going to save your sons, but first we are going to the top of this hill, where we will look to see what we can of the manor, and we are going to make a plan so we don't all get killed in the effort!" Annwr's voice went from hard to soft as she looked over at Aleswina. "Are you ready for a climb, Dear Heart?"

Aleswina nodded and started to pick up the staff, bowl, and bag that she'd dropped on the ground.

"I'll take these, Dear Heart." Annwr picked up the bowl and her staff. "And you," she snapped at Caelym as she pointed at his staff and satchel, "take those!"

Aleswina needed both hands to grab hold of shrubs and tree roots as she scrambled after Annwr and Caelym along a narrow, crumbling remnant of trail that went almost straight up the side of the ridge. Caelym reached the top first. Moving cautiously, he made his way through a copse of fir and cedar. Annwr crept after him, and Aleswina crept after Annwr. Coming to the rim, all three flattened themselves against the ground and looked over the edge.

Almost straight below them, the road they would have taken led to a gate in a high stone wall circling a cluster of wooden buildings. The first and biggest of the buildings was nearly as large as the convent's main storage barn, and the four other huts might, between them, house a full contingent of guards.

"How much money did you give him?" Easing back from the edge, Annwr stood up and stared at Caelym.

Caelym pushed up onto his knees but kept looking over the cliff as he answered, "Enough to keep the boys in comfort and reward Benyon's kin for their hospitality." Then he fell silent, staring down at the manor as Annwr muttered, "It looks as though your trusted servant must have rewarded himself quite well."

Caelym didn't need Annwr's caustic comments to see that the purse they'd sent off with the boys, though generous, could not have paid for the estate below him. All he could think was *How long was Benyon robbing our treasury? Was he a traitor for all the years I was growing up? From the days he carried me on his back, neighing and pretending to be a horse, brought me plates of sweets, helped me get dressed for my first formal ritual?*

Taking advantage of Caelym's silence, Annwr told Aleswina that the women in the kitchen had said Barnard was both miserly and vindictive—and that the orphaned boys' mother would have done them a favor if she'd taken them to the grave with her.

The look that Annwr directed at Caelym said, without words, exactly what her opinion was of the idiocy of trusting the care of children to anyone incapable of giving birth. Out loud, she confined herself to remarking that they would have to come up with a new plan since "your devoted servant" was unlikely to welcome them into his fine manor.

Recovering from his shock, Caelym was ready to offer several plans—most of which involved his getting his hands around Benyon's throat and squeezing until the miserable traitor's remaining eyeball popped out and rolled across the floor.

While granting that the idea had a certain primitive charm to it, Annwr pointed out the obvious problem—that even wearing the monk's cloak, Caelym was well known to the man who had been his "trusted" servant all those years, and who would no doubt recognize him from half a league off.

Annwr's alternative—that she should go in her disguise as a nun, ask for alms, wait until Benyon's back was turned, and then grab the boys and run with them—was met with Caelym's caustic rejoinder that since the man was a miser, there'd be as much chance of him offering her a handout as a pig playing a flute.

From there the debate between them became nasty—Annwr snorting, "Well, maybe, being the son of the Goddess, you could turn yourself into an eagle, swoop down, and snatch the boys up and carry them back here!" and Caelym sneering, "And maybe, being the sister of the Goddess, you could entice some helpful giant to take the roof off the house, pick up Benyon between his fingers, and squash him like a bug."

◆◆◆

When Annwr and Caelym had exhausted their sarcastic witticisms and became serious again, they were both forced to agree that without any way of knowing whether Benyon had guards or where he kept the boys, none of their plans had much chance of succeeding.

At this point, Aleswina surprised them (and herself) by saying that she would go and find out. "I will say . . ." She thought for a moment. "I have been sent by the monk to see whether Barnard is the man that my master is seeking."

Annwr objected to Aleswina taking such a risk on the grounds that she was not a Druid and not related to the boys in any way. Caelym agreed, without adding out loud that the girl was too cowardly to get away with it.

Somehow Aleswina did not feel afraid.

"There's no reason to worry. I am only going to see how the place is guarded and, if I can, to learn where the boys are kept. Then," she finished hopefully, "Caelym can sneak in there tonight and steal them away."

Annwr looked at Aleswina with something between concern and pride. "If you're sure, Dear Heart," while Caelym nodded silently, sat back under the shade of a tree at the edge of the overlook, took out his dagger, and started cleaning its blade with the hem of his monk's cloak.

◆◆◆

Glancing over her shoulder, Annwr saw Caelym polishing his dagger with a relish that bothered her—not because she didn't think the treacherous, thieving Benyon shouldn't have to answer for his wrongs, but because she'd yet to be convinced that men killing each other made anything better for anyone in the long run.

It tore at her heart to send Aleswina alone and defenseless into the villain's stronghold, but the sun was halfway down in the western sky and sinking steadily toward the rim of blue-gray peaks on the far side of the river plain. *Once night falls*, she thought, *there'll be no holding him back—and no telling what havoc he'll wreak with nothing but stupid, blind rage to guide him.* So she slipped Caelym's bag onto Aleswina's shoulder and, turning back to Caelym, said, "It's agreed, then. Caelym, you keep watch from here, and Aleswina will go see how the place is guarded and where the boys stay at night so you can creep in and get them without causing a row."

Caelym nodded absently, his eyes fixed on the door of the manor and his fingers stroking the dagger's shining blade.

Aleswina hugged the bag under her arm and looked from Annwr to the path down to the road, and then back to Annwr.

Annwr took Aleswina by the hand. "Well then, Dear Heart, I'll just walk with you back down to the road." She kept her voice as calm and reassuring as if she were doing no more than seeing her off to her first trip to the market—which, in fact, was not so different from what Annwr had in mind. Once they'd slipped and slid their way back to where the trail met the road, she drew Aleswina aside to sit with her on a fallen log.

"Now, Dear Heart, I want you to be careful and to take no chances. It is enough to get inside this 'Barnard's' house, look around to see what you can see, and come out safely again. But here is the pouch with our thirty-two sceattas and forty-nine penings." After pausing to glance and make sure Caelym hadn't snuck down the trail after them, she went on, "From what I heard said of him, this 'Barnard' would sell his own mother if the price was right."

Aleswina, who tended to take everything that Annwr said literally, started to ask, "Why would we want his mo—" But she stopped and thought for a moment. Brightening as she realized that anyone who would sell his own mother would certainly sell someone else's sons, she shifted to asking, "How much will they cost?"

It was a straightforward and practical question, and one that put an end to any doubt that Aleswina was Annwr's child in spirit, if not by birth.

Unfortunately, Annwr did not have a straightforward answer. While she'd done her share of trading at the main market in Strothford, she'd stayed as far away as possible from the west end where slave dealers did their trade. The one time she'd been there, she'd been on sale herself and, speaking no English, had understood nothing of the bidding around her—so, despite having a better-than-fair knowledge of what to pay for woolen goods and what price to ask for her piglets and goslings, she had no idea what to pay for children.

"Barnard is a miser and will drive a hard bargain, so you must be ready to drive a harder one," she said. "Do not act too eager to get them. Let him name his price before you name yours; if it is too high, try to bring it down with appeals to Christian charity. If you can only afford one, take the younger one; he will be cheaper, and the older one will be faster if he has to run away."

"I will, Anna," Aleswina said earnestly. "I'll keep my voice low and drive a hard bargain."

"And promise me, Dear Heart, that you'll take no chances, and that you will come away at once if you think he suspects anything!"

"I promise."

"All right. Off with you, then, but—"

"I'll be careful."

After gripping Aleswina in a last quick hug, Annwr waved her off, watched until she disappeared around the bend, and then started the long climb back up the hill, hoping that Caelym had stayed where he was supposed to be.

Chapter 38

Benyon

ews that a dark, silent monk was looking for him reached Barnard, previously known as Benyon, before Caelym stood up to leave the tavern.

Maelrwn, a sheepherder who ran his flock in the pastures next to Barnard's, was having his usual midday meal at the Spotted Hound and had followed the conversation without joining in. While Maelrwn wasn't a particular friend of Barnard's—and didn't like him better than anyone else in the village did—still Barnard was a fellow Briton and possibly a covert pagan, as Maelrwn was himself, and so, acting out of clan loyalty, Maelrwn had slipped quietly out the side way. Taking a shortcut across back fields, he'd reached the manor in half the time it took to get there by the road and rapped a quick, hard rap on the door.

Relieved that it was Barnard himself and not Wilda, Aelfgar's gossiping sister-in-law, who cracked the door open, Maelrwn whispered his warning.

Barnard blinked his eye. "A monk, looking for me? I can't think why, unless it's for a handout."

It was on the tip of Maelrwn's tongue to say, "That bishop must be falling on hard times if he's got to send a monk all the way from Lindisfarne to Welsferth for a contribution!" but he realized there was no reason for Barnard to trust him and, come to that, no reason for him to trust Barnard. "Well, good luck then . . ." he muttered, his voice trailing off awkwardly as he stepped back away from the door.

•◆•

Watching Maelrwn retreat down the path and out the gate, Barnard started to thank the Goddess that he'd answered the knock himself instead of calling for his serving woman to do it, but switched, mid-thought, to the Virgin Mary as he closed the door and leaned back against it.

Despite the scathing comments about him being bandied back and forth in the tavern, Barnard was a mild and inoffensive-looking man. His habit of cocking his head to the left to compensate for his blind side gave him a perpetually quizzical look, more in keeping with the eager-to-please servant he'd once been than the cruel, tight-fisted miser he'd become.

Barnard—or, to use his shrine name, Benyon—had worked his way up from kitchen helper to chief servant for the priests' chambers, and for his first seven years in that position, he'd been everything that Caelym had once believed him to be—honest, dependable, and devoted to the shrine. One of the few servants who could speak English, he had been the natural choice to take trinkets made by the shrine's metalsmith to trade for salt and spices at a village market within walking distance of valley's hidden entrance, and the fact that he always returned with a full and accurate account of the exchange had cemented the priests' trust in him.

In between market days, Benyon had kept up his regular duties—cleaning the priests' chambers, fetching their ceremonial paraphernalia, and polishing the shrine's sacred vessels. Moving from one task to the next, so much a feature of the shrine's life that he was almost invisible, he'd listened in on the apprentice priests' lessons and the elder priests' otherwise private conversations.

Benyon didn't start out to do anything wrong. He was just curious—and more than a little bored with what was largely tedious and repetitive work. It was only after he discovered the secret location where generations of priests and priestesses had deposited their golden tribute to the Goddess that he became greedy.

Of the dozens of major and minor ceremonies conducted throughout the year, the most important were the celebrations held on the summer solstice, fall equinox, winter solstice, and spring equinox. Each began with a public pageant at dawn, followed by a day of festivities that culminated in a communal feast served by the priests and priestess to the servants, artisans, and laborers in honor of their work throughout the year. Then, while the villagers were gathering up their sleepy children and going back to their cottages, and the shrines' servants were clearing dishes and putting away the extra tables and benches, the priests and priestess withdrew to their innermost sanctum, where they prepared to perform their secret rites.

No uninitiated person was allowed to witness these most sacred of the shrine's rituals, but one year, Benyon's curiosity got the better of him.

On the night of the summer solstice, he followed the priest and priestess who'd been chosen to reenact the courtship of the Sun God and the Earth Goddess, and he watched from the bushes as they celebrated the world's first conception.

On the night of the autumn equinox, he crept after the chanting line of priests and priestesses as they wound their way through twisting underground passageways down into a vast cavern where they danced in dizzying circles with the spirits of the dead.

On the night of the winter solstice, he hid in a side chamber of the shrine's highest tower and listened as the chief priestess led chants interceding in the lovers' quarrel between the earth and sun and calling on the sun to return to the earth and her children.

On the night of the spring equinox, he stole behind the procession of the shrine's highest priests, led by their chief oracle, who held a golden goblet above his head. They took a roundabout path to the lakeshore where they stepped on board a long narrow boat. The oracle stood at the front while the others took up paddles and propelled the craft silently across the black surface of the water toward the lake's only island, a barren outcrop of jagged boulders barely visible from where Benyon lurked in the reeds.

It was gloomy and overcast, but every now and then there was a gap in the clouds and the moonlight burst through and made the polished gold chalice sparkle as if the oracle were holding a ball of fire between his hands. The first time this happened, Benyon, who'd been crouching down out in the bushes, stood up. He stared into the darkness after the twinkling spot of light until it grew smaller and then went out for the last time. For a long time, he could see nothing, but he could hear the start of a chant that rose and fell nine times over, then stopped.

At the first sight of the Druids' boat returning across the lake, Benyon ducked back down into the underbrush. He held his breath as they disembarked and walked silently past him on their way home to the shrine. After they were safely out of sight, he stole down to the lake, eased a small boat off the dock, and paddled out to the tiny, barren island, making as little noise as he could. When he drew up the boat to the rocks, there was just enough of a ledge to climb onto for one person, much less seven Druids, unless they had mystical powers that he'd not seen in all his years of picking up after them; and if they had that much magic, he reasoned, wouldn't they have used it make themselves richer?

Squatting down, he gazed at the ripples running across the surface of the water, thinking that they must have thrown the chalice into the lake as an offering to the Goddess. Out of the blue, he recalled how the shrine's cook, purposely confusing the spirit of the Goddess embodied in the shrine's chief priestess with the cosmic entity who was the Earth Herself, had once joked, "Why do they make such a fuss when they could just hand it to her at the dinner table?"

But the haughty priests of Llwddawanden wouldn't "just hand it to her at the dinner table," and they hadn't just tossed it into the middle of the lake! They'd paddled their boat out beyond this rock, chanted their chants, and deposited it ceremoniously some-where—but where?

That was a puzzle that teased Benyon as he looked around, seeing only the shimmering black surface of the water.

Discouraged and on the verge of giving up, he sat back with his knees drawn up and his head resting on his arms and stared out at the lake as if it would show him its secrets if he just looked long enough and hard enough. There was nothing to see, how-ever, except for a log that floated some ten boat-lengths down the lake—and had been floating there the entire time he had been on the island.

With the prevailing wind through the valley pushing other floating debris to the east end of the lake, why did that log stay in one place?

Benyon climbed back into his boat, paddled out to the log, and found the chain and sunken boom that kept it in place, as well as the cleat that the Druids used to tie their boat to it. Then the clouds covering the moon parted, a shaft of light shone down through the clear waters of the lake to its deepest depths, and he saw a shimmer of gold—the chalice they'd just dropped there, and other things even more wonderful.

Dazzled by the sight, Benyon leaned over the side of his boat and reached down in an involuntary impulse to grab at the mountain of treasure glittering in the depths of the lake. The narrow boat reeled wildly, tipped over, and cast him into the frigid water. He came up splashing and coughing. Desperation overcame his panic and he managed to catch hold of the prow of the upside-down boat in one hand, grab the drifting paddle in the other, and kick his way back to the island where he forced his numb hands to turn the boat right-side up. Shaking from cold, he got into it and rowed back across the lake, vowing that if he made it to shore, he'd never pry into the Druids' secrets again.

Whether Benyon was swearing to himself or the Goddess, it was a promise he forgot the next morning and broke the next night when he again snuck out of the shrine, again took the small boat, and again paddled back out to the log. This time, he was careful not to lean out too far as he lowered an iron nail tied on a cord to see how deep the water was.

It turned out to be very deep—much too deep for him hold his breath long enough to reach the bottom, even if he dared and if he could swim, which he did not and could not.

To know where so much treasure lay unguarded would have tempted stronger men than Benyon. At first, though, he wasn't really thinking about stealing it, he just wondered if you could.

Benyon was an indoor servant. To an outdoor man, the answer would have been obvious, but Benyon did come to it before long.

He was returning home from the market, not thinking about the treasure at all, just glad to be out of the cold, dark underground passage that echoed the sounds of dripping water and the occasional clatter of a falling rock.

The trail from there ran alongside a stream, crossed over a low wooden bridge just above a deep pool, and climbed over a series of steep embankments to reach the lower gate of the shrine's thick stone wall. As he came up onto the bridge, Benyon saw the village smith wading at the far end of the pool, holding the end of a thin cord and jigging it up and down.

◆◆◆

Benyon did not, as a rule, mingle with workers who lived outside the shrine, but he knew the young artisan who made most of the things that the Druids sent to the market so he stopped and called to him, meaning to tell him which of his wares sold best. The smith, however, was an avid fisherman, and he was concentrating on a particularly elusive trout.

Ignoring Benyon, Darbin pulled his hook out of the water, stretched out his arm, and let it sink down again. His body, except for the tips of the fingers that were controlling the line, went absolutely still. Then there it was—the faint tug he was waiting for. His fingers tightened. There was another tug, but still just a curious nibble. He did a tiny jerk, just enough to make the worm on the end of the hook wiggle as if it were alive. For a moment there was nothing. And then the answering jerk as the fish snapped. Darbin grasped the line and yanked. The fish, flapping—its silver scales shimmering in the sun— was his.

His trophy in hand, Darbin turned to find out what Benyon wanted only to see him walking away.

◆◆◆

Realizing that jigging for treasure would take something bigger than a fishing hook, Benyon started searching the shrine as soon as he got there. Once he began looking, he started seeing hooks everywhere—in the kitchen holding pots, in the storerooms holding sacks of grain, and in the closets holding the priests' robes. The day he lost his left eye, he was peering over the cook's shoulder, wondering if there was some way he could take one of the heavy iron hooks that held the roasting spit.

A few days later, after the pain in his eye socket subsided, he snuck into the kitchen in the middle of the night and found a spare hook like the one he'd been looking at. The first time he used it, he brought up the golden chalice, and from then on, he thought of it as his lucky hook.

Over time, what had begun as a mental game to relieve the monotony of Benyon's daily chores grew into an obsession. At first, the thrill lay as much in the challenge as in the pieces of treasure he managed to retrieve. Hours of patient concentration might bring up a jeweled necklace or a decaying branch. Sometimes something glittering under the surface of the water would slide off the hook just before he could reach it. He might go out for weeks at a time with nothing to show for it, but then for the next two or three nights in a row bring up a goblet or torc or crown.

As his trove grew, he couldn't fit it all in the space he'd hollowed out in his mattress, so he pried up the floorboards in the closet where he kept his broom, mop, and buckets, and dug a pit to make a hidden chamber where it would be safe and he could look at it every day. Once or twice he took a bit of his treasure with him to the market and exchanged it for Saxon coins. Each time, the merchant looked sharply from the jewelry to Benyon and asked where he got it, and Benyon sensed that everyone around was staring at him and wondering the same thing. But there was nothing he could safely spend his money on anyway, since any new possessions would raise the suspicions of his fellow servants, and maybe the Druids as well.

Chapter 39

A Step Beyond Sport

or the next five years, Benyon was very much like a passionate fisherman who fished for the love of the sport but did not eat what he caught. That changed one market day when he was waiting his turn to do his trade with the salt seller near where a pair of traveling vendors were talking about the other towns on their circuit.

"Now Welsferth," one of them said, "there's the one place I know where Britons and Saxons get along without always being at each other's throats."

"And it's in Atheldom," the other replied, "where you're halfway safe as long you say you're a Christian and don't give their priests any reason to suspect otherwise"—at which both men made the sign of the cross and laughed.

Benyon left the line, sidled over to them and joined their conversation, and by the time he went back to buy the salt, he knew the road to take to reach the place they'd talked about and had begun to dream of living like a priest—or a king—with servants to wait on him.

◆◆◆

As long as the illicit hoard he'd fished out of the lake stayed hidden under the closet floor, Benyon had not seen his activity as stealing, exactly, or seen himself as a thief. Even trading the occasional piece for Saxon coins at the market hadn't seemed so bad, as long as he didn't spend any of it. To take the treasure and leave, not intending to return, was a step beyond sport—and Benyon decided to take it.

It was a surprisingly easy decision. The hard part was thinking of some way to sneak what he had come to think of as "his" treasure out of the shrine without getting caught.

Again, the answer came by accident.

He was carrying an armload of the priests' robes back from the shrine's laundry and took a shortcut through one of the side courtyards. Strictly speaking, he shouldn't have entered there without permission, but it was usually empty in the early afternoon and crossing that way saved time.

Hearing voices, a man's and a woman's, he stopped and backed off, meaning to turn around and go the long way around, but then he realized the voices belonged to the chief priestess and her consort—and they were arguing.

The union between the beautiful but aging chief priestess and the boy-priest, who was young enough to be her son, was a source of intense gossip among the shrine servants so Benyon listened in, hoping to learn some interesting tidbit to pass on.

Feywn, her voice less song-like than usual, was saying, "Ossiam has seen it in the entrails of three separate goats! We must send them now!"

There was a standing quip among the shrine's inner circle of servants that when Feywn said, "Bow!" Caelym only asked, "How low?"—so it surprised Benyon to hear Caelym protest, "We cannot send out of the valley! They are too young! And there is no longer anyone we can trust to keep them safe who speaks English and lives in the outside world!"

Benyon dodged back inside and took the servants' hallway to the priests' quarters, hugging the fresh-smelling robes to his chest. Here was the plan for how he could leave the shrine and take his treasure with him.

The next morning, he was ready to set it in motion.

One of Benyon's daily duties was to carry a tray up to the shrine's oracle, who insisted on having breakfast in his private chamber at the top of the shrine's northern tower. As he was setting out the plates and platters in the exact order that Ossiam demanded,

Benyon spoke in his most ingratiating voice, begging a thousand pardons for intruding in matters above his station . . .

"But while I was at the market, I met a cousin of a cousin on my mother's side who practices our ways and lives in the not-so-far off kingdom of Atheldom, in a village where Saxons and Britons live at peace with each other."

Ossiam, who'd been standing at the window with his back to Benyon, turned to look at him.

Struggling to keep his voice steady, Benyon went on, "He . . . my cousin's cousin . . . needs help with his flocks . . . and asks . . . that I come to stay with him for a time . . . and thinking that this might be a way for some of the young Druids to learn English, I said I would, so long as I might bring my foster sons with me."

As he was saying it out loud, Benyon saw the gaping holes in his story—*How did it just happen that he met this previously unknown cousin's cousin? Why would he, who'd never herded a sheep in his life, suddenly be the one this cousin's cousin needed? And why would he want to risk leaving the safety of the shrine for the dangers of the outside world?*

Ossiam, a tall, angular man with a jutting nose and wild, tangled gray hair, towered over Benyon, his oracle's cloak billowing in the wind that swirled through the window so that the ravens embroidered on it seemed to be flying around his shoulders.

"So, you just happened to meet your cousin's cousin, who lives in this happy village where Saxons and Britons live at peace with each other."

As he spoke, Ossiam ever so slightly nodded his head and Benyon found himself nodding along as he squeaked, "Y-yes, I just—just—"

"And this cousin's cousin said he needs your help herding his sheep."

The oracle spoke in a cold, dry voice that might almost have been a serpent's hiss.

"He—he—said he needs m-my help—"

"And at just the time we need to send the sons of our chief priestess outside of the valley to learn to speak English well enough to pass among our enemies undetected, you, out of selfless devotion, are offering to go to this not-so-distant kingdom disguised as a sheepherder fostering them there, caring for them as if they were your own flesh and blood."

Suddenly certain that the oracle could read his innermost thoughts, Benyon froze, as paralyzed as a rodent caught in the stare of a snake coiled and ready to strike. Convinced that Ossiam was about to lash out and curse him for his deceit and thievery, Benyon would have pled for a quick and not too painful death if he could have made his tongue work. Instead he dropped to his knees, still nodding, as the oracle lifted his staff and said, "I will tell the council. You will leave as soon as it can be arranged. You will need a horse and a cart big enough for the boys and all their things. Tell the stablemen I have commanded it."

With that, the oracle waved his free hand in dismissal.

Amazed, first that he was still alive and human—not transformed into some scurrying vermin and set upon by the shrine's cats—and then that he had gotten exactly what he had hoped for, a wagon big enough to carry all his treasure, Benyon backed out of the room on his hands and knees. Once he was out of the door, he must have pulled himself to his feet and climbed down the stairs, because the next thing he remembered was leaping in elation as he bounded toward the stable.

Chapter: 40

Benyon's Plan

enyon's plan was to settle into his new life, see the shrine brats learned their English, then bring them back with some excuse why he couldn't stay (and the claim to have been persuaded by Christians to convert was one guaranteed way to be expelled with no further questions asked). For the next two weeks, he spent his days rushing to do everything the priests and priestesses thought necessary to get the boys packed and ready, and his nights crafting a false bottom for the cart and packing armloads of treasure.

The day that he left Llwddawanden dawned bright and clear, a perfect spring day that seemed to promise a whole new life in a world where wishes came true and ventures couldn't go wrong.

Awake long before there was enough light to see by, Benyon lay in bed with his hands behind his head. He'd packed the wagon, making sure each urn and goblet, torc and armband was wrapped in linen and padded with wool, and all snugly tucked in with the bags of jewelry and Saxon coins. He'd fitted the false bottom over his trophies and covered it with the crates of clothes, sacks of toys, and wicker baskets of food the boys' nurse had insisted on sending with them—and covered that with an oiled wool blanket, which he'd tied down with loops of rope "to keep the rain off" (and keep any snoopers from looking under it). He'd given misleading directions to the shrine's chief priest so the map the old man was drawing would lead the wrong way if someone was sent to find him. He'd turned his duties over to his nephew, Nimrrwn, and told the simpering boy every last little detail about picking up after the priests and carrying out their chamber pots.

Benyon could hear Nimrrwn stirring in the next bed, no doubt anxious to assume his new position—and he was welcome to it!

Now he just had to collect the two boys, take his treasure, and be off.

•◆•

Of course, he should have known Druids couldn't go to the latrine without making a ceremony out of it!

All Benyon wanted to do was to get the horse harnessed and leave. Instead he had to endure a long, drawn-out farewell breakfast, sitting at the high table with the boys on either side of him, listening to Herrwn strumming his harp and telling stories about the mortal children of gods and goddesses being raised by loyal servants until they were ready to go out and perform heroic deeds.

Then there was the grand procession through the shrine, led by no less than the high priestess herself, her puffed-up consort at her side.

Instead of sneaking behind and out of sight, Benyon found himself walking in the middle of the procession, holding the boys' hands—the older one tugging and pulling ahead, the younger one prancing along and waving at the servants who were watching them go past.

The horse and wagon were waiting at the shrine's back gate. Benyon took the reins and clambered up to the wagon's seat. All that remained was for Caelym to finish hugging and kissing the two boys and lift them up.

Benyon leaned forward, reaching out his arms for whichever one of the boys Caelym relinquished first. He managed, somehow, to keep his smile fixed in place, even as he realized what his soon-to-be-former master was in the midst of saying ". . . so if you will promise me that you will both do as our good Benyon tells you, and learn your lessons quickly, I will promise you that I will come to get you and bring you home as soon as ever I can . . ."

The older of the two boys, who was the exact image of Caelym at the same age—and every bit as uppity—demanded that his father promise not just to come and get them but also to do heroic deeds on their way home.

Speaking as if he were swearing to the Goddess at the high altar stone in the center of the shrine's sacred grove, Caelym declared, "I make my vow to you, my sons, that when you have learned your lessons, I will come for you, and we will travel together on great adventures and return to your mother with gifts from all the wondrous places we have seen."

With that, he threw his arms around the boys in one last, interminable hug, before turning to Benyon to remind him which toys the boys took to bed with them at night and what stories they most liked to hear. Keeping his expression humble and his voice sincere, Benyon swore he'd care for the boys like his own flesh and blood.

With years of practice in pretending loyal devotion, Benyon made a show of comforting the younger of the two boys, who'd suddenly realized that his father truly wasn't coming along and begun to cry. The older one, who still thought this was a game, was persuaded to hold his sniveling brother on his lap while Benyon bid his last groveling farewell, made his last promise to guard the boys with his life. Even then he had to endure the shrine's chief priest making one last speech, admonishing the boys to study with diligence and to honor their hosts before he could finally snap the whip to get the horse moving.

As they rattled down the road, leaving the shrine behind, Caelym's vow to come to get his sons rang in Benyon's ears, followed by a flood of worries—*What if giving the priests false directions about where he was going wasn't enough? What if they really did have the power of second sight? What if Caelym came for the boys and found out the truth?*

Caelym's pledge to come for his sons combined with Benyon's lingering belief in Druids' supernatural abilities, merging into the conviction that he would never be safe as long as Caelym lived.

While the boys peppered him with "When are we going to get there?" "Can we go faster?" "Why are you hitting the horsie?" the only question that mattered to Benyon was, *What am I going to do?*

The answer came to him late that afternoon, when they arrived at a town with an open tavern and a lighted church.

◆◆◆

Planning for his new life had included learning about being a Christian, and Benyon had found out what he could about that during his sojourns to village market—getting both eager proselytizing from converted Britons and sarcastic counter-arguments from skeptics. In one particularly heated exchange, an earnest villager started explaining the benefits of cleansing your sin through confession only to have his unconverted cousin interrupt, "Aye, you can tell their priest anything—anything you don't mind your worst enemy hearing before the day is out." From there, the two had settled into what was clearly a well-worn dispute, and Benyon had backed off while the Christian was warning his kinsman that his soul was in peril for questioning the sanctity of holy confession, and the pagan was scoffing, "Two can keep a secret if one of them is dead!"

That cynical remark came back to Benyon just as he was pulling up the sweating, stumbling horse in front of the tavern where he bought the boys the last good meal they would have for two years before bedding them down in the back of the wagon and going back inside the inn. Although overcome by greed, he was not so devoid of conscience that he could betray the people he had spent his life with to torture and death without any qualms at all. It took four full mugs of ale for him to build the courage to leave for the church.

He got there just as the priest was coming out. Recalling what he'd been told over and over by enthusiastic converts—that Christian priests were always happy to hear about sins—he clasped his hands and, in a louder voice than he intended, announced that he needed confessing. For a nerve-wracking moment, the black-robed man just looked at him. Benyon held his breath, letting it out again when the priest nodded and led the way into the church. It didn't take long and, when he came out, he felt light and free, confident that he was saved, and Caelym was doomed.

Father Wulfric had had a long day. He was tired and hungry, and he wanted to eat supper and go to bed. Faced with a supplicant asking to confess, however, he had no choice but to agree.

Benyon was not the first penitent to come to the confessional by way of the tavern, and Wulfric had no trouble recognizing the almost overpowering odor of alcohol that wafted through the wooden grate between them. Although a generally forbearing man, he wasn't feeling much charity for a drunken Briton who thought it was funny to send a Saxon priest on a wild goose chase looking for secret Druid caves. Too tired to challenge the man's rambling story, he absolved him in the name of Christ (who was, in Wulfric's view, capable of infinite forgiveness), dispensed a routine penance and send him on his way.

Both because Wulfric did adhere absolutely to the sanctity of confession and because he was not about to be laughed at, the secret of Llwddawanden's hidden entrance would remain safe for another two years. Benyon did not know that, however, and so it was because he wanted to make a complete break from his heathen past—not because he was afraid of Caelym finding him— that Benyon changed his name to Barnard.

Lulled into a false sense of security, he also changed his mind about drowning the two boys in the first lake he came to, deciding instead that he'd keep them to be his servants as he had been a servant to their parents—the closest thing to a genuine joke he'd made since he had embarked on his plan for personal advancement all those years earlier.

Chapter 41

The Bargain

𝔄s Aleswina was making her way along the road toward the manor, Barnard was having a second tankard of ale and beginning to wonder if the story that a dark-cloaked monk was looking for him had been his neighbor's idea of a joke.

In the first heart-stopping moments after he'd answered Maelrwn's knock, Barnard had been overcome with the terror that his pagan past had been found out. His legs shaking, he'd leaned his back against the door to keep himself upright—terrified at the thought of be being accused of heresy and dragged screaming to the stake.

Then he rallied.

He ran to the kitchen to send his snooping servant woman home—certain she would betray him out of spite. Ordering the shrine brats (the mental phrase he used for the two foster sons he'd turned into slaves) to finish her work, he dashed to the storeroom where he kept the chests and crates and caskets of the things he bought at the market now that he could buy whatever he wanted. Pulling out every Christian icon and emblem he could find, he added them to the large gilded crucifix and several reliquaries he already had on prominent display in his front room. He always—even in bed at night—wore an ornate golden cross, but he hung two more around his neck for good measure.

Finally, after looking down the hall to make sure the boys weren't spying on him, he tiptoed into his bedroom. After closing and barring the door behind him, he shoved a large clothes chest aside, pried up the secret panel, lifted up the strong box of coins and jewels that was all he had left of the shrine's treasure, and counted out what he hoped would be a big enough bribe to send the monk off to burn someone else.

Walking up the front entrance of the manor house took all of Aleswina's courage. The stone walls were as thick and fortified as the ramparts of Gothroc, and while she saw no guards and heard no dogs, any hopes she had for their breaking in at night died at the sight of the iron bars on the windows.

She paused at the front door, working up her nerve to knock. Reminding herself that she was a boy now, and not afraid of anything, she straightened her shoulders and pounded on the heavy oak door.

It flew open.

She blinked.

The man peering out looked so meek and humble she would not have known it was the evil, vile, wicked Barnard, except for his having only one eye. And when she said, "God be with you, Sir. I am Codric, sent to speak to you on behalf of the blessed Brother Cuthbert, who is come on a mission for the Bishop of Lindisfarne!" he squeaked like a mouse and made his sign of the cross backwards and upside down as he bowed and waved her inside.

There was no going back now! She tramped across the threshold into a large room filled with more religious art and artifacts than the convent chapel. There were pictures of beatific Christ babies hanging next to grown Jesuses being scourged with whips or nailed to the cross, portraits of Mary smiling at hovering cherubs and of her weeping over her dead son, and paintings of martyred saints—Ignatius getting eaten by lions, Lawrence roasting on a grill, and Bartholomew being skinned alive, as well as one she didn't recognize who had an arrow sticking out of his eye. If she hadn't been hardened to the perils of sainthood by seven years in the convent, she might have quailed. As it was, she was only disappointed that there was no sign of the boys. How would she ask about buying them if she didn't see them?

Behind her, Barnard was glancing out the still open door for any sign of the actual monk.

Noticing this, Aleswina said, "Brother Cuthbert would have come himself, only he has taken a vow of silence."

"Of course! Of course! You and your high—I mean, er, *holy* master have come from afar, and you must be thirsty. Come to the kitchen and I will get you some ale, and we can talk."

The kitchen windows were barred as heavily as the front door, but the two boys were there.

Ignoring the chair Barnard pulled out for her, Aleswina sat down on one facing across the room at the counter where the bone-thin youngsters, both with an unmistakable likeness to Caelym, were moving warily about. The older one was making a show of being at work washing dishes while the younger stayed at his heels, getting in the way more than helping.

Barnard bustled about, taking two tankards from a cabinet and pouring a hefty draft of ale for each of them, before he took the seat he'd pulled out for her and cleared his throat.

"I, ah, I have not heard Brother Cuthbert's name before. Is he—"

"My master, Brother Cuthbert, is renowned throughout Christendom for his selfless devotion to the One True God in holy alliance with the revered Father Adolphus!"

Aleswina's only reason for mentioning Adolphus was to add credibility to Caelym's false identity by naming someone she had heard talked about back in the convent—where she had not paid enough attention to know that the reason for the priest's fame was his relentless pursuit and burning of heretics.

A nervous twitch appeared by Barnard's remaining eye as he babbled, "Of course! Of course! I remember now and am honored, I mean blessed, that the Holy Brother Cuthbert should honor me with his, ah, your presence."

Emboldened by seeing a man a head above her in height and three times her girth groveling, Aleswina repeated her entry line, "I am come in Brother Cuthbert's stead because he has taken a vow of silence," then added, "Brother Cuthbert labors selflessly to spread the Word of God, giving no thought for his own needs, while others, thinking only of their comfort in this world, have slaves and servants to cook their food and carry their loads."

She hoped that by dropping this hint, she might get Barnard to offer to sell the boys to her.

Instead, he fell silent, looking down at the cup in his hands. While she was waiting for him to say something, she took the chance of looking past him to give the boys a small smile that she hoped they would take as reassuring. The smaller boy peeked around his brother's side to look directly into her face, his lower lip pulled in and his eyes wide and wondering.

Kept isolated and destined for a celibate religious life, Aleswina had never given any thought to motherhood, but now she suddenly felt as if this little boy were hers, and that she would fight dragons to keep him safe.

Tearing her eyes away, she realized that Barnard was looking at her with an odd smirk on his face.

She'd given herself away, acted too much like a girl! Thinking quickly, she spat on the floor and scratched between her legs at the same time—and was relieved to see his expression turn nervous again and to hear him say, with a gasp, "Yes, well, your master must have some needs, and it cannot be an easy thing to be the only one in service and have to meet to the demands of even so devoted a monk."

Aleswina held her breath, hardly daring to hope.

"So perhaps, then, it might be a help to have one of these boys to take back with you to join in that service?"

Steadfastly keeping her voice down and prepared to spit or scratch again, she said, "It would take both of them to be of enough service to satisfy Brother Cuthbert."

"Both of them, then." Barnard's smirk returned.

"And how much?" She said in an offhanded sort of way.

Barnard was ready to have the price named as well and started by offering the lowest bribe he thought might be acceptable.

"Twenty-five sceattas."

It was, in fact, a very modest bribe, but more than Aleswina was expecting as a price for two little slaves.

The afternoon light coming in through the window was beginning to fade. If she didn't get the boys out quickly, it would be dark and Caelym would come and start wreaking havoc. Instead of making her own offer, she decided to try appealing to Christian charity. "I am sorry to say, people have been sadly lacking in their contributions of late—"

"Fifty sceattas! No, a hundred!"

Up until now, Aleswina had been feeling confident, even cocky. The last thing she expected was for Barnard to raise his price so much it so that she couldn't even pay for one of the boys unless she went to get the gold coins from Annwr. Before giving up and going back empty-handed, she made one last try.

Remembering that her earlier reference to Father Adolphus had seemed to impress Barnard, she decided to evoke his name again. "A hundred sceattas? Can you not be more charitable than that to my master, Brother Cuthbert, who is on a secret church mission for Father Adolphus?"

With that final entreaty, she silently prayed that the miserable man would name a lower price.

Instead, Barnard cried out, "Please! Please! Wait!"

He jumped up from his chair and ran out of the kitchen. Hearing him banging doors and slamming things around, Aleswina thought he must have guessed the truth, but before she could gather her wits, grab the boys, and run, Barnard burst back into the room with two bulging leather bags clutched to his chest.

"Here it is, all of it! Take it! Take them! Go tell your monk that I love Jesus and that's all I have!"

With that he broke out sobbing, but before she could ask him what the matter was, he thrust the bags into her hands, pushed her outside, tossed the two boys out after her, and slammed the door behind them.

Chapter 42

This Was the Day

Aleswina stuffed the money bags into Caelym's pouch, slung the bulging satchel over her shoulder, and called to the boys, "Come quick!"—adding, "Brother Cuthbert is waiting!" in case Barnard was listening to the door.

Both boys jumped up. Lliem rushed to her side but Arddwn, to her dismay, dashed back to the door and pounded on it—shouting that he wasn't going to leave, and neither was Lliem.

All the while Barnard and Aleswina had been talking, Arddwn and Lliem had been listening.

Terrified of Barnard, Lliem sometimes dreamed of living in a distant land where there was music and dancing and wonderful cakes to eat—and in that dream, just before he woke up cold and hungry, someone who was very tall would smile at him and hold out the most beautiful cake of all. When Aleswina (who looked very tall to Lliem) smiled at him from across the room, it seemed that the person from his dreams had come at last. All the while that he and Arddwn were being bartered over, Lliem had silently repeated, *Please, please, please,* like the word was a magic spell.

Unlike Lliem, Arddwn could clearly remember his life in Llwddawanden. He remembered his father, and he remembered Caelym's promise that he'd come to get them after they learned to speak

English. For two years, he'd whispered to himself, "We will travel together on great adventures and return to your mother with gifts from all the wondrous places we have seen," while he huddled next to Lliem in the woodshed where Barnard locked them up at night. As much as he hated Barnard (which was a hundred times more than Lliem did), they had to stay where they were or else their father wouldn't know where to find them.

So when Barnard threw them out of the house, Arddwn rebelled. He wasn't going to leave. Not now. Not after he'd learned English, like he was supposed to. And especially not today, when he'd woken up somehow certain that this was the day his father was going to come to get them. And Lliem couldn't go either. Arddwn had promised he'd take care of his brother, so when the door opened up again and Barnard poked his ugly head out, yelling at him to go away, Arddwn ran like lightning, grabbed Lliem by his shirt, and pulled him back to the door, yelling, "Our father said to stay here until he comes!" as he tried to push his way back inside.

Barnard, however, caught the boys by their collars and threw them out again, shouting, "Go on, damn you! Get out of here!"

Arddwn picked himself up and, standing with his feet set, one hand clinging to Lliem's shirt and the other balled into a fist, shouted back, "I'm not leaving! My father is coming for me!"

"Your father is dead! He's burning in hell with the rest of them!" With that, Barnard slammed the door, leaving Arddwn standing still, his lips soundlessly shaping the word "no."

Not daring to take time to comfort the boys or tell them the truth—that their father was alive and waiting not very far away—Aleswina took hold of their arms and pulled them along with her down the road and around the bend, toward the path up to the ridge.

Chapter 43

Greetings, My Son

atching the manor from their overlook, Caelym and Annwr saw the door open and Aleswina and the boys come tumbling out of it. That was enough for Caelym, who was off and running down the path before Annwr could get to her feet.

Glancing back over the edge as she gathered up the staves and the wooden bowl—which they'd still need, and she was not about to leave behind—Annwr saw the unexpected scene of Arddwn fighting to stay with Benyon. Thinking this meant that they'd misjudged a loyal servant and that he'd been a loving guardian to the boys after all, she rushed after Caelym, bent on keeping him from killing an innocent man.

She caught up with him halfway down the trail. Dropping the staves and the bowl, she grabbed hold of the rope knotted around his monk's robe for a belt, dug her heels into the dirt, and held on, shouting at him to stop and listen to her.

He did neither. Continuing to careen down the trail, he dragged her along after him. Still, she succeeded in slowing him enough that they were just skidding down the last slope as Aleswina rounded the bend, leading Lliem by the hand and gripping Arddwn's wrist as he dragged his feet and stumbled blindly after her.

◆◆◆

As he struggled to free himself from his captor's hold, Arddwn heard the birdlike whistle that had been his father's signal to call him back when he'd run off too far on their romps through the woods above the shrine.

Not about to be kept from his father by a Saxon boy who was not much taller or older than he was, Arddwn clenched his fists, determined to prove he could hit as hard he'd been hit himself. And he would have if Caelym hadn't appeared as if from nowhere and stopped Arddwn's fist mid-swing, saying sternly, "This cannot be my son who has been away from me so short a time and yet has forgotten all manners, raising his hand against one to whom he should be forever grateful and having no proper greeting for his father!"

Wrenching free from Aleswina's grasp, Arddwn launched himself into Caelym's arms with a force that would have knocked a weaker man off his feet, sobbing "Ta! Ta! Ta!" as if he were a baby even younger than Lliem.

Aleswina had no memory of her own father and if she had, it would only have been of making timid little curtsies in his presence or peeking out at him from behind nearly closed doors. Nothing in her experience at the palace or in the convent had prepared her for the sight of a grown man giving passionate hugs and kisses to a half-grown boy. Nervously, she looked at Lliem to see if he was going to follow his brother.

Equally bewildered, Lliem looked back and lifted both his arms up to her. Acting out of instinct, Aleswina picked him up and hugged him to her breast, again filled with a wave of fierce, protective love for the too-thin boy who clutched at her neck and felt so warm and fragile in her arms.

Still holding Arddwn, Caelym saw Aleswina picking up Lliem and experienced an irrational surge of jealousy mixed with heartache at the sight of his son embracing a woman who was not Feywn. Reminding himself of all he owed Aleswina for hiding him from his pursuers, nursing him back to health, and now bringing his sons to him, Caelym did not tear the boy away from her. Instead, he drew in a long, calming breath before he put Arddwn down, rushed over, and reached for Lliem, saying how much he loved and missed him—only to have the little boy shrink from him and cling tighter to Aleswina.

Arddwn saw the problem at once and assumed a knowing tone as he explained, in Celt, to his father, "He does not understand you, Ta. He only speaks English, for we were beaten if we spoke Celt, and he is a stupid little brat and has forgotten how, even though I told him he must remember." Then he added, with no small air of pride, "You may say it to me, and I will tell him for you."

"Ah, now I understand, and I thank you for this kind offer, but I myself am now somewhat learned in the use of English and so will speak for myself." Pausing a moment to nod solemnly at his older son, Caelym went on in a firmer tone, "And I will not ever again hear you call your own dear brother a 'stupid little brat,' knowing as you do that he is your closest and most beloved kin."

After kissing the tips of his fingers and touching them to Arddwn's lips to take the sting out of his rebuke, Caelym turned and edged slowly, almost timidly, over to where Aleswina was standing with Lliem, who was clinging to her like a limpet to a rock. He stopped a pace away, bent down low enough to be eye level with the quivering boy, and spoke in careful English.

"Greetings, my son. I see you do not remember me, for it has been now two years since we parted. I, however, remember you well and am most pleased to see you once again. With your kind permission, I will call you Lliem, the name your dear mother and I gave you with the blessing of our people's greatest bard."

Still clinging tightly to Aleswina, Lliem gave a barely perceptible nod.

Caelym returned it with a nod of his own and continued, "Now I will tell you that while my usual name is Caelym, I am hoping you will do me the honor of calling me 'Father' or 'Papa'—or, if you wish, 'Ta,' for that is the name that Arddwn gave to me before he could say 'Papa,' and he has used that name ever since out of fondness and affection."

◆◆◆

Too overcome with relief to be annoyed with Caelym's speech-making, Annwr stayed sitting in the grass, drinking in the sight of Aleswina hugging Lliem and rocking him in her arms.

If she'd ever admitted to having disappointment in Aleswina—which she never would have—it would have been the girl's apparent inability to care for anyone besides Annwr herself. Caelym, of course, would have added that to his reasons to disparage the innocent child who'd lost her own mother so young, but now the womanly warmth Annwr had always hoped Aleswina had inside her seemed to flow out and swirl into a warm cocoon that enveloped her and the younger of Caelym's sons. It was a moment she would keep in her heart to her dying day, one that pulled all the more on her heartstrings because Caelym had never thought to mention that Lliem had curly red hair just like Cyri's.

She would have been glad to have that moment last forever, but moments never do. Blinking back the tears that burned her eyes and swallowing the lump in her throat, Annwr got to her feet and herded the lot of them off the road and into the cover of the underbrush.

Once they were safety out of sight of any passing travelers, she explained what they would to do next, speaking in English so that little Lliem would not feel left out.

"Now that we are all together"—here, Annwr couldn't help putting out her hand to stroke each of the boys on their cheeks—"we can go back across the bridge and up the road to where we left our packs. From there, we will have to find a road or track that will take us to Llwddawanden without going through Derthwald." She intentionally left out anything about finding a convent for Aleswina, hoping that Caelym would see how unnecessary that was.

If she'd been paying closer attention, she would have noticed that—although he was making small, agreeable-sounding grunts and nodding his head as she spoke—Caelym's eyes were fixed on the bushes behind her in an unfocused gaze, suggesting that his mind was somewhere else.

Chapter 44

No Unnecessary Risks

hile Caelym was looking down from the ridge top, he'd had time to survey the features of the lands below him. His map was in the bag Annwr had taken from him and given to Aleswina, but he could see its every detail in his mind—the coiled dragon in the upper left corner, the three giants towering over snow-capped mountains, the dancing figure of a man with a stag's antlers leading the line of woodland creatures along the side of river, and the maiden standing at the edge of the lake, waving farewell. He had, of course, always understood that the greatest value of the map was in its symbolism, all of which was now clear.

He himself was the dancing man. The badger (an animal known equally for its bad temper and fierce defense of its young) nipping at his heels was Annwr. The two fox cubs skipping after the badger were Arddwn and Lliem. And the maiden waving good-bye to them all was Aleswina.

Caught off guard by the unexpected twinge of regret that accompanied this last realization, Caelym was, for one brief moment, cast back through time to the day Herrwn unrolled the map before him.

He'd been seated then, as he was now, with his knees drawn up—tense, poised to spring into action. It had been three days since the horrific events of the winter solstice. On the verge of leaving to search for his sons, he'd come to the classroom, the place that had been the center of his world during his years in training for the priesthood, to receive his teacher's blessing for his quest and to hear any final words of wisdom Herrwn might have for him.

The room's shelves, once brimming with sacred vessels and paraphernalia, were stripped bare. Only a handful of embers glowed among the last of the coals in its hearth. Herrwn had a heavy woolen shawl layered over his winter cloak and there was a bluish tinge to the tips of his fingers. They'd sat at the intricately inlaid table where Caelym had eaten his boyhood meals, the parchment spread out between them.

"Any quest," Herrwn told him, "is as much about overcoming the flaws within yourself as climbing mountains or slaying dragons."

Keenly aware of his teacher's penetrating scrutiny, Caelym looked long and hard at the three giants leering down at his illustrated self, assuming they represented the three flaws—pride, impulsiveness, and craving attention—he'd battled all his life.

He had not considered lust.

As a priest in the service of the goddess of fertility, Caelym did not view lust as a flaw—at least, not so long as his erotic passions were exclusively directed toward Feywn, as they had been from the first time he'd seen her passing by, swathed in shimmering robes so finely woven they were almost transparent.

Shaking his head to dismiss any feeling about Aleswina other than a benevolent concern for her welfare, Caelym returned his attention to the broad plain beyond Benyon's manor. Forced to conclude that Herrwn's map, for all its insights into his spiritual journey, was of no help in picking out what route to take through the maze of tracks and trails below him, Caelym had traced what seemed like the most promising way—a path that appeared to have good coverage of brush for most of its course, and which skirted a sinister cluster of barricaded buildings and came close to the edge of the forest before veering off to join a wider road to the east. He'd just finished committing the last of its several bends and turnoffs to memory when the front door of Barnard's manor swung open.

Now, torn between elation at having his sons back and fury at knowing what they had suffered, Caelym was only half listening to Annwr's nattering about going to get the packs.

It took him a moment to realize she'd finished and was waiting for some answer from him. Setting Arddwn down, he raised his dagger so that it shone in the afternoon sunlight, proclaiming, "We will go nowhere before justice is done. I will go and do it and will return with the traitor's head as a trophy."

Except for Arddwn, who jumped up and down and yelled, "Yes, Ta! Yes! I'll go too! I'll hit him and I'll kick him, and then you can cut him up in pieces!" the response to his valiant declaration was disappointing.

Annwr snorted, "And just how stupid do you think he's going to be? You think he'll unbar the door and invite you in to cut his throat?" while Aleswina whimpered, "Oh, Caelym, no! You mustn't! I think he's repented! He gave me both boys and all of the money he had and says he loves Jesus!"

None of this would have stopped Caelym if he hadn't seen Lliem shrinking away from him, terrorized by his rage. Sheathing his knife, he turned to Annwr and asked in a soft voice what she thought they should do—meaning, what she thought they should do to wreak vengeance on Benyon.

Missing his point completely, she went back to talking about going through the village and over the bridge to get their packs.

Caelym had no intention of ever again setting foot in that accursed village, where everyone had known what his sons were suffering and no one had lifted a hand to help them. As to crossing back over the bridge, risking his sons being recaptured just to get packs that were too heavy to carry on the long and arduous path that lay ahead—there was as much chance of that as of him dousing himself with honey and spending the night in a bear's den.

Mistaking Caelym's silence for assent, Annwr looked around for the staffs and bowl. In the rush to get to Aleswina and the boys, she must have left them on the bluff. Rather than climb the hill herself—and leave Caelym unwatched—she sent him to get them, breathing a sigh of relief to see him stride up the trail with Arddwn scrambling after him and then smiling when they came marching down, Arddwn proudly thumping the smaller of the staves into the ground exactly as Caelym was thumping the larger one.

It was all going much better than she expected. She gave another relieved sigh, then said, "Well, we'll be off, then, and if anyone in the village asks about the boys being with us, we'll say—"

"There will be no need to say anything, as we are not going back through the village, we are going *that* way."

Caelym—who seemed to have forgotten what Annwr had explained, or else hadn't been listening when she said it—was pointing straight across the plain to mountains that were fading into a dark blur in the rapidly failing light.

Clearing her throat to be sure she had his full attention this time, she repeated, a little louder, "We have to go back to get our packs. From there, we can follow the river through the woods and then—"

"We have no need of the packs and will not risk going back to get them. I have chosen the path we will take. We will start as soon as it's dark, so we can travel without being seen. Meanwhile, there is time for me to . . ." Caelym glanced at Lliem and went on in a mild tone of voice, "make a brief visit to the manor down the road and repay its proprietor for the tending he has given to my sons."

Loath to argue in front of the boys, Annwr moderated her tone as well. "As much as you may wish to settle your account with your loyal and trusted servant . . ." Fully intending her dig to remind Caelym that his judgment was hardly what they should go by, she allowed a long, significant moment to go by before finishing, "We must take no unnecessary risks, especially as we now have your sons' safety to consider."

By the time she realized she'd stepped directly into the trap Caelym had set for her, it was too late—he'd already burst out, "Oh, Annwr, most excellent of midwives, whose wisdom and counsel are my guiding light in this dark and dangerous world, I see how right you were in saying we must take no unnecessary risks, especially as we now have these boys' safety to consider, and I know you will agree that we will do nothing so reckless as returning through an enemy town or crossing over that watchfully guarded bridge for the sake of a few blankets and a cooking pot."

Annoyed with herself for being tripped up by what she should have recognized as a ploy, Annwr sputtered, "Our packs have no more than the bare necessities for the journey ahead of us.

Without them, what will we do for drinks and food? How do you propose we cook our meals and keep warm at night?"

"I will hold my sons to keep them warm," Caelym shot back. "We will drink water from streams, catch fish for food, and roast them without the need for a pot."

"And how will you light the fire without a flint?"

"We have my satchel. Did you think that I traveled to your door without flint or tinder?"

"And do you think that is all we will need? Your sons are dressed in rags! What in your satchel will serve to make them clothes, or—"

She was cut off as Caelym spread his arms out as if he were invoking deities of the forests and rivers to answer her question. Then, with flourish of his finger and a toss of his head, he undid the ties of his robe, lifted it off his shoulders, and swirled it around him. Shifting it from one hand to the other, he twirled it lower as he sank to his knees and let it settle in a semi-circle on the ground. Then he held one hand out to Aleswina, saying, "My bag, if you please."

Clearly dazzled by the display, Aleswina shifted Lliem to one side, slipped the bag off her shoulder, and gave it to Caelym.

Arddwn crouched down at the edge of the cloak, and Lliem loosened his grip on Aleswina's neck to watch.

Annwr pursed her lips. Of course he was putting on a show to impress the boys—but with no way to stop him without appearing to be contrary, she joined Aleswina and the boys as they gathered around Caelym's cape and watched him set his satchel down between his knees, unlace the straps, and slip his hand inside.

In a theatrical gesture, Caelym pulled out the bags Aleswina had gotten from Barnard and opened first one then the other, spilling a stream of glittering coins onto the cloak.

As the gold and silver disks flowed out, his eyebrows rose.

So Aleswina was right. Benyon had "repented," and—believing her to be the servant of a Christian priest—must be sending this trove in lieu of confessing his sins. That, to Caelym's mind, merely added insult to injury, since his sins had been against Druids and were not a matter over which any Christian priest had authority!

At this added affront, his rage, along with his resolve to exact vengeance, returned.

He was about to say as much to Annwr, when, in the final spatter of coins, a circular silver ornament fell onto the top of the heap.

While it was roughly the size and shape of a mid-size coin, this was no crudely struck token of exchange, but a perfectly round disk inlaid with gold in the shape of an oak tree, so skillfully executed that each tiny branch and each infinitesimal leaf was distinct.

It was a one-of-a-kind object, and Caelym recognized it instantly as the centerpiece from a necklace he had carried reverently in his hands as his sacred offering to the Goddess at the spring equinox when he was seventeen. As he reached out, picked it up, and felt its cool, smooth surface between his fingers, he knew he was holding the answer to the mystery of where Benyon had come by his vast wealth.

The seething rage that had risen in his breast receded, leaving only a sense of regret that he wasn't going to have the satisfaction of wringing Benyon's neck or cutting out his liver. The wretched fool had robbed the sunken trove of the Goddess Herself, and by that act he had surely doomed himself to a fate worse than a mortal could devise for him. She had, no doubt, merely held back the dread force of her fury until Arddwn and Lliem were out of harm's way.

With that heartening thought, Caelym added the gold and jewels from Aleswina's pouch to the pile of coins and flashed a smile in Annwr's direction.

A grim look on her face, Annwr answered his unspoken challenge with a sharp retort. "A great wealth we have indeed, only we cannot cook gold or eat emeralds."

Equally adamant that they would take the path he chose, Caelym scooped up a double handful of coins and let them trickle out from between his fingers. "Nor would we risk our teeth trying. I think, however, this will buy such food and clothes as we need, with some to spare. Especially"—he offered a sweeping bow to the bedazzled Aleswina—"as we will have 'Codric' to barter for us."

With that, he turned his attention to separating the gold from the silver and the jewels from the coins and scooping the piles back into their respective sacks.

◆◆◆

Seeing Aleswina beam with pride at Caelym's flattery, Annwr thought again how like Rhedwyn he was. She gave a snort, shook her head, and grumbled, "It may be days before we find a village with a market. What about tonight? Would you leave these poor babies shivering with no more than rags to wear and their little feet bare and bruised?"

But before she could finish saying—again—that they needed the supplies she had in her packs, Arddwn stamped one of his bare and bruised feet and yelled, "I'm not a baby! Lliem's a baby!"

Speaking his first words since his rescue, Lliem shouted back, "I am not a baby!"

"You are too!" Arddwn retorted. "You're always cold! I never am!"

"You are too cold!" Lliem sputtered. "You said so yesterday! And you were crying!"

From there the brothers' exchange spiraled, Arddwn screeching, "I never cry! You're the one who was crying!" and Lliem bawling, "I was not!"

"You were too! See, Ta?" Arddwn stamped his foot again for emphasis as he pointed to the tears that were beginning to spill down Lliem's cheeks. "I told you he's a stupid, crying baby!"

"I am not!"

"You are too!"

"Am not!"

"Are too!"

Having grown soft from fifteen years with the unnaturally well-behaved and always amenable Aleswina, Annwr was at a loss to stop the squabble she'd inadvertently set off. Caelym, however, had spent a good part of those same years taking care of his younger cousins and saw the row between Arddwn and Lliem as a mere bit of friendly banter compared with the epic five-way quarrels he'd had to referee on a regular basis. Taking advantage of a moment when Arddwn was drawing his breath and Lliem was wiping his eyes, he cut their spat short.

"Now hush, you both! I will not hear such discord between my two brave and grown-up sons who have stood together against a cruel foe and will always be each other's staunchest ally!"

"And," he added, to Annwr's surprise, "if Annwr, who is your mother's beloved sister, says that you must have warm clothes to wear and shoes for your feet, then that is how it must be!"

While Arddwn and Lliem were trying to work out whether they'd just been praised or admonished, Caelym got to his feet, took off his tunic and slipped it over Arddwn's head. Following suit, Aleswina put the tunic she'd been wearing on Lliem, and belted it so it wouldn't trip him.

"There," said Caelym, "now you both have a warm garment, and soon you will have new shoes for your feet. So, sit you down here."

As he spoke, Caelym pointed to a nearby log. Arddwn vaulted into place. Lliem tugged on Aleswina's hand, and she led him over to sit next to his brother. The two boys leaned forward to see what Caelym would pull out of his pack next. Their faces fell when he held up a single rolled-up piece of leather.

"This is not an ordinary piece of leather, my sons." Caelym declared as if they'd spoken their disappointment out loud. "See," he unrolled the sheet revealing a smooth surface embossed with cryptic figures, "it is inscribed with sacred symbols to defend the healing instruments that I lay upon them from the demons of fevers and festering. Now these same emblems will protect your feet from blisters on the long journey ahead."

"But how?" Arddwn asked.

"I will show you." Caelym reached back into his satchel, got his healer's kit, and took out a knife, a needle, a spool of suturing thread and the pouch of sheep's wool he kept for sopping up the ooze from draining lesions. He sliced off four thin strips from the edge of the sheet and cut the remaining piece into two larger and two smaller parts. Then, taking up each of the boys' feet in turn, he fitted and folded the leather into booties, cushioned the bottoms with a layer of wool and sewed up the sides. Finally, he punched holes for the laces, threaded them through, and tied them in neat bows at the top.

Sewing was not a talent Annwr would have credited Caelym with, but she had to give a grudging nod as he finished and stood up, saying, "And there you have your shoes!"

Arddwn leaped off the log and shouted, "Now I can really run!" before dashing up the side of the bank and jumping down, landing with a resounding thud and a grin on his face. Lliem stayed where he was, holding his feet out straight in front of him and looking wide-eyed at them. The boots were the first thing he ever remembered having that was new and just for him, and he didn't want to get them dirty, so he drew his knees up and raised his arms to Aleswina, silently pleading for her to pick him up.

She did, and, with the sun setting and Annwr resigned to abandoning their packs, the small group was ready to go.

Chapter 45

Follow Me

It was the first part of their path that worried Caelym the most. Once they got back to the forest, they just needed to follow the river as far as the start of canyons and, from there, cross over a few mountain ridges to find the place marked on Herrwn's map by the sleeping dragon where Feywn and the rest were waiting—hopefully having found a convent for Aleswina along the way.

But to get to the forest they had to skirt around Welsferth, making their way along patrolled roads and through the farmed lands, and for that they needed the cover of darkness. It was only when the sun was fully set that he picked up the repacked bag and said, with more confidence than he actually felt, "Well, then, it is time to go. Follow me and keep absolutely silent until I say it is safe to speak again!"

Lliem nodded and bit down on his lower lip. Arddwn looked like he was on the verge of saying something, but he caught his father's stern glance and clamped his teeth together.

With his satchel over his left shoulder and his staff in his right hand, Caelym pushed through the underbrush and started down the road. Arddwn followed after him, and Aleswina, hugging Lliem to her chest, followed Arddwn. Annwr clutched her staff and brought up the rear as they crept along the side of the road in single file, making no more noise than a snake slithering through dry grass.

Counting to himself, Caelym took the third turnoff on the right past the three oak trees. From there they followed a narrow lane that veered northward and away from the village proper, and only once had to duck into the bushes and wait as a trio of men heading home from the Spotted Hound staggered past singing a bawdy song suggesting that the Virgin Mary had been no better than she ought to be. After the raucous (and to Caelym's highly trained ears, painfully off-key) lyrics faded around a bend, he started on again, leading the group across a footbridge that creaked under their feet and tiptoeing past hedges and gates until they came out through a stand of muttering aspens where the track disappeared into a dark expanse of fields and pastures.

"We must wait here for moonrise." Annwr's voice came from behind Caelym, sounding so much like Feywn it took him a moment to gather the courage to stand his ground.

"We will go now, with the darkness blinding our enemy and shielding us from them!"

"So then we will stumble around, blind ourselves, getting lost and going in circles?"

"I have traveled on darker nights than this without getting lost or going in circles!" Before Annwr could make any unkind rejoinder about the night she'd found him wandering wounded and directionless not so long before, Caelym added, "I promised that I would see you safely returned to our people, and I will. You need do no more than follow where I lead!"

With that, Caelym drew in a breath of the brisk night air. Willing himself to become a creature of the wild, untroubled by human qualms and misgivings, he plunged forward, exchanging thought for impulse and deliberation for instinct.

As he picked his path along the crisscrossing trails, Caelym's senses grew sharper. Peering ahead with narrowed eyes, sniffing the air at each branch in the road, he might have been a wolf stalking its prey, if a wolf could walk upright on two legs. The wind coming from the northwest carried the scent of the forest and drew him unerringly through the web of intertwined cattle tracks to the road that separated the planted fields and grazed pastures from the edge of the forest, which loomed up on the far side of a flat expanse of low-growing brush.

Out of breath from dashing after him, Annwr gasped, "Wait—we should wait for more light. The moon will be up soon!"

"It will, and that is why we must go now," Caelym answered in a low growl. "We have just this one meadow to cross to reach the forest, and the path is straight before us, but the grass will give us no cover and it is here above all we must go in the dark."

Coming back to himself, he was relieved to realize they'd reached the entrance to the trail he'd seen from his vantage point on the ridge top—a narrow track running more or less directly to the forest across what had appeared from that distance to be a broad green field—but was actually a bog known locally as Fernley's Fen.

PART VI

Fernley's Fen

If Caelym had been better informed about the annual cycle of pasturing sheep, he would have been more suspicious of any ground that green that early in the year that wasn't being grazed. As it was, he mistook the marsh for a meadow and assumed the path leading across it was a safe shortcut to the forest.

In the drier months of late summer and early fall, the track through Fernley's Fen was passable—at least in the daylight—and was a popular route for local men going to the river to fish. Even then, however, they traveled in twos or threes and carried ropes in case any of them made a misstep off the path and into the mire, which had been known to suck a struggling ox down in a matter of minutes. This early in the year, they took the longer path that circled around the west end of the boggy expanse. None of them would have attempted crossing it, as Caelym planned to, in the wettest part of the year and the darkest part of the night.

Caelym, however, was only glad to have just this last bit of what looked like easy terrain between him and the safety of the forest. And as none of the others had any sense of where they were or what might lie ahead of them, they fell back into a line and followed him down the track into the marsh.

Chapter 46

Frogs

ounting on his ears as much as his eyes to guide him through the dark, Caelym started forward. As they made their way along the narrow track, the sounds of domestic life—the lowing of cattle and barking of dogs—dwindled and were replaced by the sounds of owls hooting, nighthawks screeching, and frogs croaking.

A lot of frogs.

Their chorus grew louder and was almost deafening, swelling up on both sides of the path and directly in front of them.

Caelym stopped mid-stride. His staff made a splash as it came down ahead of him and a sucking sound as he stepped back and pulled it out of the mire.

Arddwn, who'd been following on Caelym's heels, bumped into him.

Aleswina, still carrying Lliem, bumped into Arddwn. Annwr, who'd been hurrying to keep up, bumped into Aleswina.

"What is it?" she hissed and was about to step around to see what the problem was when Caelym hissed back, "Do not move!"

Crushed together, Annwr, Aleswina, and Arddwn stood wobbling in place.

Keeping his weight on his left foot, Caelym slid his right out to the side and felt it hit water almost at once. He eased his foot back, shifted his weight, and slipped his left foot out to the side—water lapped there as close, or closer.

He could already feel himself sinking as the ground beneath him was turning to mush, and water was beginning to creep over the top of his weight-bearing foot.

"What's wrong, Ta? Why aren't we going?" His tone wavering between crankiness and apprehension, Arddwn added, "My boots are getting wet!"

Caelym had made it a rule never to lie to his children, but at the moment the only truth that mattered was that they must not panic and flounder in the dark, so he affected a merry tone of voice as he answered, "Nothing is wrong, Arddwn, only now we are going to play a game, and the first part of the game is that we will turn around."

There was some shuffling and, more worrisome, some squishing sounds, as they did.

Still speaking cheerfully—and quite calmly, given that his right foot was sinking steadily lower, but he didn't dare shift his weight to his left before he was actually ready to start forward—Caelym said, "Now, then, Aleswina will put Lliem down just in front of her."

"Who is Aleswina?" Arddwn asked.

"Aleswina is the name we are calling Codric in our game."

"My boots will get wet!" Lliem whimpered

"My boots are already wet, and they're getting wetter, Ta!" Arddwn was tired of his little brother getting all the attention.

"I will dry your boots for you after we have played our game, but remember the rule that we all do exactly what I say, and what I say is that Annwr will take Lliem's hand, and Lliem will take Aleswina's hand, and Aleswina will take Arddwn's hand, and Arddwn will take my hand, and we will all hold on and not let go. Have we all taken hands now?"

Four "yeses" came in a single voice.

"That is excellent! Now the last part of our game is that Annwr will pull us back the way we came . . . exactly the way we came, not going off the path even a little bit."

By then Annwr understood their predicament. She reached back to take hold of Lliem's wrist and started steadily pacing exactly the way she'd come. Once she started, she didn't stop. Moving as much by the feel of the brush on either side of her skirt as by the dim sight of the gap they'd come through, she pulled Lliem who pulled Aleswina who pulled Arddwn who pulled Caelym.

Until that moment, Caelym wasn't sure whether the extra tug would be enough—or if he'd have to let go and order them on without him.

But it was, and with his right foot freed from the swamp's grasp, he lurched forward and followed the others back to dry ground.

"Is the game over? Do we get a prize?" Arddwn had distant memories of playing games with his father and his cousins, and as he recalled, there were always prizes when they finished.

Annwr—to Caelym's surprise and gratitude—said nothing about how close he'd come to drowning them all, leaving him to answer Arddwn's question as he wished.

"This part of the game is over, Arddwn, and the prize is that I will pretend I am a horse and will carry you on my back from here to the forest."

Forgetting he'd refused to be carried before, Arddwn practically leaped into place and waved triumphantly as Caelym pranced in a circle and neighed.

Lliem looked wide-eyed at their display, then turned his face up to Aleswina. Aleswina turned to Annwr, who helped with lifting him up. Once he was secure, she managed a few awkward hops and even tried to imitate Caelym's horse noises, making what Caelym would joke later was a "whiney whinny." Lliem joined in with a gaspy, giggly sound—his first laughter in two years.

Caelym might have made a longer romp of it, only Annwr pointed to the silvery glow that was spreading upward above the eastern horizon. Seeing that, Caelym gave a horse-like shake of his head, declared, "We must ride swiftly now in search of our stable for the night!" and set off down the road.

Chapter 47

Real Horses

The moon was midway up the horizon when they reached the next branch in the trail. The left-hand track—the one that Caelym guessed and hoped would take them around the edge of the marsh and into the forest—dropped abruptly down an incline and into a morass of grass and brush. Again, Annwr had her doubts, wanting to keep to the road they were on, which was admittedly more exposed but was high and dry—and empty, as far as they could see ahead.

The debate between them took place in complete silence. Caelym edged to the left and looking meaningfully toward the silhouette of treetops just visible across the expanse of ferns and gorse, while Annwr lowered her eyebrows and looked down at Caelym's soggy sandals.

Their stalemate was broken when Lliem whispered, "I hear horses! Real horses!"

Before Arddwn could say that he heard them first, his father had swung him down to the ground, and Annwr had grasped hold of his hand and was pulling him after her down the track toward the woods.

Caelym tried to take Lliem off Aleswina's back but couldn't break the stranglehold he had around her neck, so the three of them descended the first steep section of the path together, with Caelym gripping his arms around Aleswina to steady her and keep her upright. Once they reached level ground, he let her go, and she raced after Annwr.

On the verge of dashing after them, Caelym stopped. He didn't have his healer's bag or his staff and, except for holding onto Arddwn, Annwr had been empty-handed too. He dropped to his belly and wormed his way back up to the road, intent on retrieving the satchel and the staves before the oncoming riders saw them. The sound of the galloping horses grew louder as he got to the top. Pressed flat against the ground, he could feel the pounding of their hooves and knew that any moment they'd come over the rise. The satchel and one of the staves were close enough that he was able to grab them without leaving the cover of the brush. The other pole lay farther off and was practically pointing to the trail's entrance. He lunged forward, seized the end of it, and scrambled back into the underbrush—pulling the tip out of sight just as the horsemen thundered past.

Still keeping his head down, he tucked his bag under one arm and the staves under the other before scuttling, crab-like, down the slope and across the meadow, not straightening up until he reached the cover of the trees.

"You could have been—" Annwr gasped as she brought Aleswina and the boys out of hiding.

"But I wasn't!" he handed over her staff and added, "now if you will follow me." Buoyed with the satisfaction of having successfully dodged disaster, he started jauntily off, leading the way into the forest.

If he'd been alone, Caelym would have walked on through the night, breathing in the scent of pine and reveling in the bright dots of the moonlight that danced along the trail ahead of him. But with the women and children to think of, he had to find a safe place to stop and rest—preferably, a place where he could set a fish trap to catch their breakfast.

As if in answer to his thought, the path took a dip into a ravine and wended its way downward, coming to the edge of a fast-flowing stream. The main trail went straight into the water—meaning, most likely, that it could be forded. Realizing that it would be safer not to suggest to Annwr that they attempt another risky crossing in the dark, Caelym took the side track along the bank.

Chapter 48

Merna's Gift

It had been a long journey, especially for Lliem, and the splashing and splattering of the water rushing past reminded him of something important.

"Can we speak now?" Lliem hesitated, and then, in a timid whisper, added, "Ta?"

"We can, my beloved son," Caelym answered solemnly. "And you may say anything you wish to me, and I will endeavor to answer you to the fullest extent of my training and knowledge."

Lliem opened his mouth, only to close it again.

Caelym knelt down to his eye level and asked softly, "So what is it, then, that you would like to say to me?"

"I need to pee."

Hearing this, Arddwn knew there was no time to lose.

"He has to go right now, Ta, or else he'll wet all over himself."

"I will not!" Lliem squealed, hopping tensely from one foot to the other.

"He will too! And I have to go with him, because he's afraid of the dark!"

"I am not!" Liam squeaked again, but not too loudly, because he really didn't want to go into the bushes by himself, and he did need to pee and couldn't hold it much longer.

Caelym rose up and held out his hand. "Of course, you are not afraid. But we all must void sometime, so now we men will go together into the privacy of the bushes on the right side of the path, leaving the bushes on the left for the women to use as they will."

Annwr grunted and made for her side of the bushes. Aleswina was going along when Arddwn pointed at her, shocked, and sputtered, "He can't go over there! He's a boy!"

Before any of the others could explain about Aleswina being in disguise, Lliem (who was proud that for once he knew something his older brother didn't) announced, "She is not a boy." He paused for effect before declaring, with a dramatic flourish that proved he was indeed Caelym's son, "She is a goddess!" Then, with one hand firmly clasped over his crotch, he rushed into the bushes.

At that, Caelym caught hold of Arddwn's hand and pulled the confused youngster along, leaving the two women to their own affairs.

◆◆◆

When the necessities had been attended to and they were getting ready to go on, Arddwn stared at Aleswina. "So her name is really Aleswina, not Codric?"

Caelym had enough experience with children to know that to tell the boys Aleswina's name was a secret they must never reveal was to guarantee that one or both would announce, "Her name *isn't* Aleswina," at the worst possible moment. Thinking swiftly, he said, "Goddesses take many forms, each of which has its own name. The name for this goddess in this form is . . ." Here he paused, trying to think of a fitting name, as names are of grave importance and to rename even a Saxon was no small matter.

"I know! I know! It's 'Ethelwen'!" Lliem piped up, remembering the name of the goddess who saved a hero in a somewhat garbled story Arddwn had told him when they were locked in Barnard's woodshed. "Ethelwen," he repeated in a whisper as he looked up at Aleswina, his face bright in the light of the moon.

Less interested in names than in getting something to eat, Arddwn changed the subject. "Can we catch our fish now, Ta?"

"We must find a clearing and make our camp, and then I will show you how to set a trap in the river, and in the morning, we will have fish for our breakfast."

Disappointed because he was hungry now and morning was a long way off, Arddwn grumbled "Yes, Ta," and followed Caelym along the trail, occasionally kicking a stone off the path.

The clearing they found was not particularly inviting. It was surrounded by thorn bushes and there was an eerie formation in the center that turned out to be a stunted trio of dead cedars leaning into each other, their upper branches tangled together, and their long-shed needles piled in a forlorn heap between them.

Still disgruntled over Caelym's refusal to go back for their packs, Annwr grumbled, "There is a stack of firewood," when Caelym pointed to the skeletal trees and announced, "There is our shelter for the night."

"To one who has lived a year in the wild, they are more than that," he answered back, sounding irritatingly cheerful.

It was on the tip of Annwr's tongue to remind him he'd only been gone from the shrine for six months, but she held the retort back, crossed her arms, and watched while he made an elaborate show of evoking the good-will of the wood spirits and got to work.

He stripped the dry branches off the trunks up to where they meshed together and by hanging his cloak around them, created a serviceable three-sided tent. In spite of herself, Annwr was impressed, so when he turned to her and bowed, she nodded in approval and sent him off with the boys to build their fish trap. Then she crawled inside the shelter to smooth the pile of pine needles and spread her apron over them to make their bed for the night. With that done, she and Aleswina worked together to finish setting up camp, clearing away the dead leaves and broken twigs from around the tent before they scraped out a fire pit in front of the shelter's open side.

Worn out from the day's exertions, Aleswina hadn't said anything as she'd helped Annwr finish setting up the campsite. Hungry as well as exhausted, she stared at the crackling campfire and sighed. "Won't there be any fish in Caelym's trap tonight?"

"Never mind him and his fish trap, Dear Heart," Annwr answered, "look what we have here."

With all that had gone on since Caelym dashed headlong out of the Spotted Hound, Annwr hadn't had time to pull out the pouch with the supplies that the inn's Christian cook had given her. The woman had not only refused any payment but had also added a goatskin filled with the inn's best mead "to warm your souls on your holy mission."

At the time, Annwr had salved her conscience over accepting the cook's gifts under false pretenses with the rationalization that Caelym was a priest and she was a priestess, and the trek to their shrine was just as righteous a journey as any Christian pilgrimage. Now, she emptied a pile of dried apple slices, a round of hard cheese, and three fat sausages into their wooden bowl and began cutting the cheese and sausages into sections with no qualms whatsoever.

Even as a little girl Annwr had liked to see food presented so it was attractive to look at, and she wanted to make the boys' meal a special treat, so she took even more than her usual care— stacking the wedges of cheese into a miniature mountain in the center of the bowl, laying the slices of sausage around the cheese, and arranging the dried apples like a circle of crescent moons in a ring around the border. She put enough mead into her water pouch to sweeten their evening drink without making it too strong for the boys and hung the pouch from a stick propped up near the edge of the fire so it would be warm for them when they returned to camp.

Chapter 49

The Squirrel

Arddwn had given up on the idea of getting anything to eat that night. He'd had several long drinks of water from the stream and peppered his father with questions about anything he could think of to keep his mind off food. By the time the fish trap was finished, he'd found out the reason the moon changed shape, why owls hoot at night, quite a bit about the mating habits of frogs, and had almost completely suppressed his hunger pangs.

Those pangs surged back, however, at the sight of the bowl piled high with sausage, cheese, and slices of dried apples that Annwr held out in both hands as he pushed his way through the thorn bushes and into the camp. He started forward, eager to have something to eat that wasn't the kitchen waste: gristle that had already been chewed, rinds with nothing good left on them, and leftover peelings that Barnard had divided between him and Lliem and his pigs—with the pigs getting by far the better share.

"Before we partake of this unexpected feast," Caelym put a restraining hand on Arddwn's shoulder, "we must give our thanks and pay our tribute to the guardian spirits of this place and the forest creatures who make this glen their home."

"Why, Ta?" Arddwn's voice had a distinct whine to it. There wasn't enough food in the bowl for them and the forest creatures too, besides which no guardian spirit had done anything for him during any of that time he'd been slaving away at Barnard's manor, and he didn't see why he should share his newfound bounty—or his father's attention—with them.

"Patience, my son," Caelym cautioned. "We will eat soon, only first we will honor our hosts who have so generously allowed us to share their home."

"Yes, Ta," Arddwn muttered, scuffing his boot in the dirt.

With the possibility of malevolent spirits hovering nearby, listening to their every word, Caelym could hardly explain to his disappointed son that any spot as grim and bleak as this one was certain to be inhabited by the most ill-tempered of local denizens, and so they had to be especially generous in their offerings. Recalling *The quicker the invocation's begun, the sooner the chanting is done,* a rhyme that Olyrrwd, the least orthodox of his three childhood teachers, had whispered in his ear when he was Arddwn's age and complaining that it was too nice a day to spend inside learning chants, he gave Annwr a quick bow and scooped up a handful of apple slices to lay out as tribute.

What Caelym didn't know was that Arddwn loved dried apples, because they were the sweetest-tasting things he'd been able to steal out of Barnard's pantry, and he wasn't about to let some stupid sprite have them all.

As thin and malnourished as they were, Arddwn and Lliem would have been worse off (and Lliem certainly dead of starvation long since) if Arddwn hadn't learned how to steal food when Barnard's back was turned, so, while Caelym moved from one corner of the clearing to the next, depositing a few slices here and there and singing exaggerated praises for the scraggly thorn bushes and stunted trees, Arddwn trailed along—waiting for his chance to slip over and snatch them when no one was looking.

The site of Caelym's first offering, behind a patch of low-growing brush, was too close to the campfire to try anything, the second; on top of an otherwise bare rock, was too open, but the third, at the base of a tree at the farthest edge of the clearing, was out of sight. Once Caelym finished that spot's incantation and moved on, Arddwn checked that the coast was clear, then he ducked down and slunk back to get the apples before the sprites did.

He was too late. All but one of the apple slices were gone. Before he could get to that one, a squirrel darted down the side of the tree, snatched it, and ran back up the tree to the crook of an upper branch, where it sat, eating Arddwn's apple and chattering at him.

Losing his temper, Arddwn picked up a rock and threw it at the squirrel as hard as he could and almost hit it. He picked up a bigger rock and was taking aim when Caelym dashed back and caught hold of his wrist.

"Whatever are you doing, throwing rocks at he who is our host?"

"He took my apples!"

And before Arddwn knew what he was doing, he'd thrown himself on the ground, pounding it with his fists and kicking it and sobbing that it was not fair and he hated the stupid squirrel.

It was more than the squirrel Arddwn hated.

It was his mother sending him away and his father not coming to get him until now, when he'd finished learning English forever ago. It was Barnard beating him and making him eat garbage and locking him in a stinking woodshed. It was having to take care of Lliem, who was always crying and hungry and wetting himself, so Arddwn had to clean him up to keep Barnard from beating him and then having to steal him something more to eat to make him feel better when Barnard beat him anyway. It was being just as hurt and hungry and scared as Lliem but never getting to cry because he was older, and now everybody cared about Lliem and nobody cared about him, and the squirrel got his apples, and he didn't want his father to pick him up and rock him like he was a baby, and he would have told his father to let him go only he was sobbing so hard he couldn't talk, so he just kept flailing and kicking, and his father still didn't let go of him and just kept rocking him until he'd run out of tears and was too exhausted to struggle anymore.

Caelym rocked Arddwn back and forth until his sobs subsided into gasps and hiccups. Then, still clutching him close, he got up and carried him back to the tent where he settled down facing the fire with Arddwn on his lap.

The others, who'd run over when the outburst began, looked around for something to do.

Lliem, who knew how much Arddwn loved apples and also knew how his brother had always given him the best part of everything he stole for them to eat, took all the rest of the slices of dried apple out of the bowl and pressed them into Arddwn's hand. Instead of eating them, Arddwn clutched them in his fist so he could smell them while he was sucking his thumb, forgetting for the moment that only babies sucked their thumbs.

Aleswina picked up the wimple that Annwr had used to cover the bed, warmed it by holding out to the fire, and brought it over to tuck it in around the shaking, shivering boy. Annwr took the skin of mead-flavored water down from where it was hanging and handed it to Caelym. After a while, Caelym nudged Arddwn's thumb out of his mouth and slipped the spout of the water skin between his lips.

The honey-flavored water was the best thing Arddwn could remember tasting in his life—even better than dried apples, although he kept the apples Lliem gave him squished tight in his fist just in case the squirrel tried to take them from him.

Between the mead-tinged water, the warm blanket, and the steady beating of his father's heart against his cheek, Arddwn's pain-filled rage began to slip away, but he still didn't like the squirrel. Taking another swallow of the honey-water, he managed to say, "Why do we have to give (hic) our food to the for- (hic) forest animals. They're (hic) just mice (hic) and squirrels, and I don't care (hic) about them!"

Caelym loosened his grip on Arddwn a bit, shifted his position to look his son in the face, and smiled a smile so loving and proud that the last of Arddwn's anger evaporated in its warmth.

"That, my son, is a very important question! It is a question that the wisest Druids pondered even before the feud began between men and animals. It is a question that I asked when I was much the same age as you are now. And because you are wise enough to ask this question, I will tell you the story that Herrwn, who is greatest of our people's bards, told me then."

"If it's a story that Herrwn told, we'll need something to eat before it's over." Annwr brought the bowl of cheese and sausages over and set it down where they all could reach it.

Caelym waited while they got settled, Arddwn now curled up against his left side, Lliem snuggled between Arddwn and

Aleswina, and Annwr on the end, making sure that everyone was getting enough to eat and drink. Then, when the only sounds were munching noises of the boys chewing their sausages and cheese and the fire crackling, he began to tell the story that Herrwn had told him twenty years before.

Chapter 50

The Horses' Tale

As the disciple of their shrine's chief bard, Caelym had spent his formative years memorizing the hundreds of inter-connected stories, songs, and odes that, taken together, comprised the nine major sagas that lay at the heart of the belief system of the followers of the Great Mother Goddess.

Dismissed by outsiders as fables and fairy tales, those sagas were historical accounts to the Druids of Llwddawanden, and the heroes and villains in them were as important to Caelym as his direct ancestors (which many of the more notable protagonists were said to be).

Besides the divine, semi-divine, and high-born moral char-acters, there were myriad less significant beings—loyal servants, greedy merchants, kindly shepherds, or wily wood spirits—with only minor roles to play. It was the mark of a master bard that even the least important character in the most obscure tale had a unique name and some attribute that gave each of them an added dimension—not enough to distract from the major characters or the central theme, but enough to give depth and color to the story, and sometimes explain a crucial turn of events.

There was no question in Caelym's mind that their shrine's chief bard was numbered among the supreme storytellers of all times, or that "Trystwn and the Great Stallion" (or the "Horses' Tale," as it was usually called)—disregarded by some as merely a minor episode in a larger saga—conveyed an invaluable lesson despite its centering on a lesser sprite whose self-indulgence and lack of consideration for others led to his downfall. Now, looking down at the expectant faces of his two sons, their eyes sparkling in the light of the campfire, he began to tell the story as Herrwn had told it to him twenty years before.

Long ago, in the time before the feud began between men and animals and we could all still talk to each other, there was a herd of wonderful wild horses that lived in a lush green valley high up in the towering mountains. While all the horses in the herd were beautiful, their leader, a great golden stallion, and the stallion's two sons, a silver-gray yearling and a copper-red colt, were the most beautiful of all. The great stallion was not just beautiful, he was also wise and judicious, and under his shrewd leadership the herd prospered and was very happy until a wood sprite named Bervin moved into the valley.

On the day Bervin arrived, the horses were browsing peacefully on the hillside. Looking up and seeing the sprite coming over the top of the rise, they waited for him to approach their great stallion, introduce himself, and ask their permission to make his home in their valley. But he never did. Instead, he went into the middle of the richest meadow in the valley, next to the crystal-clear waters of their favorite drinking pool, and, without saying, "May I?" or "Do you have any objection?" or "By your leave," cut down the beautiful grove of whispering aspen where they rested in the heat of the summer afternoons to build himself a house.

Offended, the great stallion sent his younger son to complain to the sprite about this abuse of their hospitality, but Bervin pretended that he didn't understand horse speech and went on doing whatever he wished.

The next morning, when Bervin went to take a bath in the lake, the water was too cold, so he worked a spell to heat it up. It became so hot that all the fish in the lake were boiled. Bervin saw this and was pleased, since it saved him the trouble of making a fire to cook his breakfast.

Seeing the pool befouled and reeking from the leftover dead fish, the great stallion sent his older son to complain that now they couldn't drink the water, but Bervin didn't care, since he only drank wine brewed from thistle berries, and he threw a rock at the great stallion's son to drive him away.

Later that day, Bervin set out across the valley, look-ing for a place away from the smell of rotting fish to build another house. Flies were swarming and their buzzing bothered him, so he cast a spell that made clouds from the mountaintops gather up snow from the peaks and cover the valley floor in a thick layer of snow that killed all the insects. Since sprites can walk on the softest snow as easily as on solid ground, Bervin continued on his way, heedless of what trouble the snow meant to the horses.

This time the great stallion went himself to complain that his herd was trapped and foundering in the snow-banks, and that they would starve without the summer grass to eat! But Bervin didn't care because he didn't eat grass and didn't see why anyone would—and also because he had magical powers and the horses didn't. He dismissed the great stallion as if he were no more than a common cart horse.

By this time, the entire herd was outraged. They were stamping their feet and gnashing their teeth and crying out for revenge. The great stallion called for calm, reminding them that Bervin was right about one thing—that he had magical powers and they didn't. While true, these words added to the horses' anger, and some of the mares began to mutter amongst themselves that if the great stallion couldn't do anything about the nasty little sprite, then they'd find a stallion that could!

"I will find a way but need some peace and some time to think!" With that, the great stallion galloped away from the herd and up the side of the highest ridge above the valley.

From his lookout, he saw a figure in the distance coming toward the valley's entrance. Not only was the great stallion strong, beautiful, and wise, he also had eyes as sharp as an eagle's. He could see that the distant figure was not any ordinary wanderer but a hero, his golden hair flowing down his shoulders and his shield and armor sparkling in the sunlight.

It was Trystwn, son of the Great Mother Goddess by one of her most beloved mortal lovers, and the great stallion guessed rightly that he was coming to the valley in search of a horse to ride into battle against the giants of the northern mountains.

The great stallion moved so that he was hidden behind the trees and looked out. He watched as Trystwn cut down willow branches to build a pen and worked magic to make it invisible. The great stallion watched and waited until the trap was finished, and then he cantered back to where his herd was gathered and waiting for him.

They expected him to lead them off to safety, but instead the great stallion sent his younger son into Trystwn's trap, telling him that when he was captured, he was to plead for his freedom and promise to send a faster, stronger, and more beautiful horse in his place.

The stallion's younger son did as he was told, and when he pleaded for his freedom, Trystwn made him swear an oath that he would do as he promised and let him go.

Then the great stallion sent his older son into Trystwn's trap, again telling him that when he was captured, he was to plead for his freedom and promise, as his brother had, to send a faster, stronger, and more beautiful horse in his place.

The stallion's older son also did as he was told, and again Trystwn was persuaded to let him go after swearing to keep his promise.

The third time, the great stallion went into the hero's trap himself. When he was captured, he bowed low before Trystwn and pleaded for his freedom, offering to give the hero a faster, stronger, and more beautiful horse in his place. The great stallion was bigger and stronger and more beautiful than any horse that Trystwn had ever seen, so, as he could not believe there was a more wonderful horse anywhere, he demanded that the great stallion show him this steed before he would set him free.

The great stallion, who remained kneeling, told Trystwn to get onto his back. Once the hero was mounted, the great stallion leaped over the trap's invisible gate and landed lightly on the other side, his hooves skipping across the ground. *Together, they rode like the wind across the valley and into a glen where, from behind a thicket of hornberry bushes, they could see Bervin bathing in a steaming pool.*

"That is no beautiful stallion," Trystwn said, dark-faced and angry, "That is nothing but a common, ordinary sprite—and an ugly one at that!"

It was then that the great stallion sprang his trap.

"That is no sprite," he said. "That is my older brother, a golden stallion so beautiful that the Sun himself was jealous and turned him into a homely sprite."

Then the great stallion bit off a hair from his own tail and gave it to Trystwn, telling him to take the hair and use his magic powers to turn Bervin back into a horse—only adding that he must do this in stealth, so as not to let the Sun see what he was doing.

So Trystwn crept to the edge of the pool, keeping down so that he was hidden in the reeds, and he dropped the hair from the chief horse's tail into the water and said his magic words.

Bervin was finishing his bath, and as he rose up out of the water, his neck and arms grew longer, his face stretched out, and his hands and feet turned into hooves, and instead of standing on two legs he found himself on four. Growing tall enough to see over the reeds and the hornberry bush, he realized what was happening, and he tried to say the counter-spell and to curse the great stallion, but he could only neigh and whinny, for he had already turned into a horse that was everything that the great stallion had promised to Trystwn—a steed whose coat was the color of the sun, whose mane and tail were color of the moon, and whose eyes were as blue as the midday sky on a cloudless day, a horse that was bigger and stronger and more beautiful than any horse before or since. And so Trystwn mounted Bervin and rode off to the adventures that waited for him in other stories, leaving the great stallion and his herd to live in peace in their beautiful green valley.

As Caelym finished the story with the admonition Herrwn had spoken to him twenty years earlier—"And so now you must decide for yourself whether you will strive to understand the cares and needs of others or behave as though only your own wishes matter, as did that rude and selfish wood sprite"—Lliem drew in what began as a deep sigh but ended as a soft snore and drifted off into a dream where he and Ethelwen were riding on golden horses with silver wings and galloping up through the tops of trees and into the sky together.

Chapter 51

Family Secrets

𝕬n exceptionally imaginative boy, Lliem had found escape from the misery of his life with Barnard in his dreams—some frightening, some consoling, but no two ever the same.

Arddwn was imaginative as well, but he was weighed down with the responsibility of taking care of his younger brother, and he'd had—with minor variations—one single recurring dream. Every night for the past two years he'd dreamed that his father had come to get him. Sometimes Caelym arrived riding on a horse and sometimes sailing in a boat. Sometimes he came alone and sometimes with an army. Sometimes he led Arddwn and Lliem away playing his harp and dancing and sometimes he put them onto a wagon pulled by two huge oxen. The dream always ended the same way—Arddwn would be walking through the forest with his father and they would be talking, and suddenly he couldn't hear his father's voice anymore, and he'd look around, and Caelym would be gone, and then he'd wake up, still locked in the filthy, rat-infested wood shed.

Now, gripping Caelym's shirt with both hands, desperate to keep his father's voice from stopping, Arddwn asked one question after another about anything he could think of.

◆●◆

For Caelym, who'd been an insatiably curious boy himself, Arddwn's volley of questions was no more than he'd expect of his son and, tired as he was himself, he considered it his duty to answer each one as patiently and as truthfully as he could. The first few—*Why do we have to poop? How are babies born? What happens after we die?*—were easy enough, but as they got closer to more sensitive and challenging matters, Caelym began to feel as though he was stepping his way across a flooding stream on shaky stones. Keeping his voice even, he answered, "The journey ahead of us is long, but we are together now and that is what matters," when Arddwn asked, "How far is it to Llwddawanden?" and "Elderond couldn't be better" when Arddwn asked about his favorite goat, as this was not the time to break the news about slaughtering their entire herd for meat—or to mention that Elderond had been among the tougher and stringier of the provisions they'd had to divide.

Then Arddwn asked, "Is Mother still the Goddess or is it Arianna's turn now?"

"Your mother remains the Goddess." Here Caelym's voice did falter, but only a little, and he kept a calm—or at least a blank—countenance when Arddwn heaved a sigh and said, "Good! Arianna told us she was going to be the Goddess when we got back, and then we would have to do everything she wanted."

Arddwn had been on the verge of losing his battle to stay awake, but he rallied at the recollection of old grievances.

"And she said if we didn't, she was going to make us be consorts to troll-women and live in a bog. It made Lliem cry, but I said I'd rather be a consort to a troll than to her!"

All Caelym said was, "Your mother will be our Goddess for many years to come, and then your dear cousin Cyri will be the Goddess in her turn."

Arddwn's relationship with his older sister had been a rocky one, and her threats hung over his head more than he ever let on. Cyri, on the other hand, had never been bossy like Arianna. She brought treats when she came to visit in the nursery, she let him make up the rules when they played games together, and she never tattled to his nurse about anything he did. After a brief consideration of the new situation, he saw its advantages, and said, "I wouldn't mind being Cyri's consort, even if she is a girl."

◆◆◆

"To be chosen as the consort of so wise and beautiful a priestess as your cousin Cyri is an honor that must be earned."

With this opening, Caelym launched into the lecture he'd received from Herrwn on the day he'd entered his formal training for the priesthood.

"It is my hope you will apply yourself with diligence to your studies of all the wondrous wisdom that has been passed down through all the ages and that someday you will be ready to enter the highest ranks of our sacred order . . ."

Caelym continued the flow of elevated oration in hopes that the words Herrwn had spoken to him twenty years before would have the same effect on Arddwn they had had on him, sending him to off sleep before it was finished (and wondering belatedly whether this had been Herrwn's intention as well).

Watching Arddwn's eyes glaze over and his lids start to droop, Caelym ended in a soft whisper, "And it is my fondest wish that when you have learned all those things and have grown to be a man, your wise and beautiful cousin Cyri will find you worthy to be her consort, and you will know the joy in her service that I have found in your mother's."

For a moment Arddwn's eyelids fluttered open and, in a last flash of wakefulness, he managed to form one final question, "But what about Arianna?"

He fell asleep before he heard the end of Caelym's evasive answer: "When you are older . . . old enough to understand . . . your mother . . . or Herrwn . . . will tell you all that you must know . . ."

As Caelym gazed down at his sons, nestled together like a pair of bunnies in their nest, a shadow fell over him, and he looked up to see Annwr with her arms crossed, her eyebrows lowered, and her lips pinched in a tight line.

She jerked her head in the direction of the stream in a gesture so like her sister's that there was no question in Caelym's mind she meant for him to go with her somewhere "they could talk"—which, of course, meant that she would talk and he would apologize. Just what it was that he was needing to make amends for wasn't clear to him yet, but no doubt it would be soon.

Sighing, he slipped the folds of his tunic out of Arddwn's fingers, got up, and followed Annwr across the clearing, through the thorn bushes, and down the bank to a place just below his fish trap, where the rapidly flowing current dropped into a deep, quiet pool.

Annwr pointed to a flat rock.

Obeying her silent command, Caelym sat, drawing his knees up and making himself as comfortable as he could while he waited to find out what he had said or done that had so upset her.

His answer came in the form of an undeserved reproach: "It does no good to lie to children!"

Dismissing his protest that he didn't lie to Arddwn—and never had and never would—Annwr paced back and forth in front of him, shaking her finger as she spoke.

"You didn't tell him the truth! He asked you about Arianna and instead of telling him what happened to her, you said nothing! She was his sister! He must be told the truth—however painful and sad—so that he may grieve for her, and so that he does not dishonor her memory with childish complaints."

Stopping still and putting her hands on her hips, she finished sternly, "He must hear what happened before we reach Llwddawanden, and he must hear it from you, his father."

Annwr had no patience with family secrets. It was her view that they did far more harm than any truth could, and while she was rarely successful in convincing her inadvertently pregnant patients of that, she meant to have no such nonsense in her own family.

Certainly she could see that whatever had happened to Arianna was painful for Caelym to talk about. As a matter of fact, just how painful it appeared to be made her wonder if his grief at her death had anything to do with how much closer in age he was to Feywn's no doubt stunningly beautiful daughter than to Feywn herself.

But Arddwn and Lliem still deserved the truth. And she meant to accept no excuses from Caelym. She expected he'd wheedle and weasel a bit but would eventually agree, however reluctantly, to be forthright with her and with his sons. She wasn't expecting him to grip his arms around his chest as if he were being struck by a spear . . . or to look up at her as though she'd been the one to hurl it . . . or to say in a voice that might have come from a dying man, "There is nothing to tell. Arddwn had only one sister—the infant girl who died in my arms—and he has never spoken of her except in sorrow. He had no other sister, and Feywn had no other daughter."

Then, gazing up at her with the look of unbearable clarity she had come to associate with those who knew themselves to be on the verge of death, he whispered, "You understand, don't you?"

Annwr did understand, at least in part.

One of the many unquestioned powers of the shrine's chief priestess was her prerogative to impose the ultimate penalty of banishment on any priest or priestess whose wrongdoing exceeded forgiveness or remediation—not just from the shrine but from any acknowledgment of their existence, past or present.

It was a dire edict she'd witnessed only once.

The transgressor was just as tall, just as muscular, just as solid a presence as he had been before Feywn uttered the terse, irrevocable declaration that cast him out of their order and into oblivion, and yet no one in the crowded chamber appeared to see him anymore.

It was not that they turned their heads or even shifted their gaze. It was worse than that. As Feywn began the denunciation, they were all staring at him. When she finished it, there was some barely perceptible change in the focus of their eyes, so they were looking through him, as if the space he filled were empty.

Annwr was standing next to Herrwn and instinctively turned to him for guidance. Herrwn, however, was looking at the engravings on his staff, lost in contemplation.

When she turned back, Labhruinn was still there. If he had looked up then, their eyes would have met, and she might have said something—spoken in his defense or at least pleaded that he be given some food to take with him. He didn't. He just rose from kneeling and shuffled out of the room. For all she'd known then, he might have turned into mist and vanished like the smoke from the candle that had been blown out. She knew better now. If he hadn't starved to death in the forest or been torn apart by wolves or died some other cold, lonely death, he still walked and ate and slept somewhere in the world outside Llwddawanden.

Still, she understood what Caelym couldn't say—that Arianna had been banished. What she did not understand was how Feywn could do that to her daughter, or what wrong Arianna could have done that her mother would deny her very existence.

Annwr no longer believed that being expelled from the shrine meant people disappeared into the ether, and she no longer felt bound by the prohibition against talking about them. It was clear, however, that Caelym did, so when he repeated urgently, "You do understand, don't you?" she answered that she did in the soothing voice she'd use to calm a fretful child and phrased her next question carefully.

"But if Feywn had ever had another daughter . . . one fathered by Rhedwyn . . . and if that daughter were expelled from the shrine, what might she have done to bring this fate upon herself?"

Caelym had dropped his eyes and seemed to be gazing at the reflection of the moon in the otherwise dark pool. He wrapped his arms more tightly around his knees and rocked back and forth so pathetically that Annwr was surprised by the force in his voice when he answered, "If such a daughter had ever existed, she might have betrayed Llwddawanden to our enemies."

Chapter 52

The Last Solstice

C aelym stared into the depths of the pool. Ripples from the upper stream traveled across its surface, breaking up the shape of the half-moon's reflection, stretching it out so it took on the appearance of a ghostly female figure floating under the water. Annwr's questions seemed to come at him from far off in the distance. At first, he didn't see how he could respond, but once she made it clear that they would speak no unspeakable names and say nothing that was forbidden, he heard himself answering her as conscientiously as he had answered Arddwn.

It was the night of the last winter solstice. That night, like every winter solstice night since the founding of their cult, the celebration of the reconciliation between the earth and the sun began with the opening of the main hall of the shrine to the common people—replacing its usual solemnity with revelry as villagers wearing brightly painted masks danced to the music of drums and flutes. The sound of the ram's horn halfway between sundown and midnight signaled that it was time for the priests and priestess to withdraw from the public festivities and prepare to conduct the most important ceremony of the year—the enactment of the time when the first Druids gathered together on the highest mountain in the world, pleaded with the Sun and the Earth to put aside their differences, and convinced the Earth to call the Sun back to Her.

They filed up the stairs to the uppermost chamber of the shrine's highest tower without so much as a candle to light their way. Entering the dark room, they began the ritual by milling around the unlit hearth in what appeared to be random circles but were actually rigidly choreographed dance steps and reciting overlapping lamentations in a portrayal of the despair of human-kind, who feared they would be left to freeze in eternal night.

Gradually, the priests and priestesses took their assigned spots in preparation for the next and most critical phase of the ritual—the recitation of the chants that must be said in precise order and without the slightest deviation to ensure the sun would indeed return this year.

The moon was full that night, making the winter solstice all the more auspicious, but in spite of that, there would have been a growing tension in the chamber as they became aware that the place in the woman's line to the right of Feywn was vacant. There were, as Annwr would recall, seven stanzas that must be chanted by the chief priestess's closest female kin—and this, it went very much without saying, would have been Feywn's daughter, fathered by Rhedwyn, if such a daughter had ever been.

Caelym would have seen Feywn's lips tighten from where he stood but wouldn't have been worried himself because if Feywn had ever had a daughter fathered by Rhedwyn, then that daughter would have been forever coming late to meals and rituals, almost certainly with the express purpose of annoying her mother.

And true to form, at the last possible moment, she would have arrived. Only instead of taking her place in line, she would have stepped into the center of their circle, pulled a silver cross—the disdained symbol of the uninvited and unwelcome Christian god—out from under her robe and thrust it up like a war banner. She would have boasted that she was going to marry a powerful Saxon prince and reign with him over the vast lands around them. Then she would have openly defied her mother—saying that there were no goddesses but only a god, and that god was Jesus! Then, as they all stood frozen in their places, she would have told them that they all must convert as she had done, and never again listen to the sham of a mother goddess.

Feywn would have moved forward, lifting her staff higher than the cross.

Everyone in the chamber would have drawn back—except for Cyri, who would have stepped between the two of them in a vain attempt to make peace.

Not deigning to respond to the vile attack against herself, Feywn would have proclaimed that what they saw before them was a demon in the shape of a woman, sent by their enemies' god. Then she, Feywn, would have begun chanting the chant casting out demons and condemning their mortal manifestations to death.

At that, the demon—as she was revealed to be—would have dropped the cross and drawn her knife, would have grabbed hold of Cyri and used her as a shield as she backed out of the chamber.

He himself would have stood still, stunned and disbelieving, until he heard Feywn's voice ordering him to take up his bow and arrows and go after them.

Knowing she had no chance to escape hampered by a struggling hostage, the demon in woman's form would have hidden behind a pillar at the bottom of the tower stairs and shoved Cyri into Caelym's path as he came out. Cyri would have lurched into him, clinging to his robes as if she were trying to hold him back. He would have broken loose and taken up the chase. Cyri would not have understood. She would have run after them, calling out and pleading with him not to shoot, while his quarry dodged from one hall to the next, out of the shrine through the lower gate, and down the winding path that led to the tunnel through the underground caverns. All along the way, the demon would have been laughing—taunting and teasing him, as though this were nothing more than a game they would have played as children.

He would have reached the end of the tunnel, coming to the mouth of the cave, at the same time that she reached the edge of the pool outside. There, she would have had the choice of taking the path around the edge—making her an easy target against the cliff wall—or diving into the pool that was too wide to swim across without coming up for air.

Trapped but too proud to admit it, she would have turned and looked straight at him, her head held high, her red hair glowing golden in the moonlight, her white ceremonial robes billowing in the cool night breeze—daring him to shoot. Then, almost lazily, she would have lifted her arms and leapt headlong into the pool while he dropped to one knee, fitted his arrow to his bow, and waited.

The night sky was cloudless and there was—had he said it already?—a full moon. The water was so clear that he would have been able to see her lithe, silvery form skimming below the surface.

The echoes of Cyri's cries—pleading with him to hold his fire—would have bounced off the walls of the cavern behind him, growing louder as the shimmering white form rose up to break the surface. He would have drawn back his bowstring and launched his arrow. And then he would have doubled over in agony at what he had done. Cyri, herself racked with grief beyond tears, would have helped him to his feet, and they would have gone the long way back to the uppermost chamber of the shrine's highest tower together. He would have taken his place in the men's line, while Cyri would have stepped into the vacant place at Feywn's right side. When the time came, she would have recited each of the seven vital stanzas as though they'd been her lines from the beginning.

And when the night's ceremonies were complete, the priests and priestesses would have done what they could to fortify the shrine—setting guards at the valley's upper and lower entrances and warning their servants and the villagers to be prepared for the coming attack—before retiring to their chambers to get what rest they could before dawn.

Relieved to be done with the part of his account that required wary circumlocution, Caelym stopped rocking. He wiped an errant tear from his eye and sighed. "When we woke in the morning, it was to find that our servants and laborers had vanished overnight, taking most of the shrine's stores and all of the sheep, leaving only the herd of goats kept for milk and sacrifices—maybe out of fear of stealing animals intended to be tribute to the Goddess, or maybe they just couldn't catch the wily old ram that led the flock and trusted no one except Cyri, who'd made a pet of him years before."

"Even if," he went on, "we could have barricaded our gates against the coming invasion, we could not have withstood a siege. But then, when all seemed lost, Feywn spoke—reminding us of the prophesies of a time when we would leave Llwddawanden and return to Cwmmarwn, our ancestral home. Our hopes restored, we followed her commands. Herrwn drew the maps to guide us. What provisions we had left were gathered and packed. I, as you know, was tasked with finding you and the boys. It was thought safest for the others to travel in four groups, each to be led by a ranking priest or priestess. What hardy men we had left—the last three of the shrine's guards and our metalsmith—were parceled out between the groups like the smoked meat from the slaughter of our remaining livestock."

"Darfwyn lived, then?"

Briefly confused over what time he was in, Caelym looked around. He saw Annwr, now kneeling next to him, and recalled that she'd been carried off before any of the bodies but Rhedwyn's had been brought back to the shrine.

"Not Darfwyn. His son, Darbin, who inherited his father's place at the forge and who, alone of all the shrine's artisans, remained loyal to the Goddess." (Or, at least, to one of her priestesses—there was a story in that, but Caelym needed to finish what he'd started out to say.)

It was just as well Caelym didn't interject another topic while Annwr was grappling first with the realization that they weren't going back to Llwddawanden and then that they were heading off to who knew where, following Caelym's wildly inaccurate understanding of geography and Herrwn's useless map in hopes of somehow stumbling into those groups that had left Llwddawanden when he did. Suppressing a groan, she asked, "And how will we find the others?"

This time, Caelym anticipated her question. "There is an inn, marked by the sign of a sleeping dragon, located at the last valley below the mountains that hide our next sanctuary. It is known to be a safe haven where no one questions other visitors, and there is reason to think that the innkeeper is a secret adherent to our ways. We are to meet there. When all have arrived, we will go on together."

A cloud passed over the moon, and the pool went dark.

Caelym seemed, for the first time since Annwr had known him, to have no words left to say. He sat in the shadows, so motionless that he might have been a shadow himself.

Annwr knew the feeling—and she also knew that sometimes you just go on, whether you see any reason for it or not, so she got up and said firmly, "We are going back to camp now." When he didn't respond, she took hold of his arm, dragged him to his feet, and pointed him in the direction of their makeshift shelter. After he stumbled his way into the tent, she added another log to the fire. Instead of going back to lie with Aleswina, she settled herself next to Caelym, thinking that he was the one who most needed a mother just then.

Chapter 53

Pine Needles And Wood Smoke

he first thing Arddwn was aware of when he woke in the morning was that his clenched fists were empty, and his father was gone. The next was the sensation that he was lying on a warm, dry bed instead of the damp, splintery floor of the woodshed. Teetering between being asleep and awake, he held his breath to keep from losing the last lingering remnants of his dream to the stench of mold and rats' nests and stale pee. But when he couldn't put off breathing any longer, what he smelled was pine needles and wood smoke and roasting fish.

He didn't remember his dream having smells before.

Cautiously, he half opened his eyes and looked out of the tent— *the tent, not the woodshed*—to see five fat fish sizzling on sticks propped over a glowing campfire! If this was a dream, Arddwn wasn't going to waste it. He scrambled up and out of the tent just as Caelym came through the thorn bushes, carrying the refilled water skin in one hand and holding a second string of gutted fish in the other.

Once he'd stumbled back to camp and dropped down next to Arddwn, Caelym had plunged into a deep, dreamless sleep, like a rock dropping to the bottom of a deep, still lake. He'd woken up feeling healed and well—as he had on the morning after his festering arrow wound had been lanced, only then his thoughts had been fuzzy and confused and now they were sharp and clear.

He was on a mission from Feywn to rescue Annwr and recover his sons, and he had done both. Now he just had to take them through the forest and over a few mountains and find the inn with a sleeping dragon carved on its door, where Feywn and the rest were waiting to start on the last leg of the journey to their new sanctuary. So long as getting Aleswina to her Christian convent didn't take them too far out of the way, there was every reason to hope that he would see his sons back in their mother's arms in two or, at most, three weeks.

He eased out from between Annwr and Arddwn, stood up in the tent's doorway, stretched, and drew in an invigorating breath of the fresh forest air before setting off to collect the fish from his weir, meaning to have breakfast ready by the time the others were stirring.

Annwr woke up when Caelym did. Stiff and sore, feeling every year of her age, she got up to stoke the fire.

Cuddled together with Annwr's wimple pulled up over their ears, Aleswina and Lliem slept through the sounds of Arddwn yelling his father's name, only opening their eyes when Caelym called to them to come and get their breakfast, "before Arddwn eats it along with his own!"

No sooner were they out of the tent than Caelym had his cloak pulled off the cedar trunks. In as much a hurry to find a village market as Caelym was to reach his "sleeping dragon," Annwr joined him in doing the little that needed to be done to return the clearing to its natural, desolate state.

After paying perfunctory respects to the local spirits, they left, the cheeky squirrel chattering at them from overhead.

PART VII

Lliem's Story

Lliem would always remember that morning as the beginning of the greatest adventure of his life, and that was how he would begin the story that he would tell his own children many years later.

"But it really began when you and Uncle Arddwn were imprisoned by the horrible ogre, Barnard, and the goddess, Ethelwen, in disguise as a serving boy, came and rescued you!"

Eilwen, the first-born of the twins was a stickler for detail.

"That was last night's story! Tonight, the story will be how they went through the woods and over the mountain and to the fair where they almost got caught by the evil Christian priest!" Edriana made up for the indignity of being a quarter of an hour younger than her sister by disagreeing with everything that Eilwen said.

"Christian priests aren't all evil! There are nice ones!" Eilwen made a point of exerting her seniority by self-righteously parroting their mother's most moralistic admonitions.

"That one was! And he was going to drag Papa off and make him be a Christian!"

"But Papa escaped because he remembered what the trees said!"

Before the bickering between his two equally strong-willed daughters could go on any further, Lliem intervened in the calm but firm voice that Caelym had used to settle the innumerable squabbles he'd had with Arddwn.

"Now hush, you both! This is my story, and so you must listen and let me tell it."

Before either of them could say it was the other one who wasn't listening, he began again.

"*That morning was the beginning of the greatest adventure of my life. After we ate breakfast and thanked the spirits properly, we all followed your grandfather along the bank of the stream until we reached the swift-flowing river, and from there we turned north-wards and traveled through the woods for days and days, living on fish and frogs and wild roots and birds' eggs and even*"—here the girls chimed in, "bugs and slugs!"—"*until we finally came to the place where forest ended and the mountains began, and then we climbed—*"

"Up and up and up," the girls chorused together.

"But you never complained or said that you were tired!" Eilwen spoke up before her sister had a chance and was the one to be rewarded with her father's proud smile as he agreed, "But I never complained or said that I was tired."

This was a story, and, like all stories, the better sections were embellished while the not-so-good ones were left out, but that part was true—Lliem had never complained about being tired. He hadn't needed to, because all he'd had to do was look up and lift his arms and Aleswina had picked him up and carried him. And, of course, there were the other parts that he either forgot or never noticed because he was only five years old at the time.

Chapter 54

Annwr's Rule

Just as the hills and ridges and mountains they'd crossed would all blend into a single long climb in Lliem's memory, their trek through the forest would stretch out longer than the seven days it actually took. Each night, after a supper of whatever they'd been able to catch and gather along the way and after Caelym had told a story, Annwr tucked Aleswina and the boys in for the night, whispering "sweet dreams" to each in turn, as Caelym played his flute and sang soft, sleep-inducing songs.

Once the last of the three, which was usually Arddwn, nodded off, Caelym and Annwr would slip out of their makeshift shelter to debate what to do about Aleswina, a question that got no closer to an answer even though either of them could have repeated the other's side of the argument from memory by then.

While Caelym no longer interspersed his objections to taking Aleswina with them with disparaging remarks about her intelligence or usefulness, he was, if anything, more adamant that she be left behind, "Safe and secure in another convent, where she will not be troubled by her evil cousin's lustful pursuit!"

To which Annwr would snap, "And where is that? I failed to notice the place on Herrwn's map labeled 'The Abbey of Saint Caelym,' where hapless girls are safe from marauding packs of Gilberth's vicious guards!"

"But what you did see were hostile giants and forbidding mountains and a path leading from one danger to the next!" Caelym would sigh. "Is that the fate you wish on her?"

"That is the fate she would choose for herself if you deigned to ask her!"

"She has not the"—and here Caelym had come to insert "age or experience" in place of "wit or understanding"—"to make that choice!"

"Neither do Arddwn and Lliem, and yet you make that choice for them! Why not find them a Christian monastery and leave them behind, 'safe and secure'?"

"Because they are not Christian, and she is!"

From there the dispute would run its course, with Caelym insisting that he was only thinking of Aleswina's safety, and Annwr contending that it wasn't safe to leave her alone and defenseless when his own experience proved that Gilberth's guards had no compunctions about raiding convents in their search for her.

"Then she must learn to defend herself!"

"And I suppose you will teach her that!"

"I will, for you have not!"

"Like you have shown you can defend yourself!"

It was at this point that both would realize they'd gone too far, and retreat to the place they'd started from—that, for the time being, they would go on as they were. And that was what they did, and so, in spite of their unresolved argument, the small group's passage through the woods was for the most part as peaceful and harmonious as Lliem would later remember it being.

Late in the afternoon of their sixth day in the forest, the trees ahead of them began to thin so that there were gaps where blue sky peeped through.

There'd been no boat traffic in all the time they'd been traveling along the river bank, so, in what was to be the last uncomplicated decision Caelym and Annwr would make together for the next several weeks, they agreed it was safe to set up camp at the river's edge. By then Arddwn could build a fish trap by himself, Lliem knew how to gather sticks for the campfire, and Aleswina was as adept as Annwr at scouring the undergrowth for mushrooms and new fern fronds. With all three solemnly promising to do their chores and to stay close together, Caelym and Annwr went to see what lay ahead and decide what to do next.

As they were about to leave, Annwr looked straight at Arddwn and said for a third time, "You are to stay within sight of the camp, and you are not to go wading any deeper than your knees, and you are not to even think about going swimming until your father is back to go into the river with you!"

"I wasn't . . ."

The lie that Arddwn was about to tell crumbled under Annwr's stern gaze. Looking down at his feet and scuffing his toes, he mumbled, "I won't, Aunt Annwr."

Annwr saw no need to repeat her admonitions to Aleswina and Lliem, since the two of them were never out of sight of each other or ever went willingly into water above their ankles. Still, neither Caelym nor Annwr wanted to leave Aleswina and the boys alone any longer than absolutely necessary. They hurried on their way to look at the lay of the land ahead and returned before Arddwn had time to think of some way to accidently slip into the invitingly deep pool just upstream from his fish trap.

Although the supper they'd foraged that night was better than any Arddwn and Lliem had eaten at Barnard's manor, it hardly deserved the lavish praise Caelym heaped on it. It was clear to Annwr what was behind his exuberance. She, however, had no intention of taking Aleswina and the boys up through the rugged terrain that lay ahead without civilized food and a pot to cook it in. Her arms crossed, she let him make his case for continuing to live on "what the forest provides" and avoiding any contact with their enemies' strongholds before she pointed out that it took them half their day to gather enough to eat—and then added some uncomplimentary remarks about men who promised to fight bears and ogres but were afraid to set foot in a tiny little village.

"And what do you propose, then?" Caelym parried. "That we knock on some Saxon's cottage door and ask if they've food and clothes for five, saying we'd be glad to pay with gold and jewels and, by the way, kindly don't mention this to your friends or neighbors, as we'd prefer the king's guards don't find out that we have passed this way?"

"What I suggest is that you remember that you are going in disguise as a monk who has taken a vow of silence and leave the rest to me!"

With that, Annwr smiled at Aleswina and the boys and went on, "We will make our camp here for the night. In the morning, we will need to clean ourselves up as much as we can, and then we will play a new game, and the rule of this game will be that we all do exactly what *I* say."

Annwr paused, looked Caelym in the eye, and waited until he glumly nodded his acquiescence before she turned back to Arddwn and Lliem and went on, "And what I say is that your father will pretend to be a monk who does not speak, and we must all help him remember that, so that if he does begin to speak we must all say, 'Shhhhhhh!'" She demonstrated by putting her fingers to her lips. "And Ethelwen will pretend to be Codric again, and I will pretend to be your grandmother, and you will pretend to be my two good, obedient grandsons, and so now you may pick your own pretend names."

After some back and forth, Arddwn decided on "Elderond," which was both the name of a very exciting and adventuresome hero and also of Arddwn's favorite of the shrine's goats, while Lliem, with some help from Caelym, picked "Penddrwn," which was the name of the hero who the Goddess Ethelwen had rescued.

That settled, Annwr explained that in the morning they were going to go to market in the village, and they would use their ordinary money (of which they now had plenty, she added for Caelym's benefit) to buy supplies, as well as new packs to carry their new things in.

"For us too?" Arddwn and Lliem asked in a single voice.

"Yes, you will each have your own pack and your own cup and spoon and bowl and nice new clothes and maybe, if you remember all the rules and do exactly as I say, a toy as well."

Caelym scowled. "My sons don't need Saxon toys, they—"

But before he could get any further, Arddwn and Lliem put their fingers to their lips and said, "Shhhhhhh!"

Chapter 55

The Trees Speak

$\mathcal{A}$rddwn and Lliem lay awake late into the night, whispering about what toys to get. Their murmuring debate over balls and tops and toy boats had barely tapered off before it started up again at the first hint of dawn—or so it seemed to the exhausted grown-ups trying to sleep in the same small shelter.

"It was you that put these ideas in their heads," was Caelym's grumbling retort to Annwr's muttering about Arddwn and Lliem being his sons.

In the morning, yawning and stretching, he got up and took the boys with him to visit the bushes and get their breakfast fish out of the weir. By the time the first sun beams broke through the branches overhead, Aleswina was covering the last smoldering ashes of the campfire with an extra layer of dirt, and Annwr was shaking the pine needles off her apron.

Unable to contain himself any longer, Arddwn bolted down the path, calling, "Come on!" over his shoulder.

Lliem dashed after him, crying, "Wait for me!"

"Stop them!"

Before Annwr's command was out of her mouth, Caelym was racing to head the boys off. He caught up where the path crossed a small clearing, circled in front of them, and blocked their way.

"What is your hurry, and where are your manners?"

Thrusting out his lower lip, crossing his arms, and assuming a stance that mirrored his father's, Arddwn declared, "We thanked the forest creatures!"

Lliem had come to a stop right behind Arddwn. Peeking out around his brother's shoulder, he chimed in, "And the sprites and the spirits of the fish!"

"And so now you rush forth, leaving the shield of their good will behind you, with no thought of the dangers ahead? Do you recall nothing of what you've learned in our time together?"

"Do what you and Aunt Annwr tell us."

Confident he'd picked the right answer, Arddwn was ready to start on. When Caelym didn't budge, he elbowed Lliem for help.

"And what Ethelwen tells us, and don't eat any mushrooms that might be poisoned, and don't go swimming without you there so we don't drown ourselves, and . . ." Lliem listed off as many of the admonitions and prohibitions as he could remember, finishing with, "and cover our poo over with dirt after we do it."

"And?"

Lliem dropped his eyes as he whispered, "And don't run off into the woods by ourselves."

"But"—Arddwn picked up their defense as Lliem faltered—"we weren't running off into the woods! We were on the path! And you were right behind us!"

That was at least as close to the truth as any of the excuses Caelym had made to his teachers when they'd caught him sneaking away from his lessons to explore the forest on the upper slopes of Llwddawanden. For a moment, warm memories of roaming through the woods with no real idea of where he was going or how far he'd gone welled up in Caelym's mind. But that had been within the secure confines of Llwddawanden, where, when he was tired and hungry, all he had to do was head downhill until he reached the lake and follow the path along its shore back to the shrine.

This forest was no familiar playground with safe sides around it—it was a vast wilderness teeming with danger from savage men and hungry wolves and lurking spirits.

"And what if I was not behind you and you had left the path and were lost in a forest with wild beasts all around you? What would you do then?"

Assuming this was an actual question, Arddwn answered, "Lliem would cry and wet himself—"

"I would not!"

"Would too!"

Before his father could tell them both to hush, Arddwn rushed on, "But I would get a stick with a sharp end, and I would stab them and kill them dead!"

Not to be outdone, Lliem declared, "I'd get a stick and stab them too!" He looked at his brother. "Please, Arddwn?" he asked in a wheedling tone of voice.

But Arddwn stood firm. "No! I'm going to stab them! You can get wood and make a fire so we can cook them!"

While Arddwn and Lliem were arguing over who would do the stabbing and who would do the cooking, Caelym was thinking how like him they both were. Of course, they would venture out on their own sooner or later, in spite—or because—of adults telling them not to. In his mind's eye, he could see two frightened little figures lost in a vast, wild forest, blind with panic and running themselves into exhaustion. He ached to call out to them in that future moment—telling them to stop, stay where they were, and wait for him to find them.

For most, the notion of sending a message forward in time would seem impossible, and for most it would be. It was, he knew, a feat that could only be accomplished by a Druid master. Now, after long years in training for just such a task, it was time to prove himself.

◆◆◆

Arddwn and Lliem were still arguing when Annwr and Aleswina caught up with them.

Aleswina would have swept Lliem into her arms and Annwr would have scolded both boys up one side and down the other, only Caelym put up his hand for silence and stepped into a spot where a sunbeam pierced the branches overhead. As its shimmering light formed a halo around him, he seemed to change before their eyes into a Druid elder—assuming an aura of infinite age and wisdom that seemed to whiten his black hair and wrinkle his smooth skin.

"The woods," he proclaimed in a voice that might have come from some distant time and place, "are filled with trees."

As Caelym spoke, he gravely nodded his head. Arddwn, Lliem, and Aleswina unconsciously nodded along with him. Annwr, standing off to the side, shook her head in exasperation as she recalled how even the best of Druid priests (and by this she meant Herrwn) always had to make saying hello in the hallway into an occasion for oratory.

Paying no attention to her and looking gravely down at his sons, Caelym intoned, "The trees of this ancient forest were living long before you were ever born!"

Since Arddwn was eight and Lliem was five, this would have been true of trees in even a relatively young forest. Arddwn and Lliem were entranced, however, and Caelym swept from the mundane to the mystical.

"The roots of these trees reach down into the earth, drawing up her sacred wisdom and carrying it up through their outstretched branches and into their whispering leaves, offering that wisdom to those who enter the forest with reverence and who listen with their minds as well as with their ears."

At this, Caelym stopped speaking. His eyes bored into the boys.

Arddwn and Lliem held their breath and strove to look as though they understood—although neither of them did. Still, Arddwn stood as tall as he could, and Lliem stopped sucking his thumb. Apparently satisfied with what he saw, Caelym got to the point—that the forest itself was alive, that it harbored wonder and danger in equal measure, and that before they ventured into it on their own, they must prove to him that they understood the language it spoke as clearly as if it were their native tongue—or, he added for Lliem's benefit, English.

"Now, then, you, Arddwn, and you, Lliem, will each choose a tree from those around you, and you will listen to it and tell me what it says to you."

Arddwn quickly spotted a tall cedar with enticingly climbable branches just off the path and claimed it. Lliem drew in his lower lip and looked around and, after serious deliberation, picked a towering oak growing close by his brother's tree.

Caelym nodded his approval of each boy's choice and waited.

The boys hovered by their trees, listening with all their might, hearing the rustle of leaves or needles but nothing close to words in either Celt or English.

"So then," Caelym said. "Do you hear either of these trees shouting?"

Relieved to have a question they could answer, Arddwn and Lliem spoke as one "No, Ta."

"Do you hear them arguing?"

Arddwn could see where this was going and muttered, "No, Ta."

"Do you hear them grumbling in impatience with what their father is asking them?"

Giggling, Lliem piped up, "No, Ta!"

"What *do* you hear?"

"Nothing!" said Arddwn.

"Quiet," said Lliem.

"That is right! Quiet!" Caelym nodded at his younger son. "Now look at your tree and tell me what it is doing."

"Nothing!" Arddwn said again.

"It's standing still."

Lliem got a second nod but before Arddwn could object that that was what he meant, Caelym said, "So neither of your trees is running wildly about or stabbing at anything with sticks?"

"No, Ta." The disappointment in both boys' voices was palpable.

"And yet these trees and others like them have lived through fierce storms and freezing winds and now stand tall and unafraid—welcoming you to climb up into their branches or hide safely in their shadows should you ever be lost and need shelter while you wait for me to come and find you."

"But, Ta . . ." It was on the tip of Arddwn's lips to say it had taken his father two years to find him the last time, and that was too long to sit waiting under some stupid tree, but he closed his mouth to keep the hurt-filled words from tumbling out.

"I know how long it was that I kept you waiting when I should have come quickly at your first need," Caelym hung his head and was, for a moment, the picture of a man burdened with remorse. Drawing a breath, he looked up again and spoke with renewed strength, "But that was before I knew I would need magic whistles to find you."

It was Arddwn who saw the opening this offered, "Maybe we can get them at the market!"

"We can get many things at the market, as I've no doubt your Aunt Annwr intends to do, but I will make our magic whistles from the flute that I have played for you."

And with surprisingly little fanfare, he did. Cutting the reed flute into three, he trimmed it and taught the boys to blow notes that might not be musical but were piercing and were certain to carry farther than a child's cry for help. When he was satisfied with each boy's efforts, he tied each of the whistles to a loop of cord and hung one around each of the boys' necks and his own. Staying crouching down, eye level with them, he asked, "So now tell me what you would do if you were lost in the forest and needed me to find you?"

"Listen to our trees," Lliem guessed.

"Blow our whistles," Arddwn added.

"Wait for you," they said in unison.

Sending up a silent invocation to the Goddess by all of Her names and in all of Her forms to protect these boys who were her own precious children, Caelym nodded. With a glance at Annwr to confirm that she was willing to let him stay in the lead for now, he started up the side of the ridge that lay between them the village that—he hoped—harbored no dangers worse than what they'd encountered in Welsferth.

Chapter 56

A Village Fair

aelym was first to reach the top of the ridge. Finding it open and exposed, he turned back and said sternly, "Wait where you are!"

Aleswina and the boys obeyed his command, crouching down out of sight below the crest of the rise. Annwr dogged his heels as he crept across the ledge and looked over his shoulder as he surveyed what lay ahead.

The path they'd been following dropped abruptly downwards into a swath of pine and oak that covered the hillside below them and came out again at the bottom of the slope, where it crossed a footbridge over the broad stream and joined a wagon road on the other side. The road traveled up a rise on the far side of the valley, then disappeared into a cluster of buildings surrounded on three sides by an expanse of tents with pennants flying from their center poles.

Even from a distance and with trees blocking part of the view, Caelym could see a line of heavily loaded wagons with mounted riders alongside rolling up the road into what was not some ordinary village on market day.

"An enemy encampment!" Aware of how sound could travel in the still morning air, he barely breathed the words as he drew back from the edge.

"A fair!" Although Annwr's voice was only a shade above a whisper, it carried, and the boys dashed up to see for themselves.

Catching hold of Arddwn's tunic to keep him from scrambling over the edge and down the path, Caelym asked through gritted teeth, "And a 'fair' is . . .?"

"A fair"—Annwr sighed and rolled her eyes in the particularly annoying way she had when she was telling him for the first time about something that he had no reason to know—"is a gathering of sellers. Like a market, only with games and dancing and festivities, something like the playful parts of our rites only not a part of their Christian rituals, as their god does not approve of fun."

While Annwr was explaining the difference between markets and fairs to Caelym, Lliem stared wide-eyed at them both.

In the short time since his rescue from Barnard's kitchen, Lliem had come to believe that his father was both magical and omnipotent. How could he—how could anyone—not know the difference between a market and a fair when even Lliem, as little as he was and knowing practically nothing compared with everyone else around him, knew that a market was rows of stalls selling ordinary, everyday things, while a fair was drums and flutes and dancing and singing and acrobats leaping through the air and the smells of wonderful things cooking! Not that Lliem had ever gotten anything to eat, except for the crusts he and Arddwn had been able to snatch up off the ground before the crows did when Barnard took them along to carry all the things he got for himself, but even Barnard could not stop him from smelling the aromas or hearing the music or catching glimpses of the entertainers. And once he had seen a man breathing fire like a dragon.

Unaware of his younger son's bewildered disillusionment, Caelym shook his head at the idea of wasting rites on a god who didn't believe in fun and returned to his point.

"With so many of our enemies gathered together in one place, we must skip this village and try for the next."

"Noooo," Arddwn and Lliem pleaded together.

"No!" Annwr said in what for her was a cheerful tone of voice. "This is better than I had hoped! With the crowds of outsiders, we will be able to buy everything we need without anyone being any the wiser."

While it was at least possible that Caelym could have held out against either Annwr's assertion or the boy's entreaties, the combination of the two was overpowering. Determined to win some compensation for his surrender, he stood up straight, crossed his arms, and said, "So if we are to venture into this Saxon citadel, it is with the condition that I am allowed to speak if the need arises."

"All right, then." Reluctantly realizing there was no hope of Caelym holding his tongue altogether, Annwr settled for fussing at him in the same tone she used to remind the boys to tie up the laces of their boots and keep their fingers out of the hot fire. "As long as you remember you are to be a Christian monk and say nothing but the Latin prayers that Ales—I mean, that Ethelwen taught you!"

After giving Annwr his huffy assurance that he knew "how to behave as a monk," Caelym took a long look at the wisps of white clouds drifting across the horizon of an otherwise clear sky and did a careful count of the swallows that swooped across the path ahead of them. Deciding there were no obvious portents of impending disaster, he took up his staff, tucked his wooden bowl under his arm, and stepped boldly forward, leading their way through the pines and oaks, across the bridge, and up onto the road to join the other foot travelers hurrying along in between wagons loaded with traveling players and goods for the fair.

Chapter 57

Caelym's Tribute

The village of Girdlestone hardly counted as a citadel. Consisting of the cluster of stone and timber buildings that Caelym and Annwr had seen from the opposite ridge, along with a few dozen cottages and farmsteads spread out along the valley floor, its usual population (depending on recent births and deaths) hovered around a hundred. This number more than tripled when it played host to the increasingly popular Girdlestone Fair.

Living on a side spur off the only possible wagon road between Atheldom and Derthwald—and beyond Derthwald through the high mountain passes to the western coast—the inhabitants of Girdlestone were more used to strangers coming and going than most rural villagers. Far from objecting to the raucous mix of visitors that descended on their otherwise quiet hamlet, they'd come to depend on the brief but reliable economic boom afforded by the fair. They helped the traveling players unload their carts and set up their tents, put out their own wares to sell alongside the visiting vendors, and told anyone who asked that the best place to stay was at Ealfrid's Inn at the east end of the village.

Annwr had been to fairs in Derthwald put on by much the same set of traveling players and felt sure that even as oddly assorted a group as theirs would not stand out in the crowd so long as Caelym contained his compulsion to show off. Busy with finding the right size tunics for the boys and bartering with vendors over what their goods were actually worth, she failed to notice when he suddenly turned down a different row of stalls and wandered off on his own.

As he made his way through the bustling crowd, Caelym nodded absently at the fairgoers who approached him, and recited random bits from Aleswina's psalms as they dropped tribute into his bowl. As the coins mounted up, a new idea took shape in his mind. Well aware that Annwr had purposely not given him any of their hoard, because she had no trust in his ability to do the bartering for which she had so praised Aleswina, he now saw the opportunity to prove himself as capable of conducting business as any Saxon princess.

Casting around for something to buy that Annwr wouldn't have thought of, he saw a stall nearby selling hunting and battle gear, from child-size toys to massive lances meant to bring down wild boars. Impressed by the rows of bows and arrows and the shelves of knives for flaying anything from a mouse to a bear, he ventured, for the first time in his life, to exchange money for things. With no clear notion of what the various coins in his bowl were worth, he simply held the bowl out to the arrow smith and pointed to what he wanted.

Among the varied but mostly good-humored fairgoers there were a few—either more intensely devout or more thoroughly gullible—who put together the mysterious monk's otherworldly good looks and floating, graceful walk with his blithe indifference to the world around him and began to whisper that they were seeing an angel in disguise. As the rumor spread through the crowd, more and more of the faithful added their coins to Caelym's plate and told him their names as they did, hoping to have someone to speak in their favor at the entrance to the Gates of Heaven when the time came.

Hlother, the arrow smith and armorer, was neither devout nor gullible, but he knew that most of his customers were one or the other, and he knew an opportunity when it looked him in the face. Ostentatiously adding a handful of coins to Caelym's bowl, he took the well-made hunter's bow and the two smaller boys' training bows off the pegs that he'd pointed to, added extra arrows to the matching quivers, and commended the sainted brother on his choice in a voice loud enough to be heard a dozen stalls away. As Caelym strode off, Hlother turned back to deal with the throng of customers lining up to get the bows and arrows that were good enough for an angel.

Emboldened by his success, Caelym turned down another row, following the sound of flutes, and found a stall selling musical instruments. He walked away with a splendid little harp and a still fuller begging bowl.

Preoccupied with composing a saga of how he'd entered the enemy's camp, deceived them all, and escaped unscathed with armloads of booty, Caelym did not at first notice that he'd acquired a bevy of wide-eyed admirers whispering to each other about miracles and visions. But as the prickling sense of being followed brought him back to the present, he started paying attention.

Much of the mumbling about seraphim and cherubim made no sense to him but when a voice broke through the rest, insisting, "Well, he's no ordinary monk," it was time to take evasive action. Turning back into the crowd, he darted first one way and then another through the confused, milling throng before ducking into a narrow alleyway between a line of sheds and animal pens. He emerged from the other end with his hood pulled down over his face and the bows, arrows, harp, and bowl of coins tucked under his cloak.

With Aleswina and the boys helping, Annwr had managed to find a place under a tree to stack their goods and supplies. As she heaped up her morning's purchases, she decided they'd have to make arrangements for a room at the local inn where they could get packed up and organized away from the curious stares of passersby. Having that settled in her mind, she looked around to see where Caelym was just as he popped around a corner, grinning like Rhedwyn just returned from a successful cattle raid. Refusing to reward whatever foolish nonsense he'd been up to with any remark at all, she snapped at him to add his toys to the rest of their goods while she figured out what to do next.

"What about *our* toys?" Arddwn demanded.

The boys had, by any reasonable standard, been exceptionally good. They'd hardly whined at all about standing still to get their new clothes fitted, stayed where they were supposed to stay, and helped to carry things that didn't seem nearly so exciting now that all the sounds and smells of the fair called to them from the other side of the stands. Annwr smiled at them and said, "You have been very good boys! You've helped me get all the things we need for our travels and you have not gone off and gotten lost or done anything foolish"—here she cast a sharp glance at Caelym—"so now you have earned your reward. Codric will go with you to the fun part of the fair. He will get you some treats to eat and take you to watch a puppet show and see the jugglers, and you may each pick out one toy, and if"—here she looked at the child-sized bows and arrows Caelym had under his arm—"it is not anything sharp or dangerous, Codric will buy it for you."

"I will—" Caelym finally managed to say, getting exactly two words in edgewise before Annwr finished for him, "Brother Cuthbert will help me carry our new things to the inn, and we will take a room there so we can sleep in nice warm beds tonight. After he and I have arranged for our room and put our things away, we will come and find you and see the toy you have each chosen."

After a final reminder for the boys to stay with "Codric" and not to speak to anyone else, Annwr handed Aleswina the coin pouch and waved them off.

By the time Caelym rejoined them, Annwr had managed to get everything except his satchel and a last basket of provisions stuffed into their new packs. She'd also gotten directions to the local inn, which she'd been assured was a clean place where you could count on getting beds with blankets that were washed two or even three times a year.

Of course Caelym had to argue, fussing that it was too dangerous to risk taking a room in a Saxon tavern and that they should be off into the hills before anyone started asking why an old woman, a young monk, and three boys, their clothes in tatters and with a single small bag between them, should have pouches of silver and gold sufficient to buy up half the goods on the market.

This from a man who'd gone traipsing through the crowds drop-ping who knew what hints about his real identity!

Aware that their conversation was beginning to attract atten-tion, Annwr gave Caelym a stifling look before saying in a voice loud enough to be overheard by anyone passing by, "I am a well-en-dowed widow taking my orphaned grandsons to live with kin on the western coast before retiring to a Celtic convent. We were traveling on a boat that sank, taking all of our baggage with it, save for the small satchel holding the last of my worldly possessions. As you, along with your serving boy, are on a mission from the bishop that takes you to the coast as well, you have in Christian goodness and charity agreed to see us safely to our destination!" After the loiter-ers had moved on to attend to their own business, she lowered her voice to a softer tone—as if she were calming a cranky child—and reassured him that the inn was run by a man of mixed parentage, as much a Briton as a Saxon.

"Splendid," muttered Caelym. "He can betray us in two languages."

"Only if we talk too much!"

With that, Annwr shouldered her own pack and collected the basket and the boys' bags, leaving Caelym to grapple with the rest as she trudged up the roadway toward Ealfrid's Inn.

Chapter 58

Ealfrid's Inn

The proprietor of Ealfrid's Inn was actually named Gothreg, but he'd agreed to keep the inn's original name when he took it over from his wife's uncle, and it was easier to answer to "Ealfrid" than to explain that a dozen times a day.

Glancing out his front door and seeing Annwr and Caelym approaching, Gothreg did some quick mental calculations. News of the wealthy widow buying whatever struck her fancy for herself and her entourage had reached him early that afternoon, and he'd been wondering if they'd be turning up and where he'd put them if they did. The inn had more rooms empty than not during most of the year, but for the days of the fair in the spring and fall, every spare room, shed, and closet was filled.

A moderately devout Christian, Gothreg wasn't about to evict Father Wulfric and the two traveling friars from the room he kept for itinerant clergy. Yes, he could squeeze the monk and his boy in there, but the wealthy widow was another matter. Seeing the bulging packs the widow and monk were carrying made up his mind for him—he and his wife would join the hired help on bedrolls in the kitchen if the widow made it worth his while.

She did.

That business done, Gothreg cleared a table close to the hearth and laid out dinner for the widow and monk while his wife gathered up their things and moved them out of the two adjoining rooms they usually kept for themselves.

While his rooms were full, his dining room was empty, and likely to remain that way with both locals and visitors off to the food stands at the fair, so Gothreg, who was usually too busy to breathe at this time of day, made small talk about the weather as he unloaded his tray.

◆●◆

Before Annwr could say that he'd taken an oath of silence, Caelym spoke up, answering questions Gothreg hadn't asked.

"I am, as you see, a monk, and am on a mission to the western coast. I have promised Mistress Columbina that I will take her and her orphaned grandsons with me to find the kin with whom they, the grandsons, will live forever after, while she will enter a Christian convent, and I will go on to fulfill my sacred oath to the Bishop, which can be delayed no longer than this."

Pleased that he could now speak English in phrases as long and flowing as any he'd ever spoken in Celt, Caelym went on to cleverly lay out the specifications Annwr was demanding for the Aleswina's new convent.

"Having done things in her younger days of which she now wishes to repent, Mistress Columbina seeks her final sanctuary among other nuns of her own race in a Christian convent that is sufficiently secluded to assure that she will not be disturbed by anyone out of her past."

This was nowhere close to the most incriminating revelation Gothreg had received in his tenure as an innkeeper, and he answered without so much as raising his eyebrows, "Oh, you'd be looking for the Abbey of Saint Agnedd . . . Britons in it mostly . . . and if it's withdrawing from the world she wants, then that's the place for it." (Here Gothreg paused to find the right phrase, since 'to hell and gone again' wasn't something that he could say to a monk and an elderly widow on her way to entering a convent.) "It's a fair bit off the main road on the far side of the fourth pass going west, but still this side of the big mountains, with nothing nearby besides a hamlet called Woghop, only—"

"Only?" Caelym leaned forward attentively.

"Only it's still a grueling journey to the coast, with brigands and bandits to worry about, and not one for the mistress to take back without your protection."

"That is no problem," Caelym said quickly, before Annwr could put in her opinion about who was protecting who. "If you will kindly give us the direction to this Agnedd's Abbey, I will see her safely settled there and take her grandsons on to the kin that wait for them afterward."

"Well, there is another problem—"

"And that is?" Caelym was beginning to suspect the innkeeper was playing games with them.

But he wasn't.

"The Sisters of the Abbey of Saint Agned are holier than most," Gothreg explained, "and they recuse themselves completely for the forty days following the anniversary of the day their saint was martyred, opening their gates to no one—not for the pope himself, even if he were to kneel at their door wearing a woman's wig—until the last of those forty days is up."

"And when might that be?" Caelym's fund of patience for things Christian, never great in the first place, was evaporating.

Surprised that he'd have to teach a monk about martyrs, especially one as well-known as Saint Agned, Gothreg counted a few rounds on his fingers and said, "Well, as she was done in on the first day of March, they'd be opening up again in another twelve days—that would be the fifth of May, if I'm counting it right."

He wasn't but was close enough as to make no practical difference.

"So then, what we will do is to travel to the village there, and Mistress Columbina will take a room and wait for them to open their door and welcome her in while the rest of us go on as I have promised"—Caelym allowed himself a distinct pause before finishing—"the Bishop."

"I'm afraid you won't be finding any inn in Woghop. It's a smallish bit of a place, and those that live there don't have the accommodations we do here."

Here again Gothreg was choosing his words to fit the company, not saying bluntly that the best he'd ever hear of Woghop was that it was a filthy, stinking little pigsty where you couldn't tell the men from the hogs. Sensing Caelym's growing tension and sympathizing, since he wouldn't have wanted to be caught between the widow and the Bishop either, he offered the best alternative he could think of on the spur of the moment.

"But what the Mistress could do would be to stay at the king's lodge, which is just one valley over there."

"And the king's lodge is an inn with the excellent accommodations of your own?"

"No, the king's lodge . . . well, it's the king's lodge."

Seeing Caelym's puzzled expression, Gothreg began to wonder if the monk was a bit dull-witted in spite of his high-toned manner of speaking. Making his own words as simple as possible and speaking slowly, he explained, "It's called the king's lodge because it's the lodge that belongs to the king—or did, when he was still alive. It was his hunting lodge, though it's not hunted from anymore now he's dead."

"Which king?"

The first words that Annwr spoke since she agreed to his price for the rooms startled Gothreg a bit, but guessing she was sharper than the monk, he answered at a normal rate of speed.

"The old king of Derthwald, Theobold—not the new one, Gilberth, who must own the place, as he inherited everything from his uncle, but has never been there, so far as I've ever heard. What I'm trying to say is that the old king's lodge is still kept up by the old king's servants, sent there to live out their days when the new king came to the throne and wanted new servants around him."

Speaking in an oddly distant-sounding voice, Annwr murmured, "I knew one of those servants once. Her name was Millicent, and she was the nurse to the little princess. You wouldn't have heard of her being there?"

"Why, yes she is—or was, the last I heard."

While Gothreg's inn was well inside the boundaries of Atheldom, his wife was from Derthwald, and would be there still if her father hadn't been one of the royal guards who had been expelled from the palace when Gilberth took the throne. His in-laws remained intensely loyal to the old king's memory, and they were bitter to this day that they had been sent off "before Theobold was cold in the ground!"

Nothing Gothreg could say about its making sense that the new king would want his own guards who were loyal to him made any difference to his wife. Instead, it just set her off on a bitter tirade in which he was compared unfavorably with the faithful servants of the old king who kept up his beloved hunting lodge "as if he were still alive and going to ride up to the front door with his banners flying and horns blowing like in the old days."

Gothreg had never been to the old king's lodge or met any of its inhabitants but had heard so much about them he could name them off and describe each one as if he'd known them in person. Almost without any effort, he repeated the poignant story his mother-in-law told whenever she came to visit of how Millicent, who had been both maid to the queen and nurse to the princess, still kept all the royal gowns washed and ready for the day the princess might want them, even knowing she'd been put in a convent. It was a story that sounded better the first time it was told, and Gothreg could see that Mistress Columbina, who he'd taken for a cold, hard-hearted crone, was touched to the core, even though she said nothing more, except to ask that he tell them how to find the way there.

While the innkeeper was drawing them a map on a sheet he tore from his accounting ledger, Annwr looked past him and out through the inn's open door.

She hadn't thought of Millicent in years and was surprised the name had jumped out of her lips so quickly. She was surprised, too, by how clearly she could picture the old woman she'd seen only once in her life—rushing around in the palace nursery, desperately trying to show her where Aleswina's things were and, no doubt, heartbroken at being torn away from the little girl she dressed and cared for so lovingly. To think that for all these years, she'd held on to the hope of someday seeing the child that she, like Annwr, had come to love as her own!

"Mistress Columbina!" Caelym said softly. "It is time we take our bags to the rooms this kind innkeeper has given us for the night and go meet my helper and your grandsons at the fair, as we promised we would." He put a gentle hand under her elbow, helped her to her feet, and handed her his satchel, before carrying the rest of their bags, with the innkeeper's help, into their rooms.

Chapter 59

Brave Horse

After Annwr sent them off, Arddwn and Lliem dashed away, with Aleswina running after them. Pulled by the calls of peddlers hawking their wares, the clamor of competing musicians, and the smells of every kind of savory food imaginable, they rushed past players acting scenes from the bible and into the fun part of the fair.

By midafternoon they'd seen acrobats leaping so high they seemed to be flying. They'd watched the puppet show twice, laughing until their sides ached. They'd eaten ginger-spiced cakes and buttery fried bread and fruit tarts soaked with honey. But in all the fun and excitement, they still hadn't decided which toy they would choose for themselves.

Arddwn would have picked a real-looking wooden sword, but Aleswina stood unexpectedly firm, repeating, "Nothing sharp or dangerous," in a close approximation of Annwr's voice.

Lliem would have chosen a patchwork horse at a stand of cloth dolls and animals if Arddwn hadn't scoffed, "Those are for babies!"

Half-way through saying, "I'm not a baby," Lliem saw a tub of stick horses with leather heads and yarn manes at the far end of the stall. He dashed up to it, his eyes fixed on a spotted black and white one with a long, thick white mane.

"That one!" he squealed, adding, "Please, please, please!" as he jumped up and down.

The extremely plump woman selling the toys put down her knitting, got up from her stool, and lumbered over to the barrel. In the next moment, Lliem had his pony in his hands and was crooning, "Brave Horse, I'll call you Brave Horse," in its ear.

Arddwn was too old for stick horses. While Ethelwen was paying for Lliem's toy, he kept looking around for something he wanted that wasn't sharp or dangerous.

Not far from the toy stand, a crowd gathered around a show that was making them clap and cheer.

Dodging his way through the throng, Arddwn came out in the front row to see a juggler tossing brightly colored balls through the air in loops and figures of eight, dipping down to add one more and one more and one more again from a basket by his feet as the onlookers applauded at each new addition, until he had twelve balls in the air at once and his hands were a blur of motion. Then, far too soon for Arddwn, the juggler, Trombert, dropped off one ball after another back into the basket, until he was back to three. Keeping those going, he walked around the edge of a circle, calling for donations and offering to sell his balls for a pening each.

The crowd thinned as the act came to the end, leaving Arddwn still enthralled.

Hoping he'd had a paying customer for a change, Trombert lowered his offer to sell three balls for a single pening and include a juggling lesson in the bargain.

"They aren't sharp or dangerous!" Arddwn's response made no sense to Trombert but did to Aleswina, and she wanted to say yes only she took Annwr's directions literally and sighed, "But An—I mean, your grandmother—said you could buy just one toy."

"I'll sell you one for a pening," Trombert said quickly, "and will give you other two for free."

Aleswina was persuaded, and Arddwn got to pick his balls, which, along with his juggling lesson, took long enough that Lliem, who was anxious to ride his new pony, climbed over the stone wall behind the food stands, mounted onto Brave Horse and rode off across the open field towards a stand of trees on the other side. Caught up in his game, he danced and pranced through the grass, unaware of how far he'd gone or that he was now completely alone except for a single figure cloaked in black who'd been passing by and who left the road to follow him.

Chapter 60

Father Wulfric

father Wulfric was on his way to Lindisfarne to ask his bishop to help pray for the safe return of the novice who'd vanished without a trace from the convent in Derthwald. Although he was in a hurry, there wasn't another village to stop at before dark, so he had taken his usual bed at Ealfrid's Inn and gone out to spread the word of the mystery to the fairgoers and call on them to join their prayers with his and those of the nuns of Saint Edeth.

Having done everything he could for the moment, he was wandering around the edge of the fairgrounds when he saw Lliem dancing through the grass, the sun on his red hair and his face alight with the joy of his game.

Putting together the boy's thin, undernourished stature with his brand-new outfit and expensive toy, Wulfric had a bad feeling about what that meant.

Of the evils men did, the most abhorrent to Wulfric was the use of innocent children for an array of vile purposes unimaginable to anyone who hadn't been hearing confessions for the past forty years.

There were other possible explanations, but Wulfric was suspicious. Furthermore, he was certain that he had never baptized this boy—and as the only priest serving every village from Girdlestone to the mountain ridge that marked the northernmost edge of the Christian Saxon lands, if he hadn't baptized a child, no one had.

That settled it. Determined that this was one little soul he would save, Wulfric set out to take the boy into his care and—if it turned out his dark suspicions were correct—take him to grow up consecrated to God in the monastery where he had himself been dedicated by the earthly parents he no longer remembered.

Knowing from experience that outlaws' children, whether born, bought, or stolen, were close to feral, Father Wulfric approached his quarry carefully and silently until he was near enough to catch hold of him if he should run off.

"What a nice horse you have," he said when he was within arm's length. "May I pet him?"

The gentle, friendly opening put Lliem at ease. Nodding proudly, he trotted over and lifted Brave Horse's nose up to meet Wulfric's outstretched hand.

Tucking a firm finger around the stick pony's reins, Wulfric asked, "Who bought him for you?"

"Ethel—I mean, Codric did."

Suddenly remembering what Annwr told him about staying with Ethelwen and speaking only to her, Lliem whispered, "I'm not supposed to talk to anyone else."

Wulfric squatted down, looked Lliem straight in the eyes, and whispered back, "But you can talk to me—I'm Father Wulfric!"

Having had one father suddenly appear, Lliem supposed it was possible he had two, but thought it was better to make sure.

"Are you Arddwn's father too?"

"Of course, I am! I am father to all children who love Jesus!"

Here Lliem was disappointed because he liked having one father and would have been happy to have another one, only—

"But we don't like Jesus." He sighed, shrugged, and would have trotted off, but Father Wulfric didn't let go of Brave Horse's reins.

Like a fish suddenly aware that the worm it had just bitten into had something sharp inside it, Lliem edged backward and tried to pull Brave Horse with him.

Like a skilled fisherman with a fish not yet securely hooked, Wulfric straightened up, keeping a grip on the pony's head, "But all little children must learn to love Jesus, so if your mother and father haven't told you about Him, I will tell you now."

Tempted because his father told such good stories, Lliem hesitated a moment too long, and in a quick move, Wulfric dropped his hold on the pony's rein and grasped hold of Lliem's hand.

In the same moment that Wulfric knew he had his little fish safety caught, Lliem realized he was trapped.

Wulfric smiled. "So, now we will go back and find out who you belong to . . ."

The rest of what the well-meaning priest had to say was lost in Lliem's terror that he was going to be taken back to Barnard. Panicked, he looked around for Arddwn or Ethelwen. What he saw was a towering oak—the twin of the tree he'd chosen to be his friend in the forest.

Instead of struggling to break free, Lliem went still. And as he did, a bird in its upper branches let out a long, piping call reminding him that he had a magic whistle, so he unclenched his hands and let Brave Horse drop to the ground.

Pleased to see the child was now at ease, Wulfric relaxed his own grip and smiled at the little boy's transformed upward gaze, touched to see the innocent child's free hand move spontaneously towards his breast has if guided by a divine touch to make an untutored sign of the cross.

But what Lliem was reaching for was his magic whistle and the minute he had it in his grasp, he pulled his other hand free and ran. If he'd dashed across the open field, Father Wulfric would have caught him, but instead he ran to his tree, blowing his whistle with all his might and keeping the tree's broad trunk between him and his pursuer.

Wulfric was fast and strong for a man his age, but not quick enough to catch hold of an agile five-year-old darting first one way then the other around the tree. It was, however, just a matter of time before Lliem would eventually dodge the wrong way and be caught again.

Lliem was getting tired from blowing his whistle while he was dodging back and forth, just managing to keep the tree between them, but then, when he was almost completely out of breath, four good things happened at once:

Ethelwen appeared out of nowhere, picked him up, and carried him away.

Annwr circled around behind them, yelling "You leave that child alone!"

His father—his real, only father—rushed past to tell the pretend father to go away.

And Arddwn ran to save Brave Horse.

Chapter 61

Back to Ealfrid's Inn

aelym and Annwr were on their way to the toy stalls when they heard Lliem's whistle. Pushing through the crowd, they caught sight of Aleswina and Arddwn climbing over the fence and dashing across the field. Charging after them, they caught up midway to the tree where Lliem was barely staying out of Wulfric's reach.

Running faster than she'd ever run before, Aleswina reached Lliem first, scooped him up in her arms and fled with him clutched to her chest. Just steps behind her, Annwr paused long enough to wave her walking stick in Wulfric's direction and shout at him before she rushed after them.

Caelym would have turned to cover their retreat, except he saw Arddwn kept going on, risking capture himself to retrieve Lliem's toy horse.

It was too late to call him back.

Prepared to fight to the death to save his son, Caelym reached for his dagger, but accidentally grabbed the silver cross that Annwr insisted he wear as part of his monk's disguise instead. Hearing Herrwn's words that the wise "contend with speech, not daggers" as clearly as if his teacher were there at his side, Caelym raised the cross up and proclaimed snatches of an incantation he'd learned from Aleswina.

"*Quid gloriaris in malitia qui potens es in iniquitate,*" he cried out. "*tota die iniustitiam cogitavit lingua tua sicut novacula acuta fecisti dolum. Dilexisti malitiam super benignitatem; iniquitatem*

magis quam loqui aequitatem. Dilexisti omnia verba praecipi-
tationis in lingua dolosa. Propterea destruet te Deus in finem,
evellet te et emigravit te de tabernaculo et radicem tuam de terra
viventium. Quid gloriatur in malitia qui potens est iniquitate Tota
die iniustitiam cogitavit lingua tua sicut novacula acuta fecisti
dolum Dilexisti malitiam super benignitatem iniquitatem magis
quam loqui aequitatem Dilexisti omnia verba praecipitationis lin-
guam dolosam Propterea Deus destruet te in finem evellet te et
emigrabit te de tabernaculo et radicem tuam de terra viventium,"
infusing the words with sufficient force to make up for whatever
feeble message they contained. Then—as he would recount in
the stirring saga he would later compose about the event—his
foe, presumably a high priest of the Christians' god, knelt down
in defeat.

Caelym whirled around, triumphant, and bounded across the
field. He caught up with Annwr, Aleswina, Arddwn, and Lliem
as they slipped through the milling crowd and ducked into the
alleyway that Caelym had found earlier that day. From there they
made their way back to Ealfrid's Inn and went straight to their
room. In complete agreement about staying out of sight and leaving first thing in the morning, Caelym and Annwr walked the
boys to and from the inn's latrine before tucking them into the
innkeeper's broad bed.

Working by candlelight, Annwr and Aleswina sorted out the
packs while Caelym sat nearby with the Gothreg's map spread
next to Herrwn's, looking from one to the other with a deeply
perplexed expression.

When she was satisfied that everything was in order, Annwr
set the five packs in a row, neatly arranged by size. She put Caelym's bow and harp next to the largest one and Lliem's stick horse
next to the smallest and got into bed next to Aleswina, leaving
Caelym still awake and puzzling over his maps.

At the other end of the inn's hallway, Father Wulfric—deeply
disturbed over his encounter with the boy in the woods—stayed
up in intense prayer long after the friars sharing the room were
asleep.

Bewildered over how what had begun as a simple act of Christian charity had ended with his being confronted by a tall, dark monk hurling the words of the fifty-second psalm at him, calling him a sinner who gloried in malice, devised injustice, and wrought deceit, and warning him that God would pluck him out and destroy him, the shaken priest repeated, *"Ne proicias me a facie tua et spiritum sanctum tuum ne auferas a me ne proicias me a facie tua et spiritum sanctum tuum ne auferas a me. Redde mihi laetitiam Iesu tui et spiritu potenti confirma me redde mihi laetitiam salutaris tui et spiritu principali confirma me,"* over and over until, drained and exhausted, he got off his aching knees and climbed into his cot to fall into a strange dream of running across a field after the vanished novice, Sister Aleswina, who was dressed as a bride and riding on a stick horse.

Chapter 62

Keeping to the High Ground

nnwr was the first to wake up the next morning. She laid out a breakfast of bread, cheese, and figs along with cups of well-diluted ale before she stroked Aleswina's cheek and whispered, "It's time, Dear Heart," repeating, "It's time" as she nudged Caelym and the boys.

It was still dark when they slipped stealthily out of the inn, Caelym leading the way through back alleys, past shuttered stalls, and across the dark field where they stopped for Lliem to thank his tree and tell it goodbye.

From there they made their way through steadily steeper pastures.

By the time it was fully light, they were halfway up the next ridge.

The boys' spirits rose along with the sun, and they infected Caelym with their exuberance. As the three of them chased each other up the slope, darting and dashing from one thicket to the next in a high-spirited game of tag, Annwr talked softly to Aleswina, telling her about the king's lodge and the Abbey of Saint Agned.

Aleswina's eyes filled with tears as she whispered, "Will you . . ." choking on the lump in her throat before she could finish— *come to visit me?*

Answering the question she thought Aleswina was trying to ask, Annwr promised, "I won't leave you unless I know it's safe! You know you can trust me, don't you?"

Aleswina nodded, wiped her face with her sleeve, and even managed to smile when Lliem came galloping back on his stick horse, calling that they were almost to the top.

They stopped in a rocky hollow just below the crest of the ridge. Continuing a game of being a wolf and his cubs on a hunt, Caelym told the boys in a growly voice that this would be their wolf's den where they would wait, "while I, your pack leader, will venture cautiously on to see what lies ahead and decide what to do next."

Growling just as convincingly, Annwr corrected him, "We, your *two* pack leaders, will venture cautiously on to see what lies ahead and decide what to do next!" As she slipped off her pack, she added that Aleswina would stay with them and give them some wolf cub food.

"You mean Ethelwen!" Lliem reminded her in his most wolf-ish-sounding voice.

"I mean Ethelwen," Annwr agreed.

Leaving the boys to decide whether wolf cubs ate barley cake as well as cheese and sausage, Caelym and Annwr crept up to the ledge, where Annwr surveyed the landscape below while Caelym sat next to her with his legs crossed and his two maps spread out on his lap. Clearing his throat to get her attention, he spoke in his most dignified high-council voice.

"To the unenlightened, it must certainly appear that these two maps—one drawn by the highest priest on our council, he who is greatest and wisest of our bards, and the other by an untutored innkeeper—have no similarities between them. Further, it goes without saying—"

Annwr snorted. "If it goes without saying, why are you saying it?"

Ignoring the interruption, Caelym continued, "Were we forced to make a choice between one or the other, we would, of course, follow the map drawn by Herrwn. I, however, have, after intense study and deliberation, reconciled their differences and can say that as the innkeeper's map depicts the earthly route and Herrwn's shows us the spiritual journey, it is not only possible but essential that we take both into account, following the one but guided by the other."

"And so?"

"And so . . ." Resigned to Annwr's terseness, Caelym used his forefinger to trace a curving line through a cluster of upside-down V's on the map Gothreg had drawn for them, avoiding the wide central space labeled *D'ld,* and coming around to the *X* next to the letters *KL.* "We will bear north and west, keeping to the uplands, to reach Aleswina's ancestral lodge, where she will remain in the safe keeping of her eternally devoted nurse until the nuns of Saint Agned, whose convent will be her sanctuary forever after, open their gates and welcome her in."

Annwr gave a grunt that was neither affirmative nor negative.

Caelym went on, "And we, still keeping to the high ground, will continue to our own destination—the inn propitiously named 'The Sleeping Dragon,' where, by now, all of our beloved kin are gathered and waiting for our arrival."

Annwr nodded and said, "With the river on one side and the road on the other, even you can't get lost."

The path that Caelym chose was actually a good one. It dropped down to run along the side of that ridge without losing too much altitude, leading them into the cover of a pine forest, and—as Annwr had pointed out—with cliffs on one side and the valley of Derthwald on other, their trek was up and down but was guaranteed not to go in circles.

Still, those ups and downs were steep.

By midafternoon, Arddwn was asking, "When are we going to get to our camp?" and Lliem had switched from galloping along on Brave Horse to using him as a staff. They were all ready to stop, except for Caelym, but he was outvoted when they came into a glade that was sheltered from the wind and had a clear, babbling brook running through it.

After the supper that Annwr cooked in her new pots, and just as Caelym was starting to tune his harp in preparation for the evening's poems and songs, Aleswina shyly whispered, "I have presents for you."

She opened her pack and took out the things she'd bought at the fair while the boys weren't looking and had kept hidden from Annwr when they were packing up. She'd gotten marbles and tops for the boys and a soft woolen shawl for Annwr. Since Caelym seemed to like reciting the psalms, she'd picked a parchment prayer sheet from the ones on sale in the stall in front of the church. Written in Latin, the prayer itself had looked like all the others to her, but this sheet had the most beautiful border—one with brightly gilded flowers and butterflies so real-looking they seemed about to flutter off the page.

Touched by Aleswina's generosity, Annwr pulled gifts from her pack—a little sack of seeds she'd gathered from her cottage garden for Aleswina, a sheaf of medicinal herbs for Caelym, and the pairs of extra socks she'd gotten for the boys.

Not to be outdone, Caelym formally presented the boys with their bows and arrows.

The boys' faces beamed with delight, while Annwr's darkened with disapproval.

Seeing her lowered eyebrows and pursed lips, Caelym quickly added, "Of course, these are not toys! They are implements that you must learn to wield with skill and caution, and I will give you careful instruction about how to use them, and you will never think of pointing these arrows at anything except targets that I set for you! Is that agreed?

"Yes, Ta!" Arddwn and Lliem spoke together in the sincerest possible voices.

"Good! For if any boy were, ever so unfortunately, to forget and point his arrow at his brother or any other forbidden object, then by the power vested in me as your father and as a priest on the highest councils of our people, I should be forced to judge this a proof that this boy was too young to have them and would give him a baby's rattle to play with instead." After pausing to give this warning time to sink in, he finished, "But I know I have no reason to fear such rash or careless behavior from either of my sons!"

Both boys clutched the bows and arrows to their chests and nodded vigorously as they promised to be careful and not shoot each other or any other forbidden object.

Glancing towards Annwr and relieved that her scowl had softened to an almost smile, Caelym took up his harp and ran a finger across its strings, both to check its tuning and to give himself a moment to decide on a different story from the one he had planned. With the boys and Aleswina scrambling to their places around the campfire, he began, "So now I will tell you the story of how a carelessly fired arrow from the bow of an ill-trained archer nearly started a war between the spirit queen of the deer clan and our own ancestors."

Chapter 63

Caelym's Answer

The next day set the pattern for the weeks ahead. They woke at dawn, shared their cold breakfast with the local spirits, and hiked on until late afternoon, when they started looking for some grove or glen to make their camp for the night. When they found a good place to stop, and got the sprites' permission to spend the night, Caelym would set up an archery target for Arddwn and Lliem and spend some time teaching them to shoot while Annwr made a mix of what they gathered along the way and her carefully garnered provisions into dinner. After they'd eaten, Caelym would sing and tell stories, and they'd all curl up and go to sleep under Annwr's new blankets.

Mostly Aleswina stayed close to Annwr, but one afternoon Caelym invited her, rather formally, to come to the boys' archery lesson. Assuming he wanted her help in finding the arrows that missed the target, Aleswina was startled when it became clear that Caelym expected her to take her turn shooting along with the boys, and she was badly flustered when he stood pressed close behind her and reached his arms around her to show her how to grip the bow and aim the arrow.

If she'd been less innocent, Aleswina might have suspected Caelym of having ulterior motives—which, in fact, he did.

◆◆◆

From what Caelym could tell from the innkeeper's map, they had only one more ridge to cross before they would reach Aleswina's ancestral lodge—where, for her sake as well as their own, they would leave her in the care of loyal and trustworthy servants waiting for the gates of her soon-to-be sanctuary to open and let her in.

The phrase "loyal and trustworthy servants" was an unfortunate one. When he'd used it in discussing their plan with Annwr, she'd pursed her lips so grimly that he let another six days go by before bringing up the subject again. Even so, she seemed resolved on, or at least resigned to, leaving Aleswina behind and hadn't reopened the argument about it.

Having the highly trained memory of a Druid bard, Caelym could recall every line of their original dispute, particularly the part where Annwr had contended that it wasn't safe to leave the girl behind, "alone and defenseless and knowing full well that Gilberth's guards would raid convents in their search for her," and how he'd countered that he would teach her to defend herself.

Though spoken in the heat of their argument, it was an oath as binding as any other, and he'd been brooding ever since over what weapon she could wield or what ploy he would teach her in order to fulfill that vow.

He dismissed hand-to-hand combat immediately, certain that she had neither the strength nor the boldness to use a sword, even if he'd had one with which to teach her. But he had hope for archery. It was a skill at which he not only excelled but had also taught to Cyri so successfully that her aim and distance had come to rival his own. Now, with only days left, he was dismayed when his best attempts to show Aleswina how to aim and shoot—holding her body precisely in position, gently but firmly whispering his instructions in her ear, keeping her hands in place as he guided her to pull back and release the arrow—resulted in no more than a pitiful, wobbling shot that hit the ground far short of the target.

He returned to camp discouraged, and was on the verge of pleading with Annwr to release him from this pledge when he remembered a long-ago lesson that had taken place in the shrine's healing chambers.

It was not just any lesson but the one where Olyrrwd had asked him if he knew the difference between a surgeon's incision and a murderer's stab. Assuming this was a joke, Caelym had pretended to ponder for a moment before saying, "No, Master. What is the difference between a surgeon's incision and a murderer's stab?" He'd expected his teacher to laugh his deep, gravelly laugh and give some droll answer. Instead, Olyrrwd, with an intensely serious expression, had held up his hand with his thumb separated from his forefinger by the width of an acorn and said, "That much!"

The rest of that day's healing lesson had been taken up with Caelym's learning to maintain absolute control over the direction and depth of his lancing and excising. Now he recalled how, when his life was at stake, Aleswina had overcome her timidity and lanced his wound as perfectly as if Olyrrwd himself had been guiding her hand. So why could she not learn to plunge "that much" deeper if it were her own life that hung in the balance?

That could be the answer. It had to be the answer.

Chapter 64

Speaking of Wolves

𝕿he next afternoon, they made camp by the edge of a reed-rimmed pool where choruses of frogs were calling out, challenging Arddwn and Lliem to try to catch them. Assuming Caelym would take care of placating any necessary local spirits before going off to shoot something for their supper, Annwr gave the boys a basket and reminded them to take off their shoes and roll up their pants legs. She gave the other basket to Aleswina, saying, "You go gather the greens, Dear Heart, and I'll pull us some rush roots and keep an eye on the boys," thinking it would be better that the too-soft-hearted girl was somewhere else when it came time to show the boys how to kill their frogs quickly and painlessly before stirring them into the evening's stew.

Proud that Anna trusted her to go off gathering by herself, Aleswina wandered down the path plucking fern tips and wild celery stalks. As she went from one patch to the next, the boys' gleeful cries were overtaken by the sounds of birds singing and bees buzzing. It was almost as if she was Gwendolen going to meet a bear cub. Looking up from picking a bunch of sorrel at the edge of a flowery meadow, she saw Caelym coming toward her carrying his harp instead of his bow.

"Your basket is full to overflowing, so perhaps you will leave off your gathering and listen to the tale I've come to tell you." Making one of his sweeping bows, Caelym pointed to a circle of flat stones at the other side of the meadow.

Aleswina, who hadn't been alone with Caelym since they'd run off from the convent garden, suddenly felt shy.

"Shall I call Arddwn and Lliem?"

"When I passed them just now, they were too busy at their hunt for frogs to join us. And besides, this tale is one I mean for your ears alone."

Still a little nervous but also flattered, Aleswina took the hand Caelym held out to her and trotted along as he led her across the meadow. She took a seat on the low, flat rock he offered her with another bow. She drew up her knees and wrapped her arms around them as he sat down facing her on a taller stone. He settled his harp on his knee and gave the strings an opening strum—but instead of starting to sing about some ancient hero in the long-ago past, he let his harp strings go silent and began speaking in the formal and learned manner he used when he lectured the boys about rites and rituals.

"I do not know what is needed to become a Christian priest, but to become a Druid one requires more than simply being born to a mother who is a priestess—although that, of course, is necessary."

Supposing Caelym, like Anna, used "priestess" and "nun" interchangeably, Aleswina tried to explain that Christian priests weren't supposed to be born that way because nuns weren't supposed to have babies unless it was by immaculate conception (something she didn't actually understand any better than the other kind but knew it had only happened for the Blessed Virgin Mary).

As a priest in a cult based largely on reverence for fertility, Caelym could only shake his head at the idea that virginity was something to be blessed. Dismissing the core concept of Christianity with a wave of his hand, he went on with the point he was making.

"Having been so born and being a boy rather than a girl"— here he digressed to say that he had no regrets about being a boy, even knowing that only by being a girl was there the hope of someday becoming the living embodiment of the Great Mother Goddess, before continuing— "I left my nursery on the morning of my sixth birthday to live in the priests' quarters and devote myself to the studies necessary to take my place in the highest ranks of our order."

Again digressing, he added, "In former times, when all of our people worshiped the Great Mother Goddess above any of Her divine offspring, there would have been dozens of disciples filling our classroom. As it was, I sat alone at the feet of the three greatest of Druid masters—Herrwn, head of the High Council and our shrine's foremost bard; Olyrrwd, our shrine's beloved physician; and Ossiam, our chief oracle and master of divination."

"Then you are an oracle as well as a bard and a healer?"

Despite what Anna was always saying about Caelym's being boastful, Aleswina thought it was very modest of him not to have mentioned this before. She would have said so, only Caelym's expression clouded over, and for a moment she thought she saw tears welling up in his eyes.

He drew in a deep breath and let it out as a long, sad sigh. "It is as much honor as I, or any man, might hope for to sit on the highest councils of our shrine as a bard and a healer and as"— here his expression brightened again—"the consort to our chief priestess. But as I was about to explain, I studied with diligence, and by the age of fifteen I could recite from memory all of the stories, songs, and odes of our nine great sagas and chant the proper evocations for the twelve ranks of divinities!"

"Is that why you have learned to speak in English so quickly?" Aleswina broke in.

Caelym's justified pride in his accomplishments tipped over into boasting as he agreed, "After learning to speak the language of wolves, English is no great challenge."

"Wolves?" Aleswina gasped.

"Wolves!" repeated Caelym.

"But how—"

"That is what I am now about to tell you."

Hearing the astonishment in Aleswina's voice reawakened the awe—or, more accurately, the dread—Caelym had felt when he'd stood before the shrine's high altar at sunrise on his sixteenth birthday.

He'd risen that morning not just confident but exhilarated to think that—despite Ossiam's refusal to take him on as his apprentice—he must still retain the oracle's esteem, since it was

Ossiam rather than Herrwn or Olyrrwd who had pronounced Caelym ready to embark on his spirit quest . . . two full years earlier than ordained by tradition.

As he'd been telling Aleswina, becoming a Druid priest demanded rigorous training under the scrutiny of the elder priests—and not even Caelym's being the only son of the shrine's previous chief priestess and goddess-incarnate exempted him from any of the grueling tests along the way, or from undertaking the ultimate test to prove himself worthy to enter the final stage of his induction into the priesthood.

Divined by ritual sacrifice, the spirit quest was well-known to involve some variant of climbing to the top of a mountain, reciting incantations calling on a spirit guide (usually an animal or a bird) to reveal itself to him in a dream, and then going to sleep in order to have the dream. While the quest was a test of the apprentice-priest's endurance and a sacred rite of passage intended to bring him to a higher level of spirituality, it was also privately understood to be a last chance for adventure before settling down into another six years of demanding discipleship.

Already the acknowledged apprentice of both the shrine's master bard and their chief healer, Caelym had been eager to hear what task Ossiam would divine for him. He'd had his bow and quiver and fishing spears packed, along with his ritual paraphernalia. But his excitement had turned to despair as the oracle raised his head after staring into the entrails of the sacrificial goat long after it gave its last dying bleat. The oracle couldn't have been said to be looking at Caelym, as his eyes were rolled upwards and only their whites showed beneath his half-drooped lids. His lips, though moving, had been oddly out of pace with the shrill, eerie voice of the female spirit from the other world who spoke through Ossiam on portentous occasions.

"You must go now, at once, into the mountains to seek your animal spirit guide! You must go on this journey as animals go, without human clothes or weapons! You may not return until you have learned to speak the language of your animal spirit's tribe and to sing their songs and tell their stories!"

◆◆◆

Born a day before the spring equinox, the weather on Caelym's birthday could be anything from cold and harsh to warm and balmy.

That year, it wasn't warm and balmy.

Even in the relative shelter of the sacred grove, hail was pelting down through the branches of the towering oaks and a cutting wind was tearing at the opening of his ceremonial robes. It almost didn't matter that the task of learning to speak an animal's language was impossible, since that skill had been lost forever in the irrevocable feud between men and beasts. Going into the mountains in this weather without clothes or tools or a flint was not a quest—it was a death sentence.

He could not, of course, refuse to go, and was only taking a breath to keep his voice from quivering as he accepted his fate when Olyrrwd, who'd been standing just off to one side of the altar, spoke.

"But as animals have hide and fur, you will go in leather clothes and a fur cloak," he said, the ordinariness of his gruff and grumbly voice sounding strange after Ossiam's spine-chilling decree. "And as animals have fangs and claws, you will go armed with a knife and spear. And as you are my disciple, not even the spirit of she who speaks through the lips of our highest oracle will object to your going forth bearing a token of our sacred order."

That token, it turned out, was the healer's satchel that Caelym carried now, and it contained all the practical implements he needed to survive.

Momentarily overtaken by his memories, it startled Caelym to hear Aleswina ask, "What happened then?" and to find himself in a sunny meadow with a Saxon princess waiting for him to tell her the story of his first quest.

He blinked his eyes, cleared his throat, and began again.

On the day of my sixteenth birthday—having completed my first and second levels of study—I embarked on the quest divined for me by our chief oracle to seek my animal spirit guide and learn to speak the language of its tribe and to sing their songs and tell their stories.

Aleswina's thrilled whisper—"Oh, Caelym, is your animal spirit guide a wolf?"—was gratifying, to say the least, and he plunged into his story, strumming the strings of his harp in accompaniment.

I journeyed far up into the mountains, climbing the highest peak to chant the sacred incantations calling for the spirit of the animal that was to be my guide to come into my dreams. Buffeted by freezing winds, I heard the howls of wolves calling to each other from the peaks below me, and when I lay down to sleep, I dreamed I was a wolf myself, running swift and wild at the head of a fierce pack.

The next day, I traveled in the direction of the closest howls. After a long search, I came to the rise above a high valley and saw seven gray wolves racing after a herd of deer, cutting out the hindmost and bringing it down.

Oblivious to Aleswina's shudder, he went on to say how he'd followed the pack determined to fulfill the task he'd been given.

Keeping downwind and creeping as close as I dared, I came to understand that they spoke not only with their voices—high growls and low ones, barks and whines and sweet-sounding mewls—and with their expressions—snarling and smiling, frowning and yawning—but also with their bodies. The great gray leader of the pack stood tall and paced boldly; the lesser wolves backed out of his way and crouched down if he looked at them. For some it might have been enough to learn as much as I had, and yet I could not feel in my heart that I had fulfilled my quest, for I had not yet learned their stories or joined in their singing. But how could I do that without coming closer, and how could I come closer without being torn apart?

Aleswina held her breath, her eyes wide and wondering. Caelym strummed a rising crescendo on his harp strings.

Then, on the day of the summer solstice, as I was peering down from a rocky overlook, I saw a light brown wolf I'd never seen before come out of the bushes and trot toward the place where the pack was resting in the shade after their most recent kill.

The new wolf was a female. She was smaller by half than any of the gray wolves, and her ribs were showing through her coat. My guess—which is probably correct—is that she was the lost or orphaned cub of some other pack who was searching for her family, too young to fend for herself and too weak to run when the entire enemy pack rose up as one and stalked toward her.

As the pack surrounded her, the great gray wolf in the lead, the little brown wolf dropped down and rolled over on her back, exposing her neck and belly, as if surrendering to her death. The great gray wolf drew back his lips in a fearsome snarl and closed his teeth on the pup's throat. The pup made no move save for a small wag at the tip of her tail. I watched with tears welling up in my eyes for the poor doomed pup—but instead of biting down, great gray wolf released his grip and walked away. The rest of the pack followed him, and little brown wolf got back to her feet and crept along after them with her tail now wagging happily, even tucked as tightly as it was between her legs. Seeing this, I thought that I, too, might persuade the pack's leader to let me join their fellowship.

That night, the great gray wolf led his pack up the side of the valley to a low ridge not so far from where I was hiding. They circled into a ring to sing their songs to the moon, which was close to full. Imitating their howls, I began to sing their songs, joining in the chorus with them. And as we sang back and forth together, they came closer to me and I to them until I and the great gray wolf faced each other, no farther apart than you and I are now. The others circled and watched. Following the example of the little brown wolf, I rolled over on my back, exposing my neck and my belly. The great gray wolf put his teeth on my throat. I could feel the tips pressing sharp against my skin, and thought that, perhaps, instead of my animal spirit guide entering into me, I was about to enter into him. But the great gray wolf opened his mouth again and walked away. The rest of the pack followed and I, still in imitation of the little brown wolf, got back to my feet and joined them, keeping my head very low and wagging my hindquarters as if I too had a tail.

For months I lived together with them, adding the fish I caught with my spear to the game they brought down with their teeth, until, at the beginning of autumn, some ancestral yearning called them to leave their summer abode and journey southward. I might have gone along with them except that I too felt a yearning, equally compelling, to return to my human kin and learn to live again as a man.

"And now I say to you, who have shown such daring in our travels together"—Caelym moved on to the point he meant to make—"that if I at the age of only sixteen was able to use my wiles to survive among a pack of wild wolves, then you, who are three years older than I was then, will easily be able to learn what you must do if ever your wicked cousin or any of his evil guards should find you."

Aleswina had been listening to Caelym's story with her mouth open. At this unexpected change of subject, she closed it, biting down on her lip hard enough to draw blood.

Caelym had expected that he would have to carry on both sides of this discourse, and he continued without pausing, "I know what you are thinking, but I fear it would not work so well for you to take up your gardening trowel, giving out a battle cry, and charge against these enemies, for while it is possible they should all be so surprised at this that they would faint dead away, it is more likely that it would only serve to annoy them and make matters yet worse for you. Instead, I think you must be like the little brown wolf, pretending to be frightened and helpless."

There was no question at all that Aleswina would be able to portray being frightened and helpless, as she was doing an excellent enactment of those qualities at that moment. Pleased to see this early success, Caelym praised her lavishly before going on.

"The skills that I will be teaching you require guile and courage, both of which I know you possess in abundance. They also require that you have only a single opponent."

◆◆◆

Aleswina had no idea what to say to this, but it didn't matter since the only sound she was able to make was a small, strangled squeak.

"Yet, as we both know, men, like wolves, often travel in packs and, like wolves, will have a pack leader."

Aleswina was about to squeak again but, remembering Olfrick and his men and dogs pursuing them through the woods, she swallowed and nodded.

"So, to begin this lesson, let us say that a pack of your evil cousin's guards have come upon you—what must you do first?"

"Run."

"As the deer ran from the wolves?"

"Yes"—but even as she said it, Aleswina remembered what happened to the deer being chased by Caelym's wolves. "No, hide!"

"But it is too late for that, you are surrounded by them!"

Aleswina stammered, "I . . . you," meaning to say, *I don't know! You have to tell me.*

Before she could form all those words, Caelym broke in, "Yes! That is exactly right! You must do as I did—observing them carefully, as I did the real wolves, then determining who is their leader—and among men you will know who that leader is because he will strut boldly, while the others will do as he commands them—only remember to be careful that you do not look at them too directly, but instead let your eyes shift slyly as you glance about."

Hypervigilance was nothing new to Aleswina, and she again showed some natural talent—looking down at her toes, she kept Caelym within her peripheral vision.

Caelym nodded his approval. "Ah, that is excellent! So then you must hide any distress you may feel and instead glance up at this man with desire and invitation in your eyes."

At this point, Aleswina's natural talents, as well as her training and experience, failed her entirely. Although quite explicit in its condemnation of women as seductresses, the Bible, at least in the versions used for the readings at the Abbey of Saint Edeth, had said nothing specific about of what being a seductress entailed.

Since seduction, practiced under approved circumstances, was considered within the Shrine of the Great Mother Goddess as a skill to be learned along with other useful arts, Annwr would have been able to fill this gap in Aleswina's education. The experience of being gang-raped, however, had left Annwr soured on men as a group, and she had done nothing to encourage her timid foster daughter in this field of endeavor.

Totally out of her depth, Aleswina did her best to look at Caelym with desire and invitation but the result only suggested some embarrassing internal discomfort.

"That will not do. Watch me and I will show you."

While all of Caelym's experience in seduction had been within the sanctity of his union with Feywn, that experience was more extensive than the average man's, and he was able to reproduce a smoldering look of lust that made Aleswina's internal discomfort real. Her outward expression of this, regrettably, was to go completely blank.

Caelym, who privately considered himself irresistible, was both hurt and frustrated. Still, he was not a man to give up easily, and they spent the next half-hour making faces at each other until Aleswina was able to affect something close enough to sexual awareness to pass for it in poor light. Aleswina's best attempts were, frankly, little better than her archery, but Caelym didn't want to discourage her, so he praised her efforts before he continued his instruction.

"Now I can tell you that any man, seeing such a look as that, will certainly choose to send the others away. Once you are alone together, he will, no doubt, pull off his armor and his clothes underneath, and take you up in his arms. That is when you will swiftly pull out the sharp blade that I will give you and you will thrust it into his foul heart, and he will be too surprised to make any outcry."

Looking up at him, Aleswina chewed her lower lip—hopefully a sign that she was thoughtfully weighing his instructions.

In keeping with Olyrrwd's practice of always giving three reasons to take the remedy he was giving patients, Caelym concluded, "In this way you will have done three good things: First, you will have triumphed over your foe, bringing honor to your ancestors. Second, you will have given this foe a kind death—one that causes little discomfort and happens when he least expects it. Third, you will have done what is necessary to go on your way unharmed and in peace."

Aleswina nodded. It was a very small nod, but a nod nonetheless.

Relieved, Caelym unrolled the leather packet of healer's knives he'd brought with him. After selecting the sturdiest of the blades from his surgical kit, he began his practical instruction, both explaining and demonstrating how to plunge the point of the blade through the soft spot just below the point of the breastbone and thrust it upwards from there ("Not hesitating, and with all the force of your strong right arm!"), and cautioning Aleswina to be prepared to step back quickly to avoid the outpouring of blood.

Once she pantomimed the hand movements precisely, Caelym declared her "as dangerous as any she-wolf" and fully ready to defend herself from her wicked cousin and all his evil guards.

With a final strum of his harp strings, Caelym got to his feet, handed Aleswina her basket, and led the way back to camp, where Annwr had a pot of stew simmering—one which did not include any frogs, because, as Arddwn grumpily explained, "Lliem cried like a baby when Aunt Annwr said she'd show us how to break their necks, and we had to let them all go!"

Chapter 65

Parting Gifts

Judging from Gothreg's map, Caelym expected to get to Aleswina's ancestral lodge (as he'd come to call it) in two or at most three days. The innkeeper, however, had been under the impression that they were going to be traveling on the road—so, as it turned out, it was Herrwn's map with its three grim giants warning of unforeseen hazards that proved the more accurate.

Finally, after weeks of backtracking out of dead-end canyons, searching out fords across rivers in flood, and detouring around cliff sides, the group came to the top of the last ridge before the spot that Gothreg had marked *KL*.

The ridge, by comparison with some that they had crossed, was a low one. Looking over the edge, they could see the path switch back through scattered stands of beech and alder before it crossed a broad clearing and ran straight on to the front gate of a dilapidated fence that enclosed a cluster of rundown buildings. The largest and centermost was a long low structure with the smoke from its hearth fires rising up through a shabbily thatched roof.

"What's that?"

In two words, Arddwn captured the sense of letdown Caelym was feeling, as he'd expected a residence belonging to a king—even a dead one—would be more impressive.

"That," he said with forced enthusiasm, "is Ales—Ethelwen's ancestral lodge."

"Which log is the ancestral one?" Lliem's grasp of Celt was not yet complete, and he'd misconstrued what he'd overheard Caelym and Annwr saying to each other to mean that they were going to get some sort of magical piece of wood.

This was neither the time nor the place to resolve all of the boys' disappointments and misunderstandings, so Caelym temporized, "The earthly abodes of gods and goddesses must be kept veiled from human eyes."

Neither Annwr nor Aleswina said anything—either when they looked down at the lodge or when they went back to the hollow where they'd left the packs. There was something in their silence that silenced the boys, who whispered, "Yes, Aunt Annwr," when she told them to play quietly for a while.

With Aleswina sitting close beside her, Annwr sorted through their things, muttering, "You'll keep to your disguise as a boy, revealing your true identity only to Millicent, and she can say you are her sister's grandson come to visit. I've put your cross in with your habit, wimple, and veil for when you go on to the convent. The money Benyon gave you is in this pouch for your dowry. Remember the story you are to tell about being the daughter of a rich Briton—let's say he was a merchant who disowned you when you ran off with the son of his rival, and then that lover, whose name you will never reveal, abandoned you, and so you have come to join them, renouncing both wealth and men forever."

Aleswina nodded, took the pouch, and pushed it down to the bottom of her pack.

"This other pouch has the things for you to keep for remembrance, the gifts that the boys gave you and the seeds for your new garden, and . . ." Annwr had been busy rummaging and sorting, but now she turned to face Aleswina, holding a delicate golden brooch with a few stray threads hanging off it. "You had this when we first met. Do you remember it?"

Aleswina shook her head.

"I think it may have been your mother's, and so you should keep it."

Aleswina shook her head again.

"Well, you may want it later, so I'll put it with the rest."

⬥●⬥

Caelym, who'd been tuning his harp nearby, paused as Annwr listed off the gifts that she and the boys had given to Aleswina. He waited for her to mention his knife and when she didn't, he guessed this was no mere oversight but a renewal of her past accusations that he was ungrateful for all the things Aleswina had done for him.

Not about to let this slight go unanswered, he reached for his shoulder bag, determined to find another gift—one that Annwr could not ignore.

Sitting with his legs crossed and his satchel on his lap, he took out and laid aside his healing kit, his maps, Aleswina's parchment prayer sheet, Annwr's sheaf of medicinal herbs, and a golden pendant that had been Feywn's gift to him when she named him her consort.

Digging deeper, he found a reed flute. Did nuns play flutes? He thought not.

There was his embossed and only slightly dented box of flints and tinder—but of what use would that be to her, living indoors with others to cook her meals?

One of his protective amulets? For a moment he thought that was the answer, but he quickly realized a Druid talisman was no safe gift for anyone to carry into a Christian convent.

With almost the entire contents of his pack stacked on the ground beside him, there was nothing left except a coil of twine he'd forgotten he had.

Looking up, he saw Annwr starting to tighten the draw cords of Aleswina's pouch of gifts, so he shifted onto one knee and strummed a chord on his harp.

"I, too, have a gift to give you."

Both Annwr and Aleswina turned, looking startled—as if they'd forgotten he was there.

He struck a second chord.

"You know that Annwr has another daughter, one who is close to you in age." Here Caelym smiled at the recollection of Aleswina lying on Annwr's lap and pretending to be asleep. "Now I will tell you that when Cyri determined to be a physician as well as a midwife, it fell to me to teach her everything a physician must know—not just about healing and remedies but also understanding the living world of plants and of animals. I was then but nineteen years old, as you are now, and had only just become a physician myself, and I was afraid that I did not know enough to be teaching any other. So on the day that our lessons were to start, I took Cyri with me to a marshy spot near the edge of our sacred lake. I then took a piece of twine . . ."

Caelym set his harp aside and opened his hand to reveal the coil of twine, the way a magician might conjure a coin out of the air.

"Then I had her hold her arms straight out . . ."

With that, he took hold of Aleswina's wrists and stretched her arms out straight.

"And I measured the twine so that it was the length between her farthest fingertips."

Again, Caelym matched his actions to his words.

"Then, together, we cut small pegs from willow twigs. I used one to mark the center of what would soon be a circle. I tied the twine to that, then I stretched it out to its full length and at its far end I set in another peg. Doing this again and again, I made a ring of pegs—twice as wide across as Cyri's arms could reach. Do you see in your mind what I am saying?"

Aleswina nodded.

"Excellent! Now you can image how this was not so big a space, so you will understand how confident Cyri was when I told her that for her first task she must count everything living within that circle, and she would not be finished until I could not show her even one more thing that she had not seen for herself. Even as she was nodding her head, I could see that she expected to be finished with this and off to some more interesting lesson by the end of the day. Now, I wonder whether you can guess how long actually it took her to complete this task?"

Aleswina shook her head.

"Then I will tell you that Cyri labored on through long days and weeks and months. Time and again she proclaimed she was done, only to have me prove her wrong by showing her one more thing that she had missed, until at last, she understood that there was no end to this task. However many things you think you know about the earth, there is always more to find out. That was the lesson that Cyri learned, and forever after she has looked at all the world as carefully as she did her small circle of earth, always discovering something new and wonderful.

Caelym looped the string back into a coil, put it into Aleswina's hand, and folded her fingers around it.

"This, then, is my gift to you who have given me so much. It is my dearest hope that when you are in your new Christian convent and again have a garden, you will take this string and make a circle of earth as Cyri did, and you too will take on the task of finding everything that lives there—all of the plants and all of the creatures, down to the smallest thing that moves. You must remember that when you are inside that circle, you are to watch and seek to understand what you see without judging or interfering. And when you are doing that, you will know that my spirit is with yours, and that I am seeing those wonders as well."

Caelym got to his feet and held out his hand.

"And now, while Annwr stays here and watches over the boys, I will take you to your ancestral lodge to rejoin your loving servant, Millicent, who will guard you with her life until the nuns of Saint Agned, whose convent will be your sanctuary forever more, open their gates and welcome you in."

"Not until I have all her things ready, and I've gone first to make sure that Millicent is there, and it is safe to leave her!" Annwr spoke so fiercely that Caelym drew his hand back and stepped away as she snapped, "And you will stay here and watch the boys!"

Caelym's story about Cyri had touched Annwr deeply—as, no doubt, he'd intended it to—but she wasn't about to let him be the one to make the final judgment over whether it was safe to leave Aleswina with Millicent.

Softening her tone, she went back to what she'd been saying before he interrupted.

"Now, Dear Heart, you'll need to pick a Celtic name to give when you enter your new convent. What about 'Brighid'? That's a pretty name."

Aleswina nodded.

Chapter 66

The King's Lodge

Taking Annwr's words as his dismissal, Caelym got up and began to stride restlessly, first up the trail to the top of the ridge and then down again.

As Annwr watched him pacing back and forth, she couldn't help but wonder if he was in the throes of indecision—no longer so certain about leaving Aleswina behind. Having given up any expectation of divine intervention fifteen years before, Annwr didn't call on the Goddess to make Caelym relent, but she hoped he would, and hoped so with a desperate urgency that came very close to supplication.

Caelym, however, was more certain than ever. If he'd had any doubts (which he never did), then those doubts would have ended when he'd lain awake the night before, pondering just how easy it had been to look at Aleswina with desire and passion—far easier than it ever should have been for the consort of their shrine's chief priestess and goddess incarnate.

His rising tension was not indecision or regret . . . it was impatience to have it over and done with.

What must be done was like—here he sorted through a variety of metaphors before settling on lancing a festering boil. That was it exactly (even if he knew better than to compare Annwr's beloved Saxon princess to a pustulant boil out loud), and there was just one way to lance a boil, and that was to do it swiftly and without wavering or hesitating—poking and prodding at it only increased the pain and delayed the healing.

He made one last lap to the top and turned back, determined to tell Annwr to stop her dithering.

◆◆◆

The flickering hope Annwr had allowed herself died at the sight of Caelym's set face.

She made a last effort to break through the wall of silence that had enveloped Aleswina since they'd looked down over the edge of the ridge, pleading for her to say goodbye to the boys before they left, but Aleswina just picked up her pack and shook her head.

◆◆◆

Walking behind Annwr along the sun-speckled path through the stands of trees, Aleswina made-believe that they were just going out to pick the early strawberries that were starting to ripen on either side of the trail until Annwr spoke, dispelling that fragile daydream.

"This is close enough. You wait out of sight while I find out whether it's safe for you to stay here."

◆◆◆

After nudging Aleswina into the cover of the undergrowth, Annwr straightened her shoulders and walked on toward the manor without looking back. She kept a firm, steady pace, neither hurrying nor "dithering," and only stopped to close the gate behind her.

She'd do as she said she'd do—find out whether Millicent was still here, and if she was ready to guard Aleswina with her life. But if it turned out that the woman was gone, or if there was any trace of doubt about her loyalty, then she'd just take Aleswina back with her and Caelym could argue until he turned blue in the face.

As she lifted her hand to knock on the weathered oak door, Annwr hesitated, just a moment, imagining Aleswina and Cyri sitting with their heads together, whispering and giggling like she and Feywn had done when they were young.

Her hand was still in the air when the door swung open and, without warning, Annwr was transported back to the moment when Millicent opened the gate to the palace nursery.

That it was Millicent, Annwr had no doubt. Just like before, the woman (who'd looked ancient to her then but now seemed not so much older than she was herself) reached out, grabbed Annwr by the sleeve, and pulled her inside. Only this time the room she dragged her into was a large, bright kitchen, not a dark, shuttered child's bedroom, and, now that she was fluent in English, Annwr could understand what Millicent was saying.

Nor was there any question about Millicent recognizing Annwr.

Although she wasn't one to babble—or throw her arms around a relative stranger that she hadn't seen for fifteen years—Annwr could easily put herself in Millicent's place if their roles were reversed, and she'd been the one to long for Aleswina all that time.

Still, she answered the older woman's flood of questions—*Is the darling princess with you? Is she well? Does she have enough clothes?*—cautiously. She was also careful to make sure Millicent understood what she was agreeing to, as well as the risk she was taking on. But Millicent was unshakable; she nodded as she repeated back each provision, and she swore to care for Aleswina as she would her own daughter.

So it was settled. Leaving Millicent waiting in the doorway, Annwr went back up the path, managing to keep a steady pace all the way to where Aleswina waited huddled in the bushes.

Caelym watched Annwr come out of the lodge, climb the trail, and enter the thicket. Both women emerged a moment later—Aleswina walking downhill, back to her own people, and Annwr hurrying uphill, without a backward glance.

That was the best way, he would have told her, only she didn't stop or look at him as she rushed past, her cloak flapping behind her like the wings of a bat.

Translations of Latin Text

CHAPTER 13:

Domine, libera nos a malo
O Lord, deliver us from evil

CHAPTER 20:

Dominus regit me; et nihil mihi deerit; in loco pascuae ibi me conlocavit. Super aquam refectionis educavit me, animam meam convertit. Deduxit me super semitam iustitiae propter nomen suum.
The Lord is my shepherd; I shall not want. He maketh me to lie down in green pastures: he leadeth me beside the still waters. He restoreth my soul: he leadeth me in the paths of righteousness for his name's sake. Psalm 22:1-3 (Vulgate Bible)

in perpetuum
Forever

CHAPTER 61:

Quid gloriaris in malitia qui potens es in iniquitate? Tota die iniustitiam cogitavit lingua tua sicut novacula acuta fecisti dolum. Dilexisti malitiam super benignitatem; iniquitatem magis quam loqui aequitatem. Dilexisti omnia verba praecipitationis in lingua dolosa.Propterea destruet te Deus in finem, evellet te et emigravit te de tabernaculo et radicem tuam de terra viventium
Why dost thou glory in malice, thou that art mighty in iniquity? All the day long thy tongue hath devised injustice: as a sharp razor, thou hast wrought deceit. Thou hast loved malice more than goodness: and iniquity rather than to speak righteousness. Thou hast loved all the words of ruin, O deceitful tongue. Therefore will

God destroy thee forever: he will pluck thee out, and remove thee from thy dwelling place: and thy root out of the land of the living. Psalm 51:3-7 (Vulgate Bible)

Ne proicias me a facie tua et spiritum sanctum tuum ne auferas a me ne proicias me a facie tua et spiritum sanctum tuum ne auferas a me. Redde mihi laetitiam Iesu tui et spiritu potenti confirma me redde mihi laetitiam salutaris tui et spiritu principali confirma me. Cast me not away from thy face; and take not thy holy spirit from me. Restore unto me the joy of thy salvation and strengthen me with a perfect spirit. Psalm 50: 13-14 (Vulgate Bible)

Pronunciation of Celtic Names

Author's Note: Pronunciation of Celtic names and vocabulary in this series is based loosely on the contemporary Welsh:

Vowels:

a is always a short A, as in can, ham, or man, never long, as in may. The Welsh words am and ac are pronounced as they would be in English.

e by itself is always as in get, pet, and let. However, the letter E has a different sound in the three diphthongs.

i has the I sound, as in bin or pin, or a long E sound, as in seen or queen.

o has the O sound, as in hot, or the long sound, as in toe.

u has the sound of long EE, as in see.

w has the sound of OO, as in boot and shoot, or of U, as in pull. Note, however, that W can also be used as a consonant with the English W sound.

y has two different sounds. In one-syllable words (llyn), and in the last syllable of polysyllabic words (estyn), it is a shortened EE sound, as at the end of happy.

Diphthongs:

Ae, Ai and **Au** are all pronounced as English eye.

Aw has the sound of ow as in how and now.

Eu and **Ei** are pronounced as long A, or the ay sound in say.

Ew is difficult for English speakers because there is no direct equivalent. It is approximately eh-oo or ow-oo, but the correct sound is between those examples.

Iw or **I'w** is ee-you with the ee sound very short. It is similar to the English yew.

Oe has the sound of oi or oy.

Ow is pronounced the same as in the English row, tow, or throw.

Wy has the sound of oo-ee or a short Wi sound, as in win.

Yw or **Y'w** is the same as Iw above.

Ywy (considered a diphthong, even though it has three letters) has the sound of ow-ee, as in the name Howie.

Consonants:

B is the same as the English B, as in beer.

C is the Welsh K. It is always hard, as in can or cane, never soft, as in once.

Ch is a glottal Kh sound, as in the Scottish loch.

D is the same as the English D, as in dog.

Dd has the sound of voiced TH, as in this or there.

F always has the sound of V, as in have or very.

Ff is the same as the English F, as in first.

G is always hard, as in go or good, never soft, as in manage.

Ng has the English NG sound, as in singer, though in some words it has the NG+G sound of finger.

H is the same as the English H, but it is always pronounced, never silent.

L is the same as the English L, as in long.

Ll is a sound with no English equivalent. It is a voiceless alveolar lateral fricative formed by pronouncing L while allowing air to escape around the tongue; the English thl of athlete (or slat, pronounced with a lisp) is vaguely similar.

M is the same as the English M, as in many.

N is the same as the English N, as in no or never.

P is the same as the English P, as in poor or party.

Ph is the same as ff.

R is the same as the English R, as in right, but rolled.

Rh is pronounced as HR; that is, a slight H sound comes before the R sound.

S is the same as the English S, as in say.

Si is the same as the English Sh, as in show.

T is the same as the English T, as in turn.

Th is the English voiceless TH, as in think or three. Note difference from the voiced Dd.

W, when used as a consonant, has the English W sound, as in work.

Source: https://en.wiktionary.org

Acknowledgments

My heartfelt thanks . . .

To my writing partner, Linda, without whom Caelym, Annwr, and Aleswina would still be languishing in word-processing purgatory.

To my husband, Mark, for his unstinting support and his invaluable advice.

To my sister, Carol, for believing in this book before I did.

To my incredibly kind readers, Anne, Carrie, Connie, David, Jack, Jim, and both Joans for their insights and encouragement.

To Mirko Donninelli, scholar of classical languages and ancient history, for his generous help with Latin translations.

To my editor, Krissa Lagos, my publicist, Caitlin Hamilton Summie, and to the SheWritesPress team, with special thanks to Julie Metz for a cover that captured the essence of Caelym's journey, Shannon Green for managing to make this all come together, and Brooke Warner for taking on the quest to give women a voice.

About the Author

Ann Margaret Linden was born in Seattle, Washington, but grew up on the East Coast before returning to the Pacific Northwest as a young adult. She has undergraduate degrees in anthropology and in nursing and a master's degree as a nurse practitioner. After working in a variety of acute care and community health settings, she took a position in a program for children with special health care needs where her responsibilities included writing clinical reports, parent educational materials, provider newsletters, grant submissions, and other program related materials. *The Oath* is the first installment of The Druid Chronicles, a five-volume series that began as a somewhat whimsical decision to write something for fun and ended up becoming a lengthy journey that involved Linden taking adult education creative writing courses, researching early British history, and traveling to England, Scotland, and Wales. Retired from nursing, she lives with her husband, dogs, and cat.

SELECTED TITLES FROM SHE WRITES PRESS

She Writes Press is an independent publishing company founded to serve women writers everywhere. Visit us at www.shewritespress.com.

Light Radiance Splendor by Leah Chyten. $16.95, 978-1-63152-178-2. Set in Eastern Europe in the first half of the twentieth century and culminating in contemporary Israel and Palestine, *Light Radiance Splendor* shows how three generations of the Hebrew Goddess Shekinah's devoted mission keepers grapple with betrayal, love, and forgiveness.

Time Zero by Carolyn Cohagan. $14.95, 978-1-63152-072-3. In a world where extremists have made education for girls illegal and all marriages are arranged in Manhattan, fifteen-year-old Mina Clark starts down a path of rebellion, romance, and danger that not only threatens to destroy her family's reputation but could get her killed.

Trinity Stones: The Angelorum Twelve Chronicles by LG O'Connor. $16.95, 978-1-938314-84-1. On her 27th birthday, New York investment banker Cara Collins learns that she is one of twelve chosen ones prophesied to lead a final battle between the forces of good and evil.

Elmina's Fire by Linda Carleton. $16.95, 978-1-63152-190-4. A story of conflict over such issues as reincarnation and the nature of good and evil that are as relevant today as they were eight centuries ago, *Elmina's Fire* offers a riveting window into a soul struggling for survival amid the conflict between the Cathars and the Catholic Church.

Faint Promise of Rain by Anjali Mitter Duva. $16.95, 978-1-93831-497-1. Adhira, a young girl born to a family of Hindu temple dancers, is raised to be dutiful—but ultimately, as the world around her changes, it is her own bold choice that will determine the fate of her family and of their tradition.

Beyond the Ghetto Gates by Michelle Cameron. $16.95, 978-1-63152-850-7. When French troops occupy the Italian port city of Ancona, freeing the city's Jews from their repressive ghetto, two very different cultures collide—and a whirlwind of progressivism and brutal backlash is unleashed.